BREAKING POINT

Joe Pickett always liked Butch Roberson—a hardworking local business owner whose daughter is friends with his own. Little does he know that when Butch says he is heading into the mountains to scout elk, he is actually going on the run.

Two EPA employees have been murdered, and all signs point to Butch as the killer. Soon, Joe hears of the land Butch and his wife had bought to retire on—until they are told the EPA declared it a wetland—and the penalties the agency charged Butch until the family was torn apart. Finally, it seems, the man just cracked.

It's an awful story. But is it the whole story? The more Joe investigates, the more he begins to wonder—and the more he finds himself in the middle of a war in which he must choose sides.

continued . . .

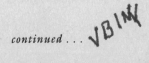

IN PLAIN SIGHT

"Edge-of-the-chair suspense . . . Heart-stopping action."
—*Library Journal* (starred review)

OUT OF RANGE

"Intelligent [and] compassionate."   —*The New York Times*

TROPHY HUNT

"Keep[s] you guessing right to the end—and a little beyond."   —*People*

WINTERKILL

"Moves smoothly and suspensefully to the showdown."
—*The Washington Post*

SAVAGE RUN

"The suspense tears forward like a brush fire."   —*People*

OPEN SEASON

A *NEW YORK TIMES* NOTABLE BOOK
LOS ANGELES TIMES BOOK PRIZE AWARD NOMINEE,
BEST MYSTERY/THRILLER

"C. J. Box is a great storyteller."   —Tony Hillerman

"A motive for murder that is as unique as any in modern fiction."   —*Los Angeles Times*

TITLES BY C. J. BOX

THE JOE PICKETT NOVELS

THE STAND-ALONE NOVELS

BREAKING POINT

C. J. BOX

BERKLEY BOOKS / NEW YORK

THE BERKLEY PUBLISHING GROUP
Published by the Penguin Group
Penguin Group (USA) LLC
375 Hudson Street, New York, New York 10014

USA • Canada • UK • Ireland • Australia • New Zealand • India • South Africa • China

penguin.com

A Penguin Random House Company

BREAKING POINT

A Berkley Book / published by arrangement with the author

For information, address: The Berkley Publishing Group,
a division of Penguin Group (USA) LLC,
375 Hudson Street, New York, New York 10014.

ISBN: 978-0-425-26460-7

PUBLISHING HISTORY
G. P. Putnam's Sons hardcover edition / March 2013
Berkley premium edition / March 2014

PRINTED IN THE UNITED STATES OF AMERICA

10 9 8 7 6 5 4 3 2

Cover design by Isabella Fasciano.

Banality of evil: A phrase coined by philosopher Hannah Arendt that describes the thesis that the great evils in history generally were not executed by fanatics or sociopaths, but rather by ordinary people who accepted the premises of their state and therefore participated with the view that their actions were normal.

You can still get gas in Heaven,
and drink in Kingdom Come.
In the meantime,
I'm cleaning my gun.

—MARK KNOPFLER, "CLEANING MY GUN"

DAY ONE

1

ON AN EARLY MORNING IN MID-AUGUST, EPA SPE-
cial Agents Tim Singewald and Lenox Baker left the Region
8 Environmental Protection Agency building at 1595 Wyn-
koop Street in downtown Denver in a Chevrolet Malibu
SA hybrid sedan they'd checked out from the motor pool.
Singewald was at the wheel, and he maneuvered through
shadows cast by tall buildings while Baker fired up the dash-
mounted GPS.

"Acquiring satellites," Baker said, repeating the voice
command from the unit.

"Wait until we get out of downtown," Singewald said.
"The buildings block the satellite feed. There'll be plenty
of time to program the address. Besides, I know where
we're going. I've been there, remember?"

"Yeah," Baker said, settling back in his seat. "I know. I
was just wondering how long it would take."

"Forever," Singewald said, and sighed, taking the turn on Speer that would lead them to I-25 North. "Wyoming is a big-ass state."

The GPS chirped that it had connected with the sky. Baker punched in an address and waited for a moment and said with a groan, "Four hundred and twenty-two miles. Six hours, twenty-seven minutes. Jesus."

Said Singewald, "Not counting the guy we need to pick up along the way in Cheyenne. Still, we ought to make it before five, easy."

"Where are we staying? Do they have any good places to eat up there?"

Singewald emitted a single harsh bark and shook his head. "The Holiday Inn has a government rate, but the bar sucks. There are a couple good bars in town, though, if you don't mind country music."

"I hate it. Six and a half hours," Baker said as Singewald eased the Chevy onto the on-ramp and joined the flow of traffic north.

IT WAS A CLEAR summer morning in mid-August. The mountains to the west shimmered through early-hour smog that would lift and dissipate when the temperature rose into the seventies. Both men wore ties and sport coats, and in the backseat was a valise containing the legal documents they were to deliver. Both had packed a single change of clothing for the drive back the next day.

Tim Singewald had thin sandy hair, small eyes, a sallow complexion, and a translucent mustache. Lenox Baker was fifteen years younger. Singewald didn't know him well at all, although his impression of his colleague was that he was overeager. Baker was dark and compact and exhibited nervous energy and a wide-eyed expression he displayed when talking with a senior staffer that said, *Keep me in mind when promotions or transfers come along.*

Singewald noticed that Baker wore a wedding band, but he'd never heard the wife's name. Singewald had been divorced for six years.

All he knew about Baker was that, like thousands of others across the country, he was new to the agency and he was gung-ho to get into some kind of action.

Baker was an EPA Special Agent (Grade 12), one of 350-plus and growing. He pulled in $93,539 a year in salary plus benefits and hoped to move up to Grade 15, where Singewald resided. Singewald made $154,615 per year, plus benefits.

As they cleared Metro Denver into Broomfield, Singewald reached up with his left hand and loosened the knot on his tie and then pulled it free and stuffed it into his jacket pocket. When Baker saw him do it, he reached up and did the same.

"Ties stand out where we're going," Singewald said.

"What do they wear? Clip-ons? String ties?"

"They don't wear ties," Singewald said. "They wear jeans with belts that say 'Hoss.'"

Baker laughed. Then: "Who is this guy we have to pick up in Cheyenne?"

"Somebody with the U.S. Corps of Engineers," Singewald said, shrugging. "I don't know him."

"Why is he coming along?"

"I don't know," Singewald said. "I don't ask."

"The secret to a long career," Baker said.

"You got it."

"Are there other secrets?" Baker asked, grinning a schoolboy grin.

"Yes," Singewald said, and said no more.

THE AGENTS DROVE another hour north and crossed the border into Wyoming. Instantly, the car was buffeted by gusts of wind.

"Where are the trees?" Baker asked.

"They blew away," Singewald said.

AS SINGEWALD WHEELED into the parking lot of the Federal Building in Cheyenne, he saw an older man in a windbreaker and sunglasses standing near the vestibule entrance. The man was conspicuously checking his watch and glancing toward them as they found an empty spot.

"Gotta be him," Singewald said.

"What was his name again?"

"Love. That's all I know about him."

The man who might be Love pushed himself off the brick wall and walked slowly to their car. Singewald powered down his window.

"You EPA?" the man asked.

"Agents Singewald and Baker."

"I'm Kim Love," the man said. "I guess we're going to the same place today."

Singewald chinned toward the backseat. "Do you have anything you need to put in the trunk before we leave?"

Love rocked back on his heels and hooked his thumbs through his belt loops. He shook his head.

"I'll follow you up," Love said. "I've got my own car."

"Sure you don't want to come with us?" Singewald asked Love.

"I'm sure."

"Suit yourself. Do you know where we're going?"

"Yes, unfortunately."

Singewald didn't react. Instead, he reached inside his jacket pocket and handed Love an official EPA business card.

"My cell phone number is on there. Give me a call when we get going so I have yours, so we can keep in touch if we get separated."

Love sighed and shook his head. "What, you think you're entering No Man's Land?"

"Yes," Baker whispered, sotto voce.

"Maybe we can stop in Casper for lunch," Love said. "I know a place there."

"We'll follow you," Singewald said with a shrug.

When Love walked away to climb into his own sedan with U.S. government plates, Baker said to Singewald, "What's his problem?"

Singewald shrugged. "Don't know and don't care," he said. "He's just another working stiff. Like us."

———

BAKER WAS PRACTICALLY SPUTTERING two and a half hours later when the brake lights of Love's sedan flashed and the Corps of Engineers car took the Second Street exit in Casper and turned in at a truck stop.

"He's yanking our chain," Baker said, leaning forward in his seat to look around. A long line of side-by-side tractor-trailers idled in a cacophony on the south side of the huge parking lot. A trucker emerged from the restaurant and convenience-store doors holding a half-gallon soft-drink container to take back to his truck cab.

"Maybe this Love knows something," Singewald said. "Maybe this place is, you know, a jewel in the rough."

"It's a *truck stop*."

"We might as well be friendly, since we're stuck with him," Singewald said, and turned off the motor.

Baker sighed. "Maybe I'll just stay in here. I can feel my arteries clogging up just looking at this place and the people coming out of it."

"You don't have to come in," Singewald said, handing Baker the keys. "If you want to listen to the radio or something."

Baker waved him off. "Believe me, there's probably nothing worth listening to here. I'm not a big fan of Buck Owens."

Singewald pocketed the keys.

"Oh, all right," Baker said with a groan, opening his door to get out.

———

THEY SAT around a Formica table in a high-backed booth; Kim Love on one side and Singewald and Baker on the other. All of the other tables and booths were occupied by truck drivers and rough-looking locals who appeared as if they'd driven into town from building sites or oil rigs. Even with their ties removed, Singewald thought the three of them stood out. Singewald thought Love seemed distant, and maybe a little hostile to them. He chalked it up to interagency rivalry and didn't let it bother him. There was no reason to make friends, he thought. He'd never met Love before, and after their joint operation later that afternoon, he doubted he'd ever see him again.

Beside him, Lenox Baker studied the plastic menu and sighed.

"Do you recommend anything in particular?" Baker asked Love.

"The chicken-fried steak sandwich," Love said without even looking at his menu. "Best in Central Wyoming. I'm from Texas, and I'm particular about chicken-fried steak. They do it right here: no pre-breaded bullshit."

Baker cringed.

Singewald ordered the sandwich as well, and Baker asked the waitress if the lettuce of the chef salad had any preservatives sprayed on it. Without a smile and with a quick glance toward her other busy tables, she said, "I wouldn't know that, hon."

"Can you ask the chef?"

"We don't have a chef. I'll ask the *cook*," she said, and spun on her heels toward the kitchen.

"Those chemicals give me diarrhea," Baker explained to Singewald.

"Can't have that," he replied.

AFTER THEY PUSHED their empty plates away and sat back—Baker had picked at his salad and claimed he was full—Love looked squarely at Singewald and said, "I can't say I like what we're doing today."

Singewald shrugged. "We're just the messengers."

"Still."

"We didn't make the decision," Singewald said. "We're just delivering the verdict."

"Yeah," Love said, shaking his head and taking a swipe at his balled-up paper napkin like a bear cub, "I read it. In fact, I read it twice and didn't like it any better the second time."

"I don't read 'em," Singewald said, looking over Baker's head in an attempt to signal the waitress. "I just deliver 'em. Reading 'em is above my pay grade."

"I hear he's a hardheaded man," Love said.

Singewald nodded.

"I get the impression he's not going to just roll over."

Baker opened his jacket and interjected, "That's why we carry these," indicating the butt of his holstered semiautomatic .40 Sig Sauer.

Love's mouth dropped open, and he turned to Singewald. "You guys carry *guns*?"

"We're trained and authorized," Singewald said softly.

"You should see what we have in the trunk," Baker said. Singewald thought of the combat shotguns and scoped semiautomatic rifles nestled in their cases.

Love's eyebrows arched when he said, "So you're prepared to shoot it out with him if necessary?"

"If necessary," Baker said, narrowing his eyes.

"I try not to predict these things," Singewald said, almost apologetically. He didn't want to continue this conversation. He wished Baker wasn't so overtly gung-ho. Then he raised his hand and waved at the waitress. He began to think she was ignoring him.

"Have you met this guy we're serving the order on?" Love asked Singewald.

"Nope," Singewald said, wondering if he should snap his fingers to get her attention. "I wasn't there the first time he was given the word. From what I understand, he was confused, mainly. I don't think he's the sharpest knife in the drawer, so to speak."

"But he sure as hell understands now," Love said, shaking his head. "Things like this . . . it makes me wonder just what the hell we're doing. It isn't the kind of thing I signed up for, that's for sure."

"What's the problem?" Baker said suddenly to Love, his tone incredulous. "The guy obviously screwed up big-time or we wouldn't be going up there. I don't understand what you're talking about."

Love leaned forward on the table and balled his fists together. "Do you know him?"

"Of course not," Baker said, defensive.

"Do you know anything about him?"

"Just his address."

"Did *you* even read the documents we're taking up there?"

"No," Baker said, looking away from Love to Singewald.

The waitress intervened and slapped the bill down on the table as she rushed by.

"Ma'am," Singewald said.

She turned toward him.

"We'll need separate checks. One for him and me," he said, gesturing to Baker, "and one for him," he nodded toward Love. "And receipts, please."

"Separate checks and receipts," she repeated with a dead-eyed stare.

"Yes."

"It'll be a minute," she said through gritted teeth.

"It's okay," Singewald said, sliding out of the booth. "I can get it taken care of at the front counter."

Baker was right behind him as he walked up to the cashier, pulling out his U.S. government Visa card. When he glanced back, Kim Love was still sitting in the booth.

AN HOUR LATER, sixty-seven miles north of Casper, Love caught up with them near Kaycee, Wyoming. Singewald looked up and saw the Corps sedan in his rearview mirror.

Baker saw him do it and turned his head toward the back. "Oh, good," he said. "Our buddy."

Singewald grunted.

"What is his problem, anyway?"

"I guess he doesn't like what we're doing."

"Why does he even care?"

"You'd have to ask him."

"I think you should mention this in our report," Baker said.

THE TERRAIN CHANGED as they drove north. Blue humpback mountains had emerged from the prairie to the west. Lines of high white snow veined down from the summits and melded into dark timber.

Baker pointed at a cluster of vivid brown-and-white dots placed on the slow-waving high grass out his window. "Are those pronghorns?"

Singewald said they were.

"And they just stand there like that? There must be a hundred of them."

"I've heard there are more pronghorn antelope than people in this part of the state," Singewald said.

"Well, at least there's something good about it," Baker said.

"THE TETONS?" BAKER ASKED, pointing toward the mountains.

"Bighorns," Singewald said. "Those are the Bighorns."

"So that's where we're going," Baker said, looking at the GPS display, and then his watch. "We should be able to get this done in time to check in to the hotel by five. We won't even have to do any overtime."

"That's the plan," Singewald said.

"I hope we can find someplace decent to eat," Baker said. "I'm starving."

"First things first," Singewald said as they took the first exit near the town of Saddlestring. The bypass would link them up with a two-lane state highway into the mountains, toward Aspen Highlands, a subdivision near Dull Knife Reservoir.

When he checked his mirror, Love's sedan was no longer there.

"Call Love and see what's happened to him," Singewald said, handing Baker his cell phone.

Baker scrolled through his recent calls and pressed SEND. After a moment, he said, "This is Agent Baker and we're on our way up the mountain. We were kind of wondering if you planned to join us."

When he punched off, he said, "Straight to voicemail. Either we lost him or he decided to go into town and check in to his hotel."

Singewald hadn't noticed whether Love had continued on I-25.

"I guess we'll do this ourselves," he said.

"That asshole," Baker said. "For sure, this will go into our report, right?"

AN HOUR LATER, Tim Singewald writhed in the grass on his back, choking on his blood. Although his legs were convulsing, causing his heels to thump against the ground uncontrollably, he couldn't feel them. He was able to roll clumsily to his right side.

Lenox Baker was also on his back just a few feet away. Baker's eyes were open, as if he were staring at the late-afternoon clouds. A bullet hole, like a third eye, looked out from his left eyebrow. He wasn't breathing.

Singewald knew he wouldn't last much longer, either. The first two bullets, he suspected, had collapsed his lungs. He couldn't draw breath, no matter how hard he tried, and he was drowning in his own blood. He gurgled when he tried to speak.

Baker's weapon lay in the dirt between them. Singewald hadn't drawn his before he was cut down.

In the distance, he heard shouting. Then a tractor started up.

DAY TWO

2

THE NEXT AFTERNOON ON THE LONG WESTERN slope of the Bighorn Range, where the sage and grass met the first lone scouts of pine preceding the army of dense timber descending from the mountain, game warden Joe Pickett encountered Butch Roberson. By the way Butch looked back at him, Joe knew something was seriously wrong.

The mid-August afternoon was uncharacteristically sun-splashed and soft under the massive blue sky, which was cloudless and clear except for a single fading vapor trail miles above. The warm air was still and perfumed with juniper, sage, pine, and mountain wildflowers: Indian paintbrush and columbine. Insects hummed at grass level, and Joe was so far away from the distant state highway he couldn't hear traffic sounds from the occasional passing vehicles.

Joe was riding Toby, his fourteen-year-old tobiano paint. The day and the surroundings brought a bounce to the gelding's step, and the horse had trouble focusing on the task. There was rich grass on both sides of the narrow trail, and Joe had to be constantly alert so Toby wouldn't dip his head to grab a bite. Joe's one-and-a-half-year-old yellow Labrador, Daisy, loped alongside or drifted behind so she could hoover up Toby's droppings, even though Joe hollered at her to stop. The new dog had joined Tube, their less-than-ambulatory corgi-Lab cross, in the Pickett household. The new dog had been dropped off at the local veterinarian's office by disgusted Pennsylvania bird hunters the winter before. They claimed she was useless. Joe knew that all year-old Labs were useless, and took her home to mature. She seemed to be settling down, now that every shoe in the house had been destroyed. And so far on this ride he'd been impressed with her, except for eating the horse droppings.

It was a rare and perfect day; so perfect, in fact, that after the year he'd had and the things that had happened, the day seemed cheap and false and somehow unearned. As he rode the Forest Service boundary, which was marked by a three-strand fence line of barbed wire, Joe had to keep reminding himself he had nothing to feel guilty about. He told himself he should just enjoy the moment because they came so few and far between. It was sunny, dry, warm, cloudless, and *calm*. After all, there he was in the Bighorn Mountains on a sunny day with his horse and his dog, and he was doing the job he loved in the place he loved. The opening days for hunting seasons in his district were weeks away, and he'd spent the summer recuperating his left hand from when he'd broken it pulling it out of his own hand-cuffs the October before. Except for the shot-up body of a pronghorn antelope found south of Winchester, he had no other pending investigations. The crime bothered him for its viciousness, though: the buck had been practically cut in two by the number of bullets, and whoever had done it had also fired several close-range shots to the head after the animal was obviously down. That kind of bloodthirsty crime was a window into the soul of the perpetrator, and Joe wanted to find whoever had done it and jack him up as much as possible. There was little to go on, though. Several rounds had been caught beneath the tough hide, and he'd sent the bullets in for analysis. But there were no shell casings, footprints, or citizen's reports of the crime. Joe could only hope whoever had done it would talk and word would get back to him.

Additionally, he had time to do preliminary elk counts in the mountains, verify the licenses of fishermen, check the water guzzlers, and actually be home for dinner with his wife, Marybeth, and his three girls. It was as if he were a character in a movie and the scene was being shot in soft focus.

Despite the setting, he found himself scanning the horizon for the ferocious snouts of thunderheads and sweeping his eyes over the ocean of trees for gusts or one-hundred-mile-an-hour microbursts or some other kind of trouble.

He thought later he should have gone with his premonition that something was coming and it wouldn't be good.

BEFORE HE RAN into Butch Roberson, he rode parallel to the western border of Big Stream Ranch, which was owned by a longtime local named Frank Zeller. It was one of the few of the big historic ranches in northern Wyoming still owned by the original family. Frank Zeller was a solid if taciturn man who managed the ranch with care. He ran huge herds of Angus cattle and pastured hundreds of saddle horses for guest ranches throughout Wyoming and Montana. He'd convinced the owners to allow the Wyoming Game and Fish Department to install water guzzlers near the forest boundary to help sustain the elk and mule deer herds not only because he cared for the wildlife, but also because he feared the spread of the brucella bacteria from the wildlife to the cattle if they mixed too much near the big creek on the valley floor.

Water guzzlers were shallow depressions in the ground covered with polyethylene fabric that captured rainwater and surface runoff—as much as five hundred to eight hundred gallons in each guzzler. The money for the guzzlers had come from an EPA grant Joe had applied for several years before, and the agency had sent an engineer up from Denver to help Joe design them. The guzzlers seemed to work. Parched herds from the mountains came down during drought years to drink, and pronghorns and mourning doves came up from the valley as well. His work, once a year, was to ride along the series of guzzlers to make sure the fabric was still intact and hadn't been blown into shreds by the vicious winter winds, and to check that the depressions hadn't been filled in with dirt or fouled by decaying carcasses.

Because water itself was rare and precious in a state that averaged less than thirteen inches of precipitation in a year—mostly snow—the wildlife literally flocked to it. As he approached each guzzler, he anticipated an explosion of doves and grouse that got Daisy excited, as well as deer bounding away through the sagebrush and elk crashing up into the timber. Once, the year before, he'd startled a black bear feeding on a deer carcass. The bear woofed at him and caused Toby to crow-hop and nearly dump Joe out of the saddle. But by the time he'd wheeled Toby around with a one-rein stop, the bear had run into the trees with startling speed and power, and it hadn't come back.

HE'D RECEIVED PERMISSION from Zeller to access the ranch. After checking in at ranch headquarters and having breakfast with Zeller and his four Mexican ranch hands, because the foreman insisted he eat, Joe parked his green Game and Fish pickup and horse trailer two miles below the line of guzzlers near a head gate.

Still, parking so far from the Forest Service boundary was a pain in the neck, Joe thought, and a fairly recent one. When they'd installed the guzzlers, the two-track ranch road had joined with a Forest Service road on the other side of the fence. They'd been able to bring their gear and equipment close to the fence so they wouldn't have to carry it across the folding foothills terrain. But two years before, the Forest Service had decided to prohibit through traffic. They'd fortified the gate, chained it, and locked it with a combination lock. Then, behind the gate, on the Forest Service side, they'd brought in a backhoe to scoop a deep hole into the road and use the dirt as a berm to prevent

vehicles from using it. The coup de grâce was a small rectangular brown metal sign that read ROAD CLOSED.

He'd saddled his horse and checked seven of nine guzzlers throughout the day. Number three had required some
dirt work, but it didn't take long, because he'd packed along
a shovel with the handle shoved down into his empty saddle scabbard.

JOE WAS RIDING between the seventh and eighth water
guzzlers, through a stand of thigh-high aspen with their
still, spadelike leaves, when he saw to his left that the three
strands of barbed wire on the fence had been severed. Each
wire was now curled back, leaving a gaping hole in the
Forest Service fence. He clucked his tongue and turned his
horse and rode Toby up through the small trees to the damaged fencing.

He swung down and grunted when his boots thumped
on the ground. His knees ached from being wrapped
around Toby's belly. He tied Toby to a midsize pine tree
with enough slack in the rope that his horse could graze,
and walked off his aches to the fence.

As he limped, he resisted saying, *Getting too old for this.*

Joe Pickett wore his red uniform shirt with the Wyoming Game and Fish Department pronghorn patch on the
shoulder, thin leather gloves, worn Wranglers, scuffed cowboy boots, and his sweat-stained gray Stetson. His duty
belt with his cuffs, pepper spray, and .40 Glock was in the
right saddlebag because it was uncomfortable to wear when

riding. His radio, citation book, uneaten lunch, and note-pad were in the left.

He thought for a moment that he should retrieve his weapon before checking out the fence, but decided against it. Joe despised his weapon, not because of its properties but because he really couldn't hit anything with it. If it weren't for a softhearted range officer, there were several times over the last few years when he shouldn't have officially qualified. Although he was comfortable and fairly accurate with a rifle and deadly at close range with a shotgun, he considered his Glock more for show and always convinced himself that he'd never pull it again for the rest of his career if he could avoid it.

The strands of barbed wire had been snipped cleanly and very recently by a sharp tool, probably a pair of wire cutters. The end of the cut was still shiny and the edges sharp. He visualized each strand snapping back as it was severed, and imagined the *pop* and the sound of singing wire.

Joe let the wire drop back to the grass and looked around. The nearest road was where Joe had parked his truck and trailer, nearly two and a half miles away. There were no other vehicles parked at that location. Whoever had cut the wire had either walked a long way from the highway—probably six to seven miles, he guessed, and across the muddy pastures and serpentine creek—or had come down from the National Forest above. The vandal had been on horseback or on foot because there were no tire tracks. But if he didn't drive a vehicle through the opening, what was the point of cutting the fence? Joe wondered.

He photographed the damage with his digital camera and took several close-in shots of the cut tips of the wire, and noted the time and location in his notebook. Then he dug his cell phone out of his breast pocket and opened it, thinking he would call Frank Zeller. Although the fence itself was the property of the U.S. Forest Service, Joe knew from experience it would take them weeks or even months to repair it due to the bureaucracy involved. Reports would have to be made and sent through channels, requests for proposal for repair of the fence would be published, bids would be taken or not from private contractors, and in the end a small army of federal employees would make their way up the mountain with newly requisitioned coils of barbed wire—probably as the first winter storm hit.

Rather, he would tell Frank Zeller, and Frank would send up his crew before nightfall so the cattle and horses belonging to the Big Stream wouldn't wander through the hole into the public forest. Frank could sort out the repercussions later, Joe thought.

But there was no cell phone signal, which wasn't unusual this far out. He closed the phone and dug out his handheld radio from the saddlebag. The static over the air made it impossible to establish communication with the dispatcher in Cheyenne 310 miles away. He squelched it down but still couldn't find a clear channel. There were squawks and snippets of conversation going on, but he couldn't determine the subject matter or the agencies of the law enforcement personnel doing the talking. He sighed and turned off the unit. He vowed to replace the batteries when he got home and request a new radio that worked better. This one, he thought, was shot.

HE WAS LATER ASKED why he hadn't simply ridden down the mountain to his pickup and used the radio inside the cab to report the fence and request assistance. But at the time, he hadn't even considered it because he couldn't have known with foresight what he'd find. Cutting a fence was a nuisance and a misdemeanor but not a major crime requiring backup. Plus, he was a Wyoming game warden, one of fifty-four in the entire huge state. He patrolled his five-thousand-square-mile district alone, and it was normal to be so far away from other law enforcement that it was pointless to call them. He was used to dealing with armed citizens in the outback on his own, and he routinely handled situations that would require backup procedure in urban settings.

What he said when asked was, "It was just a cut fence."

SO HE WALKED Toby through the middle of the gap into the timber, from private land into public land, with Daisy trailing.

The lodgepole pine forest was close, and the trunks closely packed. The canopy was open only in spots where there was rampant pine-beetle kill and the needles had dried, curled, and dropped from the branches to create a three-inch cushion of rust-colored carpet on the forest floor. The pine-beetle infestation had occurred slowly and predictably over the past fifteen years, sweeping from north to south along the Rocky Mountains. From New Mexico to British Columbia, the tiny insects burrowed into lodgepoles and deposited the larva and fungus that eventually killed the trees while they stood. Joe had read estimates that more than three million acres of trees in Wyoming were infested, and he'd seen entire mountainsides colored burnished red from dead standing timber. The only way to stop the invasion, he'd heard, was if the temperature dropped to thirty or forty below for several days in a row during the winter, which would kill the larvae. Either that or spraying the trees with insecticide when they began to show signs of infestation. The weather hadn't cooperated, and forestry officials had been too paralyzed by budgets and bureaucracy to seriously mount a defense. Now it was too late, and there were tens of millions of acres of dead standing trees like so many unlit cigarettes . . . just waiting for a match.

Joe didn't even want to think of what it would be like when the fires started. When they did, the Forest Service would be blamed for letting it happen. Joe didn't think that was entirely fair, even though he was jaded enough to know that even if the service was blamed there would likely be no firings of employees or officials, because that rarely ever happened in the federal system. Nature was nature, he thought, and it was bigger than any regional forester or forest supervisor, even if he wasn't sure they'd agree with that assessment.

As he was contemplating Armageddon as the result of fires stretching from Canada to Mexico, he smelled wood smoke. It hung thin and acrid in the mountain air.

Joe turned Toby's head slightly to the northeast in the direction of the breath of wind that carried the smoke. The smoke was too thin and close to be from a forest fire, he thought. Daisy had noted it, too, and Joe assumed by the string of drool from her mouth to the pine needle carpet that there must be an accompanying food smell too faint for him to notice.

WHEN THE DRY CAMP came into view, Joe shouted, "Good afternoon."

Although it looked like he could have gotten closer before speaking, he wanted the occupant of the camp to know he was coming. There was nothing worse than startling a likely armed man in his own camp, Joe knew.

In the clearing ahead, Joe could see a man wearing bulky camo clothing and squatting over a small fire with his back to him. A bulging pack hung on the branch of a dead pine, but there was no tent, horse, or ATV that Joe could see.

At the sound of Joe's greeting, the man wheeled around and shifted his weight toward the pack. That's when Joe saw the scoped rifle leaning against the dead tree.

"How're things going?" Joe asked in a friendly tone. As he did, he pressured Toby's right ribs with his leg so the horse would sidestep slightly and put a couple of trees between him and the man in the camp. That was another thing he'd learned long before: never approach a stranger head-on. Always come a little from the side so the scene was off-balance.

The man stood up slowly and turned toward Joe. His

posture was tense, as if he were coiled up. Smoke from the small fire outlined his body.

Joe recognized him.

"Butch?"

"Joe?"

Butch Roberson looked to be equal measures startled, aggressive, and somehow regretful. As if he were resigned to what he would have to do next.

Butch was stocky and barrel-chested, with deep-set brown eyes, a three-day growth of heavy beard, and a wide bony jaw that made his head seem even larger than it was. He had black hair flecked with gray and a once-broken nose that made him look like a fighter. He had a way of standing bent slightly forward with his arms stiff at his sides that suggested he would launch into an attack at any provocation. Until he opened his mouth, that is, and his soft-spoken tone belied the package.

Butch owned Meadowlark Construction in Saddlestring, a small company that built a few houses but mainly did renovations. He was Joe's age, mid-to-late forties, and Joe knew him because Butch was the father of Hannah, Joe's youngest daughter's best friend on earth. He'd seen Butch mainly at Lucy's plays and concerts, and the two had chatted at school functions and when one or the other was sent to pick up his daughter at the Pickett or Roberson home. But since Hannah had obtained her special learner's permit and could drive a beat-up old sedan to the Pickett house herself, he'd seen less of her parents the past year.

Joe liked Hannah, and so did Marybeth. Hannah had recently expressed an interest in horses, and Marybeth was thrilled to have some help feeding and grooming in the corral behind their house.

Joe knew Butch to be a hard worker, a devoted husband and father, and an outdoorsman who lived to hunt and fish. In that respect, he wasn't unusual at all in Twelve Sleep County, Wyoming.

Because the only times they'd talked were at social functions related to their daughters, Joe found it awkward to find Butch hunched over a fire miles from the road.

Butch seemed to find it unsettling as well, Joe thought, because the look on his face was one Joe had never seen before.

Joe said, "What brings you up here?"

Butch seemed to be searching for the answer, and Joe noted the quick flick of his eyes in the direction of the rifle. Joe hoped it had been involuntary. Men confronted by game wardens in the wild often displayed tics and gestures that were uncharacteristic in the normal day-to-day. The innocent ones, the men who hunted and fished within the regulations and took pride in their ethics and sportsmanship, often displayed signs of nervousness and anxiety because they were disturbed at the possibility of being under suspicion. It was the boastful, overly friendly and outwardly confident backslappers, Joe had found, who were more likely guilty of something.

"Just scouting elk," Butch said, finally.

Joe nodded. "Nothing wrong with that. Did you find 'em?"

Butch chinned over his left shoulder in a vague westerly direction. "Six-by-six and a six-by-seven and a dozen cows and calves," he said, meaning bulls with six and seven points on their antlers.

"That's encouraging," Joe said, climbing down. "I need to get up here and do an elk trend count soon. But it's good to hear that you found some."

Butch nodded, but his eyes stayed hard on Joe's face, like he was expecting another shoe to drop.

Joe grunted again as he stood on the ground. His lower back joined his knees and thighs in the pain parade. But he thought it important to dismount, get on Butch's level, so he wouldn't seem imperious by talking down to him.

"I didn't see your rig anywhere on the Big Stream," Joe said. "What did you do, walk here through the National Forest?"

"From the road," Butch said, peering up and over Joe's shoulder.

"That's quite a hike."

"It wasn't so bad."

"Seven, eight miles?"

"I do twenty a day when I'm hunting," Butch said without a hint of boastfulness. He was stating a fact. That was something Joe had noticed before when he talked to Butch, whether it was about hunting, or the snowpack, or roads that were still open into the mountains and break lands, or their daughters—no humor, no nuance. Butch was a serious man who didn't use many words and who seemed to regard small talk as a waste of time and calories. In that regard, Joe found him a kindred soul.

Joe led Toby twenty feet toward Butch and tied the horse to a live tree. While he did, Daisy bounded forward, tail stiffly wagging from side to side, and snuffled Butch's camo trousers. There was an etiquette about entering another man's camp, and that was to keep a distance until invited inside. Daisy had broken the rule.

"Daisy," Joe warned, dropping his voice.

"It's fine. I like dogs. She hunt?"

"We'll see," Joe said. "I'm working with her until bird season, and then I'll give her a go. Don't let her eat what you're cooking."

"Just heating up coffee," Butch said. "I already had lunch. You hungry?"

"No, but thanks for asking."

"I know I'm not supposed to have a fire."

Joe nodded. There had been an official fire ban since early that summer, placed there by the Forest Service due to the dead trees. The rule was hated by campers and hikers. Dozens of campsites had been closed in the area, and dozens more were rumored to be closed. Joe hadn't said anything because the fire ban was federally enforced and not in his purview.

When Joe didn't respond, Butch nodded, then stood there expectantly. Joe wanted to tell him to relax. Instead, he tried for common ground.

"When I left this morning, Hannah and Lucy were still asleep on the living room floor. They like to get out sleeping bags and watch movies, but I think they talk more than they watch," Joe said. Lucy and Hannah were both entering the ninth grade at Saddlestring Middle School. They'd been friends since grade school and shared the same interests in drama, choir, and dance. Lucy never hesitated to tell

Joe and Marybeth that she envied Hannah, who lived in town and could ride her bike everywhere. Unlike her, who was stuck in a state-owned Game and Fish Department house eight miles away from the action on a gravel road.

"Teenagers can sleep," Butch said.

Joe laughed. "I've got three of 'em. Three girls, that is. You're right—they can sleep."

"That's what they seem to do best," Butch said, his face suddenly wistful. Then: "Hannah used to be my little buddy. I'd get her up before dawn and we'd go out and scout game or go fishing. She kind of lost interest in that when . . ."

Joe looked up, waiting for the rest. But Butch had flushed and looked away. And Joe realized the rest of the sentence might have had to do with Lucy.

"Never mind," Butch grumbled.

Joe let it go. He knew the feeling. His oldest daughter, Sheridan, had accompanied him often into the field when she was growing up. She'd announced once that she wanted to be a game warden herself, or a master falconer, or a horse trainer. That was before Sheridan had completed her first year at the University of Wyoming, though she had yet to declare a major. She could sleep, too, and that's all she did on the days she wasn't working as a waitress at the Burg-O-Pardner to earn money over the summer before starting her second year.

April, their seventeen-year-old ward, worked part-time at a western-wear store in retail between bouts of being grounded. And when she was home and grounded . . . she slept.

"When did she get there?" Butch asked.

"Hannah?"

"Yeah."

"Last night some time," Joe said. "I saw her car parked out front."

Butch nodded. Then, without preamble: "I hope you don't mind if I ask you what you're doing up here."

Joe explained the line of water guzzlers, then finding the cut fence. As he did, he watched Butch carefully.

There was a slight reaction, a twitch on the corners of Butch's mouth.

"You wouldn't know anything about that, would you?" Joe asked breezily.

Butch shook his head and said, "They don't need to put up fences like that and close the roads. We hunted up here for a hundred years on what is supposed to be public land. Now they berm the access roads so we can't get in. Tell me what's public about that?"

Joe didn't bite, and it wasn't the answer he wanted to hear. Butch had strong feelings and opinions when it came to access to hunting areas. That wasn't unusual, either. Citizens in the area and the state took natural-resource decisions personally, and often railed against the public-lands managers who made decisions. Joe had heard the argument countless times, and sympathized to some degree. And because he was a state and not a federal employee, he often found himself in the middle. Which was why he hadn't brought up the illegal campfire.

Joe looked up and said, "I haven't called it in yet. No one knows about it except you and me. But I would guess

that if a guy went down there with a stretcher and a fencing tool, he could fix it so no one would ever even know
it was down. It's not like the Feds send out line riders to
check it."

Butch looked away. He grumbled, "I hear you."

"That's good."

"So the only reason you're up here is those guzzler
things?"

The question took Joe by surprise. "Why else?"

Butch shrugged. "Sure you don't want some coffee before I kick the fire out and move on?"

"I'm sure."

With that, Butch tossed the last of his tin cup of coffee
onto the forest floor.

"You need to borrow a stretcher?" Joe asked.

"Naw. I built fence all through high school. I know how
to fix a fence."

"Take it easy, Butch."

"You too, Joe."

Joe turned, puzzled by the whole exchange, and untied
the reins of his horse and called Daisy back.

As he pulled himself into the saddle, Butch said something Joe didn't catch.

"What's that, Butch?"

"I said, thanks for watching over Hannah."

"It's Marybeth mostly," Joe said.

"I guess so," Butch said, as he shouldered into his heavy
pack.

Joe noted how big and heavy the pack seemed to be for
a day of scouting.

———————

AFTER CHECKING the last two guzzlers—they were full and operational—Joe rode Toby slowly down the mountain toward his pickup. Daisy lagged behind, exhausted, her tongue lolling out of the side of her mouth. It was hot, mid-eighties, and Joe felt sweat run down his spine and into his Wranglers. Dense cream lather worked out between the saddle and Toby's sweaty back. As Joe cleared the trees he turned in his saddle to look at the top of the mountain where it went bald above the tree line. There was still snow up there, even in August.

He sighed and settled back into the slow gait of the horse. The previous October, during the first heavy snow of the season, he'd been on top of the summit in his department pickup and had gotten it stuck in a snowfield he never should have tried to drive across. The reason he was up there was to try and assist his friend Nate Romanowski, an outlaw falconer and federal fugitive, who was in trouble. In the process, Joe had broken his hand and watched as a wounded Nate drove away. Joe hadn't heard from Nate since, and given the circumstances and the body count that resulted, Joe didn't mind. He'd *needed* the ten months since to heal in body and mind.

Twice he'd ridden with a local tow-truck operator to the top to attempt to retrieve the pickup. Twice they'd been turned back by heavy drifts. The agency had sent up another pickup that should have been sold off because of its condition and the 190,000 miles on the odometer, but until Joe could get his new pickup out, he was stuck with the old one. The situation was the object of jokes and asides at headquarters in Cheyenne because of Joe's track record with state vehicles. It would be any day now, Joe thought, that a new Game and Fish director would be named by the governor and review his record and give him a call. He hoped to have his pickup out by then, but he wasn't sure he could make that happen.

JOE HEARD his old replacement pickup from a distance. The speaker outfit on the hood was patched to the radio inside and broadcast chatter from the mutual-aid law enforcement channel. It was set up like that so a game warden could be kept in communication when he was out of his truck, but Joe couldn't figure out how to turn it off.

As he rode closer, he was surprised by the number of transmissions, and the frequency of them, even though he couldn't yet make out the words. That happened only when something of significance occurred—a high-speed chase on the highway, a hot pursuit in the county, or a felony in progress.

He hoped whatever it was wouldn't involve him. He wanted to get home for dinner with Marybeth and his daughters.

Then he reined up for Toby to pause, and he turned in the saddle and looked far up into the timber on the mountain, where he'd last seen Butch Roberson.

3

MARYBETH PICKETT WAS GIVING AN INFORMAL
tour of the historic Saddlestring Hotel building to her
friend and county attorney Dulcie Schalk when she heard
sirens race up Main Street directly outside. In mid-sentence,
she checked her cell phone to see if there were any texts or
messages from Joe. When there weren't, she dropped the
phone back into the pocket of her summer dress.

"You do that automatically," Dulcie said.

"I guess I do," Marybeth said. "That's what happens
when your law enforcement husband is out there somewhere by himself and you hear sirens."

"I understand," Dulcie said.

Marybeth brushed a strand of hair out of her face and
wiped her hands on a cloth to remove the dust that covered
everything inside. It was hard to stay clean just walking
through the old place, and she didn't want to show up for

her afternoon shift at the Twelve Sleep County Library
smudged with grime. Dulcie had the same concern with
her severe dark business suit.

Dulcie was slim, fit, dark-haired, and tightly wound. Joe
considered her a tough attorney and too rigid in her approach, but he liked her. Marybeth had never worked with
her—or against her—but they shared a mutual interest in
western dressage and simply being around horses. When
Dulcie's stable had closed, Marybeth had offered space for
Dulcie's horse at their place, and now they saw each other
twice a day when Dulcie drove out to feed Poke, her aging
gelding. Dulcie was single and the subject of local barroom
speculation about her availability and sexual preferences,
though Marybeth knew her friend was straight—but cautious. And in Twelve Sleep County, pickings were slim.

Marybeth's secret plan was to find a man for Dulcie and
set a romance in motion. She was considering possibilities
when Dulcie said, "Back to the tour."

"Yes, where were we?"

MATT DONNELL, a local Realtor, had approached Marybeth two months before at the library and told her he had
just purchased the Saddlestring Hotel structure at a fore-
closure auction in Cheyenne. It had once been the finest
hotel in the county and *the* place where anyone of note
stayed in the area. President Calvin Coolidge, Ernest
Hemingway, Gary Cooper, and John Wayne had all stopped
there during its heyday, although it was now hard to believe, given the condition of the building. It was a sham-

bling three-level structure built of knotty pine, with a steep roof and gabled windows, a wide portico where rocking chairs had once lined up, and it gave off an overall impression of faded frontier elegance. It had also been vacant and hulking for ten years.

Donnell's idea, since home sales were slow and he and Marybeth were dedicated to historic renovation, was to figure out a use for the building that would benefit the community and restore an eyesore into something useful. He also wanted to make some money. He told Marybeth he'd always admired her business sense and entrepreneurship, and asked her if she'd like to become a twenty-five percent partner in his new venture. Since she'd once helmed a small-business consulting firm and had contacts and experience, he said he'd thought of her first.

She'd been surprised by the offer but intrigued by the possibilities. Her current schedule consisted of being the mother of three teenage girls; running the household; taking care of her two horses; and acting as unpaid research assistant, receptionist, scheduler, and sounding board for Joe. Only the library stint helped pay the bills, and family finances were tighter than ever. She knew from experience that uneven partnerships often resulted in tension and angst, but she had no capital to put into the deal. Sheridan was about to start her second year at the University of Wyoming, and both April and Lucy were on deck. Marybeth's part-time salary at the library was small, and Joe's game warden salary was hostage to an agency-wide freeze. Because of all that, though, Marybeth was frustrated with their situation—living in the battered state-owned home, scrapping for a better life—and wanted to break out of it. And she wanted to show her daughters that rewards could come by hard work and risk, especially since the only person of wealth they had known was Marybeth's mother, Missy, who'd acquired a fortune by trading up husbands for richer and richer men.

She told Donnell she'd consider it, and he said he'd get the paperwork going for the Saddlestring Hotel Development Limited Liability Company.

Joe and Marybeth stayed up late that night, and the more she thought about it and they talked about it, the more excited she got. Donnell's role was finance, compliance, permits, and materials, and her role would be restoration, recruiting, and administration. She loved the idea.

The deal wasn't in place yet, and Marybeth wanted the advice of her friend before she proceeded, which is why she'd invited Dulcie to tour the building.

"So do you know what the sirens were about?" she asked Dulcie.

"Not yet. If it's something important, they'll call me."

Marybeth slipped a rubber band off a roll of blueprints to show Dulcie the plans.

Dulcie smiled. "If I was married to Joe Pickett, I'd probably be hyperalert as well."

"Tell me about it."

"IF WE DO THIS, we'd have to gut all the old rooms and knock down half of the walls between them," Marybeth said, tracing with her finger on the blueprints, which were spread over an old door propped up by sawhorses.

"The last owners turned the place into a flophouse for transients and day workers," she said. "We want to restore it to its old glory."

She pointed to one spot on the blueprints. "We'd convert the old lobby into a central reception area," she said. "That way, we can offer the individual office holders a shared receptionist and secretarial services."

Dulcie nodded approvingly. "So you're thinking of gathering up some of the folks who are doing business in spare rooms and old houses, then? Architects, lawyers, insurance guys?"

"Exactly," Marybeth said. "The types who want a turn-key operation in a really cool environment. I know this is the kind of place I wish had been available when I had MBP," she said, referring to the business consulting firm she'd founded and run for years before the economy sank. "Of course, first we need to get it ready for business."

Dulcie put her hands on her hips and looked around, squinting. "It would really do wonders for Saddlestring and revitalize the downtown," she said. "Right now, this place just sits here like an old drunk on the corner. I'm trying to picture what it could be like."

"You really need to use your imagination," Marybeth said, deadpan.

There was so much work to be done inside—battered plaster wallboard would have to be replaced, ceilings raised, new plumbing and electricity installed—although they'd recently been encouraged when a structural engineer confirmed that the foundation's overall structural integrity was solid. In order to keep costs low, Marybeth planned to do much of the preliminary work herself with help from Joe at night and on weekends. Matt Donnell wasn't much of a hand when it came to carpentry or renovation, although he certainly put in the hours. Matt was better at dealing with local, state, and federal agencies that required permits and approvals. In fact, Matt was meeting with the building inspector and state fire marshal that afternoon. He'd confided to Marybeth that he had great relationships with the right people who could sign off on the permits.

Dulcie pointed at a large bouquet of flowers on the mantel of the old fireplace. "Those brighten up the place," she said. "Who sent them?"

"Read the card."

Dulcie read: "'Congratulations on your new hotel, Marybeth. I'm proud of you. Love, Joe.'"

"Awwwww," she said.

"I told him we can't afford flowers right now, but it's nice."

"This is the kind of place where I'd love to work," Dulcie said, imagining it. "It would be so much better than those cells they give us in the county building."

The Twelve Sleep County Building was also a relic of the 1920s, and it housed her office, two courtrooms, the road and bridge department, and the sheriff's department.

Dulcie said, "Although I have to say the atmosphere is better there now that Sheriff McLanahan is gone. There isn't as much secrecy and good-old-boy nonsense."

Marybeth nodded. McLanahan had been defeated by fewer than ten votes the year before by his deputy, Mike Reed. Although Reed was confined to a wheelchair—he'd lost the use of his legs after an on-duty assault—he had a dutiful and sunny personality that buoyed those around him. Plus, he was friends with Joe.

BOTH OF THEIR cell phones erupted simultaneously, and when they realized it, they smiled at each other before taking them. Dulcie turned and walked out of earshot, and Marybeth saw the incoming call was from her house.

It was Lucy, her fifteen-year-old daughter.

"Mom, can Hannah stay with us tonight?"

Marybeth did a quick calculation of the food available in the freezer and refrigerator, and except for the game meat Joe provided in volume, she didn't have enough items for dinner for six.

"Yes, but I need to stop at the store on the way home," she said.

"Maybe you can pick up pizza?"

"Maybe. Why is Hannah staying with us again?"

"She's my best friend, Mom," Lucy said, put out.

"I know that," Marybeth said, rolling her eyes. "Is it okay with her mom? She's stayed over at our house twice already this week."

"It was her mom's idea," Lucy said.

"Oh, really?" That sounded odd to Marybeth. Pam Roberson managed the office for the small construction company she co-owned with Butch, but she took pains to be involved in her daughter's life and activities, and she kept a fairly tight rein on Hannah, her only child. Like Lucy, Hannah was bright and attractive, although Marybeth had noted a change in her recently. Hannah had expressed an interest in horses, and Marybeth was secretly thrilled. Neither Lucy nor April shared her passion for horses, and Marybeth *loved* the idea of mentoring Hannah. Marybeth hoped this new development wouldn't create a rift between Hannah and Lucy because Lucy had no interest at all in riding.

Lucy said, "Yeah, she called a few minutes ago. She talked to Hannah and told her there were a bunch of cops at their house."

"What? Cops?"

"That's what she said."

The sirens, Marybeth thought.

"Lucy, please put Hannah on the phone."

"I can't."

"And why not?"

"Mom, she's in the bathroom. I think she's crying."

4

JOE DROVE HIS BOOT HEELS INTO TOBY'S FLANKS
and rode hard and fast back up the mountain through the
water guzzlers to where he'd last seen Butch Roberson.
Daisy ran behind, her tongue lolling out to the side. Toby
had a surprisingly smooth gait when he went all out, and
it was actually easier on Joe's aching knees and groin than
his walk or bone-jarring trot.

Toby's hooves pounded the soft ground, and Joe felt
the wind in his face. He reached up and clamped his hat
tighter on his head so it wouldn't blow off.

He yelled, "Butch!"

The name echoed back from the wall of trees beyond
the Forest Service fence—which hadn't been repaired.

WHAT HE'D HEARD over the radio wasn't reassuring. An
anonymous call had been made to the sheriff's department

reporting two federal EPA officials missing from the night before. Whoever called said the two men had never checked into their rooms at the Holiday Inn and there was no sign of their car. A uniformed sheriff's department officer was sent to where the caller said the two EPA men had been planning to go, which was a two-acre lot in a development called Aspen Highlands near Dull Knife Reservoir.

A quick check of the lot ownership with the county clerk revealed that it was owned by Butch and Pam Roberson. On arrival, the reporting officer said he could find nothing except some piles of gravel—and freshly dug soil. A quick reconnaissance of the area resulted in the location of a late-model Chevrolet Malibu SA hybrid sedan with U.S. government plates. The car was found three miles from the Roberson lot. Someone had driven the vehicle off the gravel road and into the canyon choked with heavy brush. No one was inside. The reporting officer said he could have easily driven right by the car if it weren't for the churned-up tracks on the dirt road. A tow truck, along with forensic techs, had been called to the scene.

Before climbing back into the saddle, Joe had called the dispatcher on his truck radio.

"This is Joe Pickett, GF-forty-eight. I'm located on the Big Stream Ranch . . ." He gave her the location coordinates. "I ran into Butch Roberson—the subject of the current inquiry—an hour ago and I'm going back to find him. Please relay this to Sheriff Reed's office."

When she asked, he said, "I don't want or need backup. It would take them too long to get out here, anyway."

He signed off, "GF-forty-eight, out."

GF-48 meant he was number forty-eight of the fifty-four game wardens in the state, ranked by seniority. He had once risen to GF-24 before getting into a confrontation with his superiors and losing his job and seniority number. When he'd been reinstated personally by Governor Rulon, a vindictive bureaucrat had refused to give him his old number back.

It rankled him every time he said "GF-forty-eight."

JOE'S MIND RACED, and he replayed his encounter with Butch the hour before. He had no doubt Butch knew something, and suddenly everything Butch had said carried a different, more sinister meaning. Still, though, Joe wanted to find him and tell him what had been discovered on his property. He had no authority or probable cause to arrest Roberson, but that didn't mean he couldn't question him or ask him to follow him into town.

He rode through the opening in the fence and into the timber.

Two federal agents, he thought. *Freshly turned-up ground. A car with no one in it.*

Butch would have some hard questions to answer.

THE FIRE PIT Butch had built was cold, the rocks from the fire ring kicked away. Joe dismounted and tied Toby to a tree and carefully walked around the camp. He identified his own boot prints, Daisy's prints, and large waffle-like impressions from Vibram hunting-boot soles, which he attributed to Butch. But he couldn't discern which direction Roberson had gone after breaking his camp.

"Butch?" he called out.

He stopped and put his hands on his hips and looked west, into the thousands of acres of National Forest. Most of the roads within it had been closed, so it would be tough to drive inside. Butch had grown up in the area and had hunted the mountains all his life. Beyond the summit were succeeding waves of mountains, canyons, and heavy timber wilderness.

Joe smiled bitterly. Twelve Sleep County got its name because the Indians said it took "twelve sleeps" to walk or ride a horse from the west side of the mountains to the eastern slope. That was a lot of rough country.

JOE PHOTOGRAPHED THE CAMP, the tracks, and what was left of the fire pit. He had a feeling there would be local, county, state, and federal people who would want to look at them. As he did, he questioned himself on the conversation he'd had with Butch Roberson. Had he deliberately missed something? Had his familiarity with Butch made him less than cautious?

He sighed and powered down the digital camera. Then he untied Toby and cantered him down to his pickup so he could drive to Butch's lot at Aspen Highlands.

5

BECAUSE HIS HOUSE ON BIGHORN ROAD WAS MID-way between Big Stream Ranch and the highway he'd need to take to get to Dull Knife Reservoir, Joe stopped long enough to let Toby out into the corral and dump the horse trailer. Poke, Dulcie's gelding, greeted Toby by playfully biting him on the butt. Toby kicked back at Poke and missed. Rojo, Marybeth's other horse, watched the two of them imperiously from the corner of the corral.

Joe's district was considered a "two-horse" district by the department, meaning he received reimbursement for horses, tack, food, and vet bills. It was a two-horse district because of the vast size of it—more than 1,800 square miles. He was also in charge of a department snowmobile, a boat with an outboard motor as well as a drift boat, and a four-wheel ATV. And, of course, his assigned pickup, which was stuck on top of a mountain and he might never retrieve.

As he put the three horses out to pasture, he heard Marybeth's van drive up the road and swing into the driveway in the front. He checked his watch—4:38 in the afternoon—and wondered why she was home so early.

As he unhooked the trailer hitch from the ball on his pickup, he heard Marybeth park in front. She was apparently on a break from work. Then the back door opened and slammed shut, and she emerged from the house. He thought she looked lovely: blond, slim, compact, with green eyes and nice cheekbones.

"Hey," he said, cranking the trailer hitch up and over the ball of his truck.

"You saw Butch Roberson?" she asked.

He stood and wiped away a drip of sweat that coursed down the side of his face from his hatband. "How'd you know that already?"

"Dulcie told me. She said you called it in."

"Yup."

"Joe, did you hear what happened?"

"Some of it," he said, repeating the reports he'd heard over the radio.

"Do they think Butch had something to do with it?"

"That's my impression," Joe said. "It's still too early to say. I'm not sure anyone knows anything yet."

"How did he seem to you?" she asked, concerned.

Joe shrugged. "Strange. Different. Spooked, I guess."

"But he didn't tell you anything? He didn't confess?"

"Nope. And he didn't shoot me, either."

"I don't think that's funny, Joe."

He grinned.

"Hannah is inside," Marybeth said, gesturing toward the house. "I haven't talked with her yet. She doesn't want to talk. I don't know what's going on at their house, but apparently law enforcement is there questioning Pam."

"Man," Joe said, shaking his head. It was strange to be so close to people who were apparently under suspicion.

"I feel so bad for Hannah," Marybeth said, as if reading his mind. "I don't think she really knows what's going on."

"Maybe I'll know more in a while," Joe said, telling her his intention to go back up into the mountains to Aspen Highlands. "I guess I didn't realize they'd bought a lot up there."

"Pam mentioned it to me," Marybeth said. "She said they'd scraped together enough to buy some land to build their retirement home. I don't think they've started building anything yet, though. I don't think they can afford to. The construction business hasn't exactly been booming around here, as you know."

"Could be worse," Joe said. "They could be trying to restore a historic hotel."

Marybeth's glare caught him off guard, and he realized he'd hit a nerve.

"I was just joking," he said, feeling his ears flush hot.

"I'm not amused," she said.

"I'll call when I know something," he said, giving her a good-bye kiss that she returned without much enthusiasm.

"Hannah's staying for dinner and maybe for the night," Marybeth said. "When my shift is over, I'll come back and feed everyone."

"Sheridan and April are home?"

"They will be soon. Sheridan gets off at six, and April's off at six-thirty. Sheridan's supposed to pick April up."

"Let me know if you need anything," he said. "And go ahead and start dinner without me."

"Ah," she said. "I hoped you'd be home."

"That's the way it goes," he said, climbing into the cab of his pickup. Daisy was already there.

JOE TOOK HAZELTON ROAD up into the Bighorns to Dull Knife Reservoir. Dust hung in the air on the gravel road—there had been plenty of traffic before he got there—and the waning sun fused through it to give the scene a burnished orange cast. Trees closed in and opened into mountain meadows and closed back in again, and he regretted his ill-timed joke with Marybeth about the hotel. It wasn't necessary, and he didn't harbor any resentment toward her or the prospect of the project. In fact, he trusted her business acumen and admired her tenacity, and sometimes wished he didn't love his job and these mountains so much, so he could focus his ambition on enterprises that would better benefit his family.

"Remind me to apologize," he asked Daisy. Daisy looked back as if she understood.

HE TURNED OFF the gravel road to a graded two-track at a sign in the trees announcing the Aspen Highlands development. The road plunged down into a wooded swale, then leveled out at the bottom as it got closer to the reservoir. Dull Knife had been created years before by damming the Middle Fork of the Powder River and flooding the creek basin. A smattering of cabins had been built on the east and west sides, but Aspen Highlands was obviously more preplanned. The roads through it were wide and straight and graded, and there were already a dozen or so homes built on two-acre lots in the trees.

The Roberson property was easy to find because of the collection of law enforcement vehicles he could see parked in the grass just off one of the spur roads. There were three sheriff's department SUVs, a pale green U.S. Forest Service pickup, and a highway patrol cruiser. Joe swung in off to the side of the vehicles, told Daisy to stay, and cracked the windows for her.

It was a beautiful afternoon: warm, still, almost sultry. The air was fused with pine, pollen, and wildflowers. Joe could also get a whiff of the tawny surface of the reservoir itself.

He approached the scene as if he were the first to arrive, keeping his eyes and ears open.

The lot itself was rectangular, and the borders were obvious. There were homes on both the east and west sides of the lot: an Austrian-looking chalet style on one side and an A-frame on the other. Behind the Roberson lot was a two-story log cabin built within the last couple of years, judging by the sheen on the logs and shine of the green metal roof. The cabin had a clear view of the scenic reservoir below.

Joe paused for a moment to study the other homes. By their drawn shades and the lack of any vehicles around them, he guessed no one was staying in them at the time. There were no observing neighbors standing around the perimeter of the location, or anyone talking with the deputies and other law enforcement inside.

Although he'd driven past the sign before, he'd never ventured into the development. He'd expected to find something more rural and remote, and was surprised how close the homes were to one another.

The north side of the Roberson lot appeared to be the edge of the Aspen Highlands development, and it flowed seamlessly into the National Forest. Someone—Butch?—had set up a half-sheet of plywood in front of a bermed backstop of dirt. The plywood was peppered with small holes, and had obviously been used for target practice. The paper targets had been removed. Next to the plywood was a stack of hay bales, likely used for archery practice. He looked around in the grass for the wink of spent brass and didn't see a single ejected cartridge. Whoever had been shooting had been meticulous about cleanup. The setup looked safe and well thought out to Joe, and certainly not an unusual sight in Twelve Sleep County.

Joe ducked under yellow crime scene tape that had been tacked to tree trunks and entered the lot. There was nothing on the lot except grass, an orange Kubota tractor with a loader on the front and a backhoe bucket on the back, and a mound of freshly dug soil. A knot of officers stood together off to the side of the mound, and their faces swung toward him. One of the uniformed deputy sheriffs—Joe knew him—nodded his way and detached from the others.

Deputy Justin Woods was young, tall, and angular. He

was a fairly new hire since Sheriff Reed had cleaned house of McLanahan's team of thugs. He'd recently returned from training at the Wyoming Law Enforcement Academy in Douglas, and his uniform was crisp and new. As he greeted Joe, he tipped his hat back on his head.

"Joe."

"Justin."

He gestured toward the mound of dirt. "Sheriff Reed is on the way up here with our evidence tech. We're waiting for the go-ahead to start digging."

Joe stepped to the side so he could see the mound better. It was about seven feet long and five feet wide, and the soil was so fresh some of the larger rocks poking out from it hadn't dried completely. Severed cables of tree roots were mixed with the soil.

"Sure looks like a grave, don't it?" Woods said.

"Yup." Joe nodded.

The surface around the mound was scored with V-shaped tractor-tire tracks.

Woods said, "We've got to check the backhoe for prints once the tech gets here. But it sure looks like somebody used it to dig this hole last night."

Joe agreed, and winced.

"I found the car," Woods said, gesturing over his shoulder in a vague southern direction. Joe frequently used the gravel ridge road Woods indicated. It was cut into the side of a steep mountain with a sloping grade on one side and a chasm on the other. There were turnouts for faint-of-heart drivers to return to civilization. Woods said, "It looked like somebody took it up the road and deliberately drove it off the ridge road into the canyon. They probably thought it would roll to the bottom and we wouldn't find it for months, but there were enough trees to stop it from crashing all the way to the creek."

"But no one inside?" Joe asked.

"No. But I could see those U.S. government plates easy enough from the road."

"And you're thinking this happened last night?" Joe asked.

Woods shrugged. "No way to know for sure yet, but that would be my guess."

Joe looked over at the mound again.

"Yeah," Woods said. "If somebody was buried alive . . ." He let his voice trail off.

Woods nodded toward his colleagues, who leaned on their shovels in a pool of late-afternoon sunlight. "I'd kind of like to get these guys started before it gets dark."

Joe felt a pang of frustration. He glanced at the deputies with their spades and the Forest Service ranger talking to the highway trooper. He could tell by the way the ranger was gesticulating that he was showing the size of a fish he claimed he'd caught recently in Meadowlark Lake on the other side of the mountains. He thought, *So much of law enforcement work is just standing around*.

He heard the pop of gravel under tires and looked up to see Sheriff Mike Reed's van strobing through the trees. It was a ten-year-old handicap-equipped panel Ford that had been specially purchased in Billings at an auction for the sheriff's use. Joe could see Reed was at the wheel, using the hand controls, with the evidence tech, another new employee named Gary Norwood, in the passenger seat. The election the year before had taken place while Reed was in surgery from his gunshot wounds. He'd emerged from the hospital as the paraplegic new sheriff of Twelve Sleep County. The county commissioners had agreed to buy the van, but they were balking at purchasing the motorized wheelchair he'd requested, so Reed rolled down the side ramp and was immediately stopped fast in the soft dirt. Norwood bounded over to help, but the sheriff waved him off. Instead, Sheriff Reed leaned forward and grasped the thin wheels with his big hands and shoved, powering his way to firmer ground, where Joe met him.

"I hate this," Reed said to Joe under his breath. "I'm fine in the office. I can get around. But out here it's another story. But I'm the *sheriff.* I need to get out into the county."

"Yup," Joe said, stepping aside.

"And I don't want anyone helping me, including you."

"I know."

"I don't know if I'll ever get used to this," Reed said. Joe wasn't sure he would, either. Before he'd been cut down by a desperate suspect, Reed had been tall and strapping, with a graceful, loping stride. It had been less than a year since the shooting, but Joe could see the loss of muscle mass in Reed's legs. His uniform trousers hung from bony thighs.

Reed spun in his chair toward Woods and asked for an update.

Joe listened in as Woods briefed the sheriff. Norwood tiptoed around the scene, snapping digital photos and placing evidence markers. Finally, Reed nodded, then called out to his men, "Okay, do this gently. Don't get your weight behind the shovel. Sift the dirt off and put it on a plastic tarp. You don't want to slice into anything with those shovels, gentlemen."

The deputies nodded and got to work. Reed glanced at his wristwatch and instructed Woods to call back to the sheriff's department and request a walled outfitters' tent, a generator, and portable lights.

"This may take a while," he said.

When Woods walked back to his SUV to get on the radio, Reed said to Joe, "I think I know what we're going to find."

"What?"

"At least two federal employees of the Environmental Protection Agency from Denver." His tone was solemn.

Joe looked over. The deputies were proceeding with caution, as instructed. When streams of soil were dropped on the blue plastic tarp, it made a sizzling sound.

"YOU SAW HIM, THEN," Reed said to Joe, as they watched the fresh dirt get removed from the mound an inch at a time.

"Butch Roberson?" Joe said. "Yeah, I ran into him just above Big Stream Ranch this afternoon. He told me he was scouting elk."

Joe described Butch's clothing, gear, and rifle.

"On foot?" Reed asked.

"Yup."

"And you believed his story?" Reed asked, flat.

"No reason not to," Joe said, a little defensive.

"If you'd brought him in, we might be a long way to solving this thing," Reed said, not meeting Joe's eyes.

Joe didn't respond.

"Sorry," Reed said, shaking his head. "There was no reason for me to say that, and no reason to bring him in. You didn't know anything at the time. But you know him, right?"

"Through my daughter," Joe said. "We aren't fishing buddies or anything."

Reed sighed and shifted his weight in his wheelchair from his left to his right side. Joe noticed the grimace on his face as he did it, and realized Reed was in pain. He hadn't considered that Reed still hurt from the gunshot wounds.

Joe asked Reed when the sheriff's office had first gotten the tip to check out the Roberson lot.

"This morning," Reed said. "Somebody called it in. Said he knew of two federal agents who were headed up here last night who never checked into the Holiday Inn."

"Who called?"

"He didn't give his name at first, but we tracked him down." Reed dug a notebook out of his breast pocket and flipped it open. "U.S. Army Corps of Engineers guy out of Cheyenne named Kim Love," he read. "He said he was supposed to come up here with the two EPA guys, but he got cold feet, or he felt kind of sick and needed to lie down. He said both things, so his story is a little hinky. I asked the guy to stay another night at the hotel before he headed back to Cheyenne so we could talk to him a little more. He said he'd check with his supervisor. That pissed me off, so

I told him if he tried to leave my county tonight I'd have *him* arrested," Reed said with irritation.

Joe asked, "He didn't say why he and the EPA guys were here in the first place?"

Reed said, "Something about serving a compliance order. I didn't quite understand at first. Not until I talked with Pam Roberson."

Joe was confused. "I haven't heard a thing about any conflict between the Robersons and the EPA. I'm pretty sure Marybeth doesn't know anything from Pam or she would have told me. Why is the EPA poking their noses around here, anyway?"

Reed snorted and said, "You won't believe it when I tell you. You'll want to be sitting down, if what Pam told me is true."

Joe waited, but Reed changed the subject.

"This might turn out to be my first murder investigation as sheriff," Reed said. "I used to be damned hard on Mc-Lanahan for the way he ran things. But now all I can think of is what we're missing or forgetting to do so some defense lawyer doesn't rip us up in court. This isn't easy, Joe. And I don't even have to tell you what a shit storm we're going to have if there are two dead Feds in my county."

Joe looked up. He said, "No, you don't."

"We heard they're on their way now. A couple of Fed big shots from the regional headquarters in Denver and some folks from Washington, D.C. They want to get up here and make sure we know what we're doing, I guess. They want to make sure I don't botch the investigation."

"You won't," Joe said, feeling bad for his friend.

"I should just tell them to turn around and go back. That we can handle it."

"Why don't you?"

"Because they didn't exactly ask my permission," Reed said, narrowing his eyes in anger. "You know how they can be."

ONE OF THE DEPUTIES digging into the mound gave a shout, and Gary Norwood jogged over to him. Joe and Reed saw the pops of a camera flash, then watched the evidence tech drop something into a paper evidence bag before he walked it over to show the sheriff.

Joe looked inside as the tech opened the top.

"One of our guys said it's a .40 Sig," Norwood said. "I sniffed it, and it doesn't appear to have been fired. We'll know for sure once we take it down to the lab and run it through tests."

Reed sat back in his chair and whistled.

Joe said, "Hold it. These guys were *armed*? *Armed* EPA people?"

"We haven't found any bodies yet," Norwood cautioned Joe.

"Still," Joe said, incredulous.

TEN MINUTES LATER one of the deputies with a shovel called out, "Got a body."

Sheriff Reed pursed his lips and rotated back on his wheels, then set the chair down. It was an involuntary reaction, Joe thought, as if Reed were shuffling his feet after hearing bad news. Reed whispered, "Damn it."

Another deputy said, "I'm pretty sure we've got two."

Norwood hovered around the pit taking photographs, the flash popping.

Joe left Reed and walked to the mound, which was now a shallow pit. He saw a young, waxen, square-jawed face that appeared to be looking up and out of the ground, eyes open. There was a single black hole in the brow. Next to the face was the profile of another man, older, turned on his side, his eyes closed as if sleeping. The arm of the older man was flung over the chest of the first, as if trying to cuddle. Their skin was dirty, pale, and dry, as though it were made of plastic. Norwood's camera exposed their dead white skin in bursts of flash.

Joe thought, *So indecent. So obscene. So without dignity in death.* Norwood retrieved two body bags from the back of Reed's van and unfurled them on the grass.

"Keep digging," Reed said from the perimeter. "Let's hope there's no more in there."

Joe felt his stomach constrict. He turned and stumbled out of the lot, ducking under the yellow tape. He tried to hold in his nausea, and succeeded until he heard retching from one of the new deputies. Then he bent forward, his hands on his knees, until there was nothing left in his stomach.

HE HEARD THE HEAVY bass beat of helicopter blades before he saw the lights in the still dusk sky. From the cab in his SUV, Woods said to Reed, "It's the Feds. They sent up a bird from Denver, and they want to know where they can land."

"Tell 'em the airport," Reed said sourly.

"Sir," Woods said, holding the mic away from him and covering it with his palm as though he wanted nothing more to do with it, "I think they want to land here."

"What, do they expect us to clear a landing zone like we're in Vietnam?" Reed asked. "Tell them if they have to, they can land up on the road."

"Will do," Woods said, ducking back into his vehicle because the sound of the helicopter was filling the forest.

Joe looked up as the chopper appeared, hovering a hundred feet above the treetops. The wash of wind swayed the trees and caused clouds of pine needles to drop to the forest floor. A spotlight clicked on and bathed the lot and everyone within the tape in blinding white light.

"This is Special Agent Chuck Coon of the FBI. *Clear the crime scene immediately*," came the amplified voice from the helicopter, *"and I mean immediately. Put those shovels down and step behind the tape until we give you the word."*

The deputies all looked toward Sheriff Reed, and Joe saw the man curse. Reed rarely cursed, so it surprised Joe. But the sound was so deafening he had to lip-read the words: *"Fucking Feds."*

Reluctantly, Reed motioned to his men to step away, and they did so, grumbling.

"Coon," Joe said to Reed. "Remember him? He usually doesn't come on so strong." Thinking: *Coon must have somebody senior to him up there in the chopper, barking commands.*

Coon was Joe's age, and he'd supervised the Cheyenne office of the FBI for several years. He was tightly wound and boyish-looking, with several children and a nice wife. Joe and Chuck Coon had been flung together on several cases, and despite the inherent bureaucratic tension, they'd gotten along well and Joe respected him.

The helicopter above them was still for a moment, then banked and flew above toward the road. As it did, Joe felt his cell phone vibrate in his pocket, and he turned his back to the beating sound and opened his phone. He could barely hear what the dispatcher said, so he had to keep asking her to repeat the message.

"The governor's on his way," she said, practically shouting into the other end. "And he's bringing your new director with him."

"New director?" Joe asked.

"Oh," the dispatcher said, "you haven't heard?"

6

WHILE JOE TEXTED THE QUESTION *WHAT'S THIS about a new director?* to Wyoming game wardens Biff Burton and Bill Haley for some kind of clarification, Justin Woods escorted the occupants of the helicopter from where they'd landed on a wide spot on the ridge road down to the Roberson lot.

Joe looked up to see three men behind Woods. He recognized the last in the group as Special Agent Chuck Coon, who lagged suspiciously behind the first two. Joe dropped his phone into his breast pocket and reached down to help Sheriff Reed spin his chair around to face them.

"Got it," Reed said impatiently, doing it himself.

Woods lifted the crime scene tape and stepped aside so the men could enter.

The EPA regional director—Joe would soon learn his name was Juan Julio Batista—ducked under the tape and halted, looking suspiciously from Reed to Joe to the body bags in the grass. He was slight, with a thick shock of jet-black hair and small eyes magnified slightly through rim-less glasses. He wore a sport jacket over a light blue shirt with a button-down collar and pressed khaki trousers. Joe noted Batista's fresh-out-of-the-box hiking shoes.

Batista's eyes flitted from face to face and didn't linger long enough to make a connection. To Joe, he sensed equal parts fear, indignation, and contempt. He pursed his lips before saying to Reed, "I'm Juan Julio Batista. People call me Julio. You're the sheriff in charge?"

Reed introduced himself, then started to introduce his deputies, but Batista cut him off.

"Where are the bodies?"

"In the bags," Reed said. "We left them open for your identification."

Batista paused cautiously, as if sensing a trap.

"You assume I know them personally?" he asked.

Reed shrugged. "You don't? I thought they worked in your shop."

"The EPA is not a *shop*," Batista said. "We're a very large agency with eighteen thousand full-time employees. So no, I don't know each and every employee personally."

"Sorry," Reed said, "I just assumed . . ."

"Let's not do that," Batista said, looking past the sher-iff and toward the hole in the ground. He took a deep breath and turned to the man behind him, and said, "Bring the files."

Reed extended his hand to the second man and said, "And you are . . . ?"

"EPA Special Agent Supervisor Heinz Underwood," Batista answered for him. Underwood simply nodded, and didn't shake Reed's hand.

Heinz Underwood was in his mid-sixties, Joe guessed, but he was solidly built and ramrod-straight. He had short-cropped silver hair, a bristled white mustache, pockmarked cheeks from an ancient but serious bout of acne, a heavy jaw, and piercing eyes. Unlike his boss, he seemed to revel in full-on stares designed to intimidate until the recipient looked away. After finishing off Woods and Reed, he did it to Joe, who willed himself to look back without blinking. After a beat, Underwood smiled slightly. Joe wondered what the contest had been about, who had won, and when it would resume.

Batista gestured for Underwood to follow him, and the two walked past Joe and toward the bodies. As he passed, Underwood gave Joe another look. This time, Joe smiled back. He got the impression Underwood was a tough professional who enjoyed his job.

Chuck Coon stayed where he was, and seemed suddenly fascinated by the laces on his shoes. Joe sidled up to him and said in a sarcastic whisper, "*This is Special Agent Chuck Coon of the FBI. Clear the crime scene immediately . . .*"

"Not now, Joe," Coon said sharply.

"Politics?"

"By the truckload. I got a call this morning from the second in command of the Department of Justice in Washington, right over the head of my director. He told me to drop everything I was doing to accompany Mr. Batista up here and to use our chopper. So cut me a break, Joe."

"So the FBI is now on call to the EPA?" Joe asked.

"Seems that way. But when the DOJ calls me direct, I do what I'm told."

Joe nodded and punched Coon affectionately on the shoulder.

"Don't let them see you do that," Coon hissed.

They turned to watch Batista and Underwood match up the faces of the bodies with photos from the personnel files they'd brought along. Batista said, loudly enough for everyone to hear: "Holy Mother of God." Joe noted a tinge of a Hispanic accent in the phrase he hadn't heard Batista use before.

"Where did he come from?" Joe whispered to Coon.

"Political appointee. I don't know his history, but he seems to have a lot of juice."

"Ah."

Batista turned and walked deliberately over to Reed until he was uncomfortably close, Joe thought, and so he could tower above him and make the sheriff tilt his chin up to see his face.

"Those bodies over there are EPA special agents sent up here in the line of duty," Batista said.

"That's what we thought, and my condolences. Do they have names?" Reed asked.

Batista looked over his shoulder to Underwood, and Underwood opened his files. "Tim Singewald and Lenox Baker," Underwood said. "Singewald worked for the agency for twelve years, and Baker for two and a half. Baker leaves a young family behind."

Over his shoulder, Batista said to Underwood: "Make sure you call the next of kin. Give them my deepest sympathies and say it's from my heart."

Underwood nodded crisply. "Do you want to talk to them as well?"

"No, I'm busy here. I'll have a letter sent."

"We're very sorry this happened here," Reed said to Batista, cutting in. "We'll do our best to bring the killer to justice."

Batista nodded to himself as if confirming his worst suspicions, and signaled for Underwood to come over to him. Joe watched the exchange with interest. Underwood approached Reed and Batista and said, "Sheriff, we're taking possession of this crime scene. I need you to get your men to stand down until we can get our people in place."

Reed said evenly, "That's not going to happen, gentlemen. I know how this works. This is my county and my jurisdiction. We're in the middle of a murder investigation, and we're gathering evidence and securing the scene. When you show me a court document signed by a judge ordering me to turn over my county to you, I might consider it."

Batista glared down at the sheriff but seemed too surprised to speak. He looked over anxiously to Underwood, who was stone-faced.

"Until that happens," Reed said, "I need you and your . . . assistant to move out beyond the crime scene tape and stop interfering with our work."

Batista said, "Mr. Underwood is not an assistant, Sheriff. He's our chief of law enforcement operations, and he brings years of experience from the FBI, the CIA, and Special Operations. There's no one we can trust more to carry out an investigation like this."

Joe assessed Underwood, who looked both cold and capable. Underwood showed no reaction to Batista's praise.

Batista took a half-step back, and turned to Chuck Coon, obviously anticipating backup.

Out of the corner of his eye, Joe saw Coon shrug. Batista looked as if he'd been slapped.

"You have nothing to worry about," Reed said, loud enough that his men could hear. "We know what we're doing. We'll get the bad guy, and we'll do it right. We might even request federal law enforcement assistance from Mr. Coon here," he said, nodding toward the agent, "but that's our call, not yours."

"This is a federal crime," Batista said. "Two officers of the U.S. government were murdered in cold blood. This has never happened before in my agency—*never*. I can't run the risk of turning it over to a local Barney Fife and his band of amateurs. I hope you understand. This isn't personal, but you have a small department. I can bring in the manpower and expertise of the federal government."

Joe saw Reed's face flush red, but the sheriff kept his calm. "I'm sorry you feel that way, Mr. Batista, but you're not taking over this investigation. Up here, we don't care if a murder victim is a federal employee or a local cowpoke. We treat all crimes seriously, and we vigorously investigate and prosecute them. Besides, I'm not exactly sure the shooting of two *armed men* can be considered murder in cold blood.

"At this point, Mr. Batista," Reed continued, his tone icy, "we don't know what happened yet. We are hoping you and your agency might be able to shed some light on the situation, in fact. We don't know if these two poor fellows showed up without warning on private land and waved their guns around in the air and got shot in self-defense, or perceived self-defense, or if they were ambushed or what. That's why we do an investigation."

Joe considered Julio Batista. The man looked apoplectic. His hands shook. Underwood reached out and placed his hand on Batista's shoulder to calm him. Batista shook it off.

"I will have your job for this," he said to Reed.

"No need for that kind of talk," Reed said calmly. "There are elections for that. Now please take Mr. Underwood and clear the crime scene so we can get to work. We want to make sure there aren't other bodies in that hole, and we're gathering any physical evidence we can find."

Again, Batista looked to Coon for assistance. Coon said calmly, "We might want to do that, Director Batista. We're losing our light, and it might be best to let these guys do their work while they still can."

Batista glared at Coon, obviously feeling betrayed. To Reed, Batista said, "I want you to put all of your effort and resources into finding this Butch Roberson. I want him thrown in a cage quickly for what he did to my men."

"We'll do our job," Reed said through clenched teeth.

"I'll make it known that we want this man," Batista said. "We want an example set of what happens to people when they murder public servants. I'll make it known that we'll

reward anyone who comes forward with information leading to his immediate arrest."

"You'll offer a *reward*?" Reed asked, incredulous. He
took a deep breath, and seemed to stifle his immediate
reaction. Instead, he said softly, "I'd advise against that."

"Advise all you want," Batista said. "We will do everything we can to bring this murderer to justice."

Joe shook his head, confounded by Batista's vehemence.
He looked to Coon, who pointedly refused to make eye
contact. Batista seemed determined to antagonize Reed for
reasons Joe couldn't fathom. Both Underwood and Coon
seemed to be along for the ride.

Joe was surprised when Batista turned to him. "You're
the one that let him go, right? You're the game warden who
had a nice little chat with the suspect and just let him walk
away?"

Joe said, "That would be me."

"I'll have your job, along with the sheriff's," Batista said.

"There have been many days when I'd just give it to
you," Joe said, shrugging.

He felt Coon's admonishing glare, urging Joe to keep
quiet. Behind Batista and out of his field of vision, Underwood raised his right hand and pointed his index finger at
Joe like a pistol. With his thumb, he let the hammer drop.

"I saw that," Joe said to Underwood. Underwood
smiled back with malevolence.

Then, reluctantly, Batista and Underwood moved away
from Sheriff Reed and stood just inside the crime scene
tape. Coon joined them. Batista smoldered in silence for a

moment, then retreated and pulled his cell phone and spoke heatedly to someone.

"**OUR GENERATOR AND LIGHTS** are here," Woods called out, as two more vehicles rumbled down the mountain road through the trees.

"Good," Reed said, turning toward his men with his back to Batista, Underwood, and Coon. "Keep digging, boys."

KIM LOVE of the U.S. Army Corps of Engineers arrived and got out of his sedan. There was a horrified look on his face, and he approached Joe and Reed on shaky legs.

"I could have been with them," Love said.

"Why weren't you?" Reed asked sharply.

Love looked down at his boots. "I didn't want any part of what they were doing. And the younger one was just too gung-ho. I'm getting too old for that kind of thing."

Reed told Love to drive back to town and give his statement to a uniform at the sheriff's department.

Reed said, "Make sure you leave us your contact details. We may have more questions."

"So I'm free to go home after?" Love asked, his mood improved.

"Yes."

"Good," Love said. "It's kind of crazy up here."

———

A MOMENT LATER, Joe felt a presence behind him and turned to find Heinz Underwood.

"Yes?"

Underwood did the stare again, his eyes level with Joe's. "You need to clear your plate, Mr. Pickett. Tomorrow I want to see exactly where you last talked to Butch Roberson so we can establish a forward operating base. He can't get very far on foot—if he was really on foot."

"He was when I met him," Joe said evenly. "I can't swear he didn't have a truck or ATV or even a horse stashed somewhere." Then: "The area I saw him in is National Forest. You'll need to clear it with them if you're going to set up some kind of camp."

"FOB," Underwood corrected.

"Whatever," Joe said. Then: "You won't be able to take vehicles into the forest very far. What few roads there were have been closed by the Forest Service. So if you plan to get into the mountains there, you'll need to go on horseback."

Underwood made a sour face. "Why are all the roads closed?"

"Ask *them*."

Joe continued, "And in order to get to it, we need to cross the Big Stream Ranch, which is private. You need to talk to the ranch owner. His name is Frank Zeller."

"We'll handle it," Underwood said. "Director Batista has already placed the call to the U.S. Department of Agriculture, and they're on board. They're deploying a forest ranger SWAT team to meet us here in the morning."

"A SWAT team?" Joe said, raising his eyebrows. "The

EPA has armed agents and the Forest Service has a SWAT team? When did this happen?"

"In the past few years," Underwood said dismissively, "but it's no concern of yours. Once we find the area and establish our base, you'll be cut loose to do whatever it is you do, and I don't want to see you around."

Joe felt his neck flush red. "Are you asking me or telling me? There's a difference."

"Either way, the result is the same. Besides, we've notified your governor and your new director, and they've pledged your full cooperation."

Joe blinked. The *governor*? Twice elected as a Democrat in a seventy percent Republican state, Governor Spencer Rulon was mercurial, devious, cantankerous, glib, contradictory, and wildly popular. For several years, Rulon had manipulated the agency structure to use Joe as his personal agent and point man in the field, careful to keep it him at arm's length, so if Joe screwed up, nothing would reflect back to the executive office in Cheyenne. When Joe had gotten too "hot"—according to the governor's chief of staff—he'd been temporarily shipped off into exile in South Central Wyoming and Rulon had cut off all communication. Joe had resumed his duties in the Twelve Sleep district and hadn't heard from Rulon since.

"I don't even know who my new director is," Joe said, knowing how lame it sounded.

Underwood shrugged, then leaned slightly forward so his nose was inches from Joe's.

"I know about you, Pickett," Underwood said.

"Have we met?"

"No, but your name is not exactly unknown to some of my friends. You've been around the block a few times."

"I'm just a game warden," Joe said.

"An irritating one, from what I understand."

Joe shrugged.

Underwood said, "Tomorrow," and turned and walked back to Batista.

Joe wasn't sure what Underwood had been talking about, and he couldn't connect the dots between him and the EPA chief of special agents. He'd been in the middle of so many situations in his career that involved clashes with other state and federal agencies and bureaus. It was unavoidable in a state half owned and administered by myriad federal agencies—the Bureau of Land Management, the U.S. Forest Service, the U.S. Park Service, the Bureau of Indian Affairs, the U.S. Fish and Wildlife Service, the Bureau of Reclamation, the Interior Department, the Agriculture Department—and now, apparently, the EPA.

Joe was sure he would have remembered Heinz Underwood, though, if he'd ever encountered him before. He was a memorable presence.

THE COUNTY EMPLOYEES who brought the lights and the tent weren't alone. Behind their panel van was a battered Jeep Cherokee. Joe recognized the driver and passenger as Sissy Skanlon, the twenty-six-year-old editor of the weekly Saddlestring *Roundup*, and Jim Parmenter, the northern Wyoming stringer for the daily *Billings Gazette*. Although the two were technically in competition, they pooled their limited resources so they could cover stories together.

"Here comes the media," Woods said with derision.

SKANLON AND PARMENTER gravitated to where Batista, Underwood, and Coon had grouped. Joe could hear murmured conversation. Batista took Underwood aside and spoke fervently for a minute, then stepped back. Joe was surprised Batista chose not to address the reporters himself and had apparently assigned Underwood the job. It was odd, Joe thought.

Underwood approached the two reporters and cleared his throat. Both pulled out notebooks and digital recorders to catch his words. Joe saw Underwood hand them a business card and pause while they read his title. Skanlon looked from the card to Batista and mouthed, *"Wow."*

"Underwood is telling them they're going to offer a reward—big money to anyone who can help nail Butch," Joe said to Reed. "You've got trouble."

"I know I do," Reed said, rubbing his face with his hands. Then: "Have you ever seen anything like that before? Jesus."

"You did well," Joe said. "Your guys are proud of you for the line you drew in the sand."

"I hope they'll still be proud if I get buried in it."

Joe chuckled.

"What's with that Batista guy?" Reed said under his breath. "He seems to have it out for me."

"Maybe he's just caught up in the moment," Joe said.

"This isn't the kind of situation he's used to, and he did lose two people."

"And what about Underwood? He seems to have it out for *you*."

Joe nodded. "I don't have a clue. I don't think I've ever met him before. He's not familiar to me."

"You seem to be familiar to *him*."

"Yeah, and I don't get it," Joe said. Then, to the darkening sky, "There's a lot going on I don't get, Mike."

Inside his breast pocket, Joe's cell phone suddenly vibrated with four incoming messages, one after the other. He turned and opened the phone to see who his new boss was.

7

VEHICLES WERE COMING UP HAZELTON ROAD
with their headlights on toward the Roberson lot as Joe
drove back down the mountain, against the stream. More
sheriff's department vehicles, local cops, another highway
patrolman, and pickups and SUVs from the Forest Service
and BLM. Several of the units looked like rentals from
Saddlestring Municipal Airport, Joe thought, and he
guessed they contained EPA, FBI, and other law enforcement who had arrived on the 6:40 flight from Denver. The
drivers of the rentals didn't wave back as he passed them
because, he assumed, they were unfamiliar with local custom where everybody waved at everybody simply as an
acknowledgment for sharing the road. He couldn't recall
seeing such a massive assemblage of state and federal employees before on one road, even the year before, when Nate

Romanowski was on the loose and the county was being littered with bodies.

He'd clapped Reed and Coon on the shoulder after he'd read his messages and told them to call him if he could be of any use. The scene was crowded and getting worse, and Joe could see no reason for staying around. The tent had been put up, and portable lights flooded the small lot. No additional bodies had been discovered in the hole, although the excavators did uncover a briefcase and the wallet badges of the two murdered EPA agents. Either the killer had removed the identification and tossed it into the hole with the bodies, or the agents themselves had pulled their IDs and died with them in their hands. The wallets confirmed the identification of the bodies even further.

The first message on Joe's phone was from Marybeth, asking him to pick up April at the western-wear store on his way home. The second and third were from Biff Burton and Bill Haley from other corners of the state.

Burton's message read: *Lisa Greene-Dempsey. Calls herself "LGD." Don't know a damned thing about her or where she came from.*

Haley's said: *Lisa Greene-Dempsey. The Gov has really lost it this time. Twenty-two weeks to my retirement. Counting the hours.*

So Bill Haley knew of her, Joe thought. He planned to give the other game warden a call later that evening.

The fourth was from Lisa Greene-Dempsey herself, although the number was listed as "unknown." It read: *LGD here, Joe. I'm on my way up w/ Gov. Rulon. I look forward to meeting one of our colorful wardens. Call me.*

"Colorful?" Joe said aloud.

He hesitated, then punched CALL. He was relieved that he got her voicemail. Her phone was out of range because she was likely in the state plane with the governor, flying up from Cheyenne. He haltingly said he looked forward to meeting her as well, and closed the phone.

JOE PULLED into an empty space on Main in front of Welton's Western Wear, one of the oldest retail stores in operation in Saddlestring. Because it was dark outside but all the lights were on inside despite the WE'RE CLOSED, PART-NER sign, the big display windows allowed anyone passing by to look over the jeans, boots, hats, and long-sleeved shirt display and into the store itself with the clarity of an aquarium.

He saw April right away, perched behind the counter, beaming at a couple of local boys on the other side. The boys were dressed identically in the unofficial uniform of Wyoming: T-shirts, baseball caps, faded jeans, belts with big buckles, and athletic shoes or scuffed boots. One of the boys said something, and April threw her head and hair back and laughed in what Joe thought was a provocative way. The boy who didn't tell the joke punched the other one hard in the chest, so it wasn't tough to figure out who the jibe had been aimed at.

Daisy spied April and whined, and her tail whumped the back of the truck seat.

"Okay, April," Joe said, "come on," hoping April would look out and see him waiting. He didn't want to have to

go inside and roust her and possibly create a situation with
the two boys.

Joe knew why two teenage boys would be in the store
after hours, and it didn't have anything to do with perusing
the Cinch shirts or Ariat boots. April was a stunner. She
wore a short skirt with a tooled belt, tall red cowboy boots,
and a top too tight to be subtle. And when she tossed her
hair back that way . . . Joe didn't like it.

The week before, another boy who looked the same as
these two had driven his pickup to their house to take April
out to a movie. Joe had taken the boy aside and whispered
in his ear: "I have a rifle, a shovel, and ten acres of land,
son." The boy had her back by ten.

Joe tapped on his horn, and the three teenagers inside
glanced out. Joe flashed the boys with his cab-mounted
spotlight and watched them recoil. April rolled her eyes
and shooed them away, then gestured to Joe to wait for a
moment while she closed down the store.

As the two boys walked past Joe's truck, they looked
over at him sheepishly.

"NAW, I HAVEN'T MET HER," Bill Haley told Joe, who
was waiting for April to lock up and come out of the store.
The cell connection between the two game wardens was
scratchy and poor. "I've just heard things."

"What things?"

"That she's a do-gooder with grand ideas about, and I
quote, '*dragging the agency into the twenty-first century.*'"

Joe paused. "That might not be all bad, Bill."

"Hell, Joe," Haley said, "I'm still struggling with the *twentieth* century."

Joe laughed.

"Seriously," Haley said, "I hear she considers herself progressive. She thinks the agency is a good-old-boy network, and she wants to shake things up."

Joe shrugged. "We could use a little shaking up from time to time."

"Maybe, but I'm too old and set in my ways for that. I've been around awhile and I remember a couple of other bomb-thrower directors in the past. You weren't around when there was a move to rename us 'conservation officers' or, worse, 'resource managers.' Back then, I just figured I could outlast them, and I did. This time, I'm tired and I just want out. Those types are wearing me down, Joe. I'm an old goddamned game warden and a good one, and that's all I ever wanted to be."

"Gotcha," Joe said. "Where did the governor even find her?"

"I heard it was his wife," Haley said slyly. "The First Lady has lots of friends in the smart set, I hear. The gov owes her a couple, from what I understand."

"Hmph."

Joe wasn't as plugged in to the gossip in Cheyenne as Bill Haley was, but he did recall phoning the governor's office once and having the telephone answered by Stella Ennis, who had once tempted Joe himself. Stella had been named chief of staff, and she claimed she was sitting on the governor's lap at the time. Stella compounded the problem when a reporter from the *Casper Star-Tribune* asked her about her qualifications to be chief of staff and she answered, "Have you seen these lips?"

It was a joke, but according to rumor, the response didn't go over well with the First Lady.

"All I know," Haley said, "is it's time for me to move on and leave it to you younger guys. Things are changing, and I'm not changing with them."

"I'm not that young," Joe said, and as he did, April sashayed across the sidewalk and swung into the passenger seat.

"No kidding," April said, listening in. "You're practically *fossilized*."

Joe shushed her, and said good-bye to Bill Haley.

As they passed the impressive hulk of the Saddlestring Hotel on the corner on the way to Bighorn Road, Joe said, "There it is."

April grunted something, preoccupied with text messages on her phone.

APRIL'S TRANSFORMATION from a moody, sullen, almost scary teenager into a bouncy and fashionable cowgirl had come so suddenly Joe and Marybeth were still reeling from it. It was almost as if she were trying on a new persona, Joe thought, like taking a new April for a test drive to see if she liked her. He was cautiously optimistic it might stick. Better a cowgirl than a Goth or Emo, Marybeth told him, pointing out that it had been two months since their foster daughter had worn all black or painted her mouth and nails the same color.

It could be worse: much worse, she'd said.

Joe had agreed, and still did. But the trouble with cowgirls, he knew, was the cowboys who came with them.

IT WAS FULL DARK and sultry when Joe pulled into his driveway and turned off his engine.

"Who's here?" April asked, gesturing toward the ten-year-old Ford Explorer parked in front of the house. It was parked next to Hannah's dented sedan.

"That's Pam Roberson's rig," Joe said.

"What's she doing here so late?"

Joe said, "There's a lot going on with her husband."

JOE HEARD TALKING from the kitchen table as he entered the house and took off his hat and boots in the mudroom. Daisy scrambled between his legs to engage Tube in a welcome-back wrestle-off in the middle of the front room, and Joe unclipped his Glock and placed it near his crown-down Stetson on the top shelf.

He took a deep breath before going farther. The small house seemed even smaller with all three girls home for the summer, plus Hannah and her mother. Every flat surface, it seemed, was cluttered with books, backpacks, water bottles, DVDs, magazines, and electronics. The entire place smelled of hair products.

April went straight to her bedroom and closed the door behind her without a word to anyone, as was her custom. Sheridan and Lucy shared the bedroom across the hall, but

both seemed okay with the arrangement. Neither wanted
to room with April, although they didn't say so directly.
Marybeth had let the girls sort out the sleeping arrange-
ments under a parental philosophy she described to Joe as
"Don't Ask, Don't Tell."

Joe found Marybeth, Sheridan, and Pam Roberson sitting at the kitchen table, drinking iced tea. All three looked
up expectantly, and Joe's eyes lingered on Pam for a moment, trying to read her. She looked wan and exhausted,
and thinner than usual, although she'd always been trim.
Pam had an angular weathered face, high cheekbones, and
thick shoulder-length strawberry hair feathered into an
early-eighties look. She wore a sleeveless top and jeans, and
her shoulders were freckled. Joe thought she was almost
attractive—probably had been when she was in her teens
and twenties—but looked and dressed as if she had never
left that period.

Like her husband, she was plainspoken and blunt; smart,
honest, and hardworking—if not well educated. Joe recalled
her saying once she'd attended college for a couple of years
but then dropped out when she'd met Butch. She wanted
her daughter to get a degree. She doted on Hannah, whom
she urged to strive high and accomplish something. Pam
was intensely involved in school activities and was always
there when the school administration needed a chaper-
one for a field trip or a dance, or cookies for a bake sale.
She was one of those behind-the-scenes mothers who made
everything work.

Although she'd been to their home many times to drop
off and pick up Hannah, Joe rarely saw her because it usu-

ally happened during his working day when he was out in the field. It seemed odd to see her sitting with such familiarity at his kitchen table, and he guessed she must have done it frequently over the past two years of their daughters' friendship.

"I heard they found two bodies on our lot," she said, finally.

"News travels fast," Joe said.

"Dulcie," Marybeth said, holding up her cell phone. "She's kept me in the loop."

Joe nodded, wondering if Marybeth realized that by being kept in the loop she was now sharing information with a suspect, or at least the wife of a suspect.

"I heard you saw Butch today," Pam said to Joe.

"I did."

"Did he . . . seem okay to you?"

"You haven't heard from him yourself?" Joe asked.

Pam shook her head no and lowered her eyes.

Before proceeding, Joe glanced at Sheridan, who was watching and listening intently. He didn't want her to become involved, just like he never wanted his family to become too involved, although they did. Sheridan knew the look and rolled her eyes.

It was an awkward time for them all, Joe knew. Sheridan had lived away at college for a year by herself, and now she was home. She was an adult, yet she wasn't, and it was tough for all of them to sort out what exactly she was. She liked to eat with the family when her mom cooked— usually—but often went into town to be with her friends. She often declared her independence, yet was dependent when she wanted to be. Joe wasn't sure yet how to act around her, and he thought Sheridan wasn't sure what her role was, either. They had been extremely close while Sheridan grew up, and Joe thought for a while she might follow in his footsteps. Now he wasn't so sure, and he suspected she wasn't sure what she wanted to do, either.

In two weeks, she'd be heading off to Laramie for her second year at the university. Joe didn't even want to think about it yet.

"There's pizza in the fridge," Marybeth said.

"I could make you a salad," Sheridan offered. She was still wearing her T-shirt top that read BURG-O-PARDNER over the breast.

Joe raised his eyebrows.

"Part of my job," she said. "After I take customers' orders and turn them in, I have to make the salads and get soup and bread for them. So I've turned into quite the little salad jockey."

"I don't eat salad," Joe said. "You know that."

"You should start," she said, grinning. "Man can't live on meat alone."

"I have."

He sat down with a plate of pizza slices, glanced at Pam, and said, "So here we are."

"Sheridan . . ." Marybeth said.

"Yeah, yeah," Sheridan said, pushing her chair back. "Nice to see you, Pam," she said.

Joe noted she called her Pam, not Mrs. Roberson.

Then to Joe and Marybeth: "I'll be out back in the barn with my new bird."

"New bird?" Joe asked, surprised.

"Just a little kestrel," Sheridan said over her shoulder as she went to the back door. "You'll need to come out and see it."

Joe and Marybeth exchanged glances. While Sheridan had been Nate Romanowski's apprentice in falconry, both had assumed she'd lost interest. *Apparently not*, Joe thought.

Marybeth said, "Joe, Pam wants to talk with you to see if you can offer some advice."

Joe narrowed his eyes. "I'm not a lawyer."

"I know that," Pam said.

"She doesn't need legal help yet," Marybeth continued, "but since you've been involved in this . . . *thing* all day, you might have some insight."

"Or not," Joe said.

"I trust you and Marybeth," Pam said. "Right now, I'm not sure who else I can trust. Is it true some big shot from the EPA put a reward out on Butch's head?"

"Yes," Joe said.

"Can he do that?" Pam asked, wide-eyed.

"He seems to think he can."

"Joe, what is going on?" Pam asked.

Joe chewed deliberately on a slice of pizza. He swallowed and said to Pam, "I was hoping *you'd* tell me what's going on. Sheriff Reed said it was something he couldn't even believe happened."

She nodded, and took a deep breath.

Before she began, Joe said, "Pam, you need to have something clear in your mind before you start. I'm—

we're—your friend, but I'm also in law enforcement. I have an oath to keep. I'm not officially interrogating you, and you don't have to tell me a thing if you don't want. But if you do, keep in mind that it isn't between friends, so to speak."

Pam looked desperate, and turned to Marybeth.

Marybeth said, "Do you want me to leave?"

"No," Pam said, "I want you to stay. But I already told the sheriff everything. I don't have any secrets. I'm just surprised Joe is acting like this."

"He has to," Marybeth said, reaching out and patting the back of Pam's hand. "Don't take it personally."

"I'll try not to," Pam said, gathering herself together and throwing her shoulders back. Then, to Joe, "I'll start at the beginning."

"Good place to start," he said.

8

"BUTCH WANTED A PLACE TO RETIRE IN THE mountains, on a lake," Pam Roberson said, "and he didn't want to leave Wyoming. Montana would have been okay, or Idaho, but it was his dream to own a home closer to where he hunts and fishes. He practically lives for those things, you know. He likes to say he feels like he was born one hundred fifty years too late."

Joe nodded. It was a familiar story. He knew dozens of men who were hard workers and could pull in more income if they relocated elsewhere. North Dakota was booming, and it wasn't that far away, for example. But the reason they lived and worked in Wyoming, he knew, was because of the outdoor culture, the lack of people, and the resources— specifically, big-game hunting and great trout fishing. It certainly wasn't because of the wind or the weather.

"So five years ago," Pam said, "he was talking with one

of the developers of Aspen Highlands. They wanted him
to build a spec home up there to help get it going. As you
know, we're not wealthy people and our little construction
company kind of exists week-to-week. Not many people are
building homes these days, and those that want to can't get
bank loans, so it's tough. So, financially, we really couldn't
make it work to do a spec home with no guaranteed return
right away. But the developers offered Butch and me a deal:
build the home in exchange for a lot that was worth sixty
thousand dollars. We didn't get first pick because they
wanted real money for the first few sales, but we saw it as
our opportunity to have the place Butch had always wanted
in the mountains."

"What about you?" Marybeth asked. "Is that your
dream, too?"

Pam looked away rather than answer. Finally, she said,
"I wanted Butch to be happy. I wanted him to have something to aspire to, if you know what I mean. You don't
know this about him, but he has a tendency to get down
in the dumps. He was raised in a tough household where
his dad had nothing good to say to him. Ever. He doesn't
have a lot of confidence in himself at times, even though
he should, because he's a good husband and father and he's
solid as a rock most of the time. But Butch can really be
hard on himself, and when he gets like that he's not much
fun to be around."

"That surprises me to hear that," Joe said. "I've always
found him rough and ready." As he said it, he was reminded
of Butch Roberson's haunted eyes just that afternoon.

"He comes off that way," Pam said. "He doesn't like to

talk, and sometimes I have to practically scream at him to say something. But when he told me that the most important thing to him—besides Hannah and me—was a nice home in the mountains, well, I wanted to do all I could to make that happen for him. So I agreed on the deal, even though we were taking a risk if the spec home didn't sell. We had to really beg our bankers to max out our loan ceilings, and we knew the bankers and the material suppliers were nervous about getting paid back.

"But we did it," she said, with a proud smile. "It took too long, almost eighteen months, to sell the spec home. Did you see that nice A-frame up there?" she asked Joe.

"I did."

"That was it. And when it sold, we paid off everyone and got the title to the lot you saw. I don't think I've ever seen Butch so happy. He was like a little boy because it was the first time in his life he really had his own property. Even though we can't afford to do anything with it yet, he goes up there after work and on weekends just to putter around. He's got targets set up for archery and for his hunting rifle, and he'd ask Hannah to go with him. It makes me almost cry when I think about how happy he was, how proud he was."

Joe glanced over at Marybeth and saw her eyes glisten as she listened to her friend.

"So this was five years ago," Joe said. "But it doesn't look like anything was done with the lot until very recently."

Pam placed both of her hands around her tea and focused on the glass itself.

"Not until a year ago," she said. "That's when Butch

put our company tractor on the trailer and took it up there to start leveling out the ground for the foundation. Until then, we hadn't really done anything with it except get all the permits we needed and design the house. We spent hours at night drawing floor plans and crunching numbers. I'll have to show you the plans, Marybeth," she said. "Two levels, three bedrooms, three baths, and a wraparound deck for the whole place. It really is wonderful."

"I'd like to see it," Marybeth said wistfully.

Joe got a pang. He wondered if Marybeth harbored similar dreams that were unattainable to them right now.

Pam said, "I told him it might be years before we could actually finish the house, but he took on extra work—driving the school bus and working part-time at Bighorn Liquors—to sock enough away that we could at least pour the foundation. We figured if he did most of the work himself we could save a bundle and maybe even be able to use the place once Hannah went to college."

"She didn't want to move up there?" Marybeth asked.

"Ha!" Pam coughed. "Don't get me wrong—she loved to go up there with her father, but I think it's more because she wanted to be with him. The last thing on earth she wanted was to move so far out of town away from her friends."

"Sounds like Lucy," Marybeth said, and laughed. "A social butterfly."

"Exactly," Pam said.

"So . . ." Joe prompted.

"Right," Pam said, switching back on track. "Butch saved enough to get the foundation dug out, framed, and poured. So a year ago, he went up there on a Friday and started moving dirt. He also had fill dirt brought up and dumped because the lot slopes toward the lake."

"Two acres, right?" Joe asked.

"Yeah. Not very big, but big enough."

"So tell me how this involves the EPA," Joe said. "I'm not connecting the dots."

Pam looked at him and her expression was fierce. "Even when I tell you what happened, you won't be able to connect them," she said. "Three days after Butch started grading the lot, on a Monday—Hannah was up there with him because it was Memorial Day—he was on his tractor when he looked up and saw a car coming down the road. Three middle-aged women get out, and one starts waving at him—*summoning him*—to come over. He shuts off the tractor and climbs off and walks over to where they parked, which is the road right next to our lot."

"Were you there?" Joe asked, trying to ascertain if Pam was an eyewitness or had heard the story secondhand, considering her use of the words "middle-aged" and "summoning."

"I wasn't there," she said, "but I heard the same story from both Butch and Hannah. Hannah overheard the entire exchange.

"So these three women get out of their car and stand there, glaring at my husband. There was nothing special about them—they weren't wearing suits or professional clothes or anything. Butch said he thought they were three lost tourists when he saw them," she said.

"So he goes over there and one of them says she's from

the EPA office in Cheyenne. She says he has to cease and desist moving dirt that second, that the lot is an official wetlands, and to restore the ground immediately exactly like he found it or he was breaking the law."

Joe sat back, blinked, and said, *"What?"*

"That's what they told him: that our lot was a wetlands and he was violating the Clean Water Act by disturbing it. They told him they were issuing him a verbal compliance order and that unless he restored every inch of the dirt to where it had been before he started up his tractor—and planted native grass and plants on the disturbed soil—we'd be fined every day until it was done."

"Hold it," Joe said, shaking his head. "I thought you said you got permits before you did anything."

"We did!" Pam said, smacking the tabletop with the palm of her hand. "I did it myself. We're in construction—we know how these things work. I got permits from the county and the state, and I got title to the land cleared through a title company. No one ever said anything about wetlands. And you've seen it, right?"

Joe said he had.

"Did you see anything that looks like a wetlands? Did you see any running water, or a swamp, or anything at all besides the natural slope of the land?"

"No," Joe said, trying to recall the contours of the lot. There was nothing resembling a stream or runoff ditch. And the neighboring houses were close enough, he thought, that he could throw rocks and hit them.

"So when Butch came home that night he was nearly

out of his head," Pam said. "I made him repeat the story about four times, because I couldn't believe that three broads could just drive up and tell us to stop building our home like that."

"Back up," Joe said. "I'm trying to wrap my mind around this. So walk me through it, okay?"

"Okay."

"You received no calls in advance, or any letters from the EPA?"

"No."

"Did anyone else in the subdivision or the developers have any trouble before? Did anyone else have to do anything special to develop their home?"

"No. And I know this because of the spec home we built. All our permits sailed right through."

Joe said, "These three women—were they all from the EPA office in Cheyenne?"

"Two were, they told Butch," Pam said. "The third one was from the U.S. Army Corps of Engineers, or so she said."

"Who were they, exactly? Did they give Butch paperwork or letters from the government?"

Pam shook her head emphatically. "I know the name of one: Shauna Naous. She gave Butch her business card, and I've talked to her since. Butch can't remember if the other two gave their names or not. They didn't give Butch anything at all except Shauna Naous's business card. Oh, and they said we would be fined seventy thousand dollars a day." Pam's voice was deadpan, as if delivering the punch line.

"Say again," Joe said, assuming he'd not heard correctly.

"Seventy thousand dollars a day," Pam repeated. "Starting that Monday, until we complied with the order."

"Your lot was worth . . ."

"Sixty thousand," Pam said.

"Wow," Joe said.

"That's what they told him, and then they drove away. If Butch didn't restore the lot to exactly the way it looked three days before—including the weeds and grass—we would be fined seventy thousand dollars per day. This was after three days of dirt work. As you know, there is no way possible to plant grass and weeds and make it look completely natural on a construction site for months in this country. Even if Butch hauled all the dirt out and bladed the slope back to the same grade it was, it isn't possible to have grass just magically grow again."

"Pam," Joe said firmly, "you're telling me that three bureaucrats drove all the way north from Cheyenne and showed up without a court order, or a warrant, or anything besides a single business card and told you to stop working on the property you owned or you'd have to pay seventy thousand dollars a day in fines?"

"That's what I'm telling you, Joe," she said. "I swear it."

"This is just like the Sackett case in Idaho."

Marybeth asked, "The what?" Pam looked up like she didn't know the case, either, which Joe found surprising.

"The Sacketts," Joe said. "A married couple building a home in a subdivision near Priest Lake. Out of the blue, EPA folks showed up and told them to stop and didn't provide any kind of documentation. Told them to restore the land, or they'd get a huge fine every day. The case is working itself through the legal system right now, and my understanding is it's likely to wind up in the Supreme Court."

"You're telling me this happened before?" Pam asked, as if she wasn't sure whether it was good or bad news.

"Something similar, anyway," Joe said. "Pam, be honest with me. I saw the lot, but I didn't study it. Is there any way it's actually a wetlands area? Is it conceivable Butch was filling in a swamp or a runoff stream that would go into the lake?"

"No, and that's not all," Pam said. "When this horrible Naous person finally took my call, I asked her where they had gotten the information that our property was a wetlands. She told me that it was public information and I could look it up on the Internet at the U.S. Army Corps of Engineers National Wetlands Inventory database. I was pissed because I thought the developers somehow forgot to check that or something, so I got on the computer and checked it myself. And guess what?"

"What?"

"Our property isn't listed as a wetlands. I called her to tell her that, and you know what she said?"

She didn't wait for Joe to ask.

"She said the National Wetlands Inventory database isn't definitive. She said just because our property isn't on it doesn't mean it's not a wetlands."

Joe pushed back and stood up. He crossed the kitchen to the pantry and asked, "Anybody else want a bourbon and water?"

"I'll take one," Pam said.

"I'll take one, too," Marybeth said. "And I don't even like bourbon."

JOE PLACED THE THREE GLASSES on the table, and Pam sipped hers and made a sour face, but she didn't push it away.

"So what did Butch say to this Shauna Naous and the other two when they told him to stop working?" Joe asked.

"Nothing," Pam said, and sighed. "He just clammed up and waited for them to leave. I think he was so stunned by what they told him he just couldn't speak. His dream was just crashing down all around him and he couldn't believe what was happening and he just froze up. Boy, I wish I'd have been there. I would have thrown it right back in their faces and told them to get off my property—that they had no right to even be there."

Joe believed her.

"We've never been political," she said. "I don't even know if Butch voted in the past ten years. We just don't follow that stuff, even though I'd say we're both pretty patriotic and conservative. I'm sure he just couldn't get a handle on the fact that our government could do such a thing."

"Twice, apparently," Joe said, and shook his head. "The more you tell us, the more it sounds like the same *exact* thing that happened to the Sacketts. I wonder if the same people are behind both cases?" Then: "No," he said, answering his own question. "We're in Region Eight and Idaho is in Region Ten of the EPA. So it can't be the same person, can it?"

He looked to Marybeth, and she nodded crisply. She understood what he was implying.

"I'll start doing some research tomorrow," she said to Joe. To Pam: "What happened next?"

Pam took another sip. "After Butch came home with Hannah and told me what happened, he just shook his head and sat in his chair in front of the television with the sound off. Hannah said he was quiet all the way home. I tried to discuss it with him, but he couldn't even talk about it, he was so depressed. He scared me that night. We've got plenty of guns in the house, and that was the first time I ever gathered them all up and hid them in the basement. Not that I thought he'd grab one and go after those women— I thought he might do something to himself. I wanted him to scream and yell and cuss out those women and the EPA, but he just sat there and stared. I didn't want him to let his emotions get bottled up that way, but that's how he is."

Joe asked, "Did Butch do anything with the lot? Did he blade the dirt back?"

"No," Pam said sadly. "He just walked away that afternoon and never went back. And the next day he went to work like nothing had happened."

Marybeth shook her head.

"I'm not like Butch, though," Pam said. "And the next day I was on the phone to this Naous, leaving messages every hour. Either she didn't want to talk with me or she was out of the office. I called all week. Finally, on that Friday, she called me back at four-fifty p.m. and made it a point to tell me she only had ten minutes to talk."

"What was she like?" Marybeth asked.

"She just sounded annoyed but tried to act like she wasn't," Pam said. "Like I was really imposing on her valuable time. I think if I hadn't hounded her, she might not have *ever* called me back."

She took a breath. "At first," Pam continued, "the way she explained things to me made me think Butch might have misunderstood her. She said we could clear everything up by getting what she called an after-the-fact permit once the U.S. Army Corps of Engineers did a study and said our lot wasn't a wetlands. That sounded stupid to me, because no one else had to get an after-the-fact permit, but I wrote it down and thought we shouldn't have any trouble getting one, since anyone can see there isn't any water on our property.

"When I asked her where we go to get the study started, she tells me it can't happen until we request one and the process could take years and hundreds of thousands of dollars—and it's still not a guarantee that the EPA will agree with it."

"You're kidding," Joe said, amazed and growing angrier as she went on.

"I wish I was," Pam said. "She said that even if a study said it *wasn't* a wetlands, we'd then have to apply to the EPA for something called a wetlands development permit and have it approved or rejected. See, if it was approved, we could start building, and if it was rejected we could have our day in court to try and prove them wrong. I asked how long that takes, and she said *years*. Plus, we'd have to pay application fees and lawyers' fees and that could amount to a quarter of a million dollars, she guessed. And if the wetlands development permit was rejected, all we could do then was sue the EPA in federal court, and that would take hundreds of thousands more and even more years."

"They've got you coming and going," Joe said.

"Right," Pam said, sitting back and draining her drink. "It's me and Butch going up against a federal agency with dozens of government lawyers paid by my tax money. They've got all the time and money in the world, and none of them are risking their personal bank account or livelihood like we are. And in the meanwhile, even if we started going through the process and applying for after-the-fact permits, we'd still be racking up fines of seventy thousand dollars a day. So as I was talking to this woman, I was getting more and more upset until I was crying. I might have said some things to her I shouldn't. In fact, I know I did."

Joe was confused. He said, "I still don't get it. A person gives you a business card and the fines start automatically that day? With nothing in writing at all?"

Pam said, "I begged her to send me something. I sent certified letters to her office begging for some kind of documentation of what they were doing to us and why. But she ignored me, and no one in that office would talk to me on the phone. After a couple of months, I just stopped calling."

Joe asked, "Did you try to get in touch with any of her higher-ups?"

"I sent letters and emails but never got a reply."

"Does the name Juan Julio Batista mean anything to you?"

"Sure," Pam said. "He's the big boss. I found his name in a directory, but I couldn't get past his secretary when I called, and he never replied to my emails."

"What about Heinz Underwood?"

"Never heard of him."

Joe said, "How was Butch taking this?"

"Badly," Pam said. "He just withdrew into his shell. He went to work, he came home and ate dinner, but it was like he wasn't really there. We were both waiting for the other shoe to drop—for something to happen so we could maybe find a lawyer or call the governor or some politician who might be able to help. We did talk to a lawyer, but he said he couldn't really do anything without seeing something in writing from the EPA. In fact, he kind of looked at us like we were paranoid or exaggerating. So we waited for the EPA to slap us with some kind of charge, but nothing happened."

Marybeth said, "Is that why you never said anything about it to me or anyone? Because you thought we might not believe you?"

Pam took a moment to answer while considering the question. "It's complicated. I think even though we were convinced we didn't do anything wrong we still felt . . . guilty somehow. It's just like the questions you're asking me—like you think there has to be another side to this story, because why else would they come after us like that?

"But there is no other side," she said, "unless it's something we don't know or never thought about. I think both

Butch and I always believed someone would just say, 'Hey, this is crazy. This can't happen in America,' and it would just go away."

Joe said, "You mean since that first encounter you never got a letter, or anything, from the EPA? Not even a call?"

"Nothing," she said. "I started to think it was all some kind of bad dream. Or, like I said, that it might somehow just go away. I thought maybe Shauna Naous and the EPA had lost their paperwork, or it fell through the cracks or something. I hoped maybe she got fired or something and the whole thing left with her. Then I realized federal employees *never* get fired. Still, I was starting to have some hope again. But I couldn't ever stop thinking of that seventy thousand dollars a day.

"A couple of months ago," Pam said, "Butch moved out. He said he just needed to be by himself."

Marybeth gasped and covered her mouth. She said, "Pam, why didn't you tell me?"

Pam shook her head. "I was ashamed. I didn't want anyone to know. Every day I thought he'd move back in and our life would be normal again. We still worked together at the office, but at the end of the day I'd come home and he'd go to his place. I made Hannah promise me not to tell you, but I think she told Lucy."

"Lucy never said a word," Marybeth whispered.

"She's a good friend for Hannah," Pam said. "I so appreciate her being able to spend so much time here with a *normal* family."

"Oh, we've got issues," Marybeth said, and laughed, "but we think of her as one of our own. She's a sweet girl."

"She likes you, too," Pam said.

"Where has Butch been staying?" Joe asked Pam.

"Downtown. In some grungy little apartment over the Stockman's Bar."

"I know of it," Joe said, recalling once breaking into the apartment during a case two years before.

Pam said, "The good news is Butch moved back home just last week. He said since we hadn't heard anything from the EPA in nearly a year, that maybe it was all some kind of bureaucratic snafu. He said they could at least apologize for what they put us through, but he didn't really expect anything.

"It was like having the old Butch back," Pam said with a sad smile. "It was like a black cloud had lifted from him. That's not to say I didn't resent the hell out of him for leaving us. We still have issues to work through on that one, and I don't plan to let him off the hook as easily as he expects me to let him off. But I'd be lying if I said I wasn't happy yesterday when he said he was going to go up to our lot and get back to work on it. He wasn't gone three hours before I got a call from Shauna Naous."

Joe held his breath.

"She said they were delivering the documentation I'd asked for, that it had taken a while to get it all put together."

"A *year* after you asked for it?" Marybeth said, obviously outraged.

"And she reminded me that our fine had been accumulating and was up to over twenty-four million dollars," Pam said, with a high-pitched cackle. "Over twenty-four million dollars! Here we are barely scraping along with hardly two nickels to rub together and they say we owe them twenty-four million in fines. I told her they could have the lot—that we'd just sign it over to them and they could keep it. But she said they didn't work that way."

Joe noted the rage building in Marybeth's face as she listened.

He said to Pam, "This was yesterday when she called?"

"Yes. She said there were some special agents driving up from Denver to hand-deliver the documents."

"Did you tell Butch?"

"I tried. I called his cell phone, but he didn't pick up. I figured he was on the tractor up there and couldn't hear it ring."

Joe felt his stomach growl from tension. "So those two agents drove up there to your property and Butch didn't know they were coming?"

"No."

"How did they know he'd be there?" Joe asked.

"I have no idea," she said.

"Pam," Joe said, "do you think he snapped when he saw them?"

Tears filled her eyes, but she didn't cry. She said, "That's what I keep asking myself, Joe. But what else could it be?"

"And he didn't get in contact with you? He just never came home last night?"

"That's what happened. I thought maybe he was so depressed again he just froze up. I kept waiting for him to call or come by, because I wanted to read those papers myself and call the lawyer. But instead of Butch, Sheriff Reed showed up and started asking me questions."

Joe pondered his drink, thinking he wanted another.

"So what should I do, Joe?"

"What you should do is stop talking to me," Joe said. "Get lawyered up and don't say another word to anyone."

"Won't that make us look even more guilty?" Pam asked, looking from Joe to Marybeth. "That's the whole thing here—why should I have to look guilty? We didn't *do* anything."

Marybeth said, "Pam, Butch may have murdered two federal agents."

Pam reacted as if she'd been slapped, as if the realization of what Marybeth said had finally hit her.

So did Hannah and Lucy, who had just come around the corner into the kitchen from Lucy's room but stood there with open mouths.

HANNAH ROBERSON HAD THICK, dark curls that framed her face. She was shorter than Lucy, although she had a year on her, and she had light blue eyes—now rimmed with red—and a soft, melodic way of speaking.

"Mom?" she asked. "Is it true there's a reward out for Dad?"

Joe was jarred by the words.

Pam sighed. "Where did you hear that, honey?"

"Somebody texted me."

"It's not official," Pam said. "But some idiot said some things like that."

"That's just *wrong*," Hannah said, her eyes fierce.

"I know, honey."

"But maybe he didn't do it," Hannah said. "Did they ever think of that?"

"They're not thinking right now," Pam said. "They're just reacting."

Hannah said, "He's my *dad*. They talk about him like he's some kind of animal."

Joe looked away as Pam, Hannah, Marybeth, and Lucy gathered together and began to cry. He rose and refilled his glass and wasn't sure what to say. He certainly wasn't going to join in the crying circle. There were many things wrong with Pam's story, he thought, but it resembled what he knew of the Sackett case so closely it was remarkable. It made no sense to him that something like that could happen twice. But what if it were *true*?

That was a possibility he had trouble accepting.

"I'll be back in a minute," he said, slipping out through the back door.

HE FOUND SHERIDAN in an empty horse stall under a hissing Coleman lamp, feeding strips of raw chicken to her kestrel. The bird was hooded and perched on a dowel rod she must have rigged up herself, he thought. The square rabbit cage she'd appropriated for the little hawk was sitting on a set of old sawhorses.

The falcon was the smallest of all the falcons, barely larger than a mourning dove, but Joe could see its slate-blue wings, ruddy back feathers, and a glimpse of black-and-white marking beneath the edge of the hood.

"A little male, then," he said.

"Nate once told me to start small," she said, "but I didn't want to. I wanted a prairie falcon or a red-tail, maybe even a peregrine. But I can see the sense in it now."

She nodded toward the falcon. "This guy is probably going to be a lot of work because he's hurt and he wants to eat all the time. Will you help me build a real mews in here so I don't have to keep him in a cage?"

"Sure," Joe said, "but what—"

"Am I going to do with him when I go back to school?" she said, finishing the question for him.

"Yes."

"I don't know yet. I just got him today. A customer at the restaurant hit him with his truck and he was stuck inside the grille. I think he's got a broken wing. I couldn't just let them get rid of him somewhere."

"I sympathize," Joe said, "but that kind of rehabilitation takes a lot of time and patience."

"I know that, Dad," she said. "But what else was I going to do?"

Joe shrugged. Twenty or thirty times a year, he was called to the scene of an injured animal or bird. The people who called were always happy to turn the cripple over to Joe and wash their hands of it. On rare occasions, Joe could find a shelter or volunteer who would accept the creature. Usually, though, he had to kill it. It was a necessary part of his job that he didn't enjoy at all.

"I'll help you out when I can," Joe told Sheridan. "I learned a little about falcons from Nate. But we'll have to make a decision when it's time for you to go back to Laramie."

"Thank you," she said.

He walked over and gently ran the back of his hand down the length of the bird while it ate, then did the same along both of his wings. He felt a pronounced bump under the feathers of the right wing.

"Yes," he said, "I think it's broken."

"Will it mend on its own? I know that happens sometimes."

"And sometimes it doesn't," Joe said. They both knew what would happen to the bird if the wing didn't heal itself. No veterinarians in the area accepted wounded wild birds because there was little they could do other than stabilize them. There was a rehabilitation center in Jackson and another in Idaho, but Joe didn't know when he'd have the time to get to either—or if either place would want the bird.

"Be right back," he said, and went out of the barn and around the house to his pickup. He came back with a thick roll of Ace bandage from his first-aid kit and asked Sheridan to hold the bird still. He carefully wrapped the elasticized tape around the bird so its wings were bound tight. The bird didn't squawk while he did it, and Joe was pleased with the job.

"Let's keep this on him," he said. "See if that wing mends. Who knows? Maybe he'll fly again."

Joe put his hand on Sheridan's shoulder. She was tough, and had grown up with a full awareness of the circle of life in the wild. She could deal with it, however this turned out.

"I hope so," she said. "I'm already kind of fond of him. Did Nate ever name his birds?"

"No."

"I might."

He nodded and turned to go back to the house, when she said, "The EPA isn't entirely evil."

Joe stopped short of the door. "I didn't say they were," he said. "They paid for my water guzzlers."

"I feel they mean well in most cases," Sheridan said. "The good they do outweighs the bad, I feel."

Joe turned and nodded. "Probably," he said, and no more.

"I just wanted to get that out," Sheridan said, looking away. "I don't want to get in a big argument about it."

"I'm not arguing with you. There are bad eggs in every bureaucracy, and the bigger the agency gets, the more there are. We have a few knuckleheads in the Game and Fish Department. But I can't figure out how this could have happened *twice*."

"Well," she said, "thanks for listening, anyway."

"Sure," Joe said, reaching for the barn door.

"Oh—I need to show you something else later."

"What?"

"Are you investigating a case where some idiots shot an antelope buck about a million times and left it to rot in a field?"

"Yes," he said, taken aback.

"I think I know who did it," she said.

"Did you hear something at the restaurant?" he asked.

"No. They posted some photos on Facebook."

Joe smiled. "Yes, I'd like to see it."

"Is Mr. Roberson a murderer?"

He hesitated, but when she looked hard at him, he said, "Probably."

"Poor Hannah," Sheridan said, and fed her kestrel another piece of chicken.

JOE LAY IN BED with his fingers laced behind his neck and stared at the dark ceiling. The curtains rustled slightly with a cool breeze coming down from the mountains, and he could hear the horses tussling in the corral. It was 2:30 in the morning.

Pam had left, and Hannah stayed over again. While Joe was in the barn with Sheridan, Lisa Greene-Dempsey had called his cell phone and left a message saying she was in town and he was to meet her for breakfast at the Holiday Inn the next morning at 7:30. It wasn't a request.

Sheridan had shown him the Facebook pages for nineteen-year-old Bryce Pendergast and twenty-year-old Ryan McDermott, both of Saddlestring, both classmates of hers from high school. Pendergast's page showed him cradling a used .223 Ruger Mini-14 rifle with a banana clip. McDermott's had a short video of a full-grown pronghorn getting cut down by a series of shots and someone off camera hooting about it. The photo and the video had been posted the same night a week before. Joe recognized the buck by its curled-in ivory-tipped horns.

"CAN'T SLEEP EITHER?" Marybeth asked, fully awake.

"Nope."

"I can't stop thinking about the Robersons," she said. "How horrible it is what happened with them."

Joe grunted. He said, "Something about the story Pam told us doesn't sound right."

"Do you think she was lying? Leaving something out?"

"I want to hope that," Joe said. "But it's so similar to what happened in Idaho. There's no way it can just be a coincidence."

Marybeth asked, "Is it possible it's some kind of warped policy directive? To go after people in different states in the same way?"

"Not likely," Joe said. "The EPA is getting heat and bad publicity for the Sackett case because it was so outrageous. There's no way they would encourage their people to do it again. No, this is similar, but it's different. I just can't figure out how. And I can't figure out why Pam and Butch are in the middle of it."

Marybeth sighed and snuggled in closer to him. "I know what you mean," she said. "It just always amazes me how you can know someone for years and then find out things about them you never even imagined. I never had a clue about their dispute with the EPA, or that Butch had left Pam for so long."

"They kept it in all that time," Joe said.

Marybeth placed her bare arm over his chest. She said, "Sometimes I think the most mysterious thing that exists is the interworking of a relationship. You can just never even guess the things that go on behind closed doors."

Joe said, "Nope."

"Hannah is the one I'm most worried about."

Joe said, "Yup."

JOE THOUGHT ABOUT the arrival of Batista and Underwood on the scene. Underwood seemed to Joe like a type he'd dealt with before: tough, cold, professional—doing a dirty job well if they had no choice. A little like his friend Nate Romanowski and Nate's friends. Despite Underwood's manner and innuendo, Joe thought he could deal with him.

Batista was another matter. Batista unnerved Joe in a way he couldn't put his finger on.

But when he closed his eyes, he saw the haunted face of Butch Roberson, somewhere up there in the beetle-killed forest in the dark, no doubt listening for the first sounds of the men who would be coming to hunt him down.

DAY THREE

9

EARLY THE NEXT MORNING, DAVE FARKUS AWOKE from a dream about someone pounding on his door to realize that, yes, someone *was* pounding on his door. And when someone pounded on the door, the entire twelve-by-sixty-foot single-wide trailer—perched on cinder blocks and sheathed in peeling sheet metal—shook as if it were coming apart at the rivets. He could even hear dishes tinkling in the cupboards above the sink.

"Hold on, goddamnit!" he shouted. "I'm coming, I'm coming . . ."

Farkus threw back the covers and the stray black cat that slept on his bed screeched and ran for the closet. He stood up, spine popping like a muffled series of demolitions, and rubbed his face with his hands. Pulling on a pilled pair of sweats and a T-shirt, he slid his feet into a pair of cowboy boots and staggered down the narrow hallway past the bathroom, using the walls on both sides for balance.

Dave Farkus was fifty-seven and pear-shaped with rheumy eyes, jowls, thick muttonchop sideburns, and a bulbous nose. His top left incisor had a thin slot in it from biting off fishing line. He glanced at the digital clock over the stove. It was 6:29. He wondered who would be out and about so early. In his experience, if someone knocked on his door before seven or after nine at night, trouble of some kind was waiting on the porch.

He could see a bulky silhouette through the louvered slat windows of the metal front door. The silhouette was wearing a cowboy hat, and Farkus thought, *They've come for me.*

The trailer Farkus rented sat on an acre of sagebrush south of town, with a view of the municipal dump on one side and a gravel pit on the other. Someone had once attempted to plant a garden outside but had never progressed beyond making a rectangular outline in the dirt with river rocks. A 1953 Chevrolet pickup without an engine was propped up on its rims on the side of the trailer. Over the years, the trailer had settled so it listed slightly to the south. The high-altitude sun had faded the curtains to the point that they looked like parchment paper. The Formica tabletop was scarred with cigarette burns from a previous owner, and the floors were permanently gritty. But it had a satellite dish!

"Who is it?"

"Sheriff Kyle McLanahan," the silhouette said, with a deep western twang.

"I ain't done nothing recently," Farkus said. "Besides, you ain't the sheriff anymore."

Farkus heard a heavy sigh. Then: "Just open the door. We've got something to talk about."

"It's awful early."

"What—you've got to do your yoga? Open up, Farkus."

He hesitated. He'd been renting the single-wide for five months from a woman bartender at the Stockman's Bar who had moved in with a local Realtor. Too much of her stuff was still in boxes in the closet, even though she'd promised, over and over, to retrieve them. Farkus had told her he wouldn't pay the five-hundred-dollar rent that month until she cleared her things out. So had she hired the ex-sheriff to shake him down?

Or was it because of Ardith, his ex-wife, who demanded alimony payments even though she knew he'd lost his job? Had Ardith sent McLanahan to collect?

Or maybe he was serving as the debt collector for Bighorn Fly Shop? Coming for the cash Farkus owed or the three hundred dollars' worth of natural cock ringneck pheasant skins, mallard flank wood duck sides, and peacock eyes he planned to use to tie flies to sell to tourists and local yokels? Farkus had once seen McLanahan loitering around in the Bighorn Fly Shop, he recalled. So maybe Travis, the owner, had sent the ex-sheriff along to collect.

Farkus said, "I had no idea hackles cost so damned much these days on account of all the women braiding feathers in their hair. I'm a victim of fashion, and it ain't fair!"

McLanahan said, "I don't know what the hell you're talking about. I've got a proposition for you, so *open the door*."

Dave Farkus raked his fingers through his hair that was still pressed to the side of his head from the pillow, and reached for the handle.

KYLE MCLANAHAN WAS FATTER than when Farkus had last seen him, and he'd grown a full rust-colored beard. It was easy to gauge how much the ex-sheriff had gone to hell in less than a year, because there was still a billboard just within the town limits of Saddlestring showing the sheriff with a carrot between his teeth feeding a horse and the words REELECT OUR SHERIFF KYLE MCLANAHAN. Farkus wondered if the man cursed every time he drove by it.

McLanahan squeezed into the vinyl bench seat on one side of the cluttered table but kept his hat on. It was a good hat with a Gus McCrae crease to it, which gave McLanahan a rakish frontier look. The beard helped, too.

"Why don't you make some coffee?" McLanahan said. "I like mine strong enough to pick up a cow."

"What?"

"Never mind," McLanahan said with a drawl.

Farkus had heard that McLanahan was actually from West Virginia but while sheriff had become a frontier character actor. Farkus also knew him to be wily, ruthless, and ambitious. It was no secret that after McLanahan lost the election he went on a two-month bender that ended with him in the Meeteetse town jail, howling at the bitter injustice of it all. Rumors like that traveled fast in Wyoming.

While Farkus filled the carafe of the Mr. Coffee and shoveled twice as many grounds into the filter than he usually would, McLanahan said, "Did you hear about Butch Roberson?"

The name made Farkus jerk and splash water on his hand from the tap. He turned.

"No, what about him?"

"Looks like he murdered two federal agents in cold blood two nights ago and took to the hills. You really hadn't heard?"

Farkus shook his head. He hadn't ventured from the single-wide for three days because there was no point going the two miles into town. His disability check hadn't come yet, and he was cash poor. He couldn't afford gasoline, beer, or anything else. So he'd just stayed put, tied flies, eaten out of cans the owner had left in the cupboards, and waited for the mail carrier to deliver his check and bail him out. Since he'd left his job, this had become a monthly ritual.

"Did they catch him?" Farkus asked.

"Not as of this morning. Feds are pouring in from Cheyenne, Denver, and Washington, D.C. But they aren't organized yet. Word is they'll get their marching orders later today and begin a full-scale search for Roberson in the National Forest where he was last seen."

Farkus shook his head. "That don't make any sense to me," he said. "Butch Roberson is a fugitive?"

"You used to work for him, didn't you?" McLanahan asked. He had not lost any of his cop stink-eye and tone, Farkus thought.

"For a while."

"Until he fired you, I heard."

"I'm filing for unemployment," Farkus said. "He asked me to do things I couldn't do, on account of my neck injury."

McLanahan grinned devilishly. It was hard to see his mouth because of all the whiskers, but basically his beard and mustache shifted a little.

McLanahan said, "Yeah, nothing worse than a bad neck that can't be found or detected by a doctor. It must get frustrating, always having to go on and on about how much your neck hurts when they can't find anything wrong with it."

Farkus gestured at McLanahan with the half-full carafe so a little of the water splashed out of the top: "You said you had a proposition for me, but you're just busting my balls."

"Sorry," McLanahan said. "Didn't realize you were so sensitive."

"My neck *hurts*," Farkus insisted.

"And I've got a huge pain in my ass," McLanahan drawled. "His name is Mike Reed, and he's the gimp wearing my badge and sitting in my office. I call him Wheelchair Dick, on account he's in a wheelchair and he's a dick who beat me by nine sympathy votes."

Farkus nodded, wondering where this was going.

McLanahan shifted his weight so the edge of the table wouldn't prod him in the belly.

He said, "I heard you went hunting with Butch Roberson. Is that true?"

Farkus nodded. His new employer had heard of Farkus's exploits down in the Sierra Madre, when he'd been hired to guide a team of contract killers into the mountains to hunt for two homicidal brothers. Even though he'd spent most of the time lost, Farkus had embellished the story until he came out looking pretty good. Farkus even suggested to some guys at the Stockman's Bar that he'd been known as "Pathfinder," hoping the name would catch on. It didn't. Despite that, Butch Roberson had wanted to show Farkus *his* mountains, and Farkus had agreed to go along mainly because his boss had asked him.

"It was goddamned miserable," Farkus said. "Five straight days of climbing mountains and crawling through down timber. Hardest work I've ever done in my life. Butch Roberson is a crazy man. He hunts from an hour before sunrise to an hour past sundown, and he knows every nook and cranny in those mountains. Worst of all, he passed up a half dozen shots on elk because he wanted to keep hunting. He was like a man possessed by some kind of . . . obsession."

McLanahan grinned. "Did you learn anything?"

"About what?" Farkus said, turning to pour the water into the Mr. Coffee. "What I learned is that blistered feet and sore muscles ain't my idea of a wonderful time."

"I mean, did you learn about the terrain in the mountains up above the Big Stream Ranch? Did he show you the elk-hunting areas he likes best?"

"Yeah, and it's no picnic. It's rough country up there."

"Do you think you could go back up there and know your way around?"

Finally, Farkus knew where it was headed.

"There's a reward," McLanahan said. "Federal money,

and a lot of it—hundreds of thousands, if I heard right. Probably federal stimulus funds," he said, and laughed. "But a hell of a lot of it."

"How much?" Farkus asked.

"It don't matter," McLanahan said. "What matters is me finding Butch Roberson and either bringing him in or dragging him back facedown."

Farkus shook his head. "But Butch is a pretty nice guy overall. He's just an elk-hunting fool."

McLanahan waved his hand as if swatting at a moth.

"It's not about Butch Roberson," McLanahan said, "and it's not even about the reward that I'll split down the middle with you."

He paused for effect, then said, "It's about nine voters when the next election comes around."

"Oh," Farkus said.

"You in?"

Farkus looked around the single-wide at the faded curtains and the buckled interior siding. At the quarter-inch of grease on the underside of the stove hood and the pile of cat feces in the corner of the floor near McLanahan's boots.

"I can't swear I can find him," Farkus said.

"You don't have to swear. You just have to point me in the right direction before the Feds get their poop in a group."

McLanahan struggled to pry himself out of the tight fit and took a mug of coffee Farkus poured. He said, "I'll be back in three hours with horses, guns, and gear. Can you get your shit together by then?"

"I guess so."

"Pack for a couple of days and nights, although I'm guessing we won't be up there that long. Word is Butch is on foot. He won't be able to cover that much ground."

Farkus asked, "Should I bring my thirty-aught-six?"

"Can you hit anything with it?"

Farkus shrugged. He hadn't sighted it in since he'd gone hunting with Butch, and he recalled how many times that week he'd bumped the scope on rocks and trees.

McLanahan read his expression and said, "Don't worry, I'll have enough hardware to cover us."

Farkus shook his head and said, "Butch Roberson—that just don't seem right. He always seemed like, you know, a family guy, even though he could be a hell of a hard-ass on the construction site. I just can't see him doing what you said he done. What was the deal, anyhow?"

"I didn't accuse him," McLanahan said. "Wheelchair Dick and the Feds did. I'm just along for the ride."

"Will it just be us? Just you and me?"

McLanahan warned, "Don't get all wrapped up in the details, Dave. Leave the organizing part to me. Your job is to guide, not think, okay?"

Farkus nodded, and was still nodding when McLanahan went out the door. His weight on the front step made the trailer rock.

He was right. Trouble had shown up early.

10

ON HIS WAY TO THE HOLIDAY INN TO MEET HIS
new director for breakfast, Joe drove past the Twelve Sleep
County Municipal Airport on the bench above the town.
Despite a high chain-link fence that surrounded the perimeter, a small herd of pronghorn antelope had come back
and were grazing between the two runways. Because adult
pronghorns ranged from eighty to one hundred fifty
pounds, they obviously posed a safety hazard to incoming
aircraft and themselves, although they usually had the sense
to get far out of the way.

If he didn't have the appointment, Joe thought, he
would pull over and shoo them away by firing blank .22
cracker shells. If the pronghorns continued to hang out
between the runways, he might need to dart them and
transport them somewhere else in his district. The prospect

of a small propeller passenger plane striking one or more gave him a shudder.

And beyond the grazing pronghorns, parked in front of the state-owned hangar, was a glittering eight-passenger Cessna Encore jet. On the tail was the familiar bucking-horse-and-rider logo. It was known as *Rulon One*—the governor's plane.

JOE CHECKED HIS WATCH as he walked through the aging atrium to the restaurant in the back of the hotel. He was on time. He tried to guess what she might look like, thinking: trim, probably fashionable, businesslike, professional, tightly wound and anxious. He spotted her sitting alone in a booth next to the wall, speed-reading the *Casper Star-Tribune*, an iPhone within quick reach next to her cup of coffee.

Lisa Greene-Dempsey looked up as he approached her. There was no doubting who she was, and he congratulated himself for profiling her well enough to identify. She practically fell over herself getting up, he thought, tossing the newspaper aside and striding across the carpet to greet him. She took his extended right hand in both of hers and pumped it, and said, "The infamous Joe Pickett—I'm *so* happy to meet you."

He said, "Infamous?"

"Probably the wrong choice of words," she said, pulling him to her booth, still holding his hand. "Call me LGD."

"Okay, LGD." He removed his hat and placed it crown-down next to him.

"*Director* LGD," she said with a tight smile.

She was slim and tall with severely straight light brown hair parted just off-center on the top of her head. It was streaked with gray and cut along her jawline so it gave the impression of long hair without being long. She had high cheekbones and wore designer glasses that drew attention to her already oversized blue eyes. She smiled enthusiastically with her entire mouth, upper and lower teeth framed by a box of thin lips and thrust out at him in an overeager way. Joe felt more than slightly bowled over by the sheer intensity of her studied sincerity.

He hadn't even settled in the seat across from her before she started talking.

"On my run this morning with the sun just lighting up the mountains, I thought: what a magnificent place this is," she said, waggling her fingers in the air. "Mountains and fresh air, clean water in the streams, and I even saw some mule deer along the path. Two females and their babies, just watching me run past them, and I thought: we need to preserve this for future generations. They need to see and experience nature in the same way we do, and I'm afraid we sometimes take what we've got for granted, you know?"

Joe said, "Yup."

"I think an important part of our agency's mission should be to encourage the appreciation and sense of wonder a viable wildlife population brings us. I hope that doesn't sound too touchy-feely, but I believe it."

Joe nodded in agreement, but had trouble keeping eye

contact because her look was so . . . intense. He was relieved when the waitress came over and asked for his order.

"He doesn't have a menu," Greene-Dempsey said archly to the waitress.

The server was middle-aged and overweight, with broad features, stout legs, and a no-nonsense set to her mouth. Her name badge said MAYVONNE. She'd worked at the restaurant for as long as Joe could remember, and she was known for sass. She took a deep breath, as if holding her tongue was a struggle, glanced at Joe, then glared at his new boss.

"That's okay," Joe told MayVonne quickly, trying to avert an outbreak of hostilities. "I'll have the usual."

As MayVonne filled his coffee cup she said, "Two eggs over easy, ham, wheat toast, no hash browns?"

"Yup."

"Ketchup and Tabasco on the side?"

"Yes, ma'am."

She grunted and turned on her heel for the kitchen.

"The service here could be better," Greene-Dempsey said, watching the waitress retreat. "And the food . . ." she said, making a face and gesturing to her picked-through fruit plate. "It's not exactly fresh. Who knows how long it's been sitting around back there?"

"We're a long way from fruit orchards and the ocean," Joe said. "I don't eat much that doesn't come from somewhere closer." He shrugged. "It's sort of part of the deal."

Greene-Dempsey shot a look at the swinging batwing doors to the kitchen MayVonne had pushed through.

She said, "She needs to work on her attitude."

Joe shrugged and said, "MayVonne has a boy in Afghanistan and a husband who can't find work. This is her second job. I cut her a little slack."

"Oh," LGD said, embarrassed.

GREENE-DEMPSEY SAID, "Before we discuss the matter at hand, I want to completely clear the air as far as you and the department goes."

Joe looked up. "I didn't know there was air to clear."

She laughed uncomfortably and said, "Of course there is, but not to worry. As far as I'm concerned, we all start fresh. It's a brand-new day, and it will soon be a rebranded agency, and I want all of my people—all of my *team*—to know that whatever happened in the past stays in the past. As I said, we all start fresh. The slate is wiped clean."

She said it with a sense of triumph.

When Joe didn't respond, she said, "Some people might have been troubled by things that have happened along the way. Some might say a certain game warden was a little too close in proximity when a former director was brutally killed, or a little too familiar with a certain federal fugitive who lived nearby. Some might say that a career history marked by certain periods of defiance to policy and outright insubordination are indicators of future defiance to policy and future insubordination. But those people would be wrong."

Before Joe could respond and ask who "those people" were, Greene-Dempsey said, "I have something for you."

"What—my severance papers?"

She laughed loudly, and playfully slapped the back of his hand. "You're such a character," she said.

He knew he grimaced.

"Here," she said, handing over a large, thick legal-sized envelope.

He took it.

"Open it," she said, her eyes sparkling.

Joe worked his finger under the seal, ripped it open, and dumped the contents on the table. The items consisted of a laminated card, a Game and Fish Department badge, and a smaller envelope.

"I've already got a badge," he said, puzzled.

"Look at the number," she said, gleaming.

It took him a second to realize what she meant, then he read JOE PICKETT, GAME WARDEN, #21.

"Your number has been restored to where it would have been if you'd never had that unfortunate incident a few years back," she said. "I asked my staff to do the research, and you'd now be number twenty-one. And that's what you are again, so congratulations, Joe. And welcome back."

He fingered the badge. The laminated card also indicated his new—restored—numerical designation. In one fell swoop he'd moved twenty-seven rankings.

"Thank you," he said.

"In the envelope is a letter from me making it all official."

"I appreciate it."

She nodded and said, "When they told me how important those numbers are to game wardens, how the lowest number represents the most years in service, I realized how disenfranchised you must feel. Anyone would."

She raised her index finger and touched the side of her jaw, as if demonstrating the act of thinking. She said, "So I thought, what would cause a game warden to act out? What would make a good solid employee by all accounts responsible for three times as much damage to state property than any other employee in a large agency? It puzzled me, at first, but when I asked about your history, I found out a previous director had taken away your status. You literally were disenfranchised. So I put two and two together."

Joe felt himself flushing with embarrassment.

"This really isn't necessary," he said. "I'm fine with my badge number."

"You say that," she said, mischievously, as if she knew better.

"Really," he said. "But I appreciate the effort."

"Of course," she said. "Like I said, it's a new day. There are people who thought easing out people like you might be the best thing for the department as we begin our transformation."

Joe said, "Who are these people who are always saying things?"

"Never mind that," she said dismissively. "The governor thinks the world of you."

"He does?"

"He told me so himself. He also made a reference to some special work you did for him once, but he didn't get specific."

"I see," Joe said, not elaborating. If the governor hadn't told her how the arrangement had worked and what he'd done for him, Joe took that as a cue not to tell her, either.

"Where is the governor, by the way?" Joe asked, looking around. Both the restaurant and the lobby were vacant.

"Oh, he's here," she said. "We checked in together last night. At the same time, I should say." She rolled her eyes and blushed at the implication, even though Joe hadn't made it. "So I suspect he's working in his room or meeting with local officials. You can't imagine how stressful it is to run an agency like mine, much less the entire state."

Joe could imagine. He wished, though, that LGD would stop referring to "her" agency, "her" team, and "her" staff. He hoped it was a matter of semantics.

Instead, he said, "And what do you mean by transformation?" He was thinking of Bill Haley's decision to retire.

She said, "I've reviewed the duties of a game warden. It's supposed to be one-third resource management, one-third landowner and community relations, and one-third law enforcement, right?"

"Right."

"What I see, though, is most wardens skew heavily on law enforcement at the expense of the other two. And wildlife appreciation needs to figure somewhere in that mix."

He nodded cautiously, agreeing but wondering where she was going.

"I want to change the agency for the better, Joe, and I'm asking you for your support."

"My support?"

"I'm creating a new position: field liaison. The field liaison would serve directly under me and be my eyes, ears, and advocate for new policy with game wardens and biologists across the state. I know how hardheaded and set in their ways many of these men can be, but they might be persuaded if someone they know and trust—and admire—fills the position. Someone who has been where they are and knows their issues. That someone would be you."

Joe said, "You're offering me a new job?"

"You don't have to answer right now, but I want you to really think hard about it. Believe me, there are people in Cheyenne at headquarters who think I'm crazy. You are not the most popular guy with some of them. They point to your record with state-issued vehicles, for example. But as far as the game wardens go—I haven't heard a bad word. They would listen to what you have to say."

Joe didn't respond.

She continued, "Your salary would increase by eighteen thousand dollars, and you'd move up two grades."

"Where is the job based?"

"Cheyenne, of course. I even have an office picked out next to mine, and we can share the same administrative staff."

"Cheyenne?"

"That's where our office is."

Joe had done his best over the years to avoid trips to headquarters. He knew several old game wardens who prided themselves on *never* darkening the halls of the agency building for their entire careers.

"I'm flattered you asked me," Joe said, "but I really have

to think this through and talk to my wife. She's got a business deal going here right now."

"Of course you should talk with her," LGD said. "I wouldn't expect anything different."

"I need to hear a lot more about the changes you're proposing," Joe said. "I would be a lousy advocate if I didn't agree with them."

"Of course," she said, sitting back. "We'll have time for that later. But one thing I'm adamant about is reducing the number of wardens in the field and replacing them with people more attuned to new thinking."

He looked at her. "Are you saying my job might go away?"

"Nothing is set in stone."

She leaned forward across the table, and her eyes got even bigger. "Joe, this is the twenty-first century, and it's time for a new paradigm. It isn't the Wild West anymore, and hasn't been for quite some time. I realize that it used to be that game wardens out in the field were given almost complete autonomy, and that probably worked back when Game and Fish meant Guts and Feathers. But we all need to realize we're not just here to check hunting licenses anymore. We're here to save and protect a precious resource."

Joe said, "You think all we do is check hunting licenses?"

"No, of course not, but we can get into all that later," Greene-Dempsey said. "Along with your plans to recover another department vehicle that I understand is still stuck somewhere in the mountains?"

"In a snowfield," Joe said. "I need to get it out."

"Yes, you do," she said, her face turning hard for a split second before recovering. "But first you need to know that I pledged Mr. Batista and Mr. Underwood our full cooperation in their investigative efforts. By extension, that means you."

Joe whistled.

"Is there a problem?" she asked.

MayVonne arrived with his breakfast, and he started on it while Greene-Dempsey sent her plate back and asked the waitress to bring one with only the freshest fruit. May-Vonne took another deep breath and stomped off toward the kitchen.

"THEY'RE TOO HEAVY-HANDED," Joe said when LGD asked about the status of the investigation. "I realize a terrible crime has taken place and we need to find the bad guy. But the way this Batista is going about it . . ."

"They're doing what they think they need to do," she said. "And we've pledged our cooperation and assistance. The governor is fully on board with this."

"He is?" Joe said, knowing Governor Rulon's legendary battles with the federal government over a range of contentious issues. He had once challenged the secretary of interior to an arm-wrestling match to determine a state versus federal policy on wolves, for example.

"We really don't need to get into the political weeds on this," she said. "It's not something you need to get involved in. But can you assure me you'll provide your full assistance and expertise to Mr. Batista and Mr. Underwood?"

Joe took a sip of coffee. "Yes," he said, "as long as they calm down a little. They've been offering rewards to nail Butch Roberson. That's not the way to do this."

"No caveats," she said, again instant steel. "Do I have your assurance?"

Joe took a deep breath and said, "Sure. They haven't called me yet to meet with them, but I expect that will happen later today. I might be able to help them and make sure it's not some kind of execution at the same time. I don't trust this Underwood guy. He seems like the type who would love to pull the trigger on Butch. Maybe I can stop him, and make sure Butch is behind bars where he belongs—for his own safety, if nothing else."

"That's good, Joe," she said, though without her previous enthusiasm. "You sound like you have doubts about their motives."

"I don't doubt their motives one bit," Joe said. "They've got two special agents down. I'd be the same if it were two game wardens. But they need to let the sheriff do his job."

When she looked at him askance, Joe said, "We see this kind of thing too much, and it's a big problem. Sometimes the Feds are too quick to rush in and assume everyone local is incompetent. It's like an absentee owner who over-reacts because he wants to make sure everyone knows who's boss."

"But it's a federal matter, not a local matter."

"Do you know the story behind it?" Joe asked.

"I've heard some things."

"It's one of the worst things I've ever heard," Joe said, "if true. And it's not the first time it's happened."

She said, "That isn't our concern right now. I'm sure you're aware of the conflicts going on between the state and the federal government on a variety of fronts. There has even been talk that the Department of Justice *and* the Department of Interior may sue us because of decisions Governor Rulon has made. He doesn't want another problem."

"No one does."

"Maybe," she said, reaching across the table and touching his hand again in an odd gesture that belied what she said next: "Maybe you're a little too close to the people involved."

Joe looked back, stung by the truth in it, and said, "And maybe you're too far away."

Her smile wasn't a smile at all, and he knew at that moment that one of the reasons she was offering him the new job fell partially under the category of *Keep your friends close and your enemies closer.*

Her iPhone started skittering across the table, and she caught it and looked at the display screen.

"I need to take this," she said. "See what I mean about pressures?" And she slid out of the booth. He watched her as she walked swiftly through the atrium, talking on the cell and gesticulating wildly with her free hand.

SHE RETURNED as he finished his breakfast. A new fruit plate had been delivered that, Joe thought, looked exactly like the first, except moister. He wondered if MayVonne and the cook had spit on it.

Lisa Greene-Dempsey glared at it and pushed it aside and said, "There has to be somewhere I can get fresh food in this town if I have to go to the supermarket myself. Unfortunately, I came here in the governor's Suburban and I don't know where he is right now. I assume your town doesn't have any taxis?"

"Correct. But I'd be happy to take you," Joe said.

"You would?" she asked, genuinely pleased.

"I've got an errand to run first," he said, "if you don't mind."

"Not at all."

He grabbed the check. He didn't feel right about her buying his breakfast when she didn't eat.

Joe said, "Before you make all your plans to transform the agency, do you want to come along and see a little of what I do?"

"Then you'll take me to the supermarket?" she asked, looking at her watch.

"Yup. Come with me, Director LGD."

"I'll get my jacket."

AT THE CASH REGISTER, MayVonne looked at him and shook her head.

"Piece of work you've got there," she said.

"My new boss."

"I could tell she wasn't from around here. Is she staying long?"

Joe shrugged.

"Because if she does, her and me are going to go round and round like two wet socks," MayVonne said, ringing him up.

Joe grinned. He had no idea what she was talking about, but he got the gist.

"One more thing," MayVonne said, lowering her voice in a way that made Joe take notice. "If those assholes did to Butch Roberson like I heard they did, I hope he takes out the whole damned lot of them."

Joe said, "You may not want to mention that to the governor if you see him."

She said, "I already did."

"What?"

"I saw him this morning," she said with a wry grin. "He had biscuits and gravy, and he left me a nice tip."

"Did he say where he was going?"

"Yeah," she said, smirking. "He said he was going crazy."

11

"HIS NAME IS BRYCE PENDERGAST," JOE SAID TO Lisa Greene-Dempsey, "and his partner in crime is a guy named Ryan McDermott."

She sat in the passenger seat wearing a sweater over her shoulders with her briefcase on her lap and her phone in her hand as Joe drove through Saddlestring. She looked to Joe like she was trying to be a good sport by coming along with him. He was embarrassed by the unkempt appearance of the gear and paperwork stuffed into every nook and cranny inside the cab, and he was grateful he hadn't brought Tube or Daisy along as well that morning.

"It's kind of my office," he said.

"I understand. So what is it we're doing?"

"Checking on a couple of low-life poachers," Joe said. "I've seen them around. They bounce from entry-level job to entry-level job and usually quit in a huff. Neither one of them graduated high school, although Bryce may have gotten his GED. I've seen Ryan McDermott's name in the police blotter a few times for DWI, and I think Pendergast might have been picked up once for breaking into cars. I haven't seen them out in the field, though, so I always considered them city troublemakers, not poachers."

She shook her head as he talked, and said, "It's troubling what happens to youth that are without opportunities."

Joe shook his head and said, "Bryce's parents are high school teachers, and Ryan McDermott's dad is an Episcopalian bishop. They've had plenty of opportunities—they just didn't want 'em."

"Oh," she said quickly, and looked away.

Joe said, "Sometimes people just turn out mean. You'll go crazy trying to figure out ways to prevent it from happening altogether. The only thing we can do is arrest the bad guys and put them away if we can."

She nodded and said, "This we can agree on."

"Some common ground," Joe said, smiling. He said, "People who violate our game and fish regulations often go on to do real harm to innocent citizens. It's like a gateway drug to them to worse crimes down the road. You've heard of the 'broken windows' theory of law enforcement?"

She nodded. "If we rigorously prosecute even the smallest crimes, it will set a tone and prevent bigger crimes, right?"

"Right. Well, this is the frontier version. Someone who would kill an animal out of season for the thrill of it indicates a general lack of respect for rules and laws, and sets the stage for something worse to come. That's why I throw the book at 'em if I catch 'em."

She considered what he said, and seemed to agree, he thought.

HE DROVE into an unincorporated area that hugged the west side of the town limit. The asphalt road gave way to rutted dirt, and the neat rows of suburban homes gave way to wildly incongruous houses, trailers, and lot-sized collections of junked cars and weeds.

He briefed her on the crime itself and the entries Sheridan had found on Facebook. LGD listened with interest and said, "Do you really think they're stupid enough to put the pictures up on the Internet?"

"Oh, yeah," Joe said.

"That's disgusting."

"Yup. And nothing makes me madder than slaughtering an animal and leaving it to rot."

"But to post things on Facebook . . . How dumb can they be?"

"Dumb," Joe said. "Most criminals aren't very smart—that's why they're criminals. I've caught guys because they mounted the heads of illegal trophies in their living rooms. This is a new wrinkle, though, putting up a kind of cybertrophy."

"THESE PEOPLE," she said, looking out her window at the ramshackle homes and trailers with tires thrown on the roof to keep the tops from blowing off in the wind. Then, catching herself, she said, "You know what I mean."

"They're not all bad," Joe said defensively. "The kind of crime we're investigating is actually pretty rare. Most folks around here hate poachers as much as I do, and they turn them in. They look at wildlife as a resource. They don't want it violated any more than we do.

"There are degrees of violation," Joe continued, knowing he was pushing the line. "If I find somebody who killed a deer to feed his family, I usually don't come down on him as hard as someone who killed a deer for the antlers only. And this type of thing—leaving the carcass—deserves no mercy at all."

She didn't look at him when she said, "So you're telling me you make your own rules?"

"I'd consider it discretion," he said.

Then: "Do all my game wardens make their own rules?"

"Can't say," Joe said, realizing he'd provided fuel to one of her burning fires.

"I worry that getting too close to the locals might make some of my people go . . . native," she said, looking closely at him for his reaction. "You know, it might not be as easy to arrest somebody whom you saw at PTA board the night before, for example. Or you might be a little more sympathetic than necessary to a local rancher making a damage claim if that same rancher is on your softball team."

Joe shrugged. "Seems to me we do a better job if we know the people we're working for—if we're among them."

"Unless you forget who you're working for," she said,

and shifted in her seat in a way that said the conversation was over.

HE TURNED on Fourth Street and slowed down under an overgrown canopy of ancient cottonwood trees. The duplex he was looking for, Bryce Pendergast's last known address, was one half of the house. There was a marked difference between the condition of the duplex on the left side and the one on the right. The right side was freshly painted, and there were flowers planted on the side of the porch and floral curtains in the window. The right side of the lawn was green and well maintained. An ancient Buick was parked under a carport.

On the left side of the duplex was a jacked-up Ford F-150 parked in front on the curb so it blocked the sidewalk, and the small yard between the unpainted picket fence and the front door was dried out and marked by burned yellow ovals on both sides of the broken walk between the gate and the door.

"Guess which one Bryce lives in," Joe said, pulling over and killing the engine.

He called in his position to dispatch and said he planned to question a potential suspect in a wildlife violation and gave the name and address.

"GF-forty-eight clear," he said, and racked the mic. Then he remembered and said to Greene-Dempsey: "I should have said GF-twenty-one, I guess."

She nodded nervously, her eyes dancing between Joe and the dark duplex.

Joe dug a digital audio micro-recorder out of the satchel on the floor and checked the power, then turned it on and dropped it in his front breast pocket.

She said, "Is that legal? To record somebody like that?"

"Yes. As long as one party knows the conversation is recorded, it's legal," he said patiently.

"So you're just going to walk up there and knock on the door?" she asked. "Aren't you going to call for help? For backup?"

"Don't have any," Joe said, trying to maintain his calm. "Plus, I think the sheriff's department has enough on its plate right now, don't you think?"

"Still . . ."

"Relax," he said. "This isn't unusual. I'll go up there and see if Bryce is in, and if he is, I'll check him out."

"How? You don't have a warrant . . ."

Joe said, "Here's what I do, and I've done this many times. It's my standard operating procedure. If Bryce or Ryan McDermott come to the door, I'll be friendly and professional and say, 'Hi, guys. I guess you know why I'm here.' And then I'll see what happens, whether they act like they don't know, or they start lying and overtalking, or what. I've had people confess right on the spot quite a few times. Sometimes, they blurt out confessions to crimes I didn't even know about, and sometimes they implicate their buddies."

Greene-Dempsey looked at him with obvious doubt.

She said, "Maybe you should wait a few days for this. You know—after the sheriff's department can provide some help."

He thought about it, then shook his head. He said, "It's been a week since that antelope was shot. They probably think they got away with it. But something about killing wildlife bugs many of them worse than if they'd shot a person. It's like that little tiny bit of conscience they've got tells them it's *really* wrong. So when you just ask them, sometimes they'll start spilling."

He touched the digital recorder with the tips of his fingers. "So if they confess, I've got it here."

Joe said, "Even if they keep lying and don't admit a thing or invite me in, they'll know they're under suspicion. That alone sometimes leads to them turning themselves in later or ratting on their buddy. Just showing up gets things moving in the right direction."

She shook her head and looked at him as if he were crazy.

"Tell me this isn't what you do all day."

"It isn't." He reached for the door handle.

"You can stay right here. I'll be back in a few minutes, I suspect."

"No," she said. "I want to see this. I want to see what my game wardens do. I can't be a proper director if I don't know how things work in the field."

"Deal," Joe said, swinging out and clamping his hat on his head. "You can be my backup."

She grinned nervously at that.

THE MORNING WAS HEATING UP into another warm August day. Tufts of translucent cotton from the ancient cottonwood trees were poised on the tips of the grass, awaiting a breath of wind to transport them somewhere. As he approached the broken gate, he instinctively reached down and brushed his fingertips across the top of his Glock, his cuffs, and the canister of bear spray on his belt, just to assure himself his equipment was there. The hinges on the gate moaned as he pushed it open. Lisa Greene-Dempsey maintained a ten-foot distance behind him, and followed him cautiously into the yard.

He was wondering about the burned splotches in the grass on the left side of the shared yard when a woman pushed the screen door open on the right side and stood behind it.

"Are you here about the cat urine?" she asked. "It's about time."

She looked to be in her seventies, and wore a thick robe and pink slippers. She had a cup of coffee in one hand and a cigarette in the other.

"Pardon?" Joe said.

"It reeks like cat urine," she said, gesturing next door with a tilt of her head. "When it's calm like this, the smell just about makes me sick. I've told them to clean it up, but they just laugh at me and tell me they don't own no cats."

Then Joe smelled it, the whiff of ammonia.

"I'm surprised they sent the game warden," she said, "but I'm not complaining. I expected the sheriff, but I guess you're in charge of animals around here."

"Sort of," Joe said. "But I'm here on another matter."

"Figures," she said, rolling her eyes. "Nobody seems to care that much about my problems. Even the guy who owns the place just shrugs and tells me he won't do anything because they pay the rent on time. I showed him where in the lease it said you can't have pets, but he just doesn't care."

"I'm sorry," Joe said. "I'm not here for that."

"Just make sure to ask them about the cats."

"Okay," Joe said.

She stepped back and closed the door in front of her. A moment later, Joe saw the floral curtains part an inch so she could watch what happened next.

He turned to Greene-Dempsey and shrugged. She looked nervously at the front door of the left side of the duplex.

"You can still wait in the truck," he said.

She shook her head no.

"Then make sure you stay back and to the side, please," he said.

THE ODOR GOT STRONGER on the porch when he knocked on the door. Because of the Ford pickup in front, he assumed somebody was home. When he leaned his head close to the door, he could hear and feel the thumping of bass notes from a radio or music player of some kind.

He knocked again, and heard the scuffling of feet. To his right, there was a glimpse of a face in the dirty window, and he waved at it as if to say *gotcha*.

Then, after some low murmuring on the other side of the door that indicated there was more than one person inside, a series of bolts were thrown. Joe thought, *Bolts?*

And Bryce Pendergast was standing in front of him with

the door halfway open, his face contorted into a pulled-back grimace. Pendergast was naked from the waist up, severely thin, with a sleeve tattoo on the arm. He had long, stringy hair that glistened with hair product—or grease. The tendons in his neck looked to be as taut as guitar strings, and his breathing was quick and shallow. The right side of Pendergast's body was hidden behind the door. A strong whoosh of the odor enveloped Joe on the porch.

"What do you want?" Pendergast asked, his voice high and strained.

Joe smiled and said in a friendly tone, "I guess you know why I'm here, Bryce."

"I guess I do," Pendergast said.

And in the instant it took for Joe to realize that the cat-urine smell was in fact raw ammonia from inside and the burns in the grass were from meth-making chemicals, Pendergast threw open the door and Joe saw the big pistol in Bryce's right hand that had been out of sight behind the door. The pistol suddenly swung up toward his face.

Behind him, Joe heard Greene-Dempsey gasp—and Joe ducked and flailed his hands up, managing to knock Pendergast's aim off as the gun exploded next to his ear.

Operating more out of instinct and terror than thought, Joe pinned Pendergast's wrist to the doorframe with the back of his right forearm and stepped forward and backed into him, now grasping Pendergast's wrists with both of his hands. Pendergast's arm was pinned under Joe's left armpit, the gun pointed toward the dried-out lawn, and it fired again, but Joe could barely hear the roar this time because his right ear was stunned silent. Joe recognized the weapon as an old Army Colt 1911 .45 semiautomatic, and he knew what kind of damage it could do.

Joe slammed Pendergast's wrist against the doorframe again and again, trying to make him drop the weapon. But Pendergast was younger and stronger. He could feel the hardness of Pendergast's body pressed against his back. Pendergast was now beating his free fist down on Joe's head, neck, and back, and Joe wasn't sure he had the strength or leverage to knock the gun loose.

Although he was temporarily deaf in his right ear from the gunshot and the side of his face felt stunned, he could hear yelling from behind him inside the house and Greene-Dempsey's high-pitched voice screaming, *"Call 911! Call 911!"* to the woman in the right duplex.

Pendergast's fist came down hard on the top of Joe's head, mashing his hat down nearly over his eyes and unleashing a wave of starbursts in front of his vision. He realized that if he didn't take Pendergast down soon—somehow—he'd be a dead man. He hoped whoever else was inside the house wouldn't come out front and join in on the parade of blows, or bring his own gun along.

Joe let go of Pendergast's wrist with his right hand and reached out and grasped the suspect's thumb, which was curled around the grip of the .45, and jerked back on it as hard as he could. The bone broke with a dull snap, and the thumb flopped back, held by skin alone. Because Pendergast's body was pressed tight to his back, Joe could feel him stiffen as the pain shot through him.

Pendergast howled in Joe's other ear, but the .45 dropped to the concrete of the porch and bounced into the grass. As it did, Joe let go and wheeled, ripping the first thing he could find—a big canister of bear spray—from his belt with the intention of blasting Pendergast in the eyes. But Pendergast's eyes were closed tight as he howled and hopped up and down on one foot, cupping his wounded right hand with his left, the thumb flopping from one side of his hand to the other, and Joe didn't see an opening. So he reared back and struck Pendergast solidly on the bridge of his nose with the bear spray canister, staggering him.

While Pendergast was off-balance, Joe reached in through the open door and grabbed a handful of his hair and yanked down, and the man stumbled past him and crashed facedown on the lawn, his arms windmilling. Before Pendergast could come to his senses enough to scramble for the .45, which was within his reach, Joe fell on him and forced him back to the ground and hit him three more times on the head with the bear spray canister until Bryce yelled, *"No more, man!"*

When Joe paused, Pendergast opened his bloodshot eyes and looked up. Joe quickly held the canister out and blasted the man in the face with a red burst of bear spray.

TEN MINUTES LATER, with Pendergast cuffed facedown and howling in the grass, Joe leaned against the grille of his pickup, dabbing his eyes with a moist cloth provided by the woman in the right duplex. She'd called 911, she said. He'd gotten a whiff of the bear spray's blowback himself, and it seemed like every fluid in his body was trying to pour out of his nose.

Lisa Greene-Dempsey stood a few feet away, shaken. She glared at him with her hands on her hips.

When he was able to make out her blurry image, Joe said, "You saw all that, right?"

"Of course I saw it," she said, angry. "I saw the whole damned thing. You could have gotten yourself killed."

"You didn't get hit with any of the bear spray, did you?"

"No."

"Good. It's nasty stuff."

He knew bear spray contained much more oleoresin capsicum than standard law enforcement personal-defense pepper spray, and it could turn a charging grizzly. It wasn't designed for use on humans, but at that moment Joe didn't care.

"I hope we don't have a lawsuit on our hands," she said.

"How you doing, Bryce?" Joe called out.

"I'm blind! *I'm fucking blind!*" Pendergast cried.

"Let him sue," Joe said. "I thought he was going to kill me, and the bear spray was the first thing I could grab onto."

She said, "I saw his partner run out the back and keep running down the alley."

"Was it McDermott?"

"How should I know?" she said, her voice rising.

"We'll find him," Joe said. His cheek burned where the gun had gone off, and his eyes, nose, and mouth were on fire from the blowback. There was a high whistle inside his right ear that blocked out any other sound.

"Excuse me," he said to Greene-Dempsey, and staggered past her toward the cab on his truck. "I've got to get on the radio and let everybody know to keep an eye out for McDermott. He won't get far on foot."

When he was done and hung up the mic, he turned to find Greene-Dempsey blocking his path.

"You could have been killed," she said again, shaken. "*I* could have been killed."

"I know," he said. "This isn't how it usually plays out. I had no idea things would get western."

He could feel adrenaline painfully dissipating from his muscles. He imagined she felt the same way and her method of dealing with the comedown was to upbraid *him*.

He said, "They were cooking meth—or trying to cook it. I don't think they had it figured out yet, judging by Bryce's reaction. I should have known by the smell and the chemical burns in the grass."

In the distance, several blocks away, he heard the whoop of a siren.

"Maybe they found McDermott," Joe said.

"I hope so," Greene-Dempsey said.

"They're not all meth heads," Joe said defensively, to a point she hadn't raised. To Pendergast, still crying on the ground, "You're not all bad, are you, Bryce?"

"Fuck you, I'm blind!" Pendergast shouted back.

Greene-Dempsey looked from Joe to the suspect, her anger replaced by caution.

"Joe . . ." she said worriedly.

Joe grunted and stepped around her and walked toward Pendergast in the yard. Pendergast continued to rage on that he was blind, and Joe stepped around him and retrieved the .45 and stuffed it in his belt. As he returned to the truck, he wheeled near Pendergast and reached again for the holstered canister of bear spray.

"No, no!" Pendergast screamed. "Put that back!" He tried to wriggle away in the direction of the house.

Joe turned and shrugged to Greene-Dempsey. "See, he's not blind."

She started to say something when the iPhone in her hand chimed. Joe watched her check the screen, and she looked up and said "Julio Batista" before taking the call. As she listened, her demeanor changed to one of utter seriousness, he thought.

Greene-Dempsey signed off, lowered the phone, and said, "They're ready for you now. You're supposed to meet them at some ranch outside of town, and he said you knew the place."

"Big Stream Ranch," Joe said dourly.

"That's the one," she said.

12

DAVE FARKUS FELT LIKE HE WAS BEING SHAKEN
to death, like his teeth were going to vibrate out of their
sockets, and he asked ex-Sheriff Kyle McLanahan, who was
at the wheel of the three-quarter-ton pickup towing the
long six-horse trailer, if he was going to slow down soon.
They were on an ancient two-track fire road that was wash-
boarded and marred by cross-trenches caused by spring
runoff. The center strip consisted of bumper-high sagebrush that scratched along the undercarriage of the pickup
like long fingernails on a blackboard. A long roll of dust
followed the rig.

"Why?" McLanahan asked.

"We've been on bad roads for an hour," Farkus said,
looking out at the dust-covered hood between the shoulders and heads of the two men in the front seat. "I feel like
I'm gonna get sick."

Spare tools and beer bottle caps skittered about at Farkus's feet in the back.

"We're in a hurry, Farkus."

Then McLanahan turned to the man in the passenger seat of the crew cab, a dark man Farkus had met for the first time when McLanahan picked him up, and who hadn't said two words in the past two hours.

"Jimmy, are you all right?"

"I'm fine," Sollis said.

"Jimmy's fine," McLanahan said to Farkus, making eye contact via the rearview mirror. "Time to strap in and cowboy up, buckaroo."

Farkus turned away and stared out the side window at the sagebrush flats. They were vibrating as far as he could see.

THE IDEA, McLanahan had said when he arrived at Farkus's mobile home with the horse trailer attached to his pickup and the mystery man in the passenger seat, was to drive north on the interstate, cut off at Winchester, and approach from the west the range of mountains where Butch Roberson was last seen.

"Those federal yahoos," McLanahan said, "are going to mass on the east slope at Big Stream Ranch and push west. When ol' Butch, he realizes the Feds are coming—I figure those boys will make a lot of noise and racket moving through the timber—Butch won't be stupid enough to try and make a stand. Instead, he'll stay ahead of 'em and work his way west. There are only a couple of possibilities how he'll come out, and I'm guessing he'll use the most direct route and the one he's most familiar with. That's where we'll set up and intercept him."

Farkus had nodded, not able to visualize the route McLanahan had in mind. Apparently, his puzzlement was written on his face, and it was obvious to the ex-sheriff.

"That's where you hunted with him, right?" McLanahan said. "Up there on the west side on those saddle slopes and in those canyons?"

"I think so," Farkus had said, "but we came from the other side, from the ranch. We never went up there from the west side."

McLanahan had rolled his eyes and said, "It's the same mountain, Farkus. The features don't change because you're looking at them from a different direction."

"It's wild country up there," Farkus said. "It's easy to get turned around."

Inside the cab of the pickup, Farkus had heard the mystery man snort a derisive laugh.

"Who is that?" Farkus asked, chinning the direction of the pickup.

"Jimmy Sollis. His brother used to be a deputy of mine, a good loyal guy. He was killed in the line of duty when Wheelchair Dick got it. I'll always be regretful it wasn't the other way around."

Farkus looked up, trying to connect the dots.

"He's a prize-winning long-distance shooter," Mc-Lanahan said. "He travels the country winning tournaments. He's got some kind of custom rifle and scope, and he knocks the center out of targets at a thousand-plus yards.

I figure he's a good man to have along, and he wants to test his skill."

Quiet, big, and deadly, then, Farkus thought. He'd been around too many of those types in his life, and he didn't much like them. He shifted uncomfortably from boot to boot.

"Three guys—that wasn't the deal," Farkus said.

"He'll be good to have along."

"But three guys means a three-way split, is what I'm sayin'."

"So?"

"I'm doing this for the money, Kyle. I don't have any hard feelings toward Butch."

"Jesus, Mary, and Joseph," McLanahan said, and sighed. "This ain't about the money. And don't call me Kyle. Call me Sheriff."

Farkus nodded toward his mobile home. "It's about the money for me, Sheriff."

"I told you already, this is big money. *Federal* money. They've got lots of it."

"So how much are we talking about?"

"I don't have *figures*"—McLanahan drew the word out sarcastically—"but a shitload of it, that's for sure. The Feds are the only folks who have any these days, don't you know. It'll be enough that you won't ever have to worry about when the next disability check comes in the mail so you can fill your tank."

Farkus considered pulling out. But what was his choice? There were few jobs, and he didn't want one, anyway. He liked being a free man, and busting his butt was for losers.

And this was free government money. They wouldn't even miss it.

"Okay," Farkus said.

"Then let's get the map out," McLanahan said. "I want to make sure you're familiar with the terrain before we waste our time going up there."

While the ex-sheriff unfurled the map on the hood of the pickup, Sollis got out of the truck without a word and bent over the side of the pickup into the bed. Farkus heard the sound of latches being thrown, and soon Sollis was holding a heavy and polished long bolt-action rifle with a black-matte scope. Farkus watched out of the corner of his eye.

"What's he up to?" Farkus whispered to McLanahan.

"The map," McLanahan said impatiently. "Pay attention to the map."

Farkus tried to concentrate on the features of the map McLanahan was holding flat on the hood with his bear-paw hands. The layout of the canyons *did* look vaguely familiar. He bent close and found the confluence of Otter and Trapper Creeks. To the north of the confluence was a series of saw-blade-like peaks. He was pretty sure he remembered them.

"This is where we camped," Farkus said, jabbing the location with his fingertip.

McLanahan marked it with a pencil stroke and said, "That's where we're going to be. If Butch is familiar with the camp, it's odds-on likely where he goes."

Farkus nodded.

"I don't see any roads going up there," McLanahan said.

"There were no roads. Butch likes to hunt in the wilderness, not in places you can drive to. He's crazy that way, like I told you."

As they were going over the map, Farkus kept stealing looks toward Sollis, who had jacked a cartridge into his rifle and was now at the rear of the pickup. He'd rested his rifle on the top of the corner of the bed walls and was leaning down, looking through his scope at something in the distance.

"So I think we're set," McLanahan had said, rolling up the topo map and sliding a rubber band over the roll.

As Farkus opened his mouth to speak, the air was split by the heavy boom of Sollis's rifle. Farkus jumped and looked up. In the sandy hills past the municipal dump, a plume of dirt rose in the air, leaving two black spots.

"What did you shoot at?" Farkus asked Sollis, alarmed.

"A black cat," Sollis said, ejecting the spent brass. "Eight hundred yards. Cut it right in two."

"That was *my* cat," Farkus had said.

"Not anymore," Sollis said, fitting the rifle back into its case.

THE HUGE DARK western slope of the Bighorns filled the front window of the pickup as they got closer, and the road got worse. Farkus leaned over and pressed his mouth to the gap in the open window so he could breathe fresh air and fight against the nausea he felt from being jounced around in the backseat. When he closed his eyes, he tried to picture the rough country he'd hunted with Butch Roberson the year before, but from the other direction. McLanahan seemed to think it was easy, but it wasn't. There were granite ridges and seas of black timber, and he remembered at times trying to look up through the trees to see something—anything—he recognized. A unique-shaped peak, a rock wall, a meadow, or a natural park—anything that stood out so he'd know where he was. He remembered stumbling back into the elk camp at the confluence of the creeks one night near midnight, four hours late, because he'd been turned around in a box canyon, and although he had a compass and GPS, he'd convinced himself that the instruments were wrong but he was right. Butch Roberson had been happy to see him, but concerned about the possibility of him getting lost again.

From that night on, they'd hunted together, which was a nice gesture on Butch's part, Farkus thought.

And now he was back. If it weren't for that substantial federal reward money . . .

MCLANAHAN APPARENTLY figured out how to make Jimmy Sollis open up, Farkus thought drearily: ask him about his rifle.

"It's a custom 6.5x284," Sollis said, "equipped with a Zeiss Z-800 4.5x14 Conquest scope . . ."

Jimmy Sollis was over six feet four, Farkus guessed, two hundred twenty pounds. He had olive-colored skin, black hair, a smooth almost Asian face with small, black, wide-set eyes and a flattened nose. He spoke in a flat tone with no animation at all, and he enunciated every word clearly, as if he were transcribing them on stone.

"I shoot a 140-grain Berger bullet at just over three-thousand-feet-per-second muzzle velocity," Sollis said. "I've taken the eye out of a target at fourteen hundred yards, and I can hit a man shape at eighteen hundred. I prefer a bench-rest, of course, but I've got a bipod setup that cuts down on the distance in favor of portability . . ."

Farkus tuned out. He'd never enjoyed the weaponry talk so many men loved, and it was Greek to him. If the conversation was about dry flies, streamers, or nymphs, Farkus was all over that. But gun porn? It made him tired.

Nevertheless, Farkus tried not to think of Butch Roberson at the other end of that Zeiss Conquest scope. And he thought about his stray black cat, cut in half, eviscerated, bleeding out in the sand.

THE SMELL OF HORSES and leather combined with the pine dust and dried mulch from the forest floor as Mc-Lanahan, Jimmy Sollis, and Farkus rode from where they'd parked the horse trailer at the trailhead into the trees. McLanahan led, trailing a packhorse with bulging pan-niers, with Farkus in the middle and Jimmy Sollis last. Sollis also trailed a horse, but the horse wasn't laden with anything other than an empty saddle and several coils of rope. McLanahan had explained to Farkus that the horse was for bringing Butch Roberson down from the mountain, either in the saddle or his body lashed across it.

Farkus hadn't been much help when it came to saddling the horses or gearing up, and both McLanahan and Sollis gave him a few dirty looks. Farkus had explained he was no horseman, and the time he'd spent in the saddle had been among the worst time in his life. Besides, he said, he was there to help guide them, not to be a wrangler. For revenge, he thought, they gave him a sleek black gelding with crazy eyes that looked like the devil himself. His name was Dreadnaught. And when he climbed onto Dread-naught's saddle and the mount crow-hopped and nearly dumped him before looking back with what seemed like an evil leer, Farkus knew it was a matter of time before something bad happened.

Before departing, McLanahan had packed the panniers with food, camping gear, electronics, and dozens of items—radios, body armor, gear bags—stenciled with TSCSD, or Twelve Sleep County Sheriff's Department. Things he'd "borrowed" when he cleared out, Farkus guessed. The ex-sheriff told Farkus to leave his old hunting rifle behind and instead gave him a Bushmaster semiautomatic rifle chambered for .223 with a thirty-round magazine. When he noted the TSCSD tag on the rear stock, McLanahan wag-gled his eyebrows as if to say, *Yes, so what?*

Jimmy Sollis fitted his long-distance rifle into a padded scabbard and lashed it to his saddle. He'd clipped a car-tridge belt around his waist and hung heavy-barreled bin-oculars around his thick neck.

"A QUARTER TO ONE," McLanahan declared, checking his wristwatch as they rode into the trees. "We made good time. I'll bet the Feds on the other side of the mountain aren't even organized yet."

Farkus said nothing, and of course Sollis kept quiet.

As the canopy of trees closed in above them, Farkus noted how cool and dark it was. Memories from several years before came rushing back of another horse pack trip into another set of mountains for other fugitives, as well as the previous fall with Butch Roberson in these same mountains. Butch loved the mountains as much as life itself, he'd told Farkus.

McLanahan asked, "Dave, how far until we make the elk camp?"

Farkus strained around in his saddle, looking out ahead of them—trees—and to the sides—trees. All he knew was that they were high enough into the timber where he could no longer look back and see the pickup and trailer.

"Three or four hours," Farkus said, trying to guess.

"Time to go dark, gentlemen," McLanahan said to Farkus and Sollis. "If you've got cell phones, shut them off. We can't have a phone start ringing as we're closing in on Butch. And if Wheelchair Dick finds out we're up here, he'll try to order us back. In this case, ignorance is bliss, buckaroos. We're on a mission."

Both Farkus and Sollis dug their phones out and switched them off.

Farkus asked, "What if the Feds see us and start shooting? You said they don't know we're up here, either."

McLanahan twitched his mustache—Farkus guessed it was a grin—and said, "There's a big difference between three men on horseback and one lonely and desperate guy on foot. Even those yahoos should be able to tell the difference.

"Plus," he continued, "we should be in place long before those yahoos even start their push. We should have Butch one way or other long before they even know we're here."

AN HOUR into their ride into the mountains, Farkus nudged Dreadnaught to the side of the trail and waited for Jimmy Sollis to catch up. As he approached, Sollis looked at Farkus with a hostile, deadeye stare that Farkus felt all deep in his gut.

When Sollis caught up, Farkus nudged his horse so they rode side by side.

"So what's the deal with you?" Farkus asked. "Are you going into this for the money, like me?"

"Hardly."

Farkus waited a beat, but Sollis didn't offer more. Ahead, trees were narrowing on both sides of the trail, and he knew they wouldn't be able to ride abreast much longer.

"Do you have a beef with Butch Roberson?" Farkus asked.

"Never met the man."

"So what is it, then? You and the ex-sheriff are tight?"

"Fuck, no."

The trees started to pinch in. Farkus could feel Dreadnaught start to gather beneath him, as if preparing to bolt.

"I get it," Farkus said, irritated. "You're a man of few words. Well, I'm not. And if I'm going to risk my ass going up into these mountains, I need to know what kind of company I'm keeping."

"Don't worry about it."

"I'm not kidding," Farkus said, feeling his neck flush with anger.

Sollis didn't look at him when he said, "I tried to sign up for the military, but I had a record, so they wouldn't take me. All I wanted to do was serve my country, and they wouldn't have me. I wanted to go to Iraq or Afghanistan."

At the last second, before Dreadnaught bolted or crowded Sollis's horse into the trees, Farkus clicked his tongue and moved his mount back in front. Over his shoulder, he said, "So you just want to *shoot* somebody with that rifle of yours."

"Damned right," Sollis said coldly.

AS THEY RODE, Farkus heard a high whining sound become more pronounced. At first he thought it was an insect near his ear, and he swatted at it clumsily before realizing the sound came from somewhere above the canopy of trees.

"What's that?" he asked McLanahan.

The ex-sheriff shrugged. "Sounds too high-pitched to be an airplane, but maybe the Feds are sending a spotter over the mountains to look for Butch."

The high whine passed overhead and began to recede in volume.

"Whatever it is," McLanahan said, "it's not going to see much through these trees."

"My tax dollars at work," Farkus said, and sighed.

"If you paid any," McLanahan said.

13

AFTER DROPPING LISA GREENE-DEMPSEY AT THE
Holiday Inn with a paper sack of fruits and vegetables,
and shock on her face that had been imprinted there since
the takedown of Bryce Pendergast, Joe spotted Marybeth's
van parked on the street outside the Saddlestring Hotel
and pulled behind it. Matt Donnell's Lexus was also on
the street.

Joe wanted to let Marybeth know what was going on—
that he'd been called out to Big Stream Ranch to join the
search for Butch Roberson and that his first meeting with
his new boss . . . had not gone well.

He stepped through a gap in the orange plastic fencing
on the sidewalk that indicated there was construction in
progress, and entered through the magnificent old front
doors. As he did, a heated conversation between Marybeth
and Donnell stopped him cold.

Matt Donnell stood on one side of the old lobby with a loosened tie and his hands jammed into the pockets of his trousers. He was paunchy and balding; his face was flushed. Joe could see beads of perspiration on his scalp through his thinning hair.

Marybeth stood across from him, hands on hips, bent slightly forward toward Donnell, in her coveralls, her hair tied back with a red bandanna. Even though both had stopped talking, Joe knew the look on Marybeth's face, and he knew that Donnell was in trouble. Joe had been on the receiving end of that look many times in their marriage.

To Donnell, Joe said: "Just say three words: 'You're right, dear.' Trust me on this."

Joe expected a smile, but Donnell looked straight down at the tops of his shoes. Obviously, whatever they had been arguing about was worse than Joe had thought, and he turned to his wife.

"Everything all right?"

She softened when she looked over at Joe, though, and said, "Honey, what happened to the side of your face?"

"I met my boss and got in a fight," Joe said. "I'll fill you in later."

"You got in a fight with your *boss*?"

"No—with Bryce Pendergast. We arrested him for cooking meth and shooting an antelope."

"Are *you* okay?" she asked.

"Peachy. So what's going on here? It doesn't look good."

"It isn't," she said, biting off the words. "Maybe you should ask Matt."

Joe said, "Matt?"

"I'm just the messenger," Donnell said softly, then looked up at Joe with pleading eyes. "Don't let her kill the messenger."

"Tell him, Matt," Marybeth said.

"Tell me what?"

Donnell said, "I met with the agencies and departments we needed to talk to so we could get our financing for the next stage of construction. We've got big problems."

Joe shook his head, not understanding.

Donnell said, "I knew the old state fire marshal, and he was a reasonable guy, but he retired. The new one is some kind of fire Nazi. He said we need to install a sprinkler system throughout the building, even though it's historic. We kind of figured on that, and I'd priced it in," he said, looking to Marybeth for confirmation. She nodded.

"But he threw me a curve," he said.

Marybeth cut in, still angry. "So in order for us to install the sprinkler system we have to make sure none of the old paint contains any lead, which means we have to hire special testing crews to take samples and analyze the old paint before we can do anything."

"What a pain," Joe said. "But weren't you going to re-paint anyway?"

"Of course," she said, "but it doesn't matter that we weren't going to keep any of the old paint. And it doesn't matter that in eighty years of people using this building, nobody ate any paint chips and got sick from it."

Donnell rolled his eyes and said, "They're worried flakes of the paint will come off when we strip it and kids will eat them, I guess. So we have to hire guys in hazmat suits and with special certification to strip the walls."

Before Joe could speak, Donnell said, "And that's not the worst of it."

"Tell him the worst of it, Matt," Marybeth said.

"He's worried about asbestos in these old buildings. The wallboards and the insulation might have asbestos in them. The shingles, too. And all of the wiring needs to be replaced."

Joe said, "So they want you to gut the entire building?"

"Worse," Donnell said. "We have to hire a specially certified asbestos-removal company to gut the entire structure down to the bricks and framing. Then we can't proceed until the fire marshal sends up his own personal inspector from Cheyenne to give us a permit."

Joe understood the look of panic in Marybeth's eyes now.

"And we can't do any of the work ourselves," Marybeth said, "because we don't have certified training or licenses." Then, to Matt: "Tell him about these certified asbestos-removal companies."

Matt sighed and looked away. "There aren't any."

Joe said, "What?"

"The closest one is in Salt Lake City," Donnell said. "They're backed up for eighteen months. And the cost of getting them up here to all but demolish the hotel . . ."

". . . is more than Matt paid for it," Marybeth finished for her partner. "All these new costs are way beyond what we budgeted to rebuild the hotel."

"Oh, man," Joe said, rubbing his face. He'd forgotten about the gunshot burn on the side of his head, and it stung when he touched it.

Donnell said, "No bank is going to even talk to us until we have all the permits and sign-offs."

He stepped back and raised both of his hands, palms up, toward the old vaulted ceilings.

Donnell said, "I've been buying and selling real estate in this valley for twenty-five years. There have been up and down years, but it was based on free market. It's just the way it is, and I never bitched about the bad years because the good years made up for them, and I always knew that if I worked hard and didn't screw anyone, I'd succeed—and I have, up to now."

Joe interrupted and asked, "What's it going to cost, Matt?"

Donnell made a pained face and said, "If I were to guess, I'd say rebuilding this hotel like we wanted it will cost us four times more than we thought and take three times as long."

Joe narrowed his eyes. Marybeth looked stricken. He wanted to knock Matt Donnell's head off. He said, "You're supposed to be the expert here. You're supposed to know this stuff. Marybeth trusted you."

"I know," Donnell said, lowering his arms and listing his head slightly to the side as if defeated already. "This wasn't my first rodeo. But it's the first time I ever tried to rebuild a historic building. I thought the bureaucrats would want to *help* us. I honestly thought—and I remember telling your wife this—that removing the blight from the middle of a small town and building a business incubator in its place would be cheered on. I had no idea they'd throw every possible regulation and roadblock in our way."

Joe still wanted to punch him.

"Look," Donnell said, "thousands of people passed through this hotel over the years. They ate and slept here, and nobody got sick or died. But all of a sudden, when we want to fix it up so people can use it again, it's considered a goddamned death trap. It's like it's painted with poison and infested with toxic waste. Knowing what we do now, who in their right mind would want to build *anything*, or fix *anything*, anymore?"

Donnell's face was bright red, and he looked to Joe like he might break down. Joe and Marybeth exchanged worried glances.

Then Marybeth said softly, "We're screwed, aren't we?"

Donnell looked up, took a breath, and said, "I think we should give up on this project. I'll take my losses while I still can. It's not worth it trying to push back because they hold all the cards. They've got paid lawyers and regulators with no personal financial stake in this building like we do. They can sit at their desks and tell us what we can and can't do, and they can drag this out for years or until we're both bankrupt."

"You're saying we should just walk away from our deal?" Marybeth said, and Joe noticed the welling in her eyes.

Donnell nodded. "Yes. I'll put the hotel back on the market and sell it for whatever we can get, even if we're just selling the lot itself. A corner lot on Main Street in the middle of town has to be worth something. I'll do what I can to return some of the money we've already sunk into it, I swear. I'm sorry I got you two involved."

Joe took a deep breath.

Marybeth said to Donnell, "I'm sorry you're going to take a loss, and I appreciate the opportunity you gave me." She looked at Joe. "I'm sorry."

He knew how much it meant to her. "It's okay," he said. "It's fine."

And it was a hurdle removed from not taking the job in Cheyenne, he thought but didn't say.

Then he looked at his wristwatch. "I've got to go."

"Call me," Marybeth said to his back.

14

AS JOE DROVE UP BIGHORN ROAD WITH TOBY once again in the horse trailer, the immediate anger he'd felt in the lobby of the Saddlestring Hotel subsided and was replaced by frustration. He thought about the look of utter defeat on Marybeth's face, something he'd rarely seen before. He didn't like seeing his wife so disappointed.

He wanted to fix it somehow but didn't know where to start. He wondered what she'd think about the job offer from LGD, and anticipated her response. Which is why he hadn't told her about it.

AS HE DROVE, changing channels from one problem to another, Joe tried to imagine what Butch felt like up there in the mountains, away from his wife and daughter, sleeping on the ground and listening for the sounds of approaching pursuers. Unlike Butch, Joe and Marybeth had dodged a bullet. If they'd made the hotel deal they'd have been ruined instead of disappointed.

Butch had to know, Joe thought, that his life wasn't worth anything anymore. His construction company would go bankrupt and his family would be affected in ways he could never have imagined.

Butch would know that if he turned himself in he'd be locked away for years. Did he regret what he'd done, or did he feel justified for having done it?

Joe sighed, knowing the question was academic. Butch Roberson was the only suspect in a double homicide—it didn't matter what he felt.

HE WAS SURPRISED to see a jam of vehicles in front of the gate to the Big Stream Ranch. Pickups with horse trailers, SUVs trailing pods of ATVs, law enforcement panel vans, and a dozen other vehicles were massed on the shoulder of the highway and in the right-hand lane itself—a convoy that had been made to stop. Several uniformed deputies were standing on the blacktop, directing traffic.

Joe slowed and powered his window down as he approached Deputy Justin Woods.

"What's going on?" Joe asked. "I thought they were going to set up their command post up at the forest boundary."

"That was the idea," Woods said, "but they can't get access to cross the ranch."

"What?"

"Frank Zeller won't let them through," Woods said, trying to stifle a smirk.

"Who's in charge?"

"Julio Batista and his toady," Woods said.

Joe thanked him and eased off the blacktop into the ditch and drove toward the front of the line. He could see Batista and Heinz Underwood shouting at someone through the poles of the gate, which was locked up with a heavy chain. Joe couldn't recall seeing the gate closed before. He pulled parallel with Sheriff Reed's handicapped van, shut off the engine, and swung out.

Reed was in his chair with the sliding door open, watching the action at the gate with a look of bemusement on his face. When he saw Joe, he arched his eyebrows in greeting.

"Woods told me," Joe said. "So none of these geniuses made a call to Frank to ask permission to cross his land and set up a command post on it, huh?"

"Apparently not," Reed said. "They call it an FOB, by the way."

"So how long have you been waiting here?"

Reed glanced at his wristwatch. "About a half an hour." Joe whistled.

"I heard about Bryce Pendergast," Reed said, his eyes moving to the reddened side of Joe's face. "I can't say I'm surprised, though. Pendergast and McDermott have been hanging with the tweaker crowd for a couple of years now, and I guess they thought they'd rather be buyers *and* sellers.

"Norwood called me a few minutes ago and said those idiots had all the ingredients they needed inside the house—Sudafed, iodine, phosphorus, Coleman fuel, acetone, denatured alcohol, and a bunch of flasks and beakers—but he said it didn't look like they were in production yet. He said it looked like they were trying to figure out how to cook it, but so far all they'd made were mistakes. It's a wonder they didn't blow themselves up."

"Good thing they didn't," Joe said. "There's a nice old lady next door."

"Oh—and we have McDermott in jail right alongside Pendergast. We caught him at the Kum and Go, buying a microwave burrito with his last pennies."

Joe nodded.

"Sounds like you could have gotten yourself killed," Reed said, concerned.

"Yup."

"Bear spray, Joe?" Reed asked, incredulous.

"Good stuff."

Reed grinned and shook his head, then got serious. "I think they could use your help over at the gate. You know Frank pretty well, don't you?"

"I had breakfast with him yesterday morning."

"Maybe you could talk some sense into him."

Joe looked over and saw Batista gesticulating through the rails of the gate.

"Frank's a stubborn old bird," Joe said.

"Please, Joe," Reed said. "Give it a try. We all look kind of stupid just sitting here."

AS JOE TURNED to join Batista and Heinz Underwood at the gate, Reed called after him, "Joe, they canceled their offer of a reward."

Joe looked over his shoulder, relieved. "Good."

"Couldn't get authorization for it, I guess," Reed said. "Too much red tape."

"So it wasn't like they came to their senses and realized it was too heavy-handed," Joe said.

"Nothing like that."

"Did they announce it to the press?"

"Not that I'm aware of," Reed said.

"So the word is still out there."

"I'm hoping they'll give a statement soon. I heard something about a press conference at the FOB." He nodded toward the locked gate and added, "Assuming there's an FOB."

Joe shook his head, took a deep breath through his nostrils, and approached the gate.

FRANK ZELLER STOOD on the other side of the locked gate in his Wranglers, boots, and sweat-stained silver-belly Stetson. He cradled a lever-action Winchester .30-30 rifle that was pointed loosely off to the side. Joe had last seen the weapon the morning before, in Frank's gun case. It was an old saddle carbine that had belonged to his father. The stock was scuffed, and the bluing was rubbed silver from years of rough use. He knew Frank had a large choice of rifles—every ranch house did—so he wouldn't have brought the symbolic Winchester to the gate if he didn't think the situation was profound.

Frank was short, wiry, and had a long craggy face that made him look tall in photos. Cobalt-blue eyes winked out from tanned and wrinkled skin, and his hands were so leathery it appeared he was wearing gloves. He wasn't a warm or glib man, and he'd burned through two wives, seven or eight kids, and two dozen ranch hands since Joe had been in the valley. Frank Zeller was known for being one of the few remaining scions of the original founding ranches in the area that were still intact, and for not exactly welcoming newcomers. It took three years for Frank to meet Joe's eyes as they passed on the highway, five years before Frank would raise a traditional single-digit salute of greeting from his steering wheel, seven years before Frank nodded at Joe in town, and nine years before he said Joe's name aloud. The last two years, though, they actually talked, mainly due to the water-guzzler project Joe had proposed and installed, which Frank approved of.

Like so many western characters Joe had come to know, and despite his demeanor and his constant scowl and rancher uniform of long-sleeved shirt, hat, jeans, and boots, Frank turned out to be a bundle of contradictions. He loved opera and had spent his college years in Italy attending performances at La Scala in Milan; he'd endowed the Zeller Chair of Economics at the University of Wyoming; and he kept a luxury Sikorsky helicopter in a hangar at the Twelve Sleep County Municipal Airport that he piloted himself.

Julio Batista couldn't have known any of that, though, and certainly not by the way he was talking through the gate to Frank, Joe thought. He caught the end of Batista saying: ". . . we could take this all the way if we have to,

Mr. Zeller. What you're doing here is stubbornly prevent-
ing authorized federal law enforcement from engaging in
a hot-pursuit investigation of a man who murdered two
government employees in cold blood."

Frank Zeller snorted and rolled his eyes. "So you've
already convicted him, huh? I thought you had to arrest
him first."

"We need passage, and we need it now."

Zeller said, "Not through my land, you don't. Not without a court order and compensation. This is private property, and you aren't crossing it without my say-so."

"This is insane," Batista said to Frank. "I could have
you arrested right now."

"Try," Frank said, still cradling the rifle but not raising
or pointing it. "You bust down that gate and your monkeys
will start dropping like flies."

"Is that a threat?" Batista said, his voice rising. "Did
you just threaten me? And was there a racial aspect to the
threat?"

"No threat," Zeller said. "I made a promise."

"Hey, Frank," Joe said, interrupting.

Zeller's eyes shifted to Joe, but he didn't move his head.
"Joe," he said, his voice flat.

"What seems to be the problem?"

"Isn't it obvious?" Batista said to Joe.

Joe ignored him.

"These fancy federal boys want to use my ranch to set
up some kind of camp," Zeller said. "They want to track
up my meadows with their vehicles, and open up my place

to all their friends to come in. They don't want to talk terms, or deals. They just want me to unlock this gate and stand aside while they roll through like Patton's army."

"That's ridiculous," Batista whispered.

Zeller said, "When I want to lease forest for my cattle or cut wood to build a new corral, I've got to pay these boys a fee. But when they want to charge through my ranch and use it like it was a playground, they don't want to pay *me* anything."

"He's got a point," Joe said to Batista.

The administrator's eyes flashed, and he whispered to Joe, "We don't have time to negotiate an agreement. It takes months to get this kind of thing through—you know that."

"You were quick enough with that reward last night," Joe said.

"That has *nothing* to do with this," Batista said, his voice rising again. "I thought you were here to help us."

Joe shrugged.

Frank said to Batista, "This guy you're after is on the National Forest, right? The forest is federal. So you can just turn your monkeys around and go into those mountains from the other side and I can't stop you."

"I *told* you," Batista said sarcastically, "he was last seen on *this* side of the mountains. We'd waste more than a day going around to the other side and working our way back."

"First time I ever heard of the government being worried about wasting time," Frank said. "I could tell you some good stories."

"We don't have time for your stories."

Joe watched the two as if viewing a tennis match, following each as they spoke.

Joe turned to Batista, and said, "You might try working with Frank here, instead of bullying him."

"You're useless," Batista said, waving his hand at Joe and turning away, "just like the rest of these people up here."

He strode back toward the SUV, but not without a *go-ahead* nod to Heinz Underwood. Joe saw Underwood acknowledge the signal, which had no doubt been prearranged.

Underwood stepped toward Joe, his expression hard but slightly bemused. "Walk with me," he said.

Joe cautiously fell in beside him as Underwood walked down the length of the barbed-wire fence far enough that neither Frank Zeller not the occupants of the convoy could overhear.

"You're friends with this rancher?"

"We're acquainted."

"I'd suggest you give him a little advice."

"Depends on what the advice is," Joe said.

Underwood said, "You might want to suggest to him that whatever payment he might want right now will be zilch compared to what could happen if the full attention of the EPA Region Eight office turned on him all of the sudden, is all."

Joe didn't respond.

"Just looking from here," Underwood said, gazing out

at the huge ranch spread out through the valley, "I think I see cows crapping in the streams, which might violate the Clean Water Act. I think I see clouds of methane rising from hundreds of flatulent cattle, which might violate the 1990 Clean Air Act. I think I see ranch buildings that might not be up to code, and old shingles on that big ranch house that are probably made of asbestos. An army of inspectors might just find all sorts of things that would shut down this operation or fine him boatloads of money for years to come.

"There's a lot of wildlife habitat down there in that valley," he said. "One kind of wonders if there are any protected or endangered species. It looks like good forage for the Preble's jumping mouse, or sage grouse, or maybe even some aquatic species that might be threatened by all this agricultural activity.

"Not only that," Underwood said softly. "Mr. Zeller seems to have way too many cows down there to run an environmentally sustainable operation. Look at them all."

Joe saw small knots of registered Herefords grazing far below on natural meadows.

"That's not so many," he said.

"Boy, I'm just not as certain as you are," Underwood said. "I think there might be more cows than there is grass. They might chew that grass down to nothing and leave a wasteland."

"Frank's been operating his place for forty years," Joe said. "And before that it was his grandfather and his father. Look at it. It's in great shape."

"Maybe to your eyes," Underwood said, "but when we

count the cattle and measure the forage it might be a different story."

Joe looked over with a pained expression on his face.

"It can be done very quickly," Underwood said. "Using drones."

"Drones? Like in the military?"

"We've got a few in service right now. In fact, there may even be one or two entering the airspace of these mountains as we speak."

"Are you threatening Zeller?"

"That's not a threat," Underwood said softly. "That's just offering him some good friendly advice."

Joe said, "Why don't *you* tell him?"

"Naw," Underwood said. "It would be best coming from his old pal Joe."

Joe shut his eyes for a moment, the ball of rage he'd felt earlier in the day forming again in his chest. He said, "What is it with you guys?"

Underwood shrugged and gestured toward Batista. "Comes from the top."

Through clenched teeth, Joe said, "This is the kind of scheme you ran on Butch Roberson, isn't it? You make up charges and accusations and then your target spends the rest of his life trying to prove you wrong."

Underwood shook his head and said, "We didn't write the laws. We just enforce them."

"These aren't laws," Joe said. "They're regulations you hide behind."

"We didn't write the regulations," Underwood said in a tired, singsong cadence. "We just enforce them. From what I understand, your director has ordered you to help us do that. So I'd suggest you offer some friendly advice to the rancher so we can do our job."

"Or you'll ruin *him*," Joe said.

"I never said that." Underwood smiled.

JOE STOOD shoulder to shoulder with Frank Zeller as the convoy of vehicles rumbled through the open gate. Frank was furious.

"Maybe you can sue them after the fact," Joe said.

"Or maybe," Zeller said, "I can call a meeting of the Cattlemen's Association and raise an army of ranchers and wranglers and take my ranch back. They might not do it for me, but they'll do it in memory of Butch Roberson."

"He's not dead yet," Joe said.

"Matter of time," Frank said flatly, nodding at an SUV filled with black-clad special agents that passed through the gate.

Joe looked over. "So you've seen him."

"Maybe. Won't say yes, won't say no."

"You're helping him out?"

Zeller shrugged.

"About the army—you're kidding, right?"

Frank Zeller wouldn't meet his eyes.

Joe looked to the horizon over the peaks of the mountains, expecting to note thunderheads gathering and a summer storm building, but the sky was blue and clear as far as he could see.

15

"THERE HE IS, THE SON OF A BITCH," JIMMY SOL-
lis said quietly with a sense of awe as he leaned forward
into his rifle scope.

Dave Farkus snapped his head up from where he'd been
trying to steal a few moments for a nap. His body ached.
Kyle McLanahan scrambled up from where he sat and
joined Sollis with his binoculars.

No one expected Butch Roberson to enter the camp so
soon after they'd set up.

"Damn," McLanahan said, drawing the word out.
"Looks like we guessed right. He must have been on the
move all night."

IT WAS NEARLY THREE in the afternoon when the riders
reached the eastern rim of the huge canyon. In all honesty—

Farkus knew but didn't say aloud—they'd found the canyon and the confluence of Otter and Trapper Creeks more by accident than design. Until they peered over the granite rim, he'd been convinced the giant swale they were looking for was one canyon over to the south. But they found it after all, and they'd dismounted and set up an observation point in a three-foot crack of the wall that overlooked the canyon. Sollis had methodically attached a high-tech bipod with telescoping legs to the stock of his long-range rifle and hunkered down on the floor of the opening with a range finder. When he bent down to look through the scope and study the terrain, Farkus and McLanahan had backed out of the crack into the boulders and found pools of cool shadow to sit in and wait.

Earlier in the afternoon, Farkus had been thrown when Dreadnaught had walked deliberately underneath an overhanging branch. The branch had caught Farkus in the sternum, and he'd tumbled backward and fallen on his head and shoulders, which ached. Although he'd not broken any bones, the fall knocked the wind out of him and gave him the resolve never to trust the horse again, and to keep alert.

While they secured the horses to picket pins and tree trunks in a grove of wide-spaced aspen trees, Farkus had looked Dreadnaught square in his dead black eyes and said, "Do that again, and they'll be eating you in France."

FARKUS FOLLOWED MCLANAHAN into the crack after Sollis had spoken. The shooter was on his belly, his legs splayed out in a long V, his boots hooked inward against football-sized rocks he'd rolled into place for stability. He bent into the rear lens and gently adjusted the sharpness of the image with a knob on the left side of the Zeiss Conquest scope. As Farkus lowered himself into the crack, he bumped Sollis's leg and Sollis cursed.

"Don't fuckin' touch me again," Sollis hissed without looking back. "I can't keep a bead on this guy if you're jostling me around."

"Sorry," Farkus said. Then, to McLanahan, who was adjusting the focus on his big-barreled binoculars: "Is it really him?"

"Can't tell yet," the ex-sheriff whispered. "He's a long ways away."

"My range finder says eighteen hundred yards," Sollis said. "A little over a mile. It's almost out of my comfort zone."

"Show me where he is," McLanahan said.

Sollis described the terrain, and Farkus followed along with his sight.

The canyon had sharp sides, knuckled with striated granite on the rims, and was timbered on both sides. The trees thinned as they reached the valley floor and the slopes became grassy. A small stream serpentined through the meadow, looking like a readout from a heart monitor, Farkus thought. He wondered, as he always did, if there were fish in it. Brook trout maybe, he thought.

"Follow that stream all the way up the valley," Sollis said softly to McLanahan, "to where it comes out of the trees. Can you see it?"

"Yeah, I'm following," McLanahan said, slowly swinging the binoculars from right to left.

"Right at the top in the shadows, where a little creek comes out from the south and must meet up with the spring creek coming out of the trees. That's where I saw him."

"Shit," McLanahan said, mostly to himself. "I'm having trouble . . ." He paused. Then: "Bingo. I see it. There's a cross-pole up in the trees for hanging elk."

"That's it," Sollis said.

"So where's our man? I don't see anyone."

Without binoculars of his own, Farkus saw absolutely no one, and not even the cross-pole. But the valley floor looked familiar from when he'd been hunting with Butch. In fact, Butch had passed up a shot at a five-point bull that was grazing near the bank of the creek because it wasn't big enough. Farkus remembered being frustrated by that because he was ready to go home and his back ached from sleeping in the tent.

"O-*kay*," McLanahan whispered. "I see the camp, but I don't see anyone in it."

"He left," Sollis declared after a full minute of silence. "He walked back into the trees and I lost him."

"Where the hell did he go?" McLanahan asked, obviously frustrated.

"Find some firewood, take a shit," Sollis speculated. "How would I know?"

"So you think he's coming back?"

"I can't promise anything. But he didn't look like he was on a mission to get out of there for good. He just walked from the camp into the trees real slow-like."

"He sauntered," McLanahan said.

"Yeah, like that."

"Did he look our way? Did it seem like he saw us or heard us?"

"No. We're too far away."

McLanahan expelled a long sigh through his nose, then said, "So we wait."

Farkus settled into the crack well beyond Sollis's feet and sat down with his back to the sheer rock. It was cold and penetrated his clothing. He hoped Butch Roberson just kept on walking.

WHILE THEY WAITED, McLanahan turned to Farkus and said, "I love it when a plan works. We figured out where he was likely to show up, and he did."

"Can I see?" Farkus asked, reaching out for the binoculars.

"Not now. They're perfectly focused for *my eyes*. I don't want you messing them up if he shows again. But you're sure this is the canyon, right? This is where you camped with Butch?"

"This is it."

"You're absolutely sure?"

"I'm looking at it from a different angle, but yes, where those two little creeks come together. That's where we camped."

McLanahan nodded, satisfied.

Farkus sighed and sat back. His right shoulder throbbed from the fall he'd taken. Being outside in the mountains always made him hungry, though. He thought he could use a big glass of bourbon and a steak. Some fries.

He relaxed and closed his eyes in time to hear Sollis say, "He's back."

FARKUS CONTENTED HIMSELF with not watching, but he listened as Sollis and McLanahan exchanged comments. They sounded more like they were hunting elk than a man named Butch.

"Eighteen hundred yards is a hell of a long shot," Sollis said. "I've made it in perfect conditions, but I've missed it, too."

"How far are we from perfect conditions?" McLanahan said, taking the glasses away from his eyes long enough to look around at their position.

"In perfect conditions, I've got a spotter and I can take a practice shot or two. That way, the spotter can tell me to adjust my aim a mil or two to get dead-on."

"No practice shots," McLanahan said, annoyed.

"I know. The first one has to be the one. Luckily, we don't have any wind, so I don't have to adjust much. But it gets dicey figuring the drop on the bullet when we're shooting at a downward angle. But the windage is good right now. I'm glad I brought my hot loads."

Farkus had absolutely no idea what he was talking about, and didn't care enough to ask.

McLanahan said, "We might be able to get closer if we work our way south along the ridge. My fear is he might see us moving, or we might not find such an ideal location to set up."

"I agree."

"What's he doing now?"

"He's bent over. I think he might be building a fire."

"Could you hit him?"

"I wouldn't want to try. When he's bent over like that, he's a small target. I wouldn't even dream of touching one off unless he was standing up, offering a full profile. Even then . . ."

"Shit," McLanahan said, shifting his weight against the rock so he could brace his binoculars against the wall. "I lost him while we were talking."

"He's still there," Sollis said calmly. "He's just hard to see because he's wearing camo and bent over in the grass. I think he's blowing into the fire, trying to get it started. Yes—I can see a little bit of smoke now."

"Camo," McLanahan said. "That's what he's supposed to be wearing, all right."

Sollis grunted.

Uncomfortable with the way things were playing out, Farkus swallowed and said, "Sheriff?"

"What, Farkus?"

"Don't you think we ought to consider talking to him? Maybe giving him a chance to give himself up?"

McLanahan snorted his answer.

Farkus tried another tack. "It'll be a lot easier getting him back to the truck if he's upright. I'm just sayin' . . ."

McLanahan said wearily, "Here's some wisdom that

comes from being sheriff for six years: the thing about armed men is they can shoot back. So it's best to take them down before they know we're coming. Got that?"

"What if you just wound him? What happens if you wing him and then he takes off running?"

"We follow the blood trail until we find the body," McLanahan said. "Just like hunting."

"I'm just thinking about the money, you understand. I don't want my reward money running away from us through the trees," Farkus lied.

Sollis said to Farkus, "I don't shoot to wound, you dweeb. I won't take the shot unless it's dead-on perfect."

Farkus sighed, and Sollis turned back to his scope.

That's when Farkus heard it: the high-pitched whine of an engine again. Like the one they'd heard earlier.

HE COULD SEE EVERYTHING from their vantage point, and without binoculars: the small white drone appearing over the horizon and flying just above the treetops toward the elk camp. Sun glinted from its wings and tail. The whine increased in volume as it flew closer.

"Jesus Christ," McLanahan said with irritation, "they've got an eye in the sky. Those bastards sent an unmanned drone to look for him."

Farkus had never seen one before, and it was moving so quickly in the distance he couldn't get a good look at it now. The front of the drone was egg-shaped, and there were no windows. It was tough to tell how big it was, although it stood out against the dark sea of trees.

"If the drone sees him," McLanahan said, "we've lost our advantage. He'll take to the trees again, and we might never see him again. Plus, the Feds will know where to look."

"He's got to hear it, too," Farkus observed.

"What a bad fucking break," McLanahan said, angry enough that his West Virginian drawl came through.

"He's standing up," Sollis said quietly. "Nobody talk or breathe. I may get a shot."

Farkus thought, *Run, you hardheaded son of a bitch. Don't let them see you. And don't come our direction . . .*

FOR A BRIEF MOMENT, Farkus assumed the popping noises were coming from the drone itself. They were measured but rapid, one after the other.

Pop. Pop. Pop. Pop. Pop.

Before he could open his mouth and ask what it was, the drone shivered, dropped in altitude, tilted to its left, then readjusted severely back the other way, and the right wing tip caught the top of a pine tree and exploded through it with a burst of needles and branches.

"Wow," McLanahan said.

The drone cart wheeled through the sky on the other side of the canyon and dropped into the timber with the violent sound of sheet metal buckling and tree trunks snapping. It was swallowed by the dark forest as if it had never been there at all.

And suddenly there was silence.

"He shot it down," McLanahan said with awe. "Our boy shot that bastard out of the *sky*."

Farkus barely heard Sollis whisper: "Shut up, please," then *BOOM*, his 6.5x284 rifle rocked and sounded even louder in the narrow confines of the wall crack.

Through ringing ears, Farkus heard Sollis say with triumph: "He's down."

16

JOE SADDLED TOBY AWAY FROM THE CHAOS OF A
command center of sorts that was slowly morphing from
too many disparate vehicles and law enforcement officials.
Two large canvas tents were being erected by members of
the sheriff's department—they'd borrowed them from local elk outfitters—next to two high-tech portable tent
structures marked EPA on the sidewalls. The location for
the FOB was on a bench less than two hundred yards from
the Forest Service boundary fence. Within the scrum of
tents and vehicles moved EPA special agents, sheriff's department deputies, Forest Service rangers and special
agents, BLM employees, and other men and women Joe
couldn't identify and didn't want to meet.

He could feel the tension and excitement from the FOB
as he cinched the saddle tight and Toby glared back at him
in faux discomfort. Voices were pronounced and high and

talking over one another, laughter was barked, and flare-ups of anger punctuated the hum. It was the same combi-nation of anticipation and bloodlust he'd witnessed at elk hunting camps or from within the vehicles of hunting parties setting out on opening day of the season.

Joe kept his eye on a group of four men in the temporary corral set up on the edge of the FOB. They were black-clad and sober, unlike the others, and going about their business with quiet gravitas. They seemed to have no interest inter-acting with the others in the camp. The men stood in a knot, intently listening to a local wrangler who had brought the horses as he outlined the personalities and problems with each mount. It was obvious they were unfamiliar with horses, Joe thought. As they climbed into their saddles, the wrangler adjusted stirrups and walked each horse away from the corral to await the others. Heinz Underwood shadowed the wrangler, muttering things into his ear and to his team. When all the agents were mounted, the wran-gler helped Underwood stuff gear into the panniers of a set of packhorses. It looked like too much gear to Joe, who kept his distance even as Underwood spotted him and walked his horse over.

Joe watched him come with bemusement. Underwood obviously didn't know his way around horses, and the agent didn't want to show it. But by the way he held the reins too tight and overcorrected his direction with aggressive yanks, it was obvious.

"First time on a horse?" Joe asked, as Underwood rode up.

"I've been on horses before."

"Fine," Joe said. "You're just lucky it's a brain-dead trail horse, or he might get feisty, the way you're jerking on his mouth."

Almost imperceptibly, Underwood eased up on the reins.

"Are you ready?" he asked. "My men are getting impatient."

Joe nodded and said, "What's the plan? You've got enough equipment there to last a few weeks, it looks like."

Underwood ignored the question. "You're going to lead us to where you last saw Butch Roberson, and we're going to try to determine where he went from there. At that point, you might be released from service."

"Fine by me," Joe said, but he had immediate reservations about agreeing so quickly. The team of special agents was armed with semiautomatic weapons, sidearms, shotguns, and communications equipment. They looked, he thought, like they might shoot first and ask questions later, although he was sure Underwood wouldn't admit it. If he were along, Joe thought, there would be a better chance of bringing Butch back alive. Underwood seemed to sense his concern.

"We're the advance team," Underwood continued. "If we find his track—or locate him—we'll call back and get orders and backup before we proceed."

"I'll bet," Joe said sourly.

Underwood surprised Joe by grinning.

JOE SWUNG into the saddle at the same moment a murmur rippled through the men and women at the FOB. He looked up to see most heads turned toward the road that led to the FOB through the hay meadows. Joe followed their gaze to see a huge black new-model Suburban tearing their way, sending a fat cloud of dust into the air behind it.

Before he could see the license plate or the man behind the wheel, he knew who it was. Only one man drove a new car that recklessly over bad roads.

"Do you know who that is?" Underwood asked Joe.

"Yup," Joe said. "My governor."

THE BLACK SUBURBAN hurtled at the FOB as if the driver's intention was to plow right through it, Joe thought, and he saw a few of the special agents within the tents start to sidle away. The big vehicle braked short of the parking area and skidded to a stop. Governor Spencer Rulon flew out the driver's-side door and left it open while he bellowed, *"I'm the governor of this state, and I want to know who the hell is in charge here!"*

A few beats after the governor, Joe saw Lisa Greene-Dempsey tentatively open the passenger door and step out. She appeared to have no intention of following her boss into the crowd.

Joe and Underwood exchanged glances, then both urged their horses forward toward the Suburban. Joe watched Rulon stride through the crowd of law enforcement—which parted to let him through—straight toward Julio Batista, who had come out of the EPA tent with a cell phone in his hand and a quizzical expression on his face. LGD trailed the governor. She saw Joe and nodded. She looked worried about what was going to happen next, he thought.

Underwood said quietly, "I've heard your guy is a nut-job."

Joe had seen the governor in a rage before—too many times, in fact—and fought an urge to say to Underwood, *This is gonna be good.*

Batista introduced himself and held out his free hand, palm up, to ward off the approach of Rulon, and turned away to end his call. Rulon stopped short of the outstretched palm but stood hands on hips, glaring at the EPA administrator with his upper body pointed forward and his eyes enlarged.

When Batista closed his phone and extended his hand in greeting, Rulon didn't move. He shouted, "What's this I hear about sending unmanned drones into my airspace without permission and without notifying my office?"

"We're in the middle of an operation—" Batista began calmly, when Rulon cut him off by talking over him.

"I don't care what you're in the middle of, you'll order those things back where they came from or *I'll* order the Wyoming National Guard to fly up here and blast them the hell out of the sky!"

Joe frowned. He'd seen the National Guard air fleet before and couldn't recall a single fighter plane among the helicopters and C-130 cargo planes. But maybe Batista didn't know that . . .

"It'll be shoot to kill!" Rulon thundered. "I don't care if I start a damned war between Wyoming and the EPA, because I've been threatening to start one for years."

"Look," Batista said, his eyes shooting around for support from his special agents and the others, "I know we started out on the wrong foot a few years ago. But right now we're in the middle of a murder investigation, and . . ."

Rulon jabbed his finger an inch from the EPA administrator's nose: "There are right ways to do things and wrong ways to do things in my state. When I got a call that two of your people were gunned down in Twelve Sleep County, I pledged support. We want this guy caught as much as you do. But I should have *known* not to trust any of you bastards, that you'd turn out to be the jackbooted thugs I always knew you were."

Joe smiled to himself and shook his head. He almost missed his boss approaching Rulon and grabbing gently at his arm, urging him to calm down.

Rulon said, "Now I hear you've not only offered a reward for the capture or execution of one of my constituents, you've also ordered a goddamned drone from Nebraska, where you spy on cattle feedlot operations, to fly over my airspace and spy on my land and my people. Just who in the *hell* gave you the authority to bypass the elected government of the state of Wyoming and trample over our citizens?"

Rulon's face was red, and when he paused for a breath, Batista said quickly, "First, we've retracted the reward offer. Second, I've got the authority to administrate my region."

"Governor," Greene-Dempsey pleaded, pulling him back, "Please . . ."

Then Rulon waved his arms at the assembled and astonished crowd, and said to Batista, "Get them all the hell out of here! Take down your stupid tents and go the hell away! The only agency who should be here right now is the sheriff of Twelve Sleep County. The rest of you," he said, glaring at the special agents and rangers one by one, *"beat it!"*

Batista shook his head and said, "I doubt you'd talk this way to me if I looked more like you."

"What?" Rulon sputtered, confused.

"You heard me," Batista said, crossing his arms over his chest and daring the governor to say more.

"You're accusing me . . . of what?" Rulon said. "Because you're . . ."

"A Hispanic American," Batista said, raising his chin.

Rulon shook his head, as if momentarily stunned. Then he said, "Well, I'm a Governor American, and I want your ass out of my state. We'll find your shooter, and he'll get justice. We don't want you or your thugs involved." Joe noted the governor's tone had softened, despite the words.

"And now we know why," Batista said, still smug.

Joe shook his head. In that brief exchange, Rulon seemed to have lost his momentum. And the crowd seemed to agree.

Greene-Dempsey managed to pull Rulon away again, and when he turned, Joe saw a look of spent rage crossed with befuddled realization in his face. He'd never seen the look before, and he wondered if Rulon had truly lost it after all. Rulon seemed to have the same thought, and he threw his shoulders back and gathered himself, then looked down at his feet for a moment.

Batista turned to the group of officers and said, "The show is over. It's time to get back to work."

"Jesus Christ," Underwood said, and whistled. "Your governor *is* a nutjob."

Joe said, "He might be. But he's not a racist."

Underwood said, "He is now."

WHILE UNDERWOOD WALKED his horse over to his team to get them ready, Joe dismounted and walked to the black state Suburban. He found Governor Rulon slouched in the driver's seat, shaking his head. When Joe peered inside to locate his boss, Rulon said, "She's not here. She's up in the tent apologizing to Juan Julio What's-His-Face for my racist outburst."

Joe grunted.

"I wasn't expecting that," Rulon said. "It took the wind out of my sails. He's a cunning little bastard. I would have thought these imperial Feds wouldn't be used to seeing a governor yelling into their faces, but I was wrong.

"And to play the race card like that . . . It's the lowest form of debate, because it just closes the subject down. And it's *not true*. I don't hate Hispanics. I hate federal brown-shirt *thugs named Juan Julio Batista*."

"Governor?" Joe interrupted. "Can I ask you a question?"

Rulon looked over wearily. "Shoot. I've never lied to you."

Joe hesitated, and Rulon smiled and said, "Well, not much."

"Anyway, what I was wondering is . . ."

"Why I hired her," Rulon said, finishing the wrong question. But Joe wanted to hear the answer anyway.

"I was pressured into it. But don't quote me."

"I won't," Joe said. "We had breakfast this morning. Then she came on a ride-along."

Rulon laughed and thumped the steering wheel with the heel of his hand. His usual buoyant mood returned. "I heard about that. She's still a little stunned. Bear spray, Joe?"

"It works."

"So I take it. Anyway, she's got some notions, I hear," he said. "She thinks you and your kind are too inbred. She thinks you've all gone native out here—too close to the locals."

Joe nodded.

"Have you?"

"I don't think so," Joe said. "We're like local beat cops, is the way I think about it. We know the people, so we can do our jobs better."

Rulon nodded, and said, "'Government closest to the people governs best,' some wise man once said. Do you agree?"

"I guess I do."

"So do I," Rulon said with finality. Then: "Next question?"

Joe hesitated, then said, "She told me you approved her lending me out on this investigation, that it was my duty to assist the best I can."

Rulon raised his eyebrows and said, "So?"

"I'm not sure I can do it," Joe said, surprising even himself with the words. "I know Butch Roberson. I'm not sure I can go along with this the way they're doing it."

"Why? Do you think he's innocent? Isn't this *exactly* what LGD is afraid of?"

Joe shook his head. "I don't think he's innocent. Not from what I know."

"Then what's the problem?"

Joe felt tongue-tied. After a beat, he said, "I'm just not sure how much longer I can keep doing this."

"What? Being a game warden?"

"Being a state employee," Joe said. "She offered me a desk job in Cheyenne. I've never worked behind a desk before."

Rulon, for once, didn't fire another question. Instead he said, "Do what's right, Joe. That's what you're good at. This is your decision."

Joe waited for more that didn't come. He wasn't sure what that would be, though.

Rulon, as he usually did, changed the subject again. "We've had a couple of interesting adventures together, haven't we, Joe?"

"Yup."

"I thought for a while there you were going to lose me my job," Rulon said. "You just have a knack for getting right into the middle of trouble, don't you?"

Joe nodded. He said, "Marybeth says I have a singular skill in that regard."

"She's smart and too good-looking for you," Rulon said. "You don't deserve her."

"I know that."

"What about your friend, the maniac? That stone-cold killer with the falcons you hang around with? What's he think about all this?" Rulon said, knowing Joe didn't like to talk about Nate Romanowski.

"I haven't heard from him," Joe said. "But I'm pretty sure he wouldn't like it."

"So you haven't been in touch since that trouble last year," Rulon said, and nodded. "That's probably good for you. You wouldn't want to be aiding and abetting a known fugitive."

Joe shifted uncomfortably.

"Maybe I need some guys like that on my team," Rulon mused, and gestured toward the FOB. "I could use some real muscle dealing with this tyrant Batista."

Joe looked up, puzzled. He wasn't sure if Rulon was serious.

"What's going on over there?" Rulon asked suddenly, leaning forward in his seat. Joe looked over to see Batista rushing from the tent toward a white panel communications van. The vehicle had a brace of antennas and radio dishes mounted on top. Lisa Greene-Dempsey emerged after him and walked slowly and cautiously toward the Suburban.

When she arrived and saw Joe she couldn't disguise the look of anguish on her face.

Rulon asked, "What's happening?"

She said, "His people said something happened to the drone. They lost contact with it somewhere up there in the mountains."

"It crashed?" Rulon said hopefully.

"Worse."

Rulon's smile grew into something almost maniacal. He said, "Someone shot it down?"

"That's what they're thinking," she said, shaking her head.

"Wonderful!" Rulon shouted. "Let's have more of that!"

As Joe mounted Toby to join Underwood and the others, Rulon bounded out of the SUV and called his name.

When he turned, Rulon gave him two thumbs up, then walked over toward the communications van, a skip in his step.

Joe wasn't sure what the governor meant by the signal— that everything would be fine or he was simply giddy a drone had been shot down. Everything Governor Rulon said or did, Joe had learned, had two or three different interpretations.

"Okay, men," Underwood said to the four other special agents on horseback, and pointed to Joe. "Follow *this* man."

17

APPROACHING THE ELK CAMP ON HORSEBACK ON
the floor of the canyon, Farkus felt sick to his stomach.
He'd made this kind of trek before, when a hunter in his
party claimed he'd knocked down a deer or an elk and they
set out to find it, but the only time he'd been in a similar
situation was three years before in the Sierra Madre, when
he'd been recruited on a similar mission to find those two
murderous brothers—and that hadn't gone well at all.
Jimmy Sollis's constant chatter—*he had certainly woken
up*—added to his unease.

"Look at this," Sollis said, sweeping his hand to indicate
the huge expanse around them. "Look how fucking far
this was for a perfect shot. Jesus, one shot at eighteen hundred yards. It's taking us nearly a half hour to even get
there. Man, what a rush. *What a fucking rush.*"

They rode abreast now, walking their mounts, like

outlaws in a western movie, Farkus thought. The floor of the canyon was thick with a green carpet of grass and wildflowers—columbines and Indian paintbrush, mostly. The shallow creek flowed through it. The bed of the stream was orange pea gravel, and the water was cold, shallow, and clear. He could see shadowed darts of small brook trout shoot out from beneath the grassy banks and fin madly upstream, and he wished it meant something to him. Given the circumstances, though, it didn't.

The elk camp was ahead of them, slightly elevated from the valley floor, but he could see nothing in it except a wisp of smoke from the untended campfire.

"I don't see a body yet," Farkus said, finally.

"That's because he's *down*, man," Sollis said, lapsing into druggie cadence as well as acting like he was under the influence of something stronger than adrenaline, Farkus thought. "You don't see him cause he's *down*."

"I think I liked it better when you wouldn't talk," Farkus grumbled.

Instead of feeling rebuked, Sollis threw back his head and laughed.

After a beat, McLanahan asked Sollis, "Where do you think you hit him?"

Farkus was grateful that at least the ex-sheriff appeared to understand the gravity of what they'd done.

Sollis said, "It was probably a heart or lung shot—that's what I was going for. I'm thinking heart, because the poor son of a bitch dropped like a sack of cement. He might have stood and wavered a few seconds if I blew his lungs out."

Farkus looked away.

"Any chance he's pretending to be hit so he can draw us in?" McLanahan asked. "The guy is more wily than I thought, and he can *shoot*. You saw the way he took down that drone."

"Not a chance, man," Sollis said. "At that distance the round got there long before he could have heard the shot. He'd have to be some kind of wizard to guess I was about to pull the trigger a mile away, and from what I understand he wasn't no wizard."

McLanahan nodded, apparently satisfied.

"Look back." Sollis laughed, turning in his saddle and pointing at the canyon ridge wall in the distance. "Look how damned far away it was. Jesus, what a *rush* . . ."

THEY WERE CLOSE ENOUGH that Farkus could smell the smoke. It was sharp and acrid, probably fueled by green twigs. A breath of wind shifted and took the smoke away. But there was also another smell tucked inside the smoke.

"Be alert," McLanahan said, as he reached down and peeled back the security strap of the Bushmaster in its scabbard. He drew the rifle out and seated a round. Farkus observed and did the same and laid his rifle across the pommel of his horse.

"No reason to get excited," Sollis said, and beamed, shaking his head at their precaution. "He ain't going nowhere."

Because the camp was situated on a rise from the valley floor, Farkus couldn't see into it yet. But he recognized the size of the rocks circling the fire pit, and the stumps that

had been chainsawed smooth and even to sit on. He got a
flash of a memory: *dusk, the last of the sun filtering through
the trees on the western horizon, the fire blazing high, Butch
Roberson leaning over and pouring a healthy splash of Wild
Turkey into Farkus's metal cup. He'd been talking about his
daughter, how he didn't feel like he was truly a man until
that day in the hospital when she was delivered and he looked
into her face . . .*

"THERE HE IS," McLanahan said.

The body was there just like Sollis had promised, and
Farkus saw it as they rode up the rise. The body was on its
side, facing away from them, partially curled around the fire
itself. A clump of baggy green camo with legs extended,
scarred hunting boots side by side in the grass.

Bursting through the fabric under Butch's rib cage was
a wet ball of red-and-gray intestine the size of a softball.
So *that* was the smell he'd detected earlier, Farkus realized.
The earthy, musky odor of a downed game animal being
field-dressed.

"Gut shot," the ex-sheriff declared.

Farkus waited for Sollis to say something defensive, but
there was no sound. Maybe, Farkus thought, it had finally
dawned on Sollis that his target had been a living, breathing human being.

McLanahan was still trailing the packhorse, and he
stopped both of his animals a few feet from the body and
fire ring and leaned down, studying the body. Farkus

hadn't ridden around to see the face yet, although he nearly jumped out of his skin when he thought he glimpsed movement from the body's extended right hand. After a double take, he saw the hand was still.

Then McLanahan said, "Son of a bitch. We got the wrong guy."

PANICKED, FARKUS swung down from the saddle and left Dreadnaught to wander off to graze. He didn't care. He still had the rifle in his hand as he lunged forward and grasped the body's right shoulder and pulled it to him. The body flopped to its back, and the red-haired man moaned.

"Jesus—he's still alive!" Farkus said, dropping the gun and jumping back. The man's face was square, his head blocky, and there was a five-day growth of beard. Farkus had never seen the man before, but it certainly wasn't Butch Roberson. The man's eyes were wide open but didn't move around, and there was a pink string of blood and saliva connecting the top and bottom lip of his partially open mouth.

"It isn't him, is it?" McLanahan asked Farkus, his tone neutral.

"No."

"Shit. I wonder who it is Jimmy shot?"

Farkus looked up. Sollis looked thunderstruck, but McLanahan seemed to be taking it in stride, which astonished Farkus.

He watched as McLanahan sat back and slowly surveyed

the camp. The ex-sheriff said, "I see his backpack over there against a tree. Farkus, why don't you see if you can find some kind of ID?"

"Me?"

"You. But first you better tie up your horse before it runs away on you."

Stunned by the turn of events, Farkus sleepwalked Dreadnaught over to a thick lodgepole pine and tied the lead rope over a branch. He glanced up at McLanahan and Sollis as he made his way over to the backpack because he didn't want to see the face of the gravely wounded man again. Sollis sat in the saddle staring out at nothing, slack-mouthed and frozen. McLanahan was squinting and looking into the middle distance, as if gears were working in his head.

Next to the backpack, propped on the side of the tree that had been out of their view, was a complicated compound bow with wheels and pulleys and a mounted set of razor-sharp broad-head arrows.

He called to McLanahan, "He's an elk hunter. It must be archery season on this side of the mountain."

"Gee, you think?" McLanahan said sarcastically.

"I don't see any ID," Farkus said, rooting through the pack. It smelled of stale campfire smoke and sweat, and the pack's contents were typical: camo clothing, rain gear, a sleeping bag and pad, a one-man bivvy tent, freeze-dried food packets, maps . . .

"I'll see if he's got a wallet on him." McLanahan grunted as he dismounted. To Sollis, he said, "Get down off that horse and give me a hand here, Jimmy."

Sollis simply shook his head, as if by refusing the request he was also denying the reality of the situation.

While rolling the hunter back over to his belly so he could dig through his pockets, McLanahan said, "The dumb knucklehead. He should'a known to stay out of the mountains during a manhunt or use a known murderer's camp, and especially not to wear the same damn clothes as the murderer."

Farkus quit searching and wandered toward McLanahan and the hunter. Something wasn't right, he thought, but his head was too fuzzy with the situation they were in to put it together.

McLanahan stood up holding a billfold from the hunter's cargo pants. The wallet was inside a Ziploc bag. The ex-sheriff tore through the plastic and opened the wallet, studying the ID sheathed in thick plastic. Farkus could see McLanahan's shoulders suddenly relax.

"Out-of-stater from Maine named Pete Douvarjo," McLanahan said with obvious relief. "I was worried he was a local."

"Still . . ." Farkus said, not understanding.

"Pretty likely his people have no clue exactly where he is right now. Did you find a cell phone or a satellite phone in his pack, Farkus?"

"I didn't see one, but I didn't look that close," Farkus said.

"We'll need to look."

Douvarjo made a low moaning sound, and both Farkus and McLanahan turned toward him. Douvarjo hadn't moved, and his eyes still stared at the sky.

"What are we going to do?" Farkus asked. "Do we call somebody? Can they send a helicopter here to airlift him out?"

"He isn't long for the world," McLanahan said, matter-of-fact.

Farkus covered his face with both hands, then splayed his fingers and looked out at McLanahan. "You aren't saying we leave him here, are you?"

McLanahan looked up sharply. "What can we do, Farkus? The bullet passed through all of his vital organs and made a big-ass exit wound on the other side. He's shutting down. It's just a matter of minutes."

"So we just stand here and wait?"

"For now."

"Then what?" Farkus said through his fingers.

"I haven't decided yet."

"Sheriff," Farkus said, "we just *shot* an innocent man."

"I'd call it an understandable accident, Farkus. And that's exactly what it was. This poor guy was in the wrong place at the wrong time, doing the wrong thing.

"One thing I've learned," McLanahan said, "is how important it is to control the story—they call it the narrative. I let it get away from me a year ago, and now we've got Wheelchair Dick puttering around with my job. I'm not going to let it happen again."

He gestured toward Douvarjo. "Nobody will remember this if we bring in Butch Roberson. The story will be how the ex-sheriff who really knows and understands this county went up into the mountains on his own and brought down the bad guy while the Feds and the new sheriff sat on their asses. We're on a manhunt for a killer wearing camo clothes and we happen on a man bearing that description in the act of shooting down a federal drone. What else were we to think?"

Farkus started to argue when it hit him what was wrong. It must have occurred to the sheriff at exactly the same time, because McLanahan's face went taut and he asked, "Farkus, did you see a rifle?"

From above them in the dark timber, a voice said, "I need all of you to throw down your weapons and turn around. You on the horse—climb off now."

Farkus recognized the voice.

It was Butch Roberson.

18

"THIS IS WHERE I SAW HIM," JOE SAID AS THE SIX horsemen entered the alcove. They'd ridden through the severed fence and into the burnished red forest of dead and dying trees. "Over there is where he paused to eat, and that's the tree he leaned his pack against. Right next to it was his rifle."

Underwood reined his horse to a stop, and his team followed suit. Underwood leaned forward in his saddle and took the pressure off his back by grasping the saddle horn. He looked around and said, "So he was coming off the mountain when you saw him?"

"No," Joe said, dismounting and walking Toby around the perimeter of the camp. "Butch didn't come down from the mountains. He was going up into them, from the east."

"He walked across the Big Stream Ranch to get here, is what you're saying?"

"That's right," Joe said. "He cut the fence back there and continued on."

"Why'd he cut the fence?"

"Your guess is as good as mine," Joe said, "but I think he was just frustrated. I think he was striking out at anything that reminded him of you guys."

Underwood snorted and shook his head. Then: "Didn't anyone on the ranch think it was unusual for a guy on foot to be just walking across their property? Doesn't that Frank Zeller goof have cowboys or farmhands watching the place?"

"It's a very big ranch," Joe said. "Butch Roberson could have easily stayed concealed as he came across. There are some deep irrigation ditches on the meadows down there and plenty of hills to hide behind. Or he might have crossed it before daylight—I don't know."

"Or maybe he had some help?" Underwood asked, raising his eyebrows.

"I wouldn't know," Joe said, looking up at Underwood.

Underwood asked, "So if he was coming up from the ranch when you saw him, how did he get here in the first place?"

"I'd like to know that myself," Joe said. "His truck isn't parked anywhere down there, but he indicated he'd walked all the way."

"So someone dropped him off," Underwood said.

"Yup."

"Which means someone else is involved in this whole thing. Do you have any theory on who that might be?"

Joe shrugged. It had been a question hounding him in

the back of his mind since the day before. Was it one of Butch's friends or employees? A stranger he'd commandeered on the road? Or maybe someone closer?

"I'd like to know who it was," Underwood said.

"Me, too."

"So maybe he had some help getting out here and some more help getting across the ranch."

Joe asked, "How big is this conspiracy going to get before we're through?"

"I don't trust these people," he said, squinting.

"And they don't trust you," Joe said.

"So give me your best guess," Underwood said, his eyes probing Joe's face. "Where do you think he went after you let him get away?"

"I told you," Joe said with heat, "I didn't let him . . ."

"I know, I know. You didn't know he was a murderer at the time," Underwood said sarcastically. "But putting that aside, where do you think he went?"

Joe looked around, twisting at his waist. He studied the dry forest floor and the slope of the terrain.

He said, "Because he came from the highway down there to the east, I think his intention was to continue west toward the peaks of the mountains. There's a lot of wild country up there, and plenty of places to hide out. He knows the mountains from hunting here. What I don't know is whether he planned to go over the top and drop into the canyons on the west side, or hole up here on the eastern slope."

"Why would he go over the top?" Underwood asked.

"To get farther away from you guys," Joe said. "He knows the country over there like he does here. I know that because there are two elk areas that run adjacent to each other, Area Thirty-five is this side of the mountain and Area Forty-five is the other side, and both are general elk permit areas, so special permits wouldn't be necessary. Area Thirty-five opens a week before, so I'd guess Butch hunts this side first, then moves west a week later if he wants to. It just makes sense that he'd be more comfortable hunting east to west. The terrain is easier on this side, more slope and forest broken up by natural meadows and parks. There's more open feed on this side."

Underwood said, "It's like you're speaking Greek to me."

Joe sighed and said, "Once you go over the top, the country gets tougher. There are a few brutal canyons, including Savage Run. What tends to happen is the elk herds on this side get early pressure from hunters and move over the top to get away from them and hide out in the rough country. My guess is Butch is doing the same thing."

"That's all very interesting," Underwood said. "But as you said, you're guessing."

"Yup."

Underwood sat back and sighed, then raised the satellite phone that hung from his neck on a lanyard. "I've got to check in with FOB One," he said, a hint of weariness in his voice.

"FOB One?" Joe asked, knowing the answer.

"Regional Director Batista," Underwood said. "We

need to know whether to proceed or go back. He's calling all the shots."

Joe noted the team of special agents behind Underwood exchanging cynical glances with one another that were not meant for his eyes. But he found it interesting.

WHILE UNDERWOOD TALKED with Batista—listening much more than talking, Joe observed—Joe walked down the slope until the timber thinned and opened up and he could see the expanse of the Big Stream Ranch below. The FOB, at that distance, was a small dot on a sea of sagebrush and grass.

He'd found over the years that he thought best when he was in the open, without being closed in by a tree canopy, or a ceiling, or the roof of a pickup. Somehow, his mind needed the open space of a vista to focus.

Things had been moving at lightning speed since the afternoon before, when he'd encountered Butch. Hell had broken open, and hundreds of bureaucrats were gushing out. If there was a strategic plan behind the investigation, he didn't know what it was. All he could see was a blizzard of actions and movement based on a predetermined conclusion. And now the governor was involved.

Usually, when confused by circumstances, Joe talked with Marybeth or Nate Romanowski. Rarely was their advice similar, but it helped frame the issue for him to decide. But with Marybeth understandably preoccupied and Nate who knows where, he felt unmoored and drifting out to sea.

For the second time that day, he felt empathy toward Butch Roberson, and could understand why the man had snapped.

"**Okay**," **Underwood said** to Joe and his team, "gather up. We have the word." He said "the word" with slightly disguised contempt.

One of the agents snickered, then looked away when he noticed Joe was looking at him.

Underwood said, "We're to engage hot pursuit of Butch Roberson. Joe Pickett will stay with us and help navigate. The director says that every hour that goes by is an hour wasted, so we should plan on being out all night at the very least."

One of the agents moaned but cut it off quickly after a hard glance from Underwood.

Underwood continued: "I have the coordinates of where, approximately, the drone went down. Before contact was lost, there is some video of a man—probably our subject—in a clearing of some kind. Our job is to move swiftly toward that spot and intercept him.

"On the way there, I need everyone to keep on full alert. Keep your eyes and ears open. Look for tracks, or disturbances, broken twigs, anything. This guy is dangerous, and he's desperate. But he knows the backcountry and we don't, so we can't assume he'll roll over or give himself up easily."

Underwood ordered the agents to prepare their weapons, and to mute cell phones and satellite phones. They would communicate with one another, he said, by radio. No one was to talk to anyone at the FOB without going through him first, so that lines of communication were clear.

As the agents unpacked headsets and earpieces to plug in to their radios, the man who had snickered earlier said to Underwood, "Sir, we aren't exactly wilderness types. All these horses . . . I don't know. Looking for tracks? I don't have any training in that."

He looked around at the other agents and two nodded in agreement. Underwood turned and pointed to Joe.

"What about you?"

"I've done it," Joe said, "but I'm not an expert in the field of man-tracking. I think Butch is smart enough to stay low-impact when he moves."

"You're the best we've got," Underwood said.

Another of the agents spoke up and said, "I don't think we're prepared for this kind of thing."

Joe nodded in agreement, although he knew Underwood wouldn't grant him a vote in the matter.

"I understand," Underwood said to the agent. "But you heard me. I'm relaying our orders."

"Where do we sleep?" another agent asked. "Do we have tents and sleeping bags and such?"

"No."

"What about food?" another asked.

"There's bottled water and a couple of boxes of energy bars on the packhorse," Underwood said.

"This is crazy," one of the agents said, and the others agreed.

Joe was surprised when Underwood looked to him. "What do you think—will we find him by nightfall?"

"That depends," Joe said, uneasy at the turn of events. "What are the coordinates?"

Underwood handed down a scratch pad with figures and a topo map of the Twelve Sleep National Forest. Joe sat down on the same stump he'd seen Butch Roberson sitting on and spread the map over his thighs.

When he calculated the location, he looked up. "It's over the top of the mountains."

Underwood said, "Seriously? How long would that take?"

"Most of the night," Joe said.

"Let me call FOB One," Underwood said, raising the satellite phone.

"It might make more sense to drive around to the other side," Joe said.

Underwood conveyed the situation and relayed Joe's suggestion. Joe could tell by the way Underwood's face froze that it wasn't received well. The agents looked on with stony silence.

"We proceed as ordered," Underwood said after he signed off, and tried to get his horse to walk away from the glares. But the horse didn't move.

"Click your tongue," Joe whispered to Underwood.

Underwood clicked his tongue and his mount stepped forward. He mouthed *"Thanks"* as he walked the horse by Joe.

JOE LED, followed by Underwood and his four special agents, and they climbed slowly up the mountain. The

slope wasn't steep yet, but the constant climb tired the
mounts, and he stopped every twenty minutes to allow
Toby to rest. They rode in shadow broken by shafts of afternoon sunlight that penetrated through the canopy. The
ground was barren of foliage in large stretches, and was
covered by a carpet of dry pine needles and bits of bark
fallen from dead pine-beetle-killed trees.

The trees were dead, the forest floor was dry, and the
slight breeze from the south was warm. As the horses
stepped they made a crunching sound, and the combined
cacophony of twenty-four hooves at times sounded like
applause rolling slowly up the mountain. Joe wondered how
they would ever attempt to be stealthy in the parchment-dry
forest. A dropped match or cigarette butt, he thought,
could make the whole mountain go up in flame. He was
grateful none of the special agents lit up.

WHEN HE SAW an aberration on the floor of the forest—
a disturbance in the carpet, a flap of mulch turned over—
he pointed it out to Underwood. Joe felt more than saw he
was on Butch Roberson's route.

The trunks of the trees were so dense in places that Joe
had to weave Toby through them. Sometimes, he loosened
the reins and trusted his horse to weave his own way
through. The agents followed as best they could, but their
trail horses balked at times and had to be urged to continue.
It was a dangerous situation and could turn into a wreck if
one of the horses panicked in the sea of trees, and he held
his breath at times until the small string made it through

the tightest spots. Trail horses liked trails, Joe knew. They weren't thrilled with exploration, or tight fits, or climbing mountains, unlike Toby.

Although Joe could at times only intuit the route Butch had taken, there were places where, due to obstructions or granite walls, there was no choice where he'd had to go if his goal was to traverse the range.

His intuition was confirmed when they crossed a tiny stream of springwater from somewhere above them and he saw, quite clearly, a boot track in the mud. Joe photographed it with his digital camera to compare it with any other clear tracks they found later.

AS JOE RODE, he heard bits and pieces of conversation from the agents behind him. Underwood held his tongue.

The grumbling was typical of men being charged with a pointless and ill-conceived task, he thought. They didn't like being so far from the FOB without proper food and shelter, they didn't like riding horses, and they didn't like Regional Director Julio Batista.

Joe thought he might be able to establish some common ground after all.

TWO AND A HALF HOURS after they'd left the dry camp, as the intense afternoon sun fused the forest with burnished orange, Underwood's satellite phone burred with vibration on his chest.

Joe looked over his shoulder as he walked Toby and

watched Underwood adjust the volume of the set as he listened. Something dark passed over Underwood's face at whatever he was hearing, and after a minute or two Underwood looked up and gestured with his free hand for Joe to stop.

Were they being given the word to go back? Joe wondered. He halted Toby and sidestepped so Underwood could catch up alongside him.

As Underwood approached, he lowered the phone from his ear and covered the mic with his other hand. He said, "It's for you."

"Who is it?"

"Regional Director Batista."

"What does he want?"

Underwood took a breath and extended the handset. "Our suspect somehow got ahold of a satellite phone of his own and he called the FOB. He's on the line now and they're patching it together into a conference call."

"You're kidding?"

"I'm not. He says he has a couple of hostages, including the ex-sheriff of this county. He'll let them go, but only if we agree to a list of demands. And he says the only guy he can trust to be involved in the negotiation is Joe Pickett."

19

"IS HE ON?" BUTCH ROBERSON ASKED JULIO BA-
tista. McLanahan's satellite phone was pressed tightly to
his face. Farkus noted Butch's fingers gripped the handset
so tightly they were nearly translucent white. And he noted
the line of perspiration beads under Butch's scalp. Since
the sun was sliding toward dusk and it had cooled a quick
twenty degrees in the past hour, he knew Butch wasn't
sweating because of the heat.

"We're waiting," Batista said. "Hold on—it's a technical
thing. We've got some guys trying to patch us all on together."

Farkus could hear both sides of the conversation clearly.
It was still and quiet, and Butch hadn't turned down the
volume of the speaker because he likely wasn't familiar with
the phone. Butch was nervous and twitchy, and his eyes
burned red from exhaustion.

"If you don't get him on . . . where in the hell is he?" Butch asked.

"In the field," Batista said calmly. "It's taking a while to bring all the parties together, so please be patient."

"Get him on," Butch said.

EARLIER, AFTER ordering McLanahan, Farkus, and Sollis to dismount and disarm, Butch Roberson had emerged from the shadowed stand of timber on the west slope. Farkus hadn't seen Butch since he'd quit his job, and he was surprised how he looked: thinner, slightly stooped when he walked, with furrowed lines in his face and tired eyes. He looked like he'd aged ten years, and Farkus knew it wasn't just from being on the run in the mountains for the past two days. Something had happened to Butch Roberson in the last year that had changed him physically.

Butch held a semiautomatic rifle with an extended magazine and a tactical scope mounted on it, and used the muzzle to signal that they should walk away from the camp into a grassy clearing to the south of the alcove.

"What about the horses?" McLanahan had asked.

"Let them go. All except the packhorse. I want to see what you brought me."

McLanahan protested, but Butch didn't care. He circled the three men in the clearing and unbuckled the cinch strap on Dreadnaught's saddle and did the same with the other two saddled horses. Then he slapped him on his flank. Dreadnaught took off as if the bell had rung and summer vacation had begun. McLanahan's and Sollis's horses and the spare followed, leaving only the packhorse and three crumpled saddles on the ground.

"How in the hell do you expect us to get back?" McLanahan asked plaintively.

"Who says you're going back?" Butch asked.

Butch patted them all down and made sure they had no more weapons. When he ran his hand over Farkus's clothing, he said, "Dave Farkus, I'm kinda surprised to see what kind of company you're keeping."

"Me, too," Farkus had said.

When Butch got to Sollis, he said, "Hell of a shot. Did you think it was me?"

Sollis nodded. Butch shook his head in disgust and moved to McLanahan.

"So you decided to freelance, huh?" Butch asked McLanahan.

"In a matter of speaking."

"Tell me what they're saying about me in town."

McLanahan cleared his throat. "Every Fed in the mountain west is either here or on their way. They want you for the murder of the two EPA agents. It's a clusterfuck of industrial proportion."

Farkus watched Butch carefully and noted no reaction.

"So why are you three here killing innocent elk hunters?" Butch asked.

Farkus said, "There's a big reward out for you."

Butch took that in, nodded, and said, "How much?"

Farkus looked to McLanahan with disdain and said, "I'd

like to know that myself. All I've been told is that it's a big-ass reward."

"And you were hired to guide?" Butch asked Farkus.

"Yes, Butch."

"The sheriff . . . ex-sheriff . . . hired you?"

"Yes."

Butch said, "Remind me never to take you hunting with me again."

Farkus swallowed hard and studied the tops of his boots.

Butch turned back to McLanahan. Farkus noted a desperate and sad cast in Butch's eyes, a look he'd never seen before.

Butch said to McLanahan, "Doesn't take much for you to turn on your own, does it?"

McLanahan started to defend himself, but something in Butch's expression convinced him, for once, to hold his tongue.

"Sit down, all of you," Butch said, backing away toward the packhorse. "I don't want to have to hurt anyone. I just want to see what goodies you brought me."

Roberson grinned as he pulled gear and equipment out of the panniers. Most he discarded to the side. Farkus watched as Butch found a .45 pistol, checked the loads, and put it in his pack. He also kept two satellite phones.

WITH ONE OF the satellite phones clipped on his belt and three plastic double-loop flex-cuff restraints sticking out of his cargo pants' thigh pocket for later, Butch Roberson had directed them to bury the body of the poor gut-shot hunter. He said, "I don't know who he was, but he deserves better than to leave him to the predators."

Farkus and Sollis did most of the work using a collapsible camp shovel Butch had found in the panniers. It was tough going, lots of rocks an inch beneath the carpet of grass, and it took them nearly an hour to dig a shallow grave. McLanahan spent the time trying to convince Butch to give himself up, that it would be better for him and his family if he came back with them voluntarily. Butch ignored him and finally swung his rifle over until the muzzle was a foot from McLanahan's nose.

"Say another word," Butch warned the sheriff, "and they'll be digging more graves. Did you forget you came up here to kill me? I haven't."

McLanahan's beard stopped opening for a while.

AFTER ORDERING the three of them to cover the shallow grave with big twists of pitch wood and football-sized rocks from the fire ring, Butch cinched the flex-cuffs on each of them with their wrists in front, then glared at Sollis for such a long time Farkus began to feel the hairs on the back of his neck twitch.

Butch said, "I hate to have to do this, but I can't trust you guys."

FARKUS WENT FIRST into the dark timber, followed by Sollis and the ex-sheriff.

Whenever Farkus paused, Butch prodded him on. He

seemed to have a specific destination in mind, Farkus thought, although Butch didn't reveal what it was.

They trudged past the crumpled remains of the predator drone Butch had shot down. It was shockingly white and clean but in dozens of sections on the forest floor. As they passed, Farkus could see intricate wiring through splits in the seams and smell fuel leaking out of the damaged tank. Farkus saw several well-placed bullet holes in the damaged nose of the aircraft. The crash of the drone had brought down several dead and dying trees, as well as shearing a gash in the overhead canopy.

"You've got to figure they know where it went down," McLanahan told Butch.

"Which is why we're going a long way from it," Butch had said.

"How did you know it would go down?" Farkus asked.

"I didn't," Butch answered.

THE LIGHT CHANGED as the sun kissed the tops of the mountains when they emerged from the dense trees and into a small rocky clearing. For the first time since they'd left, Farkus could get a sense of where they were and how much country there was surrounding them. He could see the last rays of the sun light the snowcapped top of the range in front of them, and the ocean of forest undulating away in the other three directions. They weren't far from the tree line, where it would be too high to sustain growth.

Butch said they could sit, which Farkus did quickly. There was a sheen of sweat beneath his clothing from the climb, and his thighs ached. McLanahan grunted an old-man grunt as he lowered himself to a boulder. Sweat streamed down his face from beneath his hatband.

Butch didn't even seem out of breath. He plucked the satellite phone out of the holster, turned it on, and hit three numbers: 911.

When he connected with the emergency dispatcher in Saddlestring, he said, "This is Butch Roberson, the man everybody's looking for. I've got Sheriff Kyle McLanahan and Dave Farkus as hostages sitting right here in front of me. I need to talk to the man in charge of hunting me down, or these two aren't gonna see another sunrise."

After five minutes of scrambling on the other end, Butch said, "Julio Batista, you said?"

Farkus could hear the man named Batista making the case for Butch to turn himself in, to spare the hostages, to not make this difficult or dangerous to anyone else. He said he had the authority to make a deal, and the power to make sure justice was done.

"I know you," Butch said, cutting off Batista. "You're the director of Region Eight, aren't you?"

"Have we met?"

Butch snorted. "No, we haven't met. My wife and I left about twenty messages for you to call us over the past year, but we couldn't get past your secretary. We sent you registered letters that were signed for, but no one responded. Now you want to talk?"

"You can trust me," Batista said. Farkus thought he heard desperation.

Butch said, "I trust you about as far as I can throw you,

you son of a bitch. Get Joe Pickett on the line. He's the local game warden."

Batista said, "I know who he is, but why can't we keep this between us?"

"No way. Get Joe on the call or I'll pop Farkus or Sollis first and the ex-sheriff second and it'll be on you."

Farkus looked up in alarm, but when he saw Butch's face he knew the threat was hollow. But Batista wouldn't know that, which was the point.

When Batista started to explain why it couldn't be done, Butch said, "You have five minutes."

FARKUS REALIZED his knees were shaking as he sat, so he cradled them between his arms. He blamed the hard climb, but he knew that wasn't all it was. Butch had a hard set to his face, and when he checked his watch he then looked up to assess Farkus and McLanahan. Butch shifted his weight so his rifle swung up and Farkus could see the black O of the muzzle.

When Butch had made the threat, Farkus thought he was bluffing. Now he wasn't sure it was a bluff. Not at all.

20

UNDERWOOD COVERED THE MICROPHONE ON
the satellite phone and whispered to Joe, "We're going to
agree with whatever he says, got that?"

Joe nodded, but it was more of an acknowledgment of
the words than agreement with them. With that, Underwood leaned over in his saddle and handed Joe the satellite
phone. When Joe took it, he heard Butch Roberson say, "Is
he on?"

"Butch, this is Joe Pickett."

"Hey, Joe."

"Butch."

"Is that asshole still with us?"

Joe's first urge was to say "Which one?" but Batista
broke in: "This is Regional Director Julio Batista. I'm still
here."

Out of the corner of his eye, Joe saw Underwood stifle

a smile. He could clearly hear the conversation in the silent and dead forest.

"Is anybody else on the line?" Butch asked.

"Just us three," Batista said quickly. Joe knew he was lying. He could picture a team of agents with headphones in one of the communications vans at the FOB, listening to every word and coordinating with technical experts to triangulate the satellite phone transmissions and pinpoint the exact location of Butch Roberson.

"I've got Dave Farkus and the former sheriff here," Butch said.

Joe shook his head. *McLanahan*. Joe and the ex-sheriff had never seen eye to eye. Joe considered McLanahan all foam and no beer.

Butch said, "I don't want to hurt them, but I've got to have some leverage with you people. I found out over the past year that you play a rigged game, so I need some insurance."

Batista said, "Butch, there's no need to take hostages. You're already in enough trouble, but that doesn't mean we can't talk it out and figure out a way for you to turn yourself in. This can all end now. You'll get a fair trial and the ability to make your case—"

"Bullshit," Butch said, cutting him off. "*Bullshit*. There's nothing fair about any of this. I'm through with thinking you people play fair, not after what you did to me and my family."

"Butch, listen . . ."

"You put up a reward like I'm some kind of desperate outlaw," Butch said, his voice rising. "Then you sent a damned drone up in the sky to look for me. I hope you know I shot the son of a bitch down."

He knows, Joe thought.

"Look, Butch . . ."

"Quit using my name like we're friends," Butch barked at Batista.

Joe guessed that over the past few minutes, Batista had received coaching from someone with experience in hostage negotiations who had told him to be calm, friendly, and reasonable . . . to try to establish a relationship with the gunman. Keep him talking. It didn't sound like it was working.

Butch said, "I need you to shut up and listen. I know you're probably trying to find me right now, so quit dragging this out. Joe, are you still there?"

"Yes, Butch," Joe said.

"I wanted to tell you yesterday, but I just couldn't. You know what they did to me, right?"

"I know some of it," Joe said. "I talked with Pam last night, and she told us. Man, I wish you would have let us know. We had no idea you were going through this."

"Pam?" Butch said, his voice softening. "Was Hannah there, too?"

"Both of them were at our house," Joe said. "Hannah was there when I left this morning."

"Are they okay?"

Joe paused for a moment. "They seem okay, Butch, considering the situation. I think they miss you."

"I miss *them*," Butch said, in a way that broke Joe's heart.

"You *can* see them again, Butch," Batista cut in with a salesman-smooth voice.

"Shut the fuck up, Batista," Butch growled. "I'm talking to Joe."

Joe was relieved Batista complied. He imagined him shrugging his shoulders with an *I tried* gesture to the hostage negotiator.

Joe said to Butch, "So Dave Farkus and Sheriff McLanahan are sitting right there with you, huh?"

"Yeah. They tried to collect the reward. Instead, they shot a hunter thinking it was me."

Joe was startled and said, "They shot a hunter?"

"Yeah, the idiots. They saw an archery hunter and gut-shot him. They brought some idiot long-range shooter along with them."

"Oh, man," Joe said. "I'll guess the hunter didn't even know what was going on."

"No shit," Butch said. "The poor guy."

"Is he dead?"

"Yeah, but it took a while."

"You know," Joe said, "for a while there I was wondering if McLanahan was really up there with you. But now I know he is because nobody else would be that much of a moron."

Butch snorted a laugh and said, "I'll tell him you said that."

"Please do," Joe said.

There was a beat of silence. Joe hoped Batista wouldn't feel compelled to fill it. But he did.

"Butch, there's really no reason to keep running. We

can bring your wife and daughter up here and you can see
them before we take you into custody . . ."

"Stay away from them!" Butch yelled. "Don't bring them
into this again or I'm punching off and I start shooting."

Joe closed his eyes and sighed. The rapport he'd been
establishing with Butch Roberson had been blown up. Joe
glanced up at Underwood and Underwood rolled his eyes
in reaction.

Through the earpiece, Joe heard a gunshot. Instinctively, he pulled down the phone and closed his eyes to find
out if he could hear it echo through the mountains. Silence,
meaning they were a long distance away. When he raised
the handset, he heard:

"That was Farkus," Butch said. "I got him right between
the eyes. Will you shut up and listen now, Batista?"

Joe couldn't believe it. Butch had killed Farkus in cold
blood.

Joe knew Farkus, and had run into him several times
over the years. The guy was a loser but had an uncanny
ability to find himself in the middle of things through no
fault—or ambition—of his own. It had seemed strangely
unsurprising to hear he'd been with McLanahan when
Butch Roberson captured them. Farkus sold a few flies to
the fly shops, fancied himself a guide, and lived off disability checks, even though he didn't seem disabled in any
way. Still . . .

"I've got three demands," Butch said to Batista. "You
meet them and McLanahan can go on living. If you screw
me around, the sheriff gets popped just like Farkus. Do
you understand what I'm saying?"

"Yes," Batista said, his voice hushed this time as if he, too, were stunned by the sudden turn in developments.

"Joe," Butch said, "I'm trusting you to make sure they follow through. You've always been straight with me. Don't let them fuck me over again, okay?"

"I hear you," Joe said, feeling a knife of shame being thrust into his heart.

"First," Butch said, "I want a helicopter sent for me. I'll give you the coordinates for where it can land. It won't be around where I am now because the terrain's too steep and I don't want to sit here like a target waiting for you to find me. And I don't want anyone on that helicopter except the pilot and Joe Pickett. I'm going to bring Joe and McLanahan with me for a while. Got that?"

"I've got it," Batista said. "Where do you want to go?"

"Somewhere where you people don't exist," Butch said. "I'll tell the pilot, but not you. Joe, are you okay with that?"

Joe glanced up to see Underwood nodding.

"I'm okay with it," Joe said.

"Don't worry—if they screw me, McLanahan will get it first."

"That's a relief," Joe said, deadpan.

Batista said, "It'll take time to locate a helicopter and send it up there . . ."

"Bullshit on that," Butch said angrily. "If you can send a drone up here, you can send a helicopter. And make sure the pilot knows what he's doing, because it'll be a night landing. I won't wait until the morning."

"What's next?" Batista said, his voice dead.

"I want a public apology for what you did to me," Butch

said. "I want you to stand in front of a national press conference and apologize for what you and your agency did to me and my family. People out there have to know what you're capable of."

Joe waited for a response from Batista, and each second that went by ratcheted up the tension. He'd lie and say he was working on sending a helicopter, but he wouldn't lie and agree to a public apology?

"He'll do it," Joe said.

"You'll make sure he does?" Butch asked.

"Yup."

"So what's the other demand?" Batista said, his tone still cold.

"Leave my family alone," Butch said. "Call off your dogs. Don't harass them anymore. No more fines or sending goons up here. *Just leave my wife and daughter alone.* If nothing else, they can build Pam's dream home with my life insurance payment."

Joe closed his eyes again. Butch had all but admitted that he saw the inevitability of what would happen to him.

"Repeat them back to me," Butch said to Batista.

Batista sighed, and said, "A helicopter, a public apology, and a dismissal of the compliance order."

"Good," Butch said. "You heard that, right, Joe?"

"I heard it."

"And you'll swear to me you'll make sure they do those things?"

"I'll do my best," Joe said, feeling the knife twist.

Butch said, "Okay, then. I'll call with the location of the landing area."

Batista said with too much force, "Keep your phone on, Mr. Roberson. That way I can keep you updated on the status of the helicopter."

There was a beat of silence, no response, and Butch's phone signed off.

But Batista was still on, and he said to Joe, "How *dare* you say I'll make a public apology," he seethed.

"You should," Joe said. "Do one thing right in this whole mess."

"That's ridiculous," Batista said, dismissing the idea.

Joe said to him, "I guess being a federal bureaucrat means never having to say you're sorry, huh?"

Batista's voice rose to a shout. Something about two dead special agents.

"I'm done talking to him," Joe said to Underwood, handing the phone back. Batista was still shouting.

Underwood held the phone out away from him without raising it to his ear. Joe turned Toby away and walked him into the standing dead trees as if trying to erect a wall between him and Underwood.

After a few moments, Joe watched Underwood raise the handset and say stonily, "So, boss, what's the plan?"

Underwood listened and nodded, grunting several assents before punching off.

After clipping the phone to his belt, he turned to his team and nodded toward the top of the summit and said, "Let's get moving."

"What about the helicopter?" Joe said. "Shouldn't I head down to the FOB to meet it?"

Underwood scoffed, "What do you think?"

Joe let that sink in.

"How long does Butch have?" Joe asked Underwood.

"Not long," Underwood said, casting an inadvertent but telling look toward the sky.

"What is it with Batista?" Joe asked.

Underwood shrugged and turned away.

21

"JOE PICKETT SAID TO TELL YOU HE THINKS you're a moron," Butch Roberson said to McLanahan.

McLanahan grunted, "Fuck him," but Farkus couldn't actually hear it. A few minutes earlier, when he saw Roberson's finger tighten on the trigger, he'd closed his eyes and hadn't seen the muzzle of the rifle swing to the right a foot from his forehead. The shot was like a punch in the air followed by extreme silence, and it took a moment for Farkus to realize he wasn't dead. The hearing was gone in his right ear, though, and he'd pissed himself. When he opened his eyes, Butch had said into the handset, "That was Farkus"; Farkus had to lip-read to understand.

He missed the rest of the conversation as well in the vacuum of white noise caused by the shot, and he thanked God he wasn't dead, because for a second there he was sure he was going to be.

THE HEARING IN Farkus's ear improved to a low hum as Butch signed off, got up, and powered down the satellite phone. Butch looked distressed as he did so, and his movements were angry. He heard McLanahan say something about letting him go—that Butch could keep Farkus as his lone hostage—and maybe some of the heat would go off once they knew he'd released the ex-sheriff of Twelve Sleep County.

Suddenly, Butch said to Sollis, "Get up."

Farkus realized why Butch had said he had two hostages, not three. Because he'd planned all along to get rid of Sollis.

"What?" Sollis sputtered.

"Get out of here. Start walking and don't look back."

"But you ran off our horses! I don't have food or water . . . I'm not even sure I know how to get back."

Butch dug a crumpled daypack out of his gear and filled it with spare clothing he'd kept from the pannier as well as a half-full canteen of water and a fold-up shovel.

"You can take this," Butch said.

"But not my rifle?"

"Are you kidding me?"

While Sollis pleaded with his eyes for intervention by McLanahan, Farkus watched Butch unbuckle the shoulder straps of the daypack and weave them under Sollis's armpits before securing them again. He roughly cinched the ties on the pack and fiddled with a side pocket. Farkus thought he saw Butch slide something into the pocket, but he wasn't sure what it was. He hoped it wasn't something good to eat. Farkus was hungry, and didn't care if Sollis starved to death out there.

Butch shrugged and said, "Go." He prodded Sollis with the rifle and spun him around.

"I might die out there," Sollis said over his shoulder. There were tears in his eyes. He held out his banded wrists. "Aren't you gonna cut me loose? I can't even get to that pack this way."

"You'll figure something out," Butch said. "At least out there you've got a chance. If you stay here around me, I'll keep thinking about what you did to that poor hunter, I'll put an end to your miserable life."

When Sollis stopped and started to turn to plead his case, Butch fired a round at him that sounded like an angry snap. Farkus felt his legs go weak.

But when he looked up, Sollis was still standing. The bullet had creased his right cheek, leaving an ugly red rip in the skin. Streams of blood dripped down his face from the wound.

"I said *go*," Butch growled through clenched teeth.

Without a word, Sollis stumbled away. Farkus could see his back through the trunks for a while. Butch watched him as well with his rifle raised, the crosshairs no doubt on the nape of Sollis's neck. Farkus waited for a second explosion and squinted his eyes in anticipation. But it didn't come, and then Sollis was gone.

"That guy makes me sick," Butch said with finality. Then, to Farkus, "Start marching."

"ABOUT WHAT I SAID . . ." McLanahan whispered to Butch after Sollis was gone.

"Naw," Butch said to McLanahan. "I'm keeping you both."

Farkus said to McLanahan, "Thanks a lot."

"I didn't think you could hear," the ex-sheriff said back. "Besides, you smell like urine."

"Get up, both of you," Butch said, gesturing at them with his rifle.

Farkus rolled to his side and got his legs underneath him and stood. His wrists were still bound with zip ties, and he was as clumsy as a cub bear. Now that he could see out beyond the pocket of gray shale they'd been in, he could see shadows reaching out from the tips of the broken rock as if they were reaching for the horizon. It wouldn't be long, he knew, before they'd be in darkness.

He asked Butch, "Why'd you do that? Shoot your rifle right by my head?"

"To make a point."

"To me?"

"To them."

"But I'm the one that's deaf now in one ear."

Butch shrugged sympathetically and said, "You'll get over it."

"Why didn't you let *me* go?" Farkus asked. "I understand why you want the ex-sheriff—he's a big fish. But why cut loose that idiot Sollis and keep me?"

Butch shrugged. "We hunted together. I guess I have a soft spot for you, even though you're a lazy bastard."

"Oh."

Butch chinned toward the south. "That way."

Farkus was confused. "I thought we were going over the top of the mountain?"

A slight smile passed over Butch's lips. "That's what I want them to think. But we're not."

Farkus looked to McLanahan for an explanation, and the ex-sheriff said, "I just figured it out myself. Butch here knows the Feds have a bead on where that drone went down, and they probably got a bead on that satellite phone before he shut it off. They'll chart the two points on a topo and connect them with a line and decide we're coming over the top of the mountain in their direction."

McLanahan sighed and said, "But I guess we're not doing that."

"No, we aren't," Butch said. "Now go."

MCLANAHAN LED, then Farkus, then Butch bringing up the rear with his rifle held loosely in his hands. Butch had secured Sollis's sniper rifle to his pack as well. Instead of going up or down the mountain, Butch indicated he wanted them to traverse it, even when they cleared some trees and looked out at a quarter-mile rock slide that had taken a good piece of the slope with it, leaving an exposed slough of loose rock.

The problem crossing the slide, Farkus figured, would be that they'd be in the open for the first time. If the Feds had another drone up or a spotter plane, they'd be sitting ducks. He didn't care if the Feds took Butch down, but he didn't want to be collateral damage. Butch must have been thinking along the same lines, because he told McLanahan to hurry.

"Hurry, hell," McLanahan said. "These slides are dangerous."

"So is being seen," Butch said. "So pick it up, Sheriff."

"This would be a lot easier if you'd cut these cuffs off."

"I'm sure it would," Butch said, "but that ain't going to happen. Now *go*. Pretend there's a box of donuts on the other side."

As they scrambled over it, Farkus looked down. The slide had not only taken the topsoil with it, but had gathered and snapped off tree trunks, which had collected into a tangle far below, almost like a driftwood hazard in a river. It was not only bad footing, but the setting sun threw knifelike shadows from the tops of trees that striped the ground like jail bars and made it hard to see.

When he shifted his weight he accidentally dislodged a football-sized rock that started rolling, then bouncing down the slide making a *pock-pock-pock* sound until it crashed into the timber below. The soles of his boots slipped a few inches as well, and he held his breath waiting for the rest of the mountain to let go and follow the rock, taking them down with it.

"This isn't a picnic," McLanahan said with emphasis to Butch, who told him to cowboy up and keep going.

The last beams of the sun had a special intensity, Farkus noticed. As if the light had been choked down into natural laser beams. He didn't mind the heat, though, because he hoped it would help dry out his trousers.

Farkus grumbled to McLanahan, "I heard you back there, trying to convince him to let you go and keep me."

McLanahan shrugged. He was crab-walking low to the ground to keep his balance.

"Is that how one partner treats another partner?"

"I was thinking strategically," McLanahan said over his shoulder. "If he'd let me go, I could help lead the Feds to him."

Farkus rolled his eyes. He said, "Aren't you tired of thinking up ways to be the hero? None of 'em have worked out very well so far."

"Shut up, you two," Butch said from behind them. "Concentrate on getting across this."

Farkus glanced back over his shoulder at Butch, who was scanning the cloudless sky.

WHEN THEY FINALLY made their way across the rock slide to solid ground and reentered the dark timber, McLanahan bent over with his hands between his knees to rest.

"Keep going," Butch said.

"I'm beat," McLanahan said between panting breaths. Sweat streamed down his face and dripped off the tips of his beard and mustache. Farkus half expected the ex-sheriff to hang his tongue out like a dog.

"Go," Butch ordered with force.

"Where are we going?"

Farkus wanted to know as well, and he looked over his shoulder at Butch.

Butch actually grinned. He said, "We don't want to be late for dinner, do we?"

22

IT WAS ALWAYS STARTLING, JOE THOUGHT, HOW quickly the temperature dropped once the sun slipped behind the rocky peaks of the mountains as if a switch had been thrown and the thin, warm air that hung in the trees was sucked with a *whoosh* into invisible vents. As they ascended toward the looming summit, he reached back and dug a well-worn Filson vest from a saddlebag and shrugged it on.

"We don't even have any goddamned *coats*," one of the special agents complained from the back, obviously observing Joe. "No coats, no food, no sleeping bags, and no fucking plan."

"That'll be enough," Underwood said wearily, not even bothering to look over his shoulder to locate the offending agent.

Joe kept his senses turned on high and tried to fight back mental threads that kept intruding from within, so he could concentrate on the situation before him. Although Underwood had no doubt been given coordinates for his handheld GPS of where the call from Butch had originated—and they certainly knew where the drone had gone down—Joe couldn't simply relax and ride. Butch Roberson had sounded angry and desperate, and he'd shot Dave Farkus in cold blood, leaving a body count of three over three days in August. Butch was also on much more intimate terms with the terrain and secrets of the mountain they were on than he was.

Joe guessed that Butch had likely figured out that the first thing they'd do was ask Joe to lead them to where he last saw him. It was logical. Therefore, Butch probably guessed that Joe was with a contingent of law enforcement and not sitting around with Julio Batista. Joe thought Butch might traverse the summit and set up an ambush Joe would lead them right into.

AFTER BEING TOLD by Underwood that the agreement to provide a helicopter was a ruse and Joe wouldn't be on it like Butch had demanded, Joe considered simply turning back. He would gladly leave the team of agents to their own devices, riding unfamiliar horses over unfamiliar terrain in an unfamiliar state. There would be consequences for Joe with Lisa Greene-Dempsey, of course. It could give her the excuse to withdraw the job offer and cut him loose.

It would set an example to all the other game wardens in the field.

And if he lost his job at the same time they were re-covering from the lost opportunity of the Saddlestring Hotel . . .

THERE WAS the very life of Butch Roberson to consider. Joe thought Butch deserved the right to make his case before a court, even if the result was inevitable. Butch should be allowed to shine some light on what drove him into such desperation, and when he was sent to prison or destined for the needle, he could perhaps attract enough attention and outrage that it couldn't happen to anyone else again. If nothing else, Joe thought, Butch deserved *that*. And the only way he might get it, given the single-minded determination of Batista, was if Joe could be along to some-how circumvent Butch's death on the mountain.

So he stayed. And with every mile, he felt more and more trapped by a career and a set of values and a mission he wasn't sure he could believe in anymore.

AS THEY RODE through clearings, he checked his phone for a signal, but he didn't get one. Joe wanted to let Mary-beth know where he was and why, and see how she was doing. He hoped Sheriff Reed thought to call her. He hated not being in contact. Bad things often happened when they weren't in contact.

WHEN THE TREES THINNED and Joe could sense the end of the tree line beneath the summit, he sidestepped Toby so Underwood would catch up and they could ride parallel. Underwood looked over at him with obvious suspicion.

"Mind if I ask you a few questions?" Joe said.

"Depends."

"We can ride up ahead if you want, so we're out of earshot of your guys."

Underwood's eyes narrowed into a squint as he considered it, then he shrugged and turned in his saddle and said to his team, "Wait here for a few minutes. We're going to scout a path over the top."

The agents pulled up and were soon forty yards behind them. Not far enough, though, that Joe couldn't hear them complain.

"I can't say I blame them," Underwood said to Joe. "This isn't the kind of thing they're trained for. Those guys are trained to storm into buildings and secure evidence of pollution and noncompliance and crap like that. They don't get any instruction on riding horses or doing this cowboy Wild West bullshit in the middle of nowhere."

Joe nodded. He was surprised at Underwood's tone. It was soft and coconspiratorial, if not exactly friendly. As if they were all on the same stupid exercise together.

"Okay, what?" Underwood asked Joe. "I'll listen to your questions, but don't expect me to answer 'em. No offense, but you're nothing to me. You're just another redneck local from the sticks."

"Gotcha," Joe said. "I guess you missed those sensitivity meetings the Feds are always holding."

"I didn't miss 'em," Underwood said. "I just don't give a shit."

Joe took a deep breath, trying to keep on track. He said, "I work for a state bureaucracy, and you work for the Feds. I've got a pretty good idea how slow things go for the most part. Getting government employees to take action isn't usually the fastest thing in the world. It's like trying to make an aircraft carrier make a sharp turn around."

Underwood shrugged, as if the statement was so obvious it didn't require any more response.

"So how is it," Joe asked, "that two agents of the EPA out of Denver would jump in their car and drive four hundred miles north to jump a landowner *the day* he starts to move dirt? Nothing happens that fast."

Underwood snorted but didn't look over. He said, "It is a little . . . unusual."

Joe waited for more.

"I already told you I'm not going to answer every question."

"That tells me something right there," Joe said. Then: "How long have you worked for Julio Batista?"

"I don't work for Julio Batista," Underwood said. "I just go to work. He just happens to be the director of the regional division right now. There have been assholes before him, and there'll be other assholes who come after."

Underwood sighed. "When I transferred out of the

Defense Department a few years ago I looked around for a soft landing—some place where I could take it easy until retirement. So I thought—the EPA. Denver. They're harmless, I thought. I could just ride out my days. That's before we got this new director."

When Joe looked over, puzzled, Underwood said, "You want to know who I work for?"

"Sure."

There was a slight smile on Underwood's face when he said, "I work for my pension, and my insurance, and my accrued vacation and sick time. I work for *me*. I show up and do whatever I have to do to get through another day. I don't give a shit what I have to do as long as those things are protected."

Joe shook his head.

"What?" Underwood said, mocking Joe's disbelief. "You expected me to say what? That I work for the American people? That I'm saving the goddamned *environment*? Is that what you expected? Look, I live in a great condo in LoDo with a view of Coors Field, where I've got season tickets for the Rockies. I have a time share in Boca. I've got a hot babe up the road in Evergreen and another babe in Florida who doesn't know anything about the one in Evergreen. *That's* what I work for. I could give a shit about everything else, including you or Julio Batista.

"Look," Underwood said, "I grew up in a little podunk town in Colorado near Glenwood Springs. My parents had a florist shop—Underwood Flowers. I watched them get up every morning at six, go to work, and not get home until eight or later. Seven days a fucking week, because people need flowers for all kinds of things. They worked their asses off and never took vacations. They thought they were building the business for me—thinking I'd take it over when I graduated from college. But that was never in my plans, you know? Why would I want to bust my ass for the rest of my life like they did? I could see the writing on the wall, and I wanted to live my life for me. I didn't want to be chained to some mom-and-pop store in the middle of nowhere."

Underwood looked over his shoulder toward the distant team of special agents.

"I don't know those guys very well," he said, "but if you asked them the same question, I'd guess you'd get pretty much the same answer."

Joe said, "You don't think any of them or the people back in the FOB have any doubts about what we're doing up here?"

"Why should they?"

"Because it's over-the-top," Joe said. "Why not let local law enforcement handle this? Sheriff Reed is competent, not like that idiot McLanahan, who used to be the sheriff and got himself caught by Butch. Reed has a different approach, and things might go a whole lot smoother if he was talking to Butch instead of Julio Batista."

"Like we care," Underwood snorted. "Grow up and look around you, Game Warden. Do you know how hard it is to find a job these days, much less a lifetime job with the government with no risk and all the security in the world?"

"You're a bunch of lifers," Joe said.

"And what a life it is," Underwood said, warming to it. "I make good money, I have great benefits, and they'll never fire me. I'm set, baby. I'll retire making four times the money my father made the best year of his life. Tell me what's not to like? You know how it is."

"It's not such a sweet deal on the state level," Joe said.

"And it shouldn't be," Underwood said. "You people are jokes to most of us, out here getting your hands dirty for next to nothing. No offense."

"Of course not," Joe said, gritting his teeth. "So what you're doing here—shoving aside the local sheriff and doing this paramilitary operation—that doesn't bother you?"

Underwood said, "No, why should it? I'm doing my job. If I wasn't here, somebody else would be. I've got nothing personal against the sheriff or that Roberson schmuck. He's a killer, after all. I'll get bonus pay for this since we're way over forty hours this week, and if I'm lucky I'll get ever so slightly injured so I can take some time off and get disability. I just don't want to get killed, because I've got a vacation planned to Hawaii with the babe from Evergreen in November. Getting killed would really ruin my plans, so I'll make sure I come out of this okay."

Joe quickly changed tacks so he wouldn't feel compelled to knock Underwood off his horse. He almost smiled when he thought how Nate Romanowski would have likely reacted to Underwood's little speech. If Nate heard it, Joe thought, Underwood would be without an ear or even his head.

Joe said, "If they're not sending a helicopter, what are they doing to find Butch Roberson? Another drone?"

"My lips are sealed," Underwood said, but smirked to confirm Joe's speculation.

"Why so heavy-handed?" Joe asked.

"I'm not the boss."

Joe felt his neck get hot. Underwood was playing with him.

"So if it's not you, and it's obviously not," Joe said, "who is driving this operation in such a frantic way?"

"Guess."

"Julio Batista," Joe said. "But why?"

Underwood scanned the trees on each side and the horizon in front of them, as if to see if there were agency spies lurking who might overhear him. Joe expected another nonanswer answer, but Underwood said, "The man has a bug up his ass. Actually, quite a few bugs. He's vindictive as hell, and he really loves his power. Before him, I was used to military guys. They can be assholes, too, but there's usually a sense of duty and tradition that keeps the really petty stuff out. This guy is different. It's like he's lived his entire life keeping a list of anyone who dissed him or disrespected him. He uses his position to get even. I've helped him do that, which is why I am where I am today."

"What do you mean?" Joe asked.

"I'll give you one example of many," Underwood said, keeping his voice low so his agents couldn't overhear. "When Batista got named director of Region Eight, his salary went up into the mid–six figures, so he wanted a new house in a ritzy neighborhood because he figured he deserved it. So he bought a McMansion in a gated horsey development named Summit Highlands out of Denver.

Two-million-dollar home with five acres, or something like that. After he moved in, he hired a contractor to outfit the roof with solar panels. You know, to set an example of how people should exist. He's big into that stuff—a true believer. Plus, he knows how to get tax credits and rebates for solar. That's what the agency does, after all."

Underwood grinned bitterly. "But Summit Highlands has a homeowners' association and the bylaws say a house can't be modified externally unless a majority of the owners agree. Apparently, those folks thought the solar panels were an eyesore. Batista fought them but couldn't get the votes. He became obsessed with beating them.

"He called me into his office one day and asked about my background and wondered if I'd be interested in helping him out. He thought I looked intimidating, I guess."

"Imagine that," Joe said, deadpan. "Go on."

"I got the message," Underwood said. "So over the next several weeks I visited every one of the board members of the homeowners' association. I asked them about the fertilizer they used on their lawns and on the golf course, and where the runoff flowed. I asked them how many lawn mowers and leaf blowers were being used and what the decibel level was. I mentioned possible violations of the Clean Water Act and the Clean Air Act, all innocent-like, and I took a lot of notes. See, the dirty little secret is, our agency oversees three things: air, water, and the earth itself. Think about it. That's a pretty damned big area to cover, and it gives us a lot of options. I never threatened anyone or initiated any action, but they were smart folks and connected A to B.

"Next homeowners' association meeting, the solar panels for Juan Julio Batista got approved by two votes. After that, I got bumped up to chief of the special agents."

"Why are you telling me all of this?" Joe asked.

"Because the son of a bitch has gone too far this time. He told me a few minutes ago he used my name with some defense guys I used to work with to get something in motion."

"What's he done?" Joe asked, feeling a shiver roll down his back.

"You'll see," Underwood said. Joe noticed a vein in Underwood's temple throbbing as he spoke. He was angry.

"Here's another little tidbit," Underwood said, leaning toward Joe and lowering his voice, "and if you ever repeat it to anybody I'll figure out a way to make your life as crappy as we did that Roberson guy's. Do you want to know my boss's name before he changed it?"

"He *changed* it?"

"John Pate," Underwood said, and laughed. "He grew up as a boring little white dude from Illinois named John Owen Pate. But after he left college, he changed it. His parents were whiter than white, but when they divorced, when he was in college, his mother married a dude named Batista. John Pate became Juan Julio Batista because he wanted to be more exotic, you know? He wanted a name that would stand out and get him noticed in the system those years. He's naturally dark-haired and dark-eyed, so it worked out for him. And he took advantage of policies to promote *people of color*."

"How do you know this?"

Underwood chuckled. "I'm an investigator, Game Warden. I investigated. I've got photocopies of his high school
yearbook when he was John Pate, and I found his parents'
divorce record and his mother's marriage announcement to
Sergio Batista when John was twenty-one. He changed his
name the year he left college. Isn't that a kick in the pants?"

"So he lied to get the job," Joe said.

"Nobody checks those things," Underwood said. "You
tick a box on your employment application and you get
moved to a special pile. And even if it was exposed, I doubt
he'd be thrown out."

"Because he's good at his job," Joe said.

"That's right. As we like to say in the agency, personnel
is policy. Batista can get things done."

"But not immediately," Joe countered. "Not unless
someone with real political juice knew how to turn that
aircraft carrier around."

"So we're back to that, huh?" Underwood said, his face
darkening. "Didn't you hear me when I said I didn't give
a shit?"

"But I do," Joe said.

Underwood sighed and said, "I don't know who put
him up to it. He didn't involve me in this one."

"Interesting. Is it possible he initiated the action himself?"

"Don't know and don't care," Underwood said. "I
doubt it, though. Batista is a political animal. He's after
big fish and headlines. Why would he waste his time on a
couple of small-town losers?"

"That's what I want to figure out," Joe said.

JOE HELD HIS TONGUE and his outrage in check while
they surveyed the treeless and tumbled scree that led to the
summit ahead of them. Despite the season, there were still
dirty strips of snow packed into broken shale where the sun
couldn't melt them. It was nearly full dark, and the glow
from the last of the sun over the top of the mountain made
their side dark, confusing, and unfocused. The stars hadn't
yet taken over the night sky enough to light up the slope.

Joe proposed a switchback route that zigged right, then
left around a sharp outcropping, then right again across a
flat snowfield.

"We can't just go straight up and over?" Underwood
asked.

"Not unless you want to cut up your horses' legs," Joe
said. "Plus, your guys aren't real riders. It's always best to
take the easiest route and let the horse pick his way."

"So be it," Underwood declared, and turned his horse
to gather his team.

Joe stayed. He turned up the collar of his Filson vest
against a slight icy breeze. When Underwood's back had
faded out of sight into the gloom below, Joe reached up
and unzipped the vest and reached into the breast pocket
of his uniform shirt.

And clicked off the digital micro-recorder he'd left in
his pocket from that morning when he'd encountered Bryce
Pendergast.

23

THE LOG LEAN-TO WAS SO OLD AND WELL HIDDEN it would have been hard to see if Butch Roberson hadn't known exactly where it was. The lean-to's roof was furry with lichen and moss that blended in perfectly in the forest, and it was set in a huge stand of thick trees that was cool and dark.

Farkus shuffled forward and was surprised there was an orange plastic cooler with a white lid set inside. After seeing nothing most of the day that wasn't rock, trees, or brush, the modernity of the cooler was like finding a highway cone in the middle of the desert. Next to the cooler was a bulging burlap sack that had been tied off with a leather string.

He stopped and shook his head. *Who put it there, and how did Butch know it would be waiting?*

Behind him, Butch said, "I trust you gentlemen will

help me with dinner, because we're just about to lose our light. Farkus, you gather some wood and kindling. Sheriff, you dig a nice fire pit inside that lean-to and get the fire going."

Then, with obvious anticipation, Butch said, "I'll cook our dinner."

He stepped through them and threw off the lid. Farkus was stunned to see what was inside the cooler. Huge, thick triangles of white butcher paper, potatoes, onions, Gatorade, and the unmistakable grinning tops of a six-pack of Coors beer. All of it nestled in ice.

"We've died and gone to heaven," Farkus said.

"It helps to have friends." Butch grinned, propping his rifle inside the corner of the lean-to.

THE SMALL FIRE licked their faces with orange light. Farkus moaned and sat back, his belly so full it was hard to the touch. Like Butch and McLanahan, he'd eaten his entire sixteen-ounce T-bone steak, a scoop of fried potatoes and onions, and washed it down with two cans of beer. Butch had doled out the food in shared portions, even though he'd been out in the wilderness longer and was probably starved, Farkus thought.

While Butch was preparing the meal, he'd balled up the wrapping paper from the steaks and tossed it toward the fire. One of the balls missed and rolled toward Farkus's foot, and he surreptitiously scooped it up and jammed it in his front jeans pocket, where it was now. He thought at the time that maybe he could write something on it and leave it for the Feds to find. But after he hid it away in his pocket, he realized he didn't have a pen or pencil with him.

THE SKY WAS FULL DARK but creamy with stars. The temperature had dropped to the mid-fifties, Farkus guessed, cold enough to make it feel uncomfortable away from the small fire inside the lean-to. Although two beers for Farkus was usually not anything more than a nice start, he felt a pleasant buzz because he was both bone-tired and dehydrated.

After they ate, he watched as Butch strapped a headlamp on from his pack and rooted through the burlap bag. He produced blankets, freeze-dried food packets, a small aluminum coffee pot and a plastic bag of coffee, binoculars, several boxes of .223 cartridges, an old Colt .45 revolver and ammunition, fleece vests, duct tape, wire and rope, and a water filter purification pump. And a fifth of Evan Williams.

"All good stuff," Butch seemed to say to himself. "All practical stuff we can use."

He jammed the pistol into the back of his pants and retied the bag closed. As he did, he glanced at Farkus as if to say, *You'll be carrying this.*

Farkus moaned, and Butch grinned in response.

"We could lighten that load if you opened the bourbon," Farkus suggested.

"Nice try," Butch said.

"So," McLanahan asked, "who is the coconspirator?"

Butch ignored him.

"AREN'T YOU GOING to get those blankets out?" McLanahan asked Butch a few minutes later, after Butch had rejoined them around the fire.

"No."

"We're gonna freeze."

"You'll be fine, it's August," Butch said, not looking over at the ex-sheriff. He seemed mesmerized by the fire, Farkus thought, or thinking deep thoughts. Licks of flame reflected from his eyes.

"We're not stopping here," Butch said, staring into the fire. "We need to keep moving. We're still too close to where that drone went down and I made the call."

Farkus groaned again. He hoped Butch would reconsider and let them sleep for a while. And he wished there was more beer in the cooler.

Instead Butch said, "We'll stay here a few more minutes and let that big dinner settle. Then we're getting up and moving south again."

When he'd been with Roberson hunting, Farkus remembered something Butch had said about the mountains to the south. That they could only go so far before they'd get cut off by a wicked canyon Farkus had heard about but never seen. The Middle Fork of the Twelve Sleep River had created a geological wonder with knife-sharp walls, a terrifying distance from the rim to the narrow canyon floor, and virtually no breaks or cracks through the rocks for a crossing. The canyon was so steep and narrow that sunlight rarely shone on the stream in the bottom.

"If I remember right," McLanahan said, "that's where Savage Run is."

"That's right."

"I don't get it," McLanahan said, shaking his head. "Why would we cut off our escape route?"

"A band of Cheyenne Indians crossed it once with women and children because the Pawnee had them trapped," Butch said. "So did Joe Pickett. He told me about it once, and I think I know where he crossed. I figure we can do the same."

Farkus and McLanahan exchanged tortured looks.

AFTER A FEW MINUTES where the only sounds were a light breeze in the treetops and the muffled popping of the fire, Butch suddenly looked up and glared at McLanahan. The ferocity in his face jolted Farkus out of his own trance. Farkus was terrified of the prospect of trying to cross Savage Run Canyon.

Butch said to McLanahan, "You know what they did, but you still came after me. What an asshole you are."

McLanahan looked away and spoke toward the fire instead of to Butch. "It isn't about you, Butch. It never was."

"Bullshit. And you brought along some great long-distance shooter so you wouldn't even have to look me in the eye before you blew my guts all over the mountain."

McLanahan started to speak, but for once thought better of it.

"You know what they did," Butch said again. "They came up here and tried to destroy me and my family. I'd like to think that the ex-sheriff might be sympathetic. I'd like to think the whole damned town would gather around one of their own. But instead, you got your guns and recruited two rubes and came after me like I was some kind of outlaw."

Farkus didn't mind being called a rube, because even he thought of himself as one.

"Butch," McLanahan said, almost pleading, "you *are* an outlaw."

Butch said, "You never gave a crap about what happened to me or my family."

"I don't know all the details," McLanahan said. "All I know is you're wanted for a double homicide."

"You didn't bother to find out the details," Butch said. "You did it for the money and the glory."

"The world's a cruel place, especially these days."

"It doesn't have to be," Butch Roberson said. Then softly, "It doesn't have to be."

AS THEY painfully gathered up, Butch ordered Farkus to make sure the fire was doused. He could use the ice water that remained in the cooler, Butch said.

Farkus carried the cooler over and the water sloshed inside. He sat it at his feet and withdrew the useless ball of butcher paper from his pocket. With his back to Butch and McLanahan, he unwrapped it and looked at the markings from the light of the flames.

T-BONE STEAKS

NOT FOR SALE

BIG STREAM RANCH AND CATTLE CO.

He put the paper into the fire, where it was quickly engulfed.

The fire hissed and steamed a pungent cloud when Farkus dumped the cooler on it. As he stirred the dying embers into black viscous soup with a stick, he knew who Butch Roberson's friend was.

24

MARYBETH PICKETT LAY FULLY CLOTHED ON HER bed with the lights off and her door shut in their bedroom. The sheer curtains undulated slowly on both sides of the open window with a breeze that had changed from warm to cool in the last hour. Coyotes were yipping in the distance, piercing the silence. Their sound was forlorn and high-pitched, and it reminded her of babies shrieking. She stared at the light fixture straight overhead, vowing to take it down soon and clean the dead miller moths out of it. She felt extremely vulnerable and alone.

She'd done all right through dinner, she thought, maintaining a cheerful veneer. She never mentioned the Saddlestring Hotel debacle to the girls and wasn't sure they'd really understood the details of it anyway—how much it had meant to her.

As she always did, she did a quick mental survey of where each member of her family was at that moment. It was something she did several times a day, and didn't know if she'd ever be able to break the habit. Lucy and Hannah Roberson were downstairs, watching television. Hannah had asked, once again, if she could stay over. Sheridan was still out with her friends but would be due home soon. April was in her room, sulking, no doubt texting all her new cowboy friends since she'd become so popular with them. And Joe was out there somewhere in the mountains, helping to lead a manhunt for a family friend.

Joe hadn't called all afternoon or evening, and she assumed he was once again in a place with no cell service. Although she should be used to it by now, it was still tough to be completely out of touch with him. She hoped he felt the same way. He'd said he did.

Throughout the day, Dulcie Schalk had kept her informed about what was going on in the mountains through texts to her phone. Marybeth knew that a command center had been established on the Big Stream Ranch, that Sheriff Reed had been marginalized (Dulcie was furious about that), and that Joe had been asked to lead a small team into the mountains where he'd last seen Butch Roberson. Butch claimed he had taken hostages, which ramped the entire horrible situation to a new level, not to mention that one of the hostages he had was ex-Sheriff Kyle McLanahan. There was some confusion about a report that an innocent hunter may or may not have been killed. Up until she heard about the hostages, Marybeth thought Joe might be able to concoct a way for it all to end peacefully.

She tried not to consider a worst-case scenario where Joe and Butch would be at each other, trying to take the other out. If it weren't for the worst-case scenarios she'd conjured up over the years that were subsequently dashed by events not quite as dire, Marybeth would have worried herself to death. She thought, as she often did, that wives who didn't have husbands in law enforcement had no idea how wrenching it could be.

IT WASN'T SUPPOSED to be like this, she thought. Her mother, Missy, had married up five times and amassed a fortune in money and land. Missy had hoped her daughter would be practical and predatory, but instead she'd married Joe. Marybeth had steeled herself to defy Missy and her ways; to show that happiness and success could be achieved without guile and calculation. And for a while there, Marybeth thought she might win that argument.

She imagined a life where she was back in business—a successful business—and Joe could change jobs. She knew how much he loved being a game warden, but frustrations with the bureaucracy and outright threats to their family over the years had taken a toll.

Sure, the journey of their marriage and their prospects seemed to follow a pattern of one step forward, two steps back. But now, it seemed, they were backpedaling furiously. The Saddlestring Hotel project had offered hope and vindication.

She sat up and rubbed her face with her hands. She hated to think like this. After all, she and Joe had two wonderful daughters they loved and who loved them, and a ward who might have recently turned the corner. The jury was still out on April, of course, and Marybeth hesitated to become too optimistic, but still . . .

WHEN HER CELL PHONE lit up on the bedstand, she scrambled to it, hoping to see it was Joe. Instead, it read: MATT DONNELL.

She didn't want to talk to him, and assumed he was calling to console her with his slick Realtor talk. He'd wrecked their lives a few hours earlier, and he was the last person she wanted to talk with again. He'd probably be scheming about ways to get around some of the regulations if she'd just hang tight, but she was still too devastated. She let the call go to voicemail.

Marybeth put the phone back down on the bedstand, listened to the chime indicating he'd left a message, and lay back on the bed.

The digital clock read 10:28 p.m.

A MINUTE LATER, she heard the sound of gravel popping on Bighorn Road and saw the sweep of headlights light up the curtains. The vehicle outside slowed, which piqued her interest, and she heard it pull off the road in front of their house. The engine revved for a few seconds and died as it was turned off.

Marybeth stood and approached the window. She hoped it wasn't a stray hunter or fisherman stopping at the house to talk to Joe about something. She could never get used to these men, often smelling of cigarette smoke and beer, thinking it was okay to simply drop by any hour of the night. Joe was usually patient with them, which was part of his job, but she wasn't as patient.

She parted the curtain to see the lights from Pam Roberson's Ford Explorer go out. She was parked next to Hannah's car. Marybeth waited for a few moments, expecting Pam to open her door and get out. But for whatever reason, she was just sitting there.

Marybeth clicked on the lights and looked at herself in the mirror over the dresser. Her eyes were dark and gaunt, and she smiled, trying to make herself look and feel happy. She hoped it worked.

LUCY AND HANNAH were huddled together under a light blanket on the couch, watching some kind of awful teen reality show featuring tattooed boys and pregnant sixteen-year-old girls. When Marybeth came down the stairs, Lucy expertly changed the channel to a nature show.

Marybeth said sternly, "You two ought to get to bed," as she passed them, her way of telling them she didn't approve of what they'd been watching and hadn't been fooled by the maneuver.

Pam Roberson sat in the Ford, her hands on her lap, staring straight ahead. When Marybeth went out the gate in front of her, Pam seemed to snap to attention and quickly got out.

"I'm sorry," Pam said. "I know it's late, but I didn't

know where to go. There are television trucks in front of my house and these people keep knocking on my door. Butch's driver's license picture—which is a really bad one—is all over the news. I just couldn't stay there, so I snuck out the back and drove over here."

Marybeth took Pam by the arm and ushered her toward their house.

"You can stay as long as you like," she said.

"I guess I wanted to see Hannah," Pam said. "I wanted to be near her."

"I understand."

Pam paused before they went in. "Marybeth, did you hear about the hostages?"

"Yes."

"I just can't believe it. It's so awful. It's like I just don't know Butch anymore. It's like there's some dangerous *criminal* up there in the mountains who has my husband's name."

Marybeth nodded and led the way inside.

LUCY AND HANNAH glanced up to see who was behind Marybeth, and Hannah looked stricken. The color had drained out of her face, and her eyes were huge. Marybeth was taken aback at first, and hoped one of her daughters never acted that way when *she* entered a room. Then she thought Hannah was likely anticipating bad news and assumed Pam was there to deliver it.

"Hey, girls," Pam said wearily.

"Mom . . ." Hannah said.

"I haven't heard anything about your dad," Pam said, trying to put up a strong front—like Marybeth.

"So he's okay?" Hannah asked.

"I just don't know. But you know your dad. *He's tougher than the rest.*"

Marybeth recognized the phrase as one from a Chris LeDoux song, and it broke her heart.

"Let's have a glass of wine," Marybeth said, leading Pam through the living room into the kitchen.

AFTER *TWO* **GLASSES OF WINE,** Marybeth sent Lucy and Hannah to bed and made up a spare bed on the couch in the living room for Pam. The wine seemed to have gone straight to Pam's head, probably from being overtired and stressed, and she slurred her words while Marybeth showed her where the towels were.

Pam went immediately to sleep and was snoring by the time Marybeth finished closing the house up for the night. While Marybeth tiptoed through the living room toward the stairs, the front door opened and Sheridan burst in.

Sheridan instinctively began to toss her backpack on the couch when she realized someone was sleeping on it, and jerked it back before it hit Pam Roberson in the face.

"Yikes," she said.

Marybeth shushed Sheridan and gestured for her to follow her out into the kitchen.

Sheridan sat down at the table, obviously puzzled. Marybeth poured a glass of wine. Sheridan grinned and asked, "Do you mind if I have a glass?"

Marybeth hesitated for a moment, then said, "Just one."

"You forget I'm in college."

"Yes, I do," Marybeth said softly, placing another glass on the table. Sheridan filled it halfway.

"What's going on?" Sheridan asked. "Is Dad home?"

Marybeth spilled, telling Sheridan about Butch and the hostages, the collapse of the Saddlestring Hotel, the arrival of Pam Roberson. She didn't want to speak loud enough to wake up Pam in the next room.

"It's been a bad day," Marybeth said, not yet sure whether she regretted saying so much to Sheridan.

Sheridan simply nodded and sipped at her wine. Although Marybeth knew it wasn't Sheridan's first drink— she was soon to be a sophomore at the University of Wyoming, after all—it was the first time they'd shared wine together.

"I'm worried about your dad up there," Marybeth said. "And I'm worried about what will happen to Butch, for Pam and Hannah's sake."

MARYBETH'S PHONE LIT UP, and she glanced at the display. The call was being made by an unknown number. She hesitated.

"Might as well take it," Sheridan said.

She did.

"It's me," Joe said.

Marybeth said to Sheridan, "Well, speak of the devil." To Joe: "Where are you calling from?"

"I borrowed a satellite phone from a guy and I don't

have much time before he wants it back. Do you have something to write down a couple of names? I really need your help with some research."

"The girls and I are fine," Marybeth said, motioning to Sheridan to hand over the pad and pen she used at the Burg-O-Pardner for taking orders. "Thanks for asking."

"I'm sorry."

"It's okay," she said, clamping the phone to her shoulder with her cheek and flipping the pad open. "Okay."

She wrote down *Juan Julio Batista*.

"Got it."

"I really appreciate it," Joe said. "Find out everything you can about him and call me back at this number. See if he links up somehow with the Sackett case. I won't be home tonight, and who knows when tomorrow. But this may be important."

"You said 'names,' plural."

"The second is Pate. John Owen Pate."

"Gotcha," Marybeth said. "By the way, I looked up the Sackett case today, and it's exactly like you said. I can't find a connection, though, with Pam and Butch. So maybe it's this Batista."

"I wouldn't be surprised."

"I have the time to do this," she said, "since I don't have to spend any more on that stupid hotel."

Joe said, "Don't worry about it. We'll get 'em next time."

She could tell by the way he said it there was something else.

"Joe?"

"I got offered a new job today by the new director."

As he described it to her, Marybeth jotted down *Chey-enne*, *desk*, and *$18K*.

"I'd become a bureaucrat," Joe said sourly.

Before she could ask for more detail, she could hear another voice in the background.

"The guy wants his phone back," Joe said. "He's waiting for a call."

"Have you found Butch?"

"Not yet."

"Is it true about the hostages?"

"I'm afraid so."

"What happened to him, Joe?"

"He broke. Now I've gotta go . . ."

AT FIVE TO MIDNIGHT as she got ready for bed, Mary-beth remembered the call from Matt Donnell on her phone. She sighed, then punched it up to listen.

Matt said, "Marybeth, I may have a line on something. We might be able to unload that piece of crap after all. I'll give you a call tomorrow and tell you more. I just hope you don't completely blame me for what happened. It's just this damned fire marshal. There's too many of those types out there. They want to be involved in every aspect of what we do . . ."

So, she thought, they'd gone from building something good to trying to "unload" it.

He went on, but she didn't want to listen to the rest.

INSTEAD, SHE PADDED downstairs in her bare feet in the dark. She could hear rhythmic breathing all around her—a house filled with anxious, sleeping females.

Marybeth slipped into Joe's tiny office off the living room and closed the door and turned on his desk lamp. She sat down and opened the browser of his computer and called up a website called themasterfalconer.com.

It was an old site, and rarely used. She was surprised it was still up. Joe and Nate had used the comment threads to communicate surreptitiously the previous year. She knew Joe still checked it from time to time to see if there was any word from Nate, but he reported that there had been nothing.

She called up a discussion thread on the training of kestrel hawks, which was the thread they had used. There had been no new comments posted for months.

When she'd been doing her inventory of her family and where they were at that time, she'd also thought of Nate. He wasn't related to them by blood, but he'd certainly been an oddball part of the family for years until all of the violence had happened and he'd gone away. She knew federal law enforcement was still looking for him, and that Joe occasionally got calls or visits to ask if he'd heard anything.

On the end of the thread, she wrote:

This is Marybeth. Do you still check this site? If so, please tell me you're doing okay, wherever you are.

She waited for a moment to see if there was a reply, then castigated herself for it. Did she really think Nate Romanowski was hovering by a computer somewhere, just waiting for her to post something?

And if he was, what would she ask him? He couldn't bail them out of the hole she'd dug, and Joe wouldn't want him around in a county filled past capacity with federal law enforcement officers.

She thought herself foolish for even posting the question, and shut down the computer.

But tomorrow, she knew, she'd check it.

AS SHE CLIMBED into bed, she heard a faint sound outside that was unusual. They were used to natural sounds: the cries of coyotes, the huffs of elk and moose from the willow-choked riverbed across the road, and assorted whistles and screeches from falcons and owls. And certainly the roar of a vehicle using Bighorn Road.

This was different. It sounded like a pair of lawn mowers in the distance. But they came from the sky.

Marybeth slid out of bed and parted the curtains, but she couldn't see what had made the noise. Then she pulled on her robe and went downstairs, back to the computer.

DAY FOUR

25

IT WAS PAST MIDNIGHT WHEN JOE REACHED THE
summit of the mountain and turned to look back. He could
see for miles and even locate the distant thread of highway
because of the lights on the few vehicles using it. Twenty-
five miles away was the tiny cluster of lights from the headquarters of Big Stream Ranch. The FOB was obscured from
view by the ocean of trees below, but he knew approximately where it was by a faint glow of lights powered by
generators.

The mountaintop was bare of trees or any kind of veg-
etation except stubborn lichen holding on to granite for
dear life, and it was illuminated by moonlight and millions
of pinprick stars. Underwood and his team were behind
him, their horses picking their way up through the icy
granular crusts of snow and loose dark shale. The wind
blew from the west into Joe's face, and he kept the brim of

his hat tilted down so his eyes wouldn't tear. The wind was surprisingly cold for August and numbed his face and hands.

Joe checked his cell phone for bars because sometimes he could get a wayward signal on the top of a mountain at night, but there was no reception. He was glad he'd made contact with Marybeth before, so she knew he was all right. He hated to have left her alone.

One of Underwood's team cursed the darkness and the cold, his voice harsh enough to cut through the wind. When the agents were close enough to start to crowd him, Joe nudged Toby on over a wide snowfield that looked like a pond or small lake in the moonlight, and led them over the mountain to the western slope. As he descended, he left the cold wind on top. And as he walked his horse into the thick stand of trees, he left the moonlight as well.

DEEP IN THE TREES, Joe could see only what the yellow orb of his headlamp would reveal. Toby could see better than he could in the dark, so he had to trust the horse wouldn't trap them in down timber or walk over a cliff. When he glanced over his shoulder, he saw the lenses of five bobbing headlamps, and sometimes the wayward beam of one slicing out to the side.

He emerged into a small mountain meadow where the canopy opened to allow moonlight. He reined Toby to a stop and waited.

Underwood joined him a few minutes later, and Joe said, "This is ridiculous. We're only going to get our horses or ourselves hurt trying to ride down this mountain in the dark."

"We have our orders," Underwood said without conviction.

"Fuck the orders," one of the team grumbled from the dark. "We need to get some rest, and my legs and butt are numb. If we ran into trouble right now, it would take me five minutes just to get out of this goddamned uncomfortable saddle."

The others agreed, and they slowly dismounted. There were plenty of moans from saddle sores and distended knees and aching buttocks. One agent said loudly this was the worst assignment he'd ever had. Joe thought it interesting that Underwood no longer reprimanded them for their loose talk.

And by painfully climbing off his own horse, Underwood seemed to agree with them. They'd gone far enough for a while.

One of the agents said, "I guess we're just supposed to sleep in the open. Oh, thank you, Regional Director, for your excellent planning."

Underwood said, "Try spooning. That's what they did in the Civil War."

Joe stifled a grin when Underwood's suggestion was met with a fusillade of angry curses. He thought for a moment that the expedition might just implode under its own combination of aimlessness and disorganization. That would be just fine with him, he thought. Joe almost felt sorry for Underwood, who was tasked with commanding a mission by a man he didn't like or respect. He was a professional, though, and his background girded him for unpleasant duties.

"And no fires," Underwood barked.

Just then, Underwood's satellite phone burred and lit up.

"Yes, Director Batista," Underwood said, loud enough to quiet the team of agents.

"Jesus Christ," one of the agents whispered. "Does the son of a bitch know we stopped?"

WHILE UNDERWOOD LISTENED to his boss and said very little except to grunt and agree here and there, Joe showed the agents how to loosen the cinch straps on their saddles, picket their horses far away from one another so that each horse could graze and not get tangled with another. Then he revealed to the agents where heavy rubber rain slickers were rolled up and tied behind the seat of each saddle itself.

"Don't unfurl the slickers with a lot of noise and force," he said to them. "You'll spook the horses. They get scared at flapping things. You can use the slickers for sleeping. They'll keep you warm enough on top and the moisture in the ground won't soak into your clothes."

"We're the fucking Wild Bunch," one of them said, pulling on a long dusterlike yellow slicker.

"I think they all died in the end," another one said sourly.

THE AGENTS WERE GRATEFUL if not happy, and Joe left them sprawled in the grass of the meadow. The yellow slickers held the moonlight. Joe thought the sight of four yellow forms writhing around to get comfortable in the grass looked sluglike and slightly comical.

For himself, he led Toby to the far edge of the meadow and unsaddled his gelding and picketed him. There was a one-man bivvy tent in the saddlebags, but Joe didn't set it up. Instead he spread it out to use as a ground tarp and covered himself with a thin wool blanket he always packed along.

He propped himself up on an elbow on the saddle he'd use as a pillow, and ate two energy bars that had been in his emergency kit for at least two years. They were dry and crumbled into dust in his mouth, and swelled into a paste when he washed them down with water from his Nalgene bottle. He waited in the dark for Underwood to sign off with his boss. Occasionally, he could hear a word or two of Batista's voice cut through the silence. He heard the words *strategic, nonnegotiable, location,* and *autopsy* very clearly.

Finally, Underwood said, "I've got some worn-out special agents here, sir. They need rest . . . I understand . . . Yes, I'll get them up and keep them moving, and I'll keep the phone on all night."

As Underwood let the phone drop on its lanyard, he said, *"Asshole."*

"Are we moving?" one of the agents asked defiantly.

"No," Underwood said. "But if he asks us later, we did."

Joe waited a beat, then said to Underwood, "I put your

horse up over here. I've got a space blanket I could lend you. Do you want it?"

Underwood said, "Is that one of those silver sheets that'll make me look like a baked potato?"

"Yup."

He sighed. "I'll take it."

Joe handed Underwood the blanket, along with the Ziploc bag with the remaining two energy bars.

"They aren't very good," Joe said.

"Thank you anyway," Underwood said, tearing into them.

AFTER UNDERWOOD SETTLED in his silver-lined blanket in the grass, Joe said, "What's the plan for tomorrow?"

"So you want to talk," Underwood said with irritation.

"I'll keep it low so your guys don't hear."

"What about me? *I'll* hear."

Joe asked, "Do they have a location on Butch?"

"Yes. His phone is on, and it has a GPS feature inside the circuitry. They know exactly where he is on the map at least."

"I knew about that," Joe said. "Butch is smart enough to know it, too, so it surprises me he kept it on."

Underwood shrugged. "Maybe he isn't so smart. Batista has been trying to contact him for hours, but he must have the phone set to mute or he just doesn't want to talk. The director wants to tell him the helicopter will be arriving at dawn."

"Which way is he headed?" Joe asked.

"West. It sounds like he doubled back after he talked to us and he's working his way down the mountain. Batista said his route is pretty erratic, though. They're guessing at the FOB that Roberson is looking for a nice flat piece of sagebrush for the helicopter to land."

"But it won't happen, will it?"

"No. There is no helicopter," Underwood said.

"What else?"

"Leave me alone."

"Not a chance. The sooner you answer my questions, the sooner you can get some sleep. Or I'll take that space blanket back. You do look like a baked potato, you know."

"Damn you."

"Has anything happened in the investigation we should know about?"

"Like what?"

"I thought I heard you say something about an autopsy," Joe said.

"Oh, yeah. There was a preliminary autopsy on our two special agents. Both were shot multiple times with small-caliber rounds. Tim Singewald was hit four times, and Lenox Baker was hit three times. Didn't you say Butch Roberson was packing a .223 semiautomatic rifle?"

"I think so. It looked like a scoped Bushmaster .223 with a thirty-round magazine. They're common around here."

Underwood said, "The rounds that killed the agents were small caliber. Once they run ballistics on them, I'm sure there will be a match."

"Lots of folks up here have .223s," Joe said. "They're a popular coyote-hunting round."

Underwood snorted. "They also found Roberson's fin-gerprints all over the car Singewald and Baker drove up from Denver. I suppose you'll say lots of people up here have the same fingerprints."

"No," Joe said. "I won't say that."

"Good. So can I get some sleep now?"

"One more question."

"Jesus—what?"

"Back to how your agency operates. How much juice would someone have to have to get a noncompliance action going the same day? Are we talking low level, mid-level, or big-shot level?"

Underwood covered his face with his hand and moaned.

"I'm just curious," Joe said.

"I told you I wasn't going there."

"But why not at this point? You seem pretty convinced Butch did it, so why does it matter who turned him in in the first place?"

"I never said anyone turned him in."

"You implied it. So which level?"

Underwood cursed and said, "Big-shot level, of course. The mid-level types might get some kind of investigation opened, but they wouldn't be able to make agents jump like that. Obviously, somebody with influence knew who to call to get them to react like that."

"So Julio Batista was in on it from the beginning, then?"

"I never said that."

"You implied it."

"Jesus fuck," Underwood moaned. "Leave me alone.

Yes, I would guess whoever called talked to the director in person. No one else could have made the decision so quickly to send agents directly from Denver. Usually, we'd let the local EPA staff handle it first."

"That's what I thought. Which means Batista knows who got this whole thing going, but he doesn't want to volunteer that information."

Underwood grunted.

"So if Butch Roberson just goes away, Batista will probably never be asked."

Underwood grunted again.

Joe thought about it, and said, "So what's our plan?"

Underwood took a deep breath and slowly expelled it through his nostrils. "We keep moving down the mountain to the west until we pick up his track. You're a tracker, right?"

"Not really," Joe said.

"I think even I could follow the prints of three guys."

"Maybe."

"Anyway, Batista said they've put together a big inter-agency task force that will be coming up this direction from the west. They're on their way now in a convoy of four-wheel-drives. The idea is they'll flush Roberson our way and we'll trap him in a pincer movement and he'll have no choice but to turn loose his hostages and we'll nail the son of a bitch in the morning."

Joe nodded in the dark. "So you'll flood the zone with people until you corner Butch."

"Yeah, I guess."

"What do you think Butch will do when he realizes there is no helicopter? Do you think he'll keep his end of the bargain?"

"Batista thinks he won't have any options at that point."

"Why is that?" Joe asked.

"Because we *will* have aircraft coming. Roberson won't know it isn't a helicopter until it's too late."

Joe felt a chill crawl down his neck. "What's coming?"

Joe could see Underwood's teeth in the moonlight as he smiled. "This is what I was worried about earlier, but I wasn't sure he could make it happen. Drones—two of 'em this time. One is assigned to the EPA, and it's just an observation unit like the last one. Just cameras and shit on board. But the second one is the kicker. Batista threw my name around and got authorization for a military drone to be assigned to us. All the way from an airbase in North Dakota. That one happens to be armed with Hellfire missiles."

Joe was speechless for a moment. Then he said, "You're going to blow him up?"

"Into a million pieces," Underwood said, shaking his head. "Just like one of the many al Qaeda number twos. That is, if Roberson doesn't release the hostages and give himself up. So he *will* have a choice in the matter."

"Aren't Hellfire missiles used to blow up tanks on the ground?"

"Yes, and terrorists in their bunkers. But they'll work pretty damned well on domestic terrorists, I'll wager."

Joe said, "If you want to start a war out here, this is the way to do it."

Underwood shrugged it off. "I'm not worried about that."

Joe said, "I am."

"Please," Underwood pleaded, turning his back to Joe, "leave me alone."

"Good night, Mr. Underwood," Joe said, and carefully reached up and clicked off the digital recorder again.

"Game Warden," Underwood said, a few minutes after Joe assumed he was asleep. "Now I have a question for you."

"What?"

"If a war started, which side would you be on?"

Joe hesitated. He said, "I'll have to get back to you on that."

JOE WAS IN HIS SLEEPING BAG, staring back at the hard white stars, when he heard Underwood's phone buzz again. Batista, no doubt, with more orders, he thought.

Instead, Underwood walked over to Joe with the space blanket over his shoulders and extended the phone.

"It's your wife," he said with irritation. "Make it quick."

"ACCORDING TO THE BIO on the agency website, Juan Julio Batista was born in Chicago in 1965," Marybeth said. "That makes him forty-eight years old—our age. There's no mention of a wife or children. He worked for an environmental group called One Globe in the Denver field office from 1989 to 2003, when he was hired by the EPA.

He was named director of Region Eight by the Washington bigwigs in 2008.

"It says he graduated from Colorado State University in 1987. Majored in sociology and minored in environmental affairs."

"Anything else?" Joe asked, aware that Underwood was hovering out of earshot.

"Tons of media mentions," she said. "He likes to give press conferences, and he's mentioned dozens of times when his agency takes action against polluters."

"Hmmmmm."

"Let's see," she said, obviously scrolling through the site. "Region Eight oversees Colorado, Montana, North and South Dakota, Utah, and Wyoming. But we knew that."

"Has he ever worked for Region Ten?" Joe asked.

"I know what you're getting at—Idaho. The Sackett case. No, he never worked there. I can't find any connection."

Joe asked, "Anything at all to tie him to Pam and Butch?"

"Nothing I can find."

"What about Pate?"

"I found some mentions, but they just stop in 1988."

"That fits," Joe said, and told Marybeth what Underwood had revealed.

"That's just . . . odd," Marybeth said. Joe could visualize her mind racing. "I'll dig deeper tomorrow at the library."

Marybeth had access to several state and federal databases from the library computers that she wasn't supposed to have. She'd assisted Joe with investigations several times.

Underwood extended his hand for the phone back.

"Good work," Joe said.

"Stay safe."

LATER, AS JOE closed his eyes, he heard the faraway sound of two unmanned drones whining through the sky.

26

JIMMY SOLLIS WEPT IN THE MOONLIGHT.

With the daypack strapped on his back and his wrists bound in front of him, Sollis stumbled on a tree root, lost his footing, and did a face-plant into the dank-smelling musky ground. He hit his head hard enough to produce spangles of orange on the inside of his eyelids, and his face was covered with dirt and pine needles.

He clumsily got to his feet again. That damned pack threw his balance off and he nearly sidestepped and stumbled to the ground again, but he got his tired legs beneath him.

And stood there and cursed and cried. He hadn't cried for years, not for anything.

It was all so damned *unfair* . . .

———

SINCE THAT SON OF A BITCH Butch Roberson had shot a crease in his cheek and sent him away, Sollis had blindly worked his way down the mountain. Without a map, a GPS, or a good sense of direction, he simply went *down*. Whenever he was given a choice to continue on a line or veer to the right or left, he chose whichever side descended. Several times, this had led him into tangled ravines he had to tear himself out of—his clothes were rags now—but sometimes it was the right choice. His goal was to get out of the black timber onto the valley floor, where at least he could see and be seen if someone was looking for him.

He'd long ago given up trying to retrace their route up the mountain, as directed by the son of a bitch Butch Roberson. Sollis hadn't paid much attention to the trail they'd taken on the way up because he'd been concentrating on his footing, and it had been in daylight. Now, everything was jumbled and confusing. He told himself that if he kept walking down he'd eventually hit the bottom. It only made sense.

The trek had been pure torture. He was without any food—although there might be some in the backpack he couldn't unshoulder or open—and his thirst was quenched only when he bumbled upon a small trickle of stream or creek.

Two hours before, he'd found a tiny ribbon of running creek and had dropped to his knees and plunged his face into it, only to find out in the dark there was less than an inch of water. He'd inhaled sand, twigs, and a floating beetle with the first gulp, and spit it out down his shirt-front. Aching of thirst, he'd pushed his way upstream through thorny brush until he located what looked like a wide and deep natural cistern bordered by rocks. Again, he dropped to his knees in the brush and lowered his head halfway between two white and spindly tree roots and drank deeply. The water was cold and cut its way down his throat and chilled him to the bone. But he kept drinking, ignoring the metallic taste.

When he was sated, he sat back and wiped his mouth dry. He could feel the hydration seep through his guts, and spread out to his extremities. Sollis couldn't remember how long a human could survive without food and water, but he knew it wasn't long without water. So he knew he'd staved off an ugly death.

Then he realized he was sitting back on something large and spongy, something that had some give to it. Something that smelled putrid. He turned and looked into the naked eyehole of a dead mule deer. He was sitting on its body, and the two long white roots he'd drunk between were its decomposing legs.

That was the first time he cried.

HE'D BEEN TWENTY YEARS OLD when he first heard about the sport of long-distance shooting. Until that time, it seemed he'd spent his life under the shadow of his muscle-bound older brother, Trent, who had landed a job as a deputy under Sheriff McLanahan in the Twelve Sleep County Sheriff's Department. Oh, how their parents loved *Trent*, who played high school football and basketball and lifted weights (and shot human growth hormone into himself) all through college until he emerged double the size he went in. Sollis, meanwhile, ran with a pack of losers and was frequently in trouble. The joke in the Sollis house—which Sollis never found funny—was that someday Trent would arrest Sollis.

Ha-ha, Sollis thought bitterly, although he admitted to himself it might have happened if Trent hadn't been killed in the line of duty the year before. He didn't miss his brother at all.

Jimmy Sollis had been on a crew of roofers who followed hailstorms around the state and into Montana, North Dakota, and South Dakota, when he first heard about long-distance shooting from the foreman. They'd been sitting on the peak of a roof eating their lunches in Lovell, Wyoming. The foreman said he still competed around the country, using high-end custom rifles to hit targets hundreds of yards away. Sollis got excited about the idea of it, and the foreman showed Sollis some of his rifles and agreed to take him to an event outside of Rock Springs.

Sollis was enthralled. He'd never been much of an athlete or a scholar, but something about propelling a small cylinder of polished heavy metal through the air to hit a target got him excited inside. It got him *hard*.

He learned about calculating windage, elevation, altitude, velocity; determining grains of gunpowder; learning how to breathe . . .

At the events he attended with his foreman, Sollis collected business cards from custom gunmakers who had booths set up, and started saving chunks of his paycheck—and supplementing his income by dealing meth to roughnecks on the side. His first long-distance rifle, a Sako TRG-42 chambered for .338, won him $2,500 at the Orem, Utah, Invitational—and he was off. He'd reinvest his winnings into more precision rifles, because a man could never have enough rifles. He sent the rifles away to custom gunsmiths who tweaked the weight of the trigger pull and equipped the weapons with specialized scope rings and high-tech optics. Sollis found he had a natural ability to calculate velocity, drop, and windage. He could hit what he aimed at.

But he wanted more. Sollis had listened to a couple of books on tape written by Marine snipers, and he desperately wanted to use his newfound skill on Iraqis, Iranians, or Afghanis. He had no strong feelings about which. So he signed up for the U.S. Marines, telling the recruiter in the White Mountain Mall in Rock Springs they were getting a blue-chip player, that they didn't realize the LeBron of snipers was standing right in front of them, actually volunteering to join their playground pickup team.

The Marines rejected him because of his rap sheet of drug-related arrests, and because of that sexual assault charge with the underage cheerleader back in high school. Furious, he tried the Army, then the Navy. But the word was out among the recruiters and he was black-balled. The foreman told Sollis about private defense contractors who might be able to use his skill, and Sollis was interested. Anything was better than roofing for a living.

So when ex-Sheriff McLanahan drove up that morning before dawn as Sollis crossed from his rental house to his pickup to go to work and offered him a chance to go with him, Jimmy Sollis jumped at it. The opportunity to use his skills for the good of humanity and on the right side of the law? He was all over that.

He had no idea that it would result in a gut-shot hunter from Maine, or a desperate hike down a mountain in the middle of the night. And all because McLanahan hadn't warned him off before he pulled the trigger on the wrong man.

It burned Sollis how McLanahan had acted once that son of a bitch Roberson had shown up. Suddenly, it was all Sollis, as if McLanahan hadn't recruited him and given him the signal to fire.

It just wasn't right.

TO MAKE matters worse, that phone Roberson had hidden in his daypack kept ringing and he couldn't even answer it. He thought:

- *He'd had his nine-thousand-dollar rifle taken away from him;*
- *He was lost;*
- *If he somehow made his way back to Saddlestring, he'd likely be arrested for gut-shooting a hunter from Maine;*
- *His belly was filled with rotten dead deer seepage;*
- *Mosquitoes were feeding on the back of his neck where he couldn't reach;*

- *His cheek ached from the bullet that had creased it;*
And . . .
- *Nobody loved him.*

And now he couldn't even answer the goddamned phone.

JIMMY SOLLIS PAUSED near the middle of a small clearing in the trees. He realized the hairs on the back of his neck and his forearms had pricked up because he'd seen, heard, or *sensed* something that was off. He stood still until his breathing returned to normal from the exertion of the trek through a long jumble of down trees and branches.

When he could hear again over the rhythmic pounding of his own heart, he slowly turned his head to the right, then the left. He wondered what it was that had made him stop, made the hairs prick up. Sollis had a creepy thought that someone might be watching him.

The terrain had leveled somewhat after an hour of clawing his way over and through the timber on a steep slope. The moon, straight overhead, lit up the grassy meadow in a shade of light blue. The wall of trees on all four sides of the clearing was dark and impenetrable by the light, though, which made him think that whatever or whoever was watching him hung back in the shadows.

"Who's there?" he croaked. "Come on out, or I'll come in after you."

He regretted how the end of his sentence had risen in pitch and revealed his fear.

He listened for a response. Nothing.

Then a small puffball of a cumulus cloud drifted across the face of the moon and plunged the meadow into gloom. Sollis waited for the cloud to pass so he could see again.

He tried to recall what it had been that spooked him, something out of the corner of his eye, something he glimpsed or thought he'd glimpsed: a huge human face. It made no sense.

But because the moonlight was muted, his eyes adjusted, and the face, measuring two feet wide by three feet tall, emerged from the utter darkness just inside the trees to his right. Sollis gasped and squared off against it, his bound hands out in front of him to ward off the Attack of the Face.

He saw eyes the size of charcoal briquettes, a wide nose, a thick mustache, and a sardonic grin. He realized he was looking at the side of an ancient cabin or line shack, and some bad artist years before had painted the face on the siding.

"Jesus Christ." Sollis sighed, dropping his hands and letting his shoulders relax. It was just an old shack.

He went to it, and saw what a crude and stupid face it was. He wondered if the mountain man or cowboy who had painted it had been doing a self-portrait or if it'd been the face of someone he knew. Not that it mattered now.

Sollis moved around to the front of the structure and saw the open misshapen door, and two broken-out windows that seemed to squint up and to the right because the building was leaning that way and about to fall over. There was no roof on the shack because it had buckled and fallen inside, which left no room in there to stretch out and sleep and no reason to go in.

He walked to the other side of the shack and found the rusted frame of what looked like a Model T Ford pickup in a small grove of aspen trees. The rubber was gone from the tires and the fabric on the seats had long before been eaten away. Three eight-foot trees sprouted up from beneath the car frame, one from where the motor should have been.

Sollis cursed again. There wasn't anything in the shack or around it that could help him. The crappy old cabin looked to have been built in the 1920s or 1930s—long before there was any electrical or telephone service available. Back before the Forest Service had closed all the roads to the public. Whoever had driven up there, built a shelter, painted the face, and left his pickup, was long gone.

Then he stared at the rusted frame of the Model T, and he got an idea.

THE FRONT BUMPER was thin and insubstantial by modern standards, he thought, but the top edge was fairly sharp. Sollis was on his knees in the grass, working his arms and the plastic bindings back and forth along the edge, sawing at the zip ties. It made a low moaning sound.

It took him nearly an hour to feel some give, and another ten minutes to saw completely through. The shards of the ties fell to the ground.

Sollis cried "Yes!" and stood up and rubbed at his sore wrists. His mind had wandered a couple of times as he sawed away mindlessly and the sharp rim of the bumper had scratched his skin, but the bleeding wasn't bad.

Feeling unbelievably free, he loped from the old car frame into the open meadow and slung the daypack to the ground. He felt so much lighter without it, and he opened the top flap and rooted through it to see what the contents were. Clothing, mainly, which he had no use for. But he found a filled plastic bottle of water, and he opened it and drank. It nearly washed the taste of the deer water out of his mouth.

He found no food except a can of Van Camp's Pork and Beans. He started to root through the pack for a knife or can opener when the phone started ringing once again. He'd nearly forgotten about it, and Sollis found it in a side pocket of the pack.

The display showed a number with a 307 area code with no name attached to it. The face of the phone was confusing at first, but he saw the icon of a standard telephone handset and punched the button and held it up to his ear.

"Who is this," Sollis said, "and why do you keep calling?"

There was a beat of silence, as if the caller was surprised there was someone on the other end.

A high voice with a slight Hispanic accent said, "This is Juan Julio Batista."

"Who?" Sollis asked.

"Who is *this*?"

"Who do you think it is?" Sollis said cautiously.

"Butch Roberson."

"Yeah, right," Sollis said sarcastically.

"Let's not play these games."

"Fine, I'll hang up."

"No," Batista said urgently. "Please stay on the line."

"Technically, it isn't a line," Sollis said.

He could hear muffled voices from the other end, as if the caller had placed his hand over the microphone. Sollis found it annoying, and was prepared to turn off the phone and call one of his roofer buddies to come get him, when Batista came back on.

Batista said, "Can you hear the helicopter coming? It should just about be right above you."

Sollis was confused. Then he recalled Butch Roberson's demands, and smiled a second time. Maybe, he thought, he could get the pilot to take *him* away. Off the mountain, away from everything, maybe far enough the cops couldn't find him right away.

He heard the sound in the night sky. It increased quickly in volume. Sollis had never been close to a helicopter in his life, but in the movies a helicopter made a whumping sound when it flew. This sounded more like a flying lawn mower.

"Stay right where you are so the pilot can see you," Batista said. "Is there enough clear space where you are for it to land?"

"I'm not sure," Sollis said, looking around at the small meadow.

"Stay where you are."

"I am. I can hear it coming, but I can't see anything."

"It's coming, believe me. Look up," Batista said.

There was more muffled talking in the background.

Sollis did, and saw a dark cigar shape hovering over the

eastern wall of trees. There were no lights on it, and he could see it only because it blocked out a line of stars. It didn't move but stayed in one place, which didn't seem natural.

"That doesn't look like a helicopter to me," Sollis said, as a red ball of flame appeared from underneath the unmanned drone.

He heard the *whoosh* coming straight at him.

And he never heard anything else.

27

JOE PICKETT'S EYES SHOT OPEN AT THE SOUND of a sharp concussion. Instinctively thinking *thunder*, he expected the night sky to be filled with storm clouds, but it was still clear, the stars sharp and endless.

Then, like a distant thunderclap, the echo of the explosion rolled through the mountains. He sat up and rubbed his face, and noticed other bodies were stirring in the moonlight, disturbed by the sound. But no one else seemed awake.

At that moment, Underwood's satellite phone went off and Joe got a sick feeling in his stomach.

Grunting himself awake and patting around in his blanket for the phone, Underwood sat up.

Joe was close enough that he heard Batista's triumphant voice say, *"We got him."*

Joe closed his eyes. He thought of Pam and Hannah Roberson, hoped they were sleeping, and hoped they'd be spared the news as long as possible, because their lives had just been changed forever.

THE TEAM OF SPECIAL AGENTS grumbled and thrashed as Underwood walked among them, nudging them with his boot to get up and get ready. Joe had already stowed his sleeping bag and pad in his saddlebags and was carrying his saddle toward Toby when Underwood said to his men, "Listen up, guys. I just talked to Director Batista. He said they located Butch Roberson west of us with the military drone and they fired a Hellfire missile and took the bastard out."

Joe paused to hear the rest, and saw the faces of the team turn to Underwood. One of them said, "Holy Christ—a Hellfire missile?"

"Our drone used night-vision technology to pinpoint Roberson and transmit the video back to the FOB," Underwood said. "He was standing in the middle of a small clearing, talking to Director Batista on the satellite phone. He didn't have the hostages with him and he was in the clear, so the determination was made right then to fire."

"Is he dead?" one of the agents asked.

"Deader than dead," Underwood said. "With no collateral damage we know of. Director Batista is concerned Roberson might have killed his hostages before he was located, but our job is to confirm that. We're supposed to

establish a perimeter around the kill zone and keep everyone away until the FBI can send their forensics team to get
a positive DNA identification."

"Hold it," Joe said to Underwood. "If they got video
of him and determined it was Butch, why do they need to
send in forensics to the site? Can't they do the work later
in their lab?"

"I don't know the answer to that," Underwood said. "I
wasn't the one who issued the kill order."

"Who did?"

"Director Batista," Underwood said. "He made the call
himself. That much I know."

"It's over," one of the agents said. "Riding horses, sleeping in the open—all this bullshit for nothing."

"At least he won't be shooting at us," one of the agents
said with relief.

"Let's get ready, guys," Underwood said. "We need to
be at the kill zone as soon as we can. I've got the coordinates, and Batista said it's about eight miles away."

He looked up at Joe. "How long do you think that will
take?"

Joe said, "Two hours if we can stay out of the down
timber, a lot longer if we get tangled up in the forest."

Underwood grimaced and nodded. He said, "Let's not
do that. Let's get this over so we can get the hell off this
mountain."

As Underwood painfully climbed up into his saddle,
Joe said, "So this is how it happens now?"

"What?"

"You don't even bother with making an arrest or taking them to court. You just see them on a video screen and push a button."

"Wasn't my call," Underwood said. "But I can't say I'm all busted up about it. Better they blow him up than risk any of us getting hurt."

Joe said, "And here I always thought part of the job of law enforcement was the risk of getting hurt."

Underwood smirked and shook his head. "You and your old-school crap."

"Let me borrow your phone again," Joe said, reaching out.

"Not now. We have to stay off the line in case . . ." Underwood's argument petered out as he saw the illogic in it. "I guess Butch can't use his phone if he's blown up in a million pieces."

"Yup."

Underwood sighed and unslung the lanyard for the phone over his head. "Why do you need it?" he asked.

Joe said, "I need to quit."

"What—this mission?"

"My job," Joe said.

"Then you can't have it," Underwood said, pulling the phone back before Joe could grasp it. "I need you until we find the kill zone. You know these mountains better than anyone here."

Joe took a deep breath and expelled it slowly through his nose. He felt the need to be a witness at the kill zone since he'd already come this far.

"That and no farther," he said.

"Don't worry," Underwood said. "I'll be as glad to get rid of you as you are to leave."

Joe could see the reflection of his grinning teeth in the moonlight.

That's when Underwood's phone lit up again and trilled. Joe expected it to be Batista with more orders or more self-congratulation.

He was close enough to hear Butch Roberson's bass voice ask Batista, *"What the hell did you idiots just do?"*

Joe looked up at the night sky and was a little surprised and ashamed by his sense of relief.

Then it hit him: If it wasn't Butch Roberson who'd been hit by the missile, who was it?

28

MOMENTS BEFORE, DAVE FARKUS HAD BEEN jolted by what he thought must be a gunshot, and he spun on his heels and writhed and held his bound hands out in front of him as if they'd ward off an oncoming bullet. The sound was a big *CRACK!* that seemed to split open the very night itself and he was surprised that it took a second for the trees to the northwest to sway as shock waves blew through them.

Behind him, Butch Roberson hissed: "Get moving!" and the three of them sprinted across a rock- and grass-covered field toward the shelter of a broken cirque of rocks that looked to provide cover.

Farkus had glanced over his shoulder as he ran and saw a rose-colored ball of flame roll up from the dark sea of trees several miles away to the northwest. The explosion looked to have happened in the timber short of the valley floor they'd come through the afternoon before.

Safely in the rock formation, Butch ordered Farkus and McLanahan to get down. They sat with their hands bound and resting between their knees while Butch Roberson climbed up a coffin-shaped outcropping with a squared-off top large enough for him to pace back and forth. He seemed to be planning their next move, Farkus thought. Either that, or Butch had been seriously thrown by the explosion.

As Butch paced on the top of the rock, his reverse silhouette could be seen only because he blocked out the wash of creamy stars in the sky. Then Farkus could see a glimpse of the ambient light of the satellite phone lighting up Butch's cheek.

"What was it?" Farkus asked McLanahan.

"Something big."

"Thanks, expert," Farkus said.

McLanahan gestured toward Butch, who was activating his phone.

"Maybe he's had enough," McLanahan said. "Maybe Butch is ready to give himself up."

"What the hell did you idiots just do?" Butch yelled into the handset.

BECAUSE BUTCH WAS ABOVE HIM holding the handset tight to his face and walking back and forth on the rock, Farkus could only hear one side of the conversation.

"Don't try to tell me that was the helicopter, Batista. What do you take me for? I was a Marine. I *flew* in helicopters. I know the hell what one looks like and sounds like, and that wasn't a helicopter . . ."

Then: "Stop it with your lies. You sent another drone, but this one was loaded for bear. Don't deny it, you liar. Do you know what you did? You blew up a miserable loser I'd sent away. I can't say he was an innocent man, because he wasn't. His name was Jimmy Sollis, and he's the one who gut-shot that hunter. But you killed him, Batista . . ."

Then: "I had a feeling you'd try something like this, but I was stupid enough to think you'd just divert your men to the signal and chase the wrong guy. I never thought you'd be stupid enough to blow him up with a missile because of a phone he carried in his backpack. Now you've got real blood on your hands, Batista. How does it feel?"

Then: "Stop it, just stop it. There was never going to be a helicopter, was there? The whole thing was a lie, wasn't it?"

Then: "You're treating me like a goddamned *terrorist*— firing missiles at me without ever looking at me face-to-face. That's how you people are, isn't it? You don't return calls, you don't talk to actual citizens because what they say might make you uncomfortable. And you do this the same way, don't you? Everything at a comfortable distance, where you never have to get your hands dirty or worry about someone actually fighting back . . ."

Then: "So what's next? Are you going to drop bombs on me? Hit me with a nuke? The drones I'm familiar with are MQ-1 Predators and they can only pack one Hellfire missile, and that's the one you used to blow the hell out of Jimmy Sollis . . ."

Then: "So you've shot your wad, Batista. Now you're going to have to decide if you want to face me one-on-one like a man, or are you going to send that helicopter you promised?"

Farkus turned to McLanahan. He said, "There isn't any helicopter, is there?"

"Nope. There never was."

"I wonder if this changes our strategy?"

McLanahan shrugged. "I'd guess we'll keep heading for that canyon. What I can't figure out is why he called them. Now they'll get a fix on this location."

Farkus shivered. He hadn't thought of that. He wondered how long it would be before a missile came screaming at them out of the sky.

"Let's hope Butch was right that they only had one for the time being," McLanahan said. "But that doesn't mean they won't order up some more."

Farkus barely heard him because as he watched, something strange was happening to Butch Roberson. He had started to *glow*.

"Look," Farkus whispered.

Where before Roberson could be seen only because his form blocked out the stars, he was now bathed in slight orange. Farkus could see Butch's features and clothing. When Farkus leaned to the side and looked out at the forest from between the rocks, he saw that the trees had begun to glow orange as well.

"Oh my God," Butch said into the handset. "Now look what you've done."

Without giving Batista a chance to reply, Butch powered down the handset and threw it down the mountain. Farkus heard it strike a branch, then hit a rock a beat later.

"Let's go," Butch said to them.

"What's happening?" Farkus asked. "What's out there?"

Butch Roberson shook his head. He said, "First they put up fences and blocked all the roads to the public. Then they sat on their butts behind their desks and watched pine beetles kill millions of trees for thousands of miles.

"Now," Butch said, his face a mask of weariness, "they're going to burn it all down and maybe us with it."

"The missile started a fire?" Farkus asked.

"That's what he's saying, genius," McLanahan said sharply.

29

JOE URGED TOBY DOWN THE MOUNTAIN IN THE
dark but let his horse choose the route. Toby chose well
and stayed on a well-established game trail that skirted
most of the hazards and kept them out of situations where
they'd need to back out. It was mindless riding except
for the occasional branch Joe had to duck under, and he
spent the next two hours letting facts and questions about
the situation float through his mind, hoping they would
somehow string together into some kind of plausible thread
that would explain why he was there and what he was doing and what Butch Roberson had set in motion. He'd
learned over the years to let his subconscious work on
problems, and more often than not it had led to good re-
sults. Thunderclap-like revelations came not when he was
puzzling them over or talking them out, but while he

was putting up elk-fence on a rancher's hayfield or cleaning out his garage or taking a shower.

So he focused on the task at hand—getting down the mountain in the dark and relying on Toby to get him there—and let his mind try to make order out of disorder.

The rapid response by the EPA the same day of resuming construction of Butch's home still nagged at him. It was as if someone on-site had been poised and ready to make the call. Pam had not identified any business competitors or personal enemies whom she thought capable of such an act, and Joe couldn't imagine someone in the valley harboring such hatred toward Butch—and such patience—that he or she wouldn't be known. Everybody knew everything about each other in Saddlestring, and word would have been out if someone was gunning for Butch, Joe thought. So it must have been someone unknown to Butch, or someone he'd never suspect—and someone who had the power to fire up Batista.

Then there were the acts that followed the murders; acts that seemed desperate and out of character for Butch. Burying the two agents on his own land, then disposing of their car in the canyon. Neither was well thought-out, and Butch must have known that both would quickly be discovered within days if not hours. Both pointed straight at Butch, except something didn't jibe in the sequence for Joe.

Butch didn't come off as a runner, Joe thought. After shooting the agents, it seemed much more in character for Butch to drive to the sheriff's office and turn himself in. Or even turn the rifle on himself. But to run?

And who lent a ride to Butch as far as the Big Stream Ranch? Was it an innocent, or someone complicit in the murders? As far as Joe knew, no one had stepped forward to admit they'd given the newly infamous fugitive a ride.

There were plenty of locals Joe knew who had animus toward the Feds and who would be sympathetic to Butch's situation. But despite that, how many would actually assist an armed man who had just committed a double homicide? Who would potentially implicate themselves in such a crime out of empathy for Butch?

Joe thought about what Butch had gone through in the past year, how he'd been persecuted to the point that his mental health and his family were nearly destroyed. He wondered why Pam had kept the situation to herself—both the compliance order and Butch's depressed reaction—while the pressure built. And how Hannah had remained close friends with Lucy but had never given away what was going on in her own home between her mom and her dad.

And there was something else, and Joe wasn't sure he wasn't attaching more significance to it than it warranted. But he now thought about how Butch had looked at him the other afternoon, the way his eyes seemed to implore something to Joe that Joe couldn't read at the time. Joe had sensed guilt or panic, but now he thought it might have been something else. It was as if Butch thought Joe might somehow *understand*, which Joe didn't at the time and wasn't sure he did now.

Understand what? Joe thought. Why did Butch think Joe would understand why he was acting that way? Even though they got along well, the basis of the relationship between Butch and Joe was based on the fact their daughters were best friends. Outside of that, Joe didn't think the two of them would be any closer than any local Joe met in the field or around town.

Then he recalled the layout and details of the two-acre lot. The Kubota tractor. The plot of dug-up ground where the agents were found. The surrounding homes in the trees of the subdivision. The shot-up target Butch had used to sight in his rifles and blow off steam.

That's when Joe thought the unthinkable. A thread tied together what he knew.

And he didn't like it one bit.

HE WAS JOLTED out of his dark theorizing when he heard the cracking of branches directly in front of him. Toby's ears pricked up, and Joe could feel the horse tense between his legs. Something was coming up the game trail fast and hard in the dark, and it was not concerned with stealth.

He strained forward in the saddle, squinting in hope of seeing better through the gloom. His headlamp wouldn't throw light far enough into the trees to see anything yet.

Behind him, one of the agents lost control of his horse when the mount started crow-hopping and the man fell heavily to the ground with a shout.

The sound of twigs and dry branches breaking rose in volume, and a small constellation of glowing blue lights like manic fireflies filled the trees. They were eyes reflecting back from his headlamp.

Elk—cows and calves and spikes and bulls—were suddenly pouring up through the forest. Heavy antlers of the bulls, still in velvet, thunked tree trunks with the sound of muffled baseball bats. Joe watched the herd draw close and part around him like a river coursing around an island, only to rejoin farther up the mountain.

"Easy, easy, easy," Joe cooed to Toby, whose muscles were taut with tension. *"Easy, easy, easy . . ."* as the huge herd poured around them and kept going.

Behind him, the agents were having their own private rodeo. Their horses bolted, and soon there were more men on the ground than in the saddle. Underwood's horse reared, but somehow he stayed on.

When the elk were gone, leaving the air heavy with their musky smell, Joe was still mounted. Agents moaned and cursed and writhed in the grass, and two of the horses ran behind the herd of elk in a panic, their stirrups flapping and striking their flanks as if to goad them on.

"Jesus Christ!" Underwood hollered. "What in the hell just happened?"

"Elk," Joe said calmly.

"I know that! But what made them charge into us like that? We've lost most of our horses, and I've got injured agents on the ground."

"Something spooked them," Joe said, turning in his saddle to look west, the direction the elk had come.

There was a slight rose-colored tint to the sky that threw him off. Not only was the sun rising in the wrong direction, he thought, it was coming up an hour too early.

Then he smelled the smoke.

"**ARE YOU TRYING** to get us killed?" Underwood yelled into the satellite handset to Juan Julio Batista. "Why didn't you fucking tell us the forest was on fire?"

Joe was still mounted, and he listened while leaning forward in his saddle with his arms crossed over the pommel. The agents who still had horses held them by the reins. The two without horses just stood there. One man said he thought his arm was broken and another said he couldn't walk because of a sprained ankle.

"I don't care," Underwood bellowed at Batista. "This isn't worth it. We might burn to death if we stay here, and I won't waste the lives of these men. You need to send an evacuation chopper *now*. We'll figure out where it can land and how to get to it."

The agents were nodding and urging Underwood on.

"I don't care if your ass is on the line," Underwood shouted. "We're not going to fry up here for you or anybody else."

Underwood punched off, furious. He said, "The missile started the forest on fire, and it's already out of control. The fire is spreading out to the east, north, and south."

"We're east," one of the agents said.

"Not for fucking long," Underwood said. "Those elk had the right idea. We're evacuating. We're going to go right back up that trail where we came from until we can get above the tree line. I'm hoping they'll send a chopper to get us out of here before the whole fucking mountain goes up."

"How fast is the fire moving?" someone asked.

"Fast," Underwood said, and Joe noted the real panic in his voice.

"What about those of us who don't have horses?" an agent asked.

Underwood extended his hand and let the agent double up on the back of his horse.

"If you don't have a horse," Underwood said to the other man on foot, "you'll have to share."

With that, he turned his horse and cantered through the trees up the trail. One of the mounted agents helped the crippled agent get behind him on his horse and the two of them followed the others.

The agents left weapons, gear bags, and body armor scattered on the ground.

Before they all vanished into the dark timber, Underwood returned and cocked his head at Joe.

"Aren't you coming?"

"Nope."

"Then where are you going?"

"I'm going to go find Butch," Joe said, and turned Toby south, toward Savage Run.

"Joe!" Underwood called. Joe turned around in his saddle just in time to catch the satellite phone Underwood had tossed through the air.

"Call in your position if you get in trouble," Underwood said before he waved good-bye and rode away.

30

DAVE FARKUS COULD NOW SEE WHERE HE WAS running due to an unnatural, hellish light that filled the sky and illuminated the ground and penetrated the scrub trees they'd entered. The entire sky was fused orange and streaked with gray bands. Ash, like snow, filtered down through the air. He assumed it was dawn, but there was no way to tell because he couldn't see the sun through the cover of smoke.

Butch Roberson no longer enforced the decorum he'd insisted on before the fire started and the three of them jogged abreast, zigzagging around trees and clumps of brush. Sweat poured down Farkus's spine into his jeans, and his shirt clung to his back. It was worse for McLanahan, though, he noticed. McLanahan looked like he'd just stepped out of a shower fully clothed. His face was flushed red, and his breathing was ragged and forced.

Behind them was a roar of white noise. The temperature had risen, and it was getting warmer by the minute. The air itself was hot and acrid, and Farkus tried to filter it by holding his shirtsleeves up to his face while he ran.

His throat was raw from breathing in smoke-filled air, and his eyes watered. It was like standing in front of a campfire, filling his lungs with the smoke.

"Hold up," Butch said, nearly out of breath himself. *"Hold up."*

Farkus stopped and looked over to see Butch pulling a long knife out of a sheath and approaching him. Had he decided to do them in and proceed alone?

"Hold out your hands."

Relieved, Farkus did as he was told.

Butch cut the zip ties free and turned to do the same for McLanahan, who now held his hands out.

Butch said, "You're both free to go."

"Go where?" McLanahan replied angrily.

"Anywhere you want."

McLanahan gestured behind them. "There's fire *everywhere*. Where do you expect us to go?"

"I'm sticking with you," Farkus said to Butch. Butch nodded reluctantly.

He said, "I can't guarantee your safety if you stay with me."

"I'd rather take my chances with you than stay with Fatty."

McLanahan reacted with anger and panic, and turned so he could look behind them, as if to find a path through the oncoming fire. He spat a curse and shook his head.

At that moment, less than a mile away, was a loud popping sound, followed by another.

"Is somebody shooting?" Farkus asked Butch.

"No," Butch said, shaking his head. "Those are trees exploding. When the sap in the trees gets superheated, trees literally blow up."

"Jesus," Farkus said. "Exploding trees."

"That's going to be us if we don't get moving," McLanahan said. His eyes were wet and bloodshot, rimmed with red.

Butch unshouldered his pack and dug into it and emerged with a spare long-sleeved shirt. He used his knife to cut it into wide strips, then doused the strips with water from his Nalgene bottle.

"Tie these around your mouths," he said. Then, to McLanahan: "Tie yours extra tight."

"Are we still headed for the canyon?" Farkus asked as he covered his mouth with the cool, wet cloth and knotted it at the nape of his neck. It felt good.

Butch nodded. "I don't think we have any choice but you can do whatever you want. I doubt the fire can jump the canyon, and I know Batista can't. So if we can get there, we might have a chance to get out of this."

Farkus nodded, ready to go.

"How in the hell are you going to get across?" McLanahan said.

Butch threaded his arms through his pack and buckled it back on.

"I guess we'll find out," he said.

"That's bullshit," McLanahan said. He looked over his

shoulder at the oncoming fire. They couldn't actually see leaping flames yet, but the air was getting hotter and exploding trees signaled the approach of the flames.

"I'm going to make my stand," McLanahan said. "I'll find a ditch, cover myself with dirt, and let it pass over the top of me."

"Fine," Butch said. "Suit yourself. Have you ever heard of the Mann Gulch fire in Montana?"

"The *what*?"

"That's right, you're from West Virginia," Butch said. "In 1949, smoke jumpers got caught in a situation like this and thirteen died. Those that didn't suffocate from the smoke tried to hunker down and ride it out like you were describing. They were baked like potatoes."

At that moment, a long and heavily muscled mountain lion appeared out of nowhere and ran right through the three of them, threading silkily around their legs, and ran toward higher ground. Farkus was astounded.

"He didn't even care we were here," Farkus said.

"Okay," McLanahan said to Butch. "I'll go with you."

"You can stay," Butch said. "Mountain lions have to eat, too."

"I'm going with you," McLanahan said, defeated. "But no one knows how to get across. I can see us standing there on the edge as the fire comes straight at us."

"I know that canyon has been crossed."

"That's Indian hokum," McLanahan said. "Have you *seen* it?"

Farkus had, that time he was hunting with Butch. They'd stood on the rim and looked down. Butch had pointed out the knife-sharp walls, a terrifying distance from the rim to the narrow canyon floor, and virtually no breaks or cracks through the rocks to assure a crossing. The canyon was so steep and narrow that sunlight rarely shone on the surface of the Middle Fork. Butch said it cut through eight different archaeological strata before it hit the bottom.

"It's been done," Butch said, holding McLanahan's eye. "Once by those Cheyenne back in the old days when the Pawnee closed in on their camp, and they did it at *night*. And Joe Pickett did it."

McLanahan shook his head in disgust. "He *claims* he did it. He's a pain in my ass, you know."

"If Joe says he did it, he did it," Butch said.

"And there he is," Farkus said, doubting his eyes, as Joe appeared on horseback through a haze of smoke and rode right toward them.

31

"YOU'RE NOT GONNA SHOOT ME, ARE YOU, Butch?" Joe called out, after reining Toby to a stop. He knew the answer, though, because Roberson was lowering the rifle he'd raised instinctively when Joe appeared.

"I don't think so," Butch responded, "or I'd have already done it."

"That's good," Joe mumbled aloud to himself, and nudged Toby's flanks toward the three men who stood staring at him from within a sparse stand of twisted and ancient mountain juniper that was just a little taller than themselves.

Through burning eyes, he noted that Farkus wasn't dead after all, and that both Farkus and McLanahan weren't cuffed or bound. They stood on either side of Butch Roberson, who squinted at him through the haze and waves of heat, wearing his backpack and cradling his AR-15.

HE'D FOUND THEM more by intuition and strategic luck than anything else, Joe thought. After he'd left Underwood and the agents, he'd ridden south, cutting across the face of the mountain from clearing to clearing so he could look back and down and see the progress of the fire. He tried to skirt dry grassy areas and stick to the shade and rock on the side of the meadows because he knew how fast fire could consume it and he didn't want to be trapped.

The fire was amazing and terrifying to behold, and as he rode he got the clear feeling that all rules had been suspended, all bets were off, all was forgotten, and it was suddenly every man for himself. Even the wildlife had jettisoned its instincts and caution, and ran across his path up the mountain with no more than a passing glance. Elk, mule deer, mountain lions, bobcats, three black bears (two with cubs), and a lone black wolf he thought he'd seen before. Only the wolf hesitated as it loped along, and locked eyes with Joe for a momentary and primal exchange of information—*run*—before vanishing into the timber.

"You again," Joe had said.

WHEN HE COULD SEE clearly from the edges of the meadows, which wasn't often, Joe noted how the fire was racing up and across the mountain in what looked like reverse molten rivers of flame. It was ravenous and craven, without thought or mercy, and it either roared up ravines from the ground up or jumped from crown to crown of high dead pine trees like a manic gremlin, consuming everything it wanted to consume. The fire was so huge and so voracious that it seemed to be creating its own weather; hot blasts of air rocketed up the mountain and primed the dry timber for oncoming destruction. Long-standing trees went *whumpf* and exploded into flame, and the underbrush snapped and crackled with a high-pitched fury.

At one point he saw a wall of flame shoot through a stand of aspen, linger a moment among the live green trees as if taking a breather, then squirt out the side onto low-hanging dead pine boughs and continue its course. Ash behaved like snow, either swirling horizontally along the ground as if in a ground blizzard or floating down softly through the air, depending on the wind speed and direction of the moment.

It was a maelstrom. The hot, dry wind blew steadily to the east, but at times it swirled and reversed direction and blew like a blowtorch and blew north, then west.

Twice, he witnessed fire whirls that emerged from the trees in thirty-foot columns of flame. The whirls whipped back and forth as if they were being shaken. One fire whirl was slapped down by a gust of wind but continued to burn as a horizontal fire worm that ignited all the grass in its path.

Joe knew from the speed of the fire's advance that there would be no putting it out. This fire, in perfect conditions of hot, dry weather with an endless supply of dead and low-moisture fuel, would burn until it burned out. Joe had heard of fires that burned so hot they literally sterilized the ground for years after they'd passed through, and he guessed this was going to be one of those.

He could only speculate how big the fire would become, because it was already out of control and growing. If it found enough fuel at the summit, it could flow over the top and into Big Stream Valley. Airborne embers could be blown through the wind to land on dry trees hundreds of yards from the source. He felt both sick to his stomach and humbled by the awesome power of nature at the same time. It wasn't the first forest fire he'd seen—far from it—but it was already the biggest and fastest. Previously, he'd observed fires from a safe distance.

Fire was natural, he knew that. Forests had to regenerate, and fire jump-started the process by opening the canopy, clearing debris, and activating aspen shoots and pine seeds. The mountain had burned countless times over the ages, long before there were humans to run from it.

Yet . . .

So he continued to head south, toward Savage Run Canyon. Not only because he'd speculated that Butch had chosen the same route and everything else was misdirection but because it was the only terrain that wasn't yet in flames.

AS JOE RODE UP on the three men, he said, "Butch, when this is over I'm going to place you under arrest. You understand that, right?"

Butch nodded.

Joe said, "Just so we're clear. I'm going to try to get this handled aboveboard and locally. I'll get Dulcie involved, and we'll do our best to keep the Feds out."

"I appreciate that."

"But right now we're going to put that all aside and try to survive this. Does that sound like a deal to you?"

"Yes, Joe."

"Okay, then."

"How far from here to the canyon?" McLanahan asked Joe, without any preamble.

"Couple of miles," Joe said.

"Can you get us across?"

"I can't promise it," Joe said. "It's been years and I haven't been back."

"Jesus Christ," McLanahan said. "We're going to burn to death up here."

Joe shrugged. He didn't have the time or inclination to talk to McLanahan, even when there wasn't a forest fire racing toward them.

"I thought you were dead," Joe said to Farkus, as he climbed off Toby.

"So did I," Farkus said, rolling his eyes toward Butch Roberson. "That trick was his idea."

Joe asked Farkus, "Why is it you always seem to be in the middle of every bad situation there is?"

"I don't know!" Farkus said, almost howling. "But the same could be said about you."

"Point taken," Joe said.

"It was spur of the moment," Butch said, referring to his claim that he killed Farkus. "That guy Batista just pissed me off so bad I needed to convince him I was a serious man and I'd kill hostages if I had to."

"Why not McLanahan, then?" Joe asked. "That would make the world a better place."

"Hey!" the ex-sheriff cried, hurt. "That was uncalled for."

But Joe noticed Butch was stifling a grin.

"You know there was never any helicopter," Joe said.

"I figured as much."

Joe said, "Did you know when you sent the shooter away they'd try to blow him up?"

"No," Butch said.

"Then why'd you give him that satellite phone?"

"I knew it had GPS. I figured they'd track him thinking it was me and give me some time to get out of here. I had no idea they'd shoot a goddamned *missile* at him."

"This fire isn't the only thing out of control," Joe said.

JOE LOOKED AROUND where they stood. It was dry and rocky except for the junipers. He said, "I've read where you can start a personal grass fire and lay down in it when it goes out. That way, the fire will go around you because you've already used up the fuel."

The others looked at him optimistically. Except Butch.

"That won't work here, though," Joe said. "Not enough grass and the brush is over our heads. Plus, the fire is burning too hot. People die from smoke and heat, mostly. They don't burn up."

"The canyon is our only choice," Butch said.

"Yup."

While Butch, Farkus, and McLanahan waited anxiously, Joe said, "Give me a minute."

"We don't have a minute," McLanahan shouted. He was looking at actual flames advancing on them from tree to tree in the direction from which Joe had come.

"You're free to go on ahead," Butch said to McLanahan, which shut him up.

Unsaddling Toby, Joe quickly dug into his essentials bag for a canvas evidence pouch and a length of leather string. He dug out the digital recorder from his pocket, put it in the pouch and cinched it, and wrote FOR GOV RULON ONLY on the canvas with a black marker. He tied the string around Toby's neck and said, "Be safe, buddy," and slapped his horse on the flank.

Toby bunched up and took off. He looked back only once.

"Go!" Joe hollered.

"He's got a better chance without my weight and that saddle," Joe said. But as he watched his horse thunder up the mountain, his eyes stung, and it wasn't from the smoke.

He dug the satellite phone out of the saddlebag.

He turned to Roberson. "Butch, I'd jettison that pack if I were you."

Butch looked back, conflicted.

"Remember our deal," Joe said.

Butch nodded and lowered the pack. "What about my rifle?"

"I'd leave that, too."

"No. It goes with me."

Joe didn't want to argue. The look in Butch's eyes said it wouldn't be productive.

"Then let's go," Joe said, walking through them toward the south, still clutching the phone. He looked down and noticed there was a message on the screen. In all the commotion, he hadn't heard it ring.

He'd retrieve it as soon as he had a moment.

"I hope you can find that passage again," McLanahan shouted.

"Yeah," Joe said dourly. "Me, too."

32

JOE COULD FEEL HEAT ON HIS BACK WHEN THEY reached the southern rim of Savage Run Canyon. The wind had kicked up, blowing from the northwest, and supercharged the wall of oncoming fire behind them. Occasionally, an ember carried by the wind blew across his vision and one had landed on his shoulder, burning a hole in the fabric. He'd slapped at it as if it were a wasp.

The air was so hot it burned his lungs to breathe it, and each breath seemed hollow, devoid of oxygen. The smoke was thick and he felt more than saw the opening of the canyon ahead of him, and stopped short. Farkus bumped into him because he was apparently walking with his eyes shut.

"Don't *do* that," Joe warned.

"Sorry."

An arched eyebrow of prickly juniper rimmed the canyon, the foliage biting into the rocky soil and holding on for dear life. It made it hard to tell where the real edge of the canyon began.

Joe looked up and was surprised to find out that at eye level he couldn't even see the opposite rim of the canyon because of the smoke. Only when he ducked and trained his eyes down could he vaguely make out the opposing wall. The sheer cliff face was as vertical and slick as he remembered it in his nightmares, and he could see no sign of the passage.

"How far?" Butch Roberson croaked, his voice thick with mucus.

"I don't know," Joe said over his shoulder.

Because he couldn't see farther than thirty feet, he didn't know if he was even in the vicinity of the old switchback trail he'd once found. He tried to conjure up a clear memory and convinced himself that he'd need to walk west, not east, along the edge of the rim to find it. The wrong choice, he knew, could be fatal.

The problem with moving parallel to the rim of the canyon was that the fire would no longer be pushing them from the back, but from the side. The only way to escape as the flames closed in on them would be to jump and plunge into the void. There was no way he would do that. Even if he somehow avoided bouncing off the canyon wall on the way down, the impact of hitting the surface of the shallow river would kill him.

IT HAD BEEN ten years since he'd made the crossing. At that time, he was with an environmental terrorist named

Stewie Woods and Woods's girlfriend, Britney Earth-share. They were being pursued by a couple of aging hit men, and the only place to escape them was to cross the canyon. Joe had heard of the legend of the crossing. Sup-posedly, a band of Cheyenne Indians—mainly women and children because the warriors were hunting in another part of the mountains—defied certain death and made the crossing in the middle of the night before a murderous group of Pawnee closed in on them. No one knew if the Cheyenne knew about the location of the crossing before they were forced to find it, or whether it had been pure crazy luck. But most of the Cheyenne made it across, leaving tepee poles, travois, and a few broken bodies along the descent. Joe had originally found the location of the crossing because he discovered an ancient Cheyenne child's doll made of leather and fur that had been discarded. The doll was displayed in his home.

Now he wished he'd left the doll where he'd found it so he'd have some idea where the trailhead was located.

More burning embers, like fireflies, floated through the air. The roar of the fire was so loud it was difficult to hear anything else.

HE REMEMBERED STEWIE had blundered over an out-cropping of rock hidden in the brush, and had nearly fallen to his death in the canyon. The rock—if he'd gone the right direction and could find it again—would indicate the mouth of the trailhead to the Cheyenne Crossing. In the intervening years, the brush had become even taller and thicker than before.

Joe felt panic start to set in. He hoped it wouldn't turn into mindless shock, and he shook his head to clear it while he walked. His left shoulder, side, and leg were hot from the proximity of the flames. His skin tingled with it, and he tried to maintain a stride where he could avoid letting the hot fabric touch his flesh.

"Oh God, oh God, oh God," McLanahan moaned. "We're going to die in the worst way."

"I always thought freezing would be worse," Farkus said, his voice muffled through the wet cloth over his mouth.

Butch said nothing but kept prodding McLanahan along ahead of him whenever the ex-sheriff stopped to rest. He couldn't get air, either.

Joe dragged his right boot through the edge of the juniper, hoping to bump up against the hidden rock.

As he'd done before when he found himself in a similar situation, he thought of his family. Marybeth had no idea where he was, or what was happening. She was likely at home, watching with horror as smoke billowed from the mountains that filled their front room window. There was likely no real information yet about where the fire started, how it started, or who was caught within it, because it took a while for official spokesmen to get organized to give statements. And it had all happened so fast.

Joe saw the faces of Sheridan, Lucy, and April all turned toward the fire from different vantage points: Sheridan as she drove her truck toward Saddlestring wearing her waitress uniform to go to work at the Burg-O-Pardner, April scowling beside her in her cowgirl outfit, Lucy—and Hannah—bookending Marybeth in the front room. All their faces turned his direction but not knowing it.

He wondered how far the fire had spread north. Was it burning the face off Wolf Mountain, which was the closest to their home? Had it advanced into the river cottonwoods of the Twelve Sleep Valley? Was it racing toward Saddlestring itself?

MCLANAHAN SCREAMED, and Joe turned to find him hopping up and down. An ember had lit on his back, and his shirt was on fire. Butch slapped at the flames while McLanahan danced away, Butch yelling at McLanahan to stop moving. Farkus looked on as if paralyzed.

Joe ducked around Farkus and threw himself at McLanahan and rode him down to the ground, where he landed on his side. Both Joe and Butch flipped the ex-sheriff to his belly and threw handfuls of dirt on McLanahan's back. As the man writhed, they whacked at the flames with open hands until the fire was out. The flesh on the ex-sheriff's back was wet crimson, and large yellow blisters were blooming. The tatters of his shirt were scorched black.

As McLanahan moaned beneath them, Butch looked up with a red-eyed squint and said, "Joe, I hope we're getting close."

BECAUSE THE FIRESTORM CREATED its own ecosystem, occasionally the wind reversed for a few seconds. When it did, the air cleared and the intensity of the heat was reduced, and Joe could see ahead along the rim.

After McLanahan had staggered to his feet again, his face a mask of pain, the wind stopped blowing for a moment. Joe cautiously pushed through the juniper to peer into the canyon itself. The palms of his hands stung on contact with the brush because he'd burned them slapping out the fire on McLanahan's back. But he managed to part the branches and poke his head through them. He wanted to drink in and remember every feature of the canyon before the smoke came roiling back.

When he looked straight down, he could see the river, which looked like a twisted thin strip of sheet metal in the shadow of the canyon floor. *How cool it must be down there,* he thought.

And when he looked ahead a quarter-mile upriver from where he stood, he could see a number of tepee poles scattered haphazardly along the side of the cliff. They looked like silver toothpicks because of their age, and they were still there ten years later, just as they'd been there for the previous hundred and fifty years. He'd chosen the right direction.

"Found it!" he hollered back.

"The trailhead?" Butch asked hoarsely.

"Yup."

"Thank God."

Joe said, "There's still the 'getting down' part."

As if to highlight his statement, the wind whirled around

them and resumed blowing south and the flames roared toward them, advancing by jumps from tree to tree.

WITHIN FIVE MINUTES, the toe of Joe's boot thumped against the rock he'd been looking for. It had been completely obscured by the juniper bush. Edging toward the abyss, Joe parted the brush until he could locate the two-foot ledge just over the rim. He recalled Stewie standing on the ledge after he'd tripped on the rock.

Only half the ledge was there—a one-foot-by-two-foot outcropping. The other half had fallen away. That would make it difficult to lower themselves down the face of the wall to where the trail actually began.

"Oh, man," Joe said.

"Hurry, hurry," McLanahan cried in full panic.

Joe looked back and saw why. The fire was less than ten feet behind them, and tendrils of it were shooting across the ground toward them, igniting pine needles and tufts of dried grass.

"Listen to me," he said, trying to stay calm. Three sets of bloodshot eyes bored into him from masked, soot-blackened faces.

"There's a flat rock down here no bigger than the top of a stepladder. You'll need to use it to lower yourself off the edge to the trail below. Stay tight to the side of the wall, because the trail isn't any wider than a foot or so. Drop down to that trail and keep your balance. Got that?"

Nods. Scared-but-frantic nods.

"I'll go first," Joe said. "I'll try to steady each of you

when you lower yourself down. Don't panic, and don't start thrashing around or you might take both of us over. Okay?"

"Just fucking hurry," McLanahan said through his mask. Joe could tell his teeth were clenched as he said it.

"How far is the drop to the trail?" Butch asked.

"Seven feet or so, if I remember," Joe said. "But it will seem farther when you're dropping through the air."

"Sweet Jesus," Farkus moaned.

JOE GRIMACED as he lowered himself on the shelf to grasp the ledge. His legs and back weren't as flexible as they'd been ten years before. Even if he dropped safely to the trail cut into the canyon wall, he had no idea if stretches of it—like the ledge itself—had dropped away. He tried to not even think of what it would be like for the four of them to be isolated on the trail itself with no way to get down, their only other choice being to try and work their way back to the top and burn to death.

He turned to face the wall and reached down on either side to grasp the sharp edge of the rock, and backed off until he dropped and was suspended. While he hung in the air, he looked down his shirtfront to confirm the trail was still there below him. It was. Joe said a prayer and let go.

The soles of his boots hit the surface of the trail with a heavy thump, and his knees screamed from the impact. He didn't remember *that* from ten years before. Far below, he heard something smack against the rocks, and he realized the phone had fallen out of his jeans from the jump. He wouldn't be able to call Marybeth for a while, and he cursed.

"Hurry!" McLanahan shouted.

"Okay," he shouted up. Because of his angle, he couldn't see the other three above him. "You can come on. The trail is here, and I'm standing on it. Come one at a time so I can help steady you and guide you down when you let go."

A few seconds later, Joe recognized Farkus's Vibram-soled work boots dangling above him. Even though the fire was roaring and snapping on top, Joe could hear Farkus mewling with fear.

"It's okay," Joe said, reaching up until he could grasp the back of Farkus's belt. "You can let go."

"Sweet Jesus," Farkus cried, still hanging.

"Let go," Joe shouted.

Farkus dropped and landed clumsily on the trail, and Joe kept a grip on the belt so the man wouldn't lose his balance and plunge into the canyon.

With Farkus now standing and hugging the wall, Joe shinnied carefully around him. He could feel Farkus trembling.

"Move a few feet down the trail so I have some room to work," Joe said to him. Then to McLanahan and Butch: "Next!"

"We're burning up here," Butch's voice croaked.

"Then *hurry*," Joe replied.

He looked up in time to catch a small rock that bounced off his cheekbone from the shelf above. Then, more quickly than he could react, the entire bulk of Kyle McLanahan flew silently by and vanished into the canyon below.

Joe had seen just a flash of the ex-sheriff's face as the

man plunged past him feetfirst. McLanahan's expression wasn't terror—he simply looked annoyed that he'd lost his footing. It happened so quickly Joe hadn't even had the chance to reach out for him, although if he had, the weight and momentum of the body would have likely taken him down with it.

As he processed what he'd just seen, Joe heard a heavy impact far below that sounded like a bag of ice being dropped on a sidewalk.

"What just happened?" he yelled up at Butch.

"The stupid son of a bitch missed the shelf when he stepped down," Butch said. "I tried to grab him, but he was gone."

Joe shook his head to clear it, then said, "Okay, now you, Butch."

"Here I come."

Joe tapped on Butch's ankles to assure him he was there. The fabric of Butch's clothing was smoking from heat. Then, like he'd done with Farkus, Joe grasped Butch by the belt and steadied him down to the trail. Joe noted that Butch had left his rifle behind, although he still had a pistol shoved into his waistband.

JOE AGAIN HAD FARKUS mash himself against the cliff wall while he shouldered around behind him.

"Is he dead?" Farkus asked.

"Probably."

"Too many damned donuts," Farkus said, shaking his head.

———

HUGGING THE WALL, Joe sidestepped down along the narrow trail, calling out hazards such as a break in the trail or loose rocks. Farkus followed, then Butch.

After the first switchback, the trail widened and they were able to square their shoulders and hike down it slowly. Joe kept one hand on the canyon wall at all times. In case he slipped on loose earth, he wanted to fall into the wall and not plunge into the canyon like McLanahan had.

As they descended, the roar of the fire muted, but the sky above was still smudged with smoke. Joe could see no glimpse of blue in it. The light filtering through the smoke cast everything with a dirty yellow tint.

He had never gotten along with McLanahan from the beginning, but Joe felt no sense of relief from what had just happened. He doubted he would ever forget that look of utter *annoyance* on the ex-sheriff's face as he flew by.

JOE MEASURED THEIR progress by studying the opposite wall of the canyon as they descended. They were barely halfway down after twenty minutes of trekking. He could make out the trail on the other side as it switchbacked up the wall, although lengths of it looked overgrown by brush.

"I'm looking forward to getting into that cold water," Butch said with a tight mouth. He was obviously in pain because of the intense heat he'd endured waiting on top for Farkus and McLanahan to lower themselves to the trail. Heat blisters rose everywhere his skin had been exposed.

Joe grunted. He was pleased the trail wasn't broken, but there was still a long way to go.

THEY FOUND MCLANAHAN'S body plastered facedown on an outstretched boulder just below the trail. He was absolutely dead. His arms and legs were splayed out as if he were trying to make a snow angel, but his body was oddly misshapen. There was very little blood, but Joe didn't doubt that most of his bones had been broken on impact. The ex-sheriff's head sagged toward the downhill side of the boulder like a water balloon propped on a sloping table.

"At least it was quick," Joe said, removing his hat for a moment. Butch did the same.

"Just for the record," Butch said, "I didn't push him, in case anyone was wondering."

"I wasn't," Joe said.

"Not that I'd blame you," Farkus said. "After all, he did come up here to kill you."

"If I wanted to kill him, he'd already have been dead," Butch said.

"Poor fat idiot," said Farkus. "He should have stayed back in West Virginia."

Joe hated to leave McLanahan's body splayed out like that. It wouldn't take long for the local scavengers—rodents, ravens, even the bald eagles that nested in the canyon—to locate and feed on the remains.

"We've got to try and take the body with us," Joe said.

"How?" Butch asked.

"I'm not sure."

"Leave it, I say," Farkus said flatly.

Instead, Joe and Butch flattened out on the narrow trail and reached down to the body, each grasping an ankle.

Joe said, "One-two-three . . ." and they heaved.

McLanahan's body was heavy, though, and severely broken. Joe realized to his horror he was pulling on the leg but it was elongating and narrowing as he did so because the bones were broken inside and the trunk of the body wasn't lifting. Joe grunted and pulled and so did Butch, but all they managed to do was upset the equilibrium of the body until it slipped over the side of the boulder toward the river below.

"Let go!" Joe shouted, so they wouldn't be carried down with it.

The body thumped against another rock outcropping on the way down, and cartwheeled into the river with a booming splash.

Joe gathered himself up. He was winded and couldn't shake the sensation he'd had when the leg stretched.

"That probably wasn't my best idea," he said.

Butch simply nodded in agreement.

"OH, NO," Butch said in a whisper a few minutes after they'd dropped McLanahan's body. Joe turned to him to find out the source of his concern.

Butch stood rigid on the trail, looking straight up.

Joe followed his gaze.

Twists of orange flame—fire whirls—could be seen darting over the rim of the canyon where the trailhead began. Like snake's tongues, they shot out into the opening and snapped back.

"The wind must really be whipping up there," Joe said.

As he spoke, flaming embers crossed the slice of sky above them from the south rim to the north. A moment later, the brush on the northern rim ignited with a flash.

"It jumped the canyon," Joe said.

"How are we gonna get out of here?" Farkus wondered aloud.

33

THE CORE OF HIS BODY WAS SO HOT FROM THE
fire that when he lowered himself to his chest in the Middle Fork of the Twelve Sleep River, Joe expected the water
to sizzle and steam to rise, but it didn't. Clamping his hat
on tight so it wouldn't float away, he slipped beneath the
surface. It was instantly quiet, and the water was clear and
cold. Joe opened his eyes to see the multicolored riverbed
of smooth potato-sized rocks, and three fat cutthroat trout
finning in the current near an undercut bank. The fish just
held there with a minimum of effort, something Joe wished
he could do.

He lowered his boots to the riverbed and stood up.
When he broke the surface the sounds came back: the well-
muscled flow of the river, the roar of the fire hundreds of
feet above. Joe let the cool water chill and soothe him.

"Oh, God," Butch said after resurfacing, "it feels so good."

Joe looked over to see Butch standing with his eyes closed and a smile of sweet relief on his face. He imagined how wonderful the cold water must feel on the open blisters and burned skin.

Farkus entered slowly, tentatively, cautious step by cautious step, until he was in to his knees.

"Come on in," Joe said. "It's great."

"I can't swim."

"It isn't deep enough to drown. We're both standing."

Farkus winced. "Any water is deep enough to drown." With that, he stepped forward, slipped on a river rock, and flailed his arms and went under. He came up sputtering and cursing several feet downstream.

THE THREE OF THEM stood in the river without speaking after that, each with his own thoughts. Joe let his body cool until he had goose bumps on his flesh. He looked straight up at the narrow opening of the canyon as if at another world. It was hell up there.

Although it was mid-morning, the sky was dark and mottled. Tongues of flame slashed out from both sides of the canyon. Despite how far away they were from the top, ash fell softly around them to be carried downstream.

Finally, Farkus said, "How long do we stay here before we climb out?"

"We're not climbing out," Joe said. "That fire will be burning all around us for a long time."

"Then what do we do?" he said, a high note of panic in his voice. "Do we build a tepee and stay down here?"

"We could borrow those poles up there," Butch said as a joke, but Farkus didn't smile. Joe noted that Butch's mood had improved markedly since they'd found the water.

Joe said, "The only thing we can do is go down the river."

"Have you ever been down it?" Farkus asked.

Joe shook his head. The Twelve Sleep Wilderness Area had been so designated because the canyon and the river were nearly impenetrable. There were no roads in and very few trails. It was wild and steep and ancient and not navigable except by adventurers in kayaks in the early runoff season.

"I've always wanted to see it, though," Joe said.

"There's something wrong with you," Farkus replied.

Joe grinned. Marybeth had often said the same thing.

WITH FARKUS AND BUTCH clinging to a dry pileup of debris, Joe scouted downriver.

There wasn't enough water in the river to swim freely, and the canyon walls were so sheer they couldn't walk more than a few feet on the dry bank. Going downstream was their only option, but there didn't seem to be an easy or practical way to do it. Because of the pitch of the riverbed, Joe assumed the river conditions changed around every bend. There would be long, deep pools leading to furious rapids to stretches where it looked like a boulder field that just happened to have a river going through it.

He stood knee-deep in an eddy with his hands on his hips, shaking his head.

When he returned to the others and told them what he could see downriver, he stopped in mid-sentence.

"What?" Farkus said. "What's wrong?"

"Nothing's wrong," Joe said, studying the debris pileup. For years, trees that had been dislodged upriver had been washed down during flood years and runoff months. The pile they were on was dense with interlocked driftwood that had been washed smooth and was pale white in color. It looked like some kind of boneyard. But simply because the pile was wood, Joe knew, didn't mean it would float. Most of the lengths, he guessed, were fatally waterlogged.

Butch seemed to read his mind and swiveled where he sat. He pointed at a broken tree trunk near the top of the pile that was eighteen inches in circumference and eight or nine feet long. It was high enough on the pile, Joe thought, that it might be a recent addition and wouldn't be heavy with water. It looked stout enough to hold them all, and there were enough nubs on it where branches had once been that could serve as handgrips.

"That just might be our boat," Joe said.

IT TOOK NEARLY a half hour to free the log from the pile because it was so entangled in the debris, but they finally were able to free it and roll it down the river. The log bobbed in the water and didn't submerge, and Butch held it in place while Joe and Farkus reached around it and found places to hang on.

The surface of the log was smooth and slick, the bark blasted off by scouring water, but it was dry and buoyant. On the count of three, they lifted their feet off the riverbed and pushed it out into the deepest part of the river.

It floated.

"This might just work if we can keep it pointed down-river," Joe said. "If we let the back end swing around, we might get hung up on rocks or more debris. That would be bad."

They found their grips and balance on the log—Joe was on the left side of the log with his right arm draped over the top, Butch was on the right a few feet behind, and Farkus switched between the left and right side around the stump of the log depending on which way it drifted.

"Are you guys about ready?" Joe asked.

Before either could answer, there was a large explosion on the surface of the water between the log and the bank, and the splash slapped across their faces.

Joe's first thought was that rocks were being dislodged from the canyon walls and dropping down into the river. But when he squeezed the water out of his eyes, he looked up to see the silhouette of a large mule deer, the antlers in velvet, dropping through the sky right toward them. It was trailing a stream of smoke like a shot-up fighter plane about to crash.

"*Duck*—it's coming right at us . . ." he shouted, before letting go of the log and submerging.

A herd of deer had been trapped, he guessed. They'd retreated as far as they could to the rim of the canyon, but there was no way to outflank the fire. They'd bunched on

the rim as the flames burnt their hides until they actually
tried in vain to *jump the canyon*.

The buck deer hit the log with a concussive impact that
boomed through the water. Joe looked up to see thrashing
arms, legs, and hooves in a cloud of white bubbles and
swirls of blood. The end of the log itself was driven down
in front of his vision by the weight of the buck—before
rolling out from beneath it and righting itself.

When he came to the surface, he looked into the frightened eyes of Butch Roberson, who was standing a couple
of feet away. Their boat-log was floating slowly downriver,
just out of reach.

And there was no sign of Dave Farkus.

"You get the log," Joe said to Butch. "I'll look for
Farkus."

Joe took a deep breath and again dropped beneath the
surface.

He could see two still bodies a few feet downstream,
tumbling in lazy slow motion along the river rocks. One
was the buck—its back broken, ribbons of blood streaming
out from its snout, its hide horribly burned—and the other
was Farkus.

Joe closed the distance quickly and managed to grasp
Farkus by his shirt collar. There was no resistance—no
indication of life or struggle—as he pulled him up. The
river was shallow enough that he could stand and breathe,
and he kept Farkus above the surface by reaching under
the man's arms and pulling Farkus's back tight to his chest.
Joe backed his way to the narrow bank and lowered Farkus
to the river rocks.

The man was breathing, but his breath was soft and shallow. Farkus's left shoulder was asymmetrical, and when Joe bent over and loosened his shirt he could see the shoulder—and possibly the clavicle and sternum—had been crushed by the impact.

Farkus moaned, opened his eyes briefly, then passed out again.

"Only *you* would nearly get killed by a *falling deer*," Joe said to Farkus, hoping the power of the fall hadn't broken too many bones inside the man.

BUTCH SPLASHED HIS WAY over with the log in tow. They lifted Farkus and placed him facedown on the log as if straddling it, with his hands and legs dangling down into the water and his head resting on its ear on the trunk itself. They decided not to bind him to the log in any way so he wouldn't slip off, but try to keep him balanced between them. If they tied him on, Joe thought, and the log flipped or got away from them in a rapid . . .

JOE AND BUTCH walked the log into the deepest part of the river, until the current leaned into them from behind. They pushed off and raised their feet out in front a foot or so below the surface and let the log float them.

As if he were guiding a fisherman on a drift boat, Joe kept his eyes downriver at all times. The river was technical and challenging; the trick was to anticipate the deepest runs and try to stay in the faster-moving water most of the time. But when the current looked like it would speed up and suck them into exposed boulders or dead trees or the cliff face itself, they'd have to maneuver the log so it would skirt the hazards but still keep floating.

It didn't take long for Joe and Butch to sync, to read each other's thoughts and keep the log—and Farkus—moving forward. When the bow of the log started to drift to the left, Joe's side, Butch would drop a boot deep until it caught on a rock and the makeshift craft would correct to the right. They learned to slow it by dragging their feet on the riverbed like anchors, and turn it quickly if one man set his feet and the other lunged forward. They spoke very few words and navigated by feel and intuition.

"River right," Joe would say, and Butch would either anchor a foot or shift his weight to cajole the log in that direction.

"River left—*hard*," Joe would grunt, digging in so Butch could swing the craft over to avoid a series of blade-like rocks that blocked the right channel like a row of tombstones in a Civil War cemetery.

THE SOUND of the river was omnipresent, but Joe could tell the intensity of the fire above was dissipating. Either the timber on top there was already burned to the ground or the fire hadn't yet reached it—he couldn't tell. The narrow band of sky was still choked with smoke and light diffused through it.

Despite how dire their situation was, Joe allowed himself to be astounded by some of the sights and features they floated by. He vowed to himself to come back someday, maybe with an experienced kayaker, and run the river with time to appreciate it. There was no wilder river in the mountains. It had never been dammed because it was impractical in the canyon, and there wasn't enough water in it to be used for navigation or even to float ties or lumber when the railroad had been built downstream or the towns constructed. It was useless for irrigation because of the canyon walls. The Middle Fork was rocky, foamy, untamed, and amoral. Few human beings had left a mark on it of any kind.

Joe knew that the Middle Fork would eventually feed into the North Fork of the Twelve Sleep River several miles downstream, according to maps he'd studied. But river miles were different than map miles, and included bends, channels, and meanders that could double or triple the actual distance on paper. At the confluence of the Middle Fork and North Fork was a popular Forest Service campground that would likely be occupied by campers—if they hadn't yet been evacuated. Joe thought it unlikely, since the fire had spread so fast.

Campers meant vehicles, cell phones, and possibly medical supplies for Farkus. It also meant the end of the trail for Butch Roberson, one way or other. Joe thought Butch had to know that.

But first they had to get there.

IN SOME STRETCHES where the canyon walls were especially close and the spray hung in the air, the fast river created an ecosystem of its own, Joe noted. There were ponderosa pines growing almost parallel to the canyon wall itself that were eight feet in circumference and reached sixty feet in the air. They were the tallest—and oldest—trees Joe had ever seen in the mountains. Unfamiliar orchidlike wildflowers in vibrant colors clung to small shelves along the way, nurtured by the steady spray and almost constant shadow. Butch nodded at ancient hieroglyphics drawn on slatelike slabs. Joe could make out human forms, spears, bows and arrows. The stick men appeared to be hunting bison, although the bison looked more like wildebeests than the buffalo Joe was used to. He wished he had a camera.

But whenever Joe's concentration wandered from studying the river ahead, they'd drift one direction or the other and have to overcorrect. Or Farkus would moan pitifully or vomit. Joe noted that Farkus's shoulder seemed to have doubled in size since the deer hit him, and dark discoloration was creeping out on his neck from under his collar. He continued to drift in and out of consciousness, but something inside him kept him clinging to the log regardless.

THE WATER WAS COLD and was fed by springs and snowmelt high above. While it had been welcome at first, given the heat of the fire, Joe was wary of hypothermia setting in. His limbs were numb and tight and at times not responsive. It was as if the cold water was sapping his strength away. When they floated through a patch of sunlight, he basked in it and tilted his face up toward the source of the warmth.

When he glanced at Farkus, he saw that he, too, was cold. His skin was ghostly white, and his lips were pale and tinged with ultramarine.

THEY FLOATED THE FIRST HOUR—Joe guessed it had been three miles at best—without any serious mishaps. Given the circumstances, Joe felt almost ashamed of himself for enjoying the ride.

Until they heard the roar up ahead of them that sounded like the booming of thunder.

But it wasn't thunder.

34

SAVAGE RUN CANYON PUSHED IN ON THE NAR-
row river, which pinched the flow of water and speeded it
up. Joe looked frantically right and left, looking for a place
they could lay up so he could detach from the craft and
scout ahead, but there were no banks—only slick vertical
walls.

Ahead, the river narrowed in even more, and Joe
couldn't see beyond a sharp V of rock a hundred yards
ahead of them. Beyond the V there was no sign of the
river in the distance. Which meant it dropped sharply in
elevation.

"Oh, man," Butch said.

Joe tried to climb up the side of the log to get a glimpse
of what was in front of them, but when he did he nearly
tipped Farkus into the water.

"Have you ever heard of Middle Fork Falls?" Joe shouted above the growing roar.

Butch looked over with fear in his eyes. "No."

"I haven't, either," Joe said. "So maybe it's just a drop or rapid ahead and not a waterfall."

"What should we do?" Butch shouted.

The river seemed to rise and bunch up with coiled power, as if it were gathering to propel them through the V. The walls on both sides shot by. Joe tentatively dropped his left boot to gauge the depth of the river, but he couldn't touch bottom.

"Keep us in the middle and hold on tight," Joe said. "Shout if it looks like we're going to hit something."

Butch nodded frantically, then turned to face the V as they powered into it.

Joe shouted into Farkus's ear: *"Wake up, Dave, and hold on."*

Farkus raised his head, looked ahead, and screamed.

THE FIRST SENSATION as they plummeted through the V was of exploding sunshine and weightlessness. The bow of the log was suspended in the air for a moment, and when Joe glanced up the length of it, he saw not river but tree-tops. Then it tipped and plunged.

There was a Middle Fork Falls after all, and the log rode it almost straight down in a twenty-foot drop. Joe could do nothing other than wrap his arms around the trunk and press his face into the slick wood. The momentum of the plunge knocked his legs back until they were parallel with the log itself, and they knifed into a deep pool below—immense silence, again—before floating back to the surface.

Joe did a quick inventory. Butch Roberson was sputtering and choking on water, but had held on. Farkus was moaning and had slipped over to Joe's side, so Joe shoved the man back up on top and in balance.

While he did, Joe almost didn't notice that the log was once again picking up speed.

"Jesus—look what's ahead," Butch yelled.

Farkus shouted, "I'm holding on!"

Joe swung around and could see the river. It was a terrible sight. From where they were until the river finally made a sharp bend to the left a quarter-mile below, it was angry white foam punctuated by rocks. The pitch of the river dropped steadily toward the bend below. Joe could detect no theme to the river, no central current or deeper passage where they could safely avoid the hazards. It was as if the river itself was being fed down a rocky chute.

Joe swung himself around back into position and got his feet out ahead of him. He craned his head up to look for deeper water—the darker, the deeper—and he judged by the speed they were going they'd be literally on top of navigable water before they could see it. Running the rapids would demand split-second adjustments.

"I'll call it out if I can," Joe said. "If you get thrown off, just lean back in the current and keep your feet out in front of you."

"Gotcha," Butch hollered. "Take us through it, Captain!"

Joe almost smiled.

THEY FLEW DOWN the rapids like a pinball bouncing from post to post, bumper to bumper. Joe called out, *"Left, left, right, left, right-right-right! Left, left, right . . ."*

All senses on high, Joe didn't think; he saw and reacted and yelled. The nose of the log swung from side to side to avoid rocks, sometimes riding up the side of a boulder for a moment before settling back down in the current. The chutes between the rocks were so narrow he banged his knees and thighs on them as they caromed down, and Joe's left knee hit a boulder so hard he felt the impact all the way into his hip socket. His left leg was so numb he actually glanced down immediately after the impact to see if it was still attached. It was.

Halfway down the rapids, Farkus regained consciousness and raised his head. When he saw what they were in the middle of, he shrieked and clung even harder to the log.

Which was good. Joe had almost forgotten about Farkus.

THEY BANKED HARD RIGHT around a huge boulder with Joe on the outside pushing and scrambling and Butch on the inside at pivot. When the front of the log nosed around the rock, Joe glanced up to see a hollow-eyed Kyle McLanahan, propped up as if sitting in a pile of driftwood, staring back at him. McLanahan's torso was out of the water, and his arms were propped up on lengths of debris as if he were leaning back in his easy chair watching a football game. His head was cocked slightly to the side. His face was bone-white and slack, his mouth slightly open.

In reaction, Joe nearly lost his grip on the log, but he realized McLanahan was still dead and his body had washed all the way downriver from his fall until it caught in the pileup.

Several thoughts came to Joe at once before the current built up again and swept them away:

- *It still hadn't sunk in yet, the fact that ex-sheriff Kyle McLanahan was dead.*
- *McLanahan had been in the valley just slightly longer than Joe. They'd known each other for twelve miserable years. Although he'd schemed and plotted against Joe and had made decisions that cost good men their lives and mobility, McLanahan was a worthy adversary.*
- *Sheriffs didn't seem to do very well in Twelve Sleep County.*

And . . .

- *Dead bodies in cold mountain rivers took on unique characteristics of their own—the skin remained well preserved, predation was rare, they didn't bloat. Dead bodies in cold rivers became mountain mummies, at least for a while.*

THEY GOT THROUGH the worst of the rock garden with bruises, abrasions, and no broken bones. They were able to lay up in an eddy with a hundred yards still to go, and fortunately the eddy was shallow enough they could stand again on the riverbed.

Joe and Butch panted until they got their breath back and once again Joe was grateful the water was so cold. If it wasn't, he knew, he'd be able to feel the injuries he'd sustained. When he looked down into the water, he could see several small spirals of blood coming from gashes on his left leg. The pant leg of his Wranglers was tattered, ribbons of it floating in the current. He was surprised he hadn't lost his boot.

"I can't believe we got through that," Farkus said in a croak, looking back up at the rapids above them.

"We?" Butch said.

"I'm hallucinating, I think," Farkus said. "I had this dream I saw Sheriff McLanahan sitting on some wood, watching us go by."

WITH BUTCH HOLDING the log in place, Joe splashed to the foot of the eddy and scouted ahead. The last hundred yards wasn't as rocky, but it was a steep narrow flume that ended in a wide slow run before it went around a bend. After what they'd been through, it looked like a picnic.

He realized, as he gazed downstream, that there was warm sun on his shoulders. He turned. The mouth of the canyon was behind them now. The terrain surrounding them was still mountainous but softer, flatter, tamer, with folds rather than cliffs. And although the sky was thick with smoke that gave every vista a sepia-toned look, the fire hadn't advanced this far downriver yet.

Joe felt a huge weight lift from his shoulders. They'd gone through the worst. He'd never heard of anyone running the Middle Fork in August when the water was so low—probably because no one in his right mind would try, he thought. He stanched back a feeling of guilty pride.

When he returned to the log, he saw that Farkus had passed out again. Butch stood waist-deep in the water, keeping the log in place. His expression was pained but stoic, and Joe wondered if the reason was because of the many injuries he'd sustained or because he knew, like Joe did, that the campground would be less than an hour away.

ALTHOUGH THE FLUME wasn't marred by rocks, it was steep and fast. Joe felt exhilarated by the descent, which was fueled by a combination of momentum and adrenaline. He felt intense sun on his face and his hat wanted to lift off his head in the wind. They shot the pitch like seasoned professionals, Joe thought. He'd grown attached to the floating log, and thought that he'd like to load it on a trailer and take it home. Then he remembered it was only a tree trunk, although a special and much-loved tree trunk, and that Marybeth would rightly wonder why it was in the garage.

When they hit the pool at the bottom and slowed down, he secretly wanted to do it again.

———

TEN MINUTES LATER, Joe and Butch tugged the log along behind them through the warm shallows. It was no longer a boat, Joe thought, but a kind of floating stretcher for Dave Farkus.

The riverbed was soft and sandy, and the water was warm. His cuts and bruises came to life as he warmed up and slogged along, and he noticed Butch grimacing as well. Now that they were out of the rapids and falls, the price they'd paid to run them was coming due.

Joe looked downriver. The water was knee-deep and still. Behind them, the fire raged out of control, but the wind wasn't blowing north yet. When it did, and it was a matter of time, everything he could see on both banks would go up in flames. He felt small and powerless. It was a feeling he appreciated for the pure truth of it in a situation like that.

Joe thought this was the time to talk with Butch. Soon he wouldn't have the chance. As he took a long breath and began to speak, Butch interjected: "Joe, thank you for getting me through this. I couldn't have done it on my own."

Joe grunted.

"I mean, I've spent a lot of time in the mountains. I know my way around, and I've put myself in situations I had to think and work myself out of. But I've never run a river, and I never could have done what we just did."

Joe said, "Thanks."

"I'll remember this for the rest of my life," Butch said. "I'll remember what you did. This could have gone a bunch of different directions, I know that. But you saved my life. And the idiot Dave Farkus—you saved him, too."

Joe didn't respond to that. Instead, he said, "Butch, I know you had opportunities to make this go another way. You could have shoved Farkus off the log, or knocked me on the head, or just let go of the log and let me try to do this on my own. You could have escaped, is what I'm saying. It would have been easy. But you hung in there, and I appreciate that."

Joe glanced back to see if Farkus was awake. He was glad he wasn't.

"He's out again," Joe said. "I don't know how long he'll be under. So while we're just walking along here . . ."

Butch grinned in response, as if he'd been anticipating the questions.

"You know we're going to be at the campground pretty soon," Joe said. "Who knows who will be there, or what will happen. So since it's just you and me, and before we show up . . ."

"What?"

"There are decisions that need to be made."

"Yeah, I know," Butch said, resigned. "When you agreed to make sure that helicopter was coming, were you lying to me?"

Joe said, "Yes. It was out of my hands."

Butch nodded to himself, as if checking off a box in his mind.

"Were you setting me up?"

"No," Joe said. "I was hoping I could be there to intervene. That's the only reason I stayed with the EPA agent team. I wanted to be there when they found you so I could arrest you and keep you alive. Batista wanted blood."

Butch glanced over sharply, as if he hadn't considered that.

"The guy really wants to kill me, doesn't he?"

"Yes, he does."

"Do you know why?"

"Not yet. But you'll be the first to know when I find out. And I *will* find out."

A HALF HOUR LATER, Butch nodded in the general direction of Saddlestring. "Are the people down there with me or against me?"

Joe shrugged. "I don't know. It's all happened so fast and the facts aren't out yet. You haven't had the opportunity to tell your side. But when you do, you'll have some support, I think. Not when it comes to killing those agents, though. But no one in their right mind will think what Batista did to you is the right thing."

Butch nodded to himself and didn't turn his head to look at Joe. He seemed to be in turmoil, Joe thought.

Joe said, "Like I said, let's handle this locally. Turn yourself in to Sheriff Reed and Dulcie Schalk. You won't walk, but they'll be fair."

"And you'll make sure of that?" Butch asked with skepticism.

"I'll do my best," Joe said, and bit his tongue. He didn't want to say more.

"Okay, then," Butch said. "Let's do this right."

"Thank you, Butch."

Butch snorted, as if he really didn't have a choice. Although he did.

JOE CAME right out with it: "Butch, did you kill those two EPA agents?"

Butch feigned shock at the question, then said, "Of course I did."

"Were you alone at the time it happened?"

"Damn right."

"They just showed up and got out of their car and you happened to have your .223 and you just blew them away?"

"That's right."

"Did either one of them threaten you, or draw a gun?"

Butch paused, as if recalling the moment. He said, "The first one, the younger one, never should have pulled his gun. He didn't have a chance. I shot him first and he went down. The older one went for his weapon, and I got him before he could clear it. Hell, until that second, I didn't know those bastards were armed."

Joe felt his stomach clench. He wasn't sure if it was the aftereffect of the morning, the lack of food, or what Butch had just confessed. Or all three.

Joe said, "So you're saying you killed them without even knowing who they were?"

"That's what I'm saying, Joe."

"How do you feel about that?"

Butch hesitated, then said, "Just fine."

"You know one of them had a family, like you and me?"

"How would I know that?"

"You wouldn't, I guess," Joe said. "But you should care."

The bend of the river leading into the campground was in sight. For the first time that morning, he could hear the sounds of other people: motors racing, gravel crunching under tires, snatches of voices.

He didn't have much time left.

JOE SAID, "So after it was done, after those two agents were down, then what?"

"What do you mean?"

"What did you do next?"

"I fired up my tractor and buried them."

Joe nodded. "Why right there on your lot? I mean, it seems so obvious."

"I wasn't thinking clearly," Butch said. "It isn't every day I kill two guys. I just wanted them out of my sight, you know? I couldn't just leave them on the ground with holes in them."

"Right. So then what? You took their car?"

"Yeah," Butch said. "They left the keys in it when they got out. I drove it up Hazelton Road to a place where I knew I could dump it. I aimed it at the edge of the road and jumped out of the car and watched it go over. I was hacked off it didn't go all the way down the canyon to the bottom, but it got hung up in some trees instead."

"So that was you?"

"Of course," Butch said.

Joe trudged along, his legs on fire from cuts and bruises, his burned hand, his head wounds from the fight with Pendergast, and his muscles aching.

"So clear this up for me," Joe said. "You drove the EPA car off the road, but how did you get back to your lot?"

Butch started to answer, then set his mouth.

"I can't figure that one out," Joe said.

Butch shrugged but wouldn't meet Joe's eyes.

"And when you came out here, to Big Stream Ranch," Joe said, "you had to have had a ride or I would have seen your truck on the side of the road. How else would you get here?"

Butch shrugged.

Joe pressed, "When we first saw each other a couple of days ago, you know what we talked about."

"Yes."

"So I'm starting to get it, I think," Joe said. "You could have just shot me at that point and no one would know. I didn't know what had happened, or that anyone was looking for you. But you let me ride away."

Butch looked over and squinted as if he couldn't believe Joe even contemplated the fact that he could have hurt him.

Joe said, "I've been thinking a lot about it, the things you said and what we talked about. So I want to run something by you. This isn't an official interrogation, Butch. This is just you and me. But I need to know."

Butch took a deep breath and trudged ahead. Joe looked hard at the man, and saw himself.

And that's what it was.

Simple as that.

He almost didn't need to float his darkest theory out loud. But he did, anyway.

"YOU KNOW," Butch said softly after confirming it, "when you think about all of this, it's hard not to want to just throw up your hands and give up."

Joe looked over, still partially stunned by what they'd discussed.

"These guys," Butch said, "the EPA. They're supposed to protect the environment, right? That's why they exist."

Joe didn't respond.

Butch said, "They burned down the whole fucking mountain."

Joe said gently, "I know."

Butch barked a bitter laugh.

Joe said, "We're close to the campground, Butch."

THEY TRUDGED AROUND the bend of the river in the shallows and Joe noted the current had picked up slightly. The log bumped up against the back of his legs, as if it were a Labrador wanting to run again.

"We can float right through them," Joe offered. "They may not even know we're there. But that isn't our deal."

"A deal is a deal," Butch said.

Since he'd confirmed Joe's theory, Butch Roberson seemed to have deflated in height, power, and confidence. He seemed to Joe like a shell of his former self.

"I wasn't kidding," Joe said. "This was just between us."

"Thank you."

"Are you going to stick with your story?"

"Absolutely. And I trust you to keep it between us."

Joe nodded.

"You'd do the same thing, wouldn't you, Joe?" Butch asked.

Joe hesitated before saying, "Don't ask me that."

"You would. You're a good man."

Joe changed the subject.

"So do you want to float right through or pull over and give yourself up?"

Butch seemed overwhelmed that Joe had suddenly given him a choice. He said, "The second."

Then, with resignation: "I can't outrun them. There are too many of those guys."

Joe hesitated a moment and said, "You might find allies who will help keep you out of their hands. I have a friend who has operated off the grid for years. I'm sure he'd give you some help."

Butch nodded. "Yeah, I know there are people out there who could help me, like Frank Zeller. But why get other folks in trouble? This is my problem, not theirs."

"They may not think of it like that," Joe said.

"My mind is made up. Don't give me any more chances to change it."

"Okay, then," Joe said. "You'll need to give me that pistol. You won't be needing it anymore."

Butch reached back and handed it over. Joe tossed it toward the bank.

———

THE CAMPGROUND WAS BUSTLING, and it didn't take long to figure out why. Joe recognized vehicles, tents, communications vans, and personnel from the forward operating base on the Big Stream Ranch. They were establishing a new FOB, he reasoned, since the old one was being consumed by the fire. He assumed Batista had ordered the campground evacuated, and was establishing a new beachhead. Joe was impressed they'd been able to assemble and move so quickly. But he dreaded the fact that he was delivering Butch Roberson into the Lion's Den.

As they nosed the front of the log into the muddy bank of the campground, the cacophony of voices and activity went silent. Dozens of federal men and women turned their faces toward Joe and Butch, and there were gasps and open mouths.

Someone said, "Jesus, there he is."

Joe searched the crowd for Governor Rulon, but didn't see him. His new director, Lisa Greene-Dempsey, was there, however. She looked shocked to see him, and her eyes blinked quickly behind her designer glasses. Joe thought he must look like quite a sight: wet and torn clothing, disheveled appearance, streams of blood pouring down his legs into his boots.

Heinz Underwood shouldered through the crowd. To Joe, he grinned and said, "You made it, you crazy bastard." He pointed at Butch and said, "Arrest that man."

Several agents Joe didn't recognize started to advance. Beside him, Joe could feel Butch stiffen.

"No," Joe said, stepping in front of Butch and placing his right hand on the grip of his Glock.

The agents halted and looked back at Underwood for further instructions.

"Where's Batista?" Joe asked.

"He said he was called back to HQ," Underwood said, with a twinkle in his eye. "He's been gone an hour. He left in a hurry."

Joe acknowledged the news with a curt nod. It fit.

Lisa Greene-Dempsey said, "Warden Pickett, you need to stand aside. You need to cooperate."

"I'm through cooperating," Joe said, his tone flat.

To Greene-Dempsey, Joe said, "Call Sheriff Reed and get him down here now. This man will surrender to him and him only. He'll be in county lockup if you need to see him."

Underwood said to Greene-Dempsey, "This is a federal matter. You'll have to order your employee to turn over that man."

"Warden Pickett—" she said without enthusiasm, but Joe cut her off.

He said, "I made Butch a deal. He agreed to turn himself in to the sheriff."

Silence.

Joe meant it. His insides roiled, and he didn't want to draw his weapon.

Greene-Dempsey stepped forward, and Joe said softly, "That includes you, too, I'm afraid. Just make the call."

She stopped there and gasped for air. Then she raised her iPhone.

BEFORE JOE CLIMBED into the sheriff's department handicap van behind Butch Roberson in handcuffs, he plucked his badge off his uniform shirt and placed it in Lisa Greene-Dempsey's outstretched palm. She closed her fingers around it and shook her head sadly.

"You don't have to do this," she said.

"Yeah, I do," Joe said. "This has all put such a bad taste in my mouth, I don't think I'll ever shake it."

"You're in bad shape," she said. "You might feel different when this is all behind us."

"Is the governor still around?" Joe asked.

"He's somewhere in town," she said.

"Did my horse survive?"

"Your horse?"

"I let him go."

The director shrugged and shook her head. She didn't know anything about Toby.

Joe grunted and climbed into the van and slid the door shut behind him.

"Mike," Joe said to the sheriff, "can I borrow your phone? I need to call my wife."

Sheriff Reed handed his phone over.

As the van cleared the campground, spewing a roll of dust, Joe looked through the back window. Lisa Greene-Dempsey was saying something to Underwood, shaking her head while she did, and still clutching his badge.

Behind them, massive columns of yellow smoke rolled into the sky from the mountains.

"Thank you for what you did back there," Butch Roberson said.

Joe nodded.

"Ask Marybeth to tell Pam and Hannah I'm all right, okay?"

Joe and Roberson exchanged a long look of understanding.

"I will," Joe said.

AFTER HE'D TOLD MARYBETH he was safe but injured and he might be in the hospital for a few days, and she expressed relief, she said, "Something really odd happened this morning. Did you get my message?"

"No, what happened?"

"Pam asked to use the computer so she could check her email, and I pointed her to it. I'd left it on from last night when I called you. But when she sat down at it, her face turned white as a sheet. The EPA site was still up on the screen with Batista's photo and bio . . ."

Joe felt something flutter in his stomach.

". . . and Pam pointed to the photo of him and said, 'What is this asshole doing here? And why are they calling him Juan Julio Batista?'"

"Let me guess," Joe said. "She knew him as John Pate."

"And that's where things start to connect."

Joe noticed that as he spoke the name, Butch's head had snapped up sharply.

ONE WEEK
AFTER

35

WITH NATE ROMANOWSKI IN THE PASSENGER
seat of the pickup, Joe turned from the interstate onto the
state highway that led to the burning mountains. Joe wasn't
wearing his uniform anymore, which made him feel incom-
plete. Seven red shirts were in a pile in the corner of the
bedroom, where he'd thrown them as if they were radioac-
tive. Spare badges, name tags, his weapon and gear belt,
and a dog-eared laminate of the Miranda warning had been
tossed on top of the pile.

Joe glanced down. His personal Remington shotgun
was muzzle-down on the bench seat between them. He'd
loaded it with double-ought buckshot.

NATE WAS TALL AND ANGULAR, with piercing blue eyes
and a hatchet nose, and a short blond ponytail since he'd

grown his hair back from a year before. The leather strap of the shoulder holster that held his .500 Wyoming Express handgun stretched across a white T-shirt beneath his open pearl-button cowboy shirt.

As they climbed, Joe hit his headlights. Smoke was still heavy in the air, and he hadn't seen the sun or blue sky for a week. It was as if someone had placed a lid over the valley to keep it from boiling over.

There were no living trees on either side of the road, just skeletons with crooked black limbs. The ground was scorched and there were places where it still smoked. The air was bitter and sharp, and Joe's lungs ached from breathing it in.

"This reminds me of black-and-white footage from World War One," Nate said. "It looks like a moonscape."

Joe grunted.

"How big is the fire now?"

"Last I heard, it stretches a hundred miles to the north and sixty miles to the south. It moves about twenty to twenty-five miles a day depending on the wind."

"Big," Nate said.

"And getting bigger."

The local news was dominated by fire reports and stories of cabins and ranches being burned down, communities evacuated, smoke jumpers killed or injured. People wore masks when they went outside, and public health authorities cautioned young parents to keep their children indoors. Most of the residents of the Saddlestring retirement home had been flown to other locations where they could breathe.

"Where did you say we were headed?" Nate asked.

"A subdivision called Aspen Highlands."

"I hate cutesy names like that."

NATE HAD SIMPLY shown up on their doorstep three nights before. He'd been sitting on the porch reading a book when Marybeth drove Joe home from the hospital after they'd treated and released him for all of his injuries. Joe had been injured many times before without three days of hospital care, and cynically figured he'd been stuck there to give affidavits and statements regarding Butch Roberson rather than for the severity of his wounds. Dave Farkus was in the next room and he was recovering well. Joe had overheard Farkus telling an attractive nurse how he'd escaped death by bullet, fire, and a whitewater river. How he planned to sell his story to Hollywood.

When Nate saw them drive up, he raised his head and smiled a goofy smile, for Nate.

Marybeth braked a little too hard for Joe and flew out of the van to hug the falconer. She didn't even close her door.

Joe limped around the van and shut it, and turned to Nate and Marybeth. It was good to see Nate again, he thought.

Nate gestured toward the burning mountains and said, "Sorry. It looks like I'm too late."

Nate said to Marybeth, "I leave for a year and look what happens. Your husband burns the entire place to the ground."

"Actually," Joe said, "you're right on time."

"You've got something for me to do?"

"Yup."

"Now?"

"Give me a couple of days to sort it out," Joe said.

Nate nodded. "Good. I hear Sheridan has a kestrel. I'd like to see it."

Marybeth clapped her hands girlishly and said, "I know she'd love to show it to you, Nate."

JOE HAD TO SLOW DOWN the pickup as a yellow roll of smoke blew across the road. As he peered into the gloom, he couldn't see actual flames anywhere and he wondered what there was left to burn.

Nate said, "In the long run, the fire will be a good thing. New growth, aspen, all that."

"Yeah, yeah," Joe said. "Like I haven't heard that a thousand times in the last week."

"You're getting grumpy," Nate said.

"I keep thinking about Butch. How he could be me."

"Stop thinking so much."

"I've missed that kind of brilliant advice. Wait, no, I haven't," Joe said with an edge.

"So what's this guy's name we're going to visit?"

"Harry Blevins," Joe said. "Harry S. Blevins."

"And you learned about him how?"

"Matt Donnell, the real estate mogul," Joe said. "When he came by the house to tell Marybeth he'd sold the hotel, I asked Matt to use his contacts at the county records department to do a title search. He's the one who came up with Blevins."

"Ah."

Donnell had been practically bursting with the good news. He'd learned that the Bureau of Land Management was in the midst of a search for more space in the county because they'd outgrown their old building. Donnell had swooped in and offered the Saddlestring Hotel lot, and the supervisor in charge liked the location—right in the middle of town.

He'd get all his money back, Matt told Marybeth. There would be no profit and what he'd spent on repairs was lost, but the bulk of the investment would be returned. Joe had expected Marybeth to be pleased with the news, but she wasn't.

"They'll tear it down, won't they?" she had asked Donnell.

"Most certainly," he said, nodding.

"So they can throw up a perfect new nothingburger government office building," she said.

"Yes."

"Don't you see the irony in this, Matt?"

"Of course I do," he said. "But I'm not in the business of irony. I'm in the real estate business."

"It's a good place for you," Marybeth said to him, doing a shoulder roll and climbing the stairs toward their bedroom.

"I thought she'd be *happy*," Donnell said to Joe. He was obviously distressed.

Joe said, "Give her some time."

"It wasn't easy, convincing the BLM to buy that lot. What I'm saying is it cost me a little money, if you know what I mean."

Joe understood.

That's when he asked Donnell to do the title check.

"SO YOU'RE UNEMPLOYED," Nate said as they drove up Hazelton Road.

"Yup."

"When do you have to move out of your house?"

"We haven't gotten that far yet," Joe said. "I think they'll give me to the end of the month at least. The new director wants to spin it so it doesn't look like I quit. The wheels of government turn pretty slow, you know."

"Except when they don't," Nate said, and grinned. "So what are you going to do?"

Joe shrugged. "Something different. Something honest. I have to be able to look at myself in the mirror in the morning."

"And what would that be?"

"I'm figuring it out, Nate. Governor Rulon has called my cell phone twice in the last couple of days. He says he wants to offer me a job."

"Really?"

"Really."

"And you haven't called him back?"

"Not yet."

Nate nodded and didn't say anything for a few minutes. Then: "Since I've been gone, I've come up with a few projects of my own. It's worked out pretty well. I'm in demand. Do you want to hear about it and maybe partner up?"

Joe looked over and squinted. "I don't know. Do I?"

Nate smiled wolfishly. "It depends if you've completely shucked that Dudley Do-Right thing of yours."

"I haven't."

"Then this is a subject best left for another time," Nate said.

Joe was curious but not curious enough to ask. There was something disconcerting about Nate, he thought. Nate seemed too jolly, too devil-may-care, where in the past he'd been intense yet honorable in his way. Joe chalked it up to the terrible things that had happened to Nate in the past year, and understood how those tragedies could affect a man.

Still . . .

COUNTY ATTORNEY DULCIE SCHALK had come to their house two days before and had told Joe and Marybeth the governor was on a rampage against Batista.

It turned out rancher Frank Zeller had noticed an extra horse grazing in his pasture several days before that turned out to be Toby. Zeller had retrieved the digital recorder and delivered it in person to Rulon, who'd listened to it.

Although Dulcie said she didn't know any of the details, Julio Batista had been placed on administrative leave pending an investigation of his actions—not the least of which was the unauthorized use of a Hellfire missile. The governor wanted Batista arrested and was making the case for it to anyone who would listen, including Dulcie.

Dulcie said she was pursuing charges against Juan Julio Batista for the murder of Jimmy Sollis. So far, the federal agencies were refusing to turn over the audio and video footage of the drone strike, but Dulcie was tenacious, and she was certain she'd receive it in the weeks ahead. When she did, she said, she'd file the papers to have Batista extradited to Twelve Sleep County.

Joe said, "The murder of Jimmy Sollis? That's it? He'll claim fog-of-war stuff. If you're lucky, you'll get him on manslaughter."

"It's better than nothing," Dulcie said, defensive.

"There's more," Joe said, and waited for Marybeth to hand Dulcie the file she'd put together.

"And maybe," Joe said, "we can get him to deliver *himself.*"

JOE HAD VISITED Butch Roberson in the county lockup the day before. Roberson wore an orange jumpsuit with TSCDC—Twelve Sleep County Detention Center— stenciled across his back and over a breast pocket. He was shaved and cleaned up, although his arms were covered with bandages from his wounds. He looked smaller through the thick glass of the visiting booth, Joe thought.

Joe asked Butch if he'd changed his mind about his confession.

Roberson said he hadn't.

"I need to ask you about representation," Butch said. "I don't know anything about being a criminal. I'm supposed to show up tomorrow before Judge Hewitt for a charging ceremony or whatever they call it. I built an addition on Hewitt's house. He knows me, so I think that's good. The county has said they'd give me a lawyer free of charge."

"Duane Patterson," Joe said. "He's the public defender. He hasn't handled any high-profile cases like yours."

"He seems like a nice guy, though."

"He is," Joe said. "You could do worse."

"I got a call from some public defense firm," Butch said. "They said they have a team of lawyers who want to screw the EPA. I'm fine with that. I was starting to wonder if there was anyone out there who cared at all what they did to us."

"That's good to hear," Joe said.

Butch shook his head. "It's kind of out of my hands now, isn't it? Now I'm just a peon in the system."

"There are some good people out there," Joe said. "You should at least listen to them. Even if they take you on to prove a point, it's *your* point."

THEN JOE ASKED HIM if he knew the name Harry S. Blevins.

It took a moment for Butch to understand. When he did, his face flushed and he said, "That son of a bitch. So it was him, huh?"

"I think it was," Joe said.

"Then why didn't he ever call me? Why didn't he talk to me man-to-man?"

Joe said, "I don't think they do that."

"SO WHAT do you want me to do?" Nate asked as Joe turned past the half-burned sign for Aspen Highlands. "Do you want me to put him down?"

"No," Joe said, not sure if Nate was kidding. "Just be scary. Follow my lead and be the scary Nate."

"I think I can do that."

A TEAM OF SMOKE JUMPERS out of Missoula had been dropped on the location and had saved the structures within Aspen Highlands by igniting a backfire around the perimeter of the subdivision that destroyed the dry fuel before the wildfire could get to it. The crowns of many of the trees had burned, though, as well as a buck-and-rail fence that marked the development. Aspen Highlands was an oasis of green within a desert of scorched earth. Joe credited the smoke jumpers, of course, but wondered who had the clout to convince them to divert resources to spare the development when the wildfire was threatening every town and city throughout the front range of the northern Rocky Mountains.

Joe eased to a stop adjacent to the Roberson lot. The tractor was still there, and the hole where the agents had been found hadn't been filled in. The grass inside the perimeter tape was trampled down flat by so many law enforcement personnel.

"This is where it happened, eh?" Nate asked quietly.

"Yup."

"I imagined more land. This isn't much."

Joe nodded. He left the truck running and opened the door and said, "I'll be right back."

He returned to the faded plywood that had been

used as a target. He tossed it into the empty bed of his pickup.

"What was that about?" Nate asked.

"Nothing," Joe said. Then he gestured toward the two-story log cabin above them with the green metal roof. He remembered looking at it the day the agents were found.

"That's the retirement home of Harry Blevins," Joe said.

"Nice place," Nate said.

"Nice pension," Joe said.

THERE WAS A NEW-MODEL Jeep Cherokee parked beneath a carport on the side of the cabin.

"He's home," Joe said.

"Does he live alone?" Nate asked.

"As far as I know. From what Matt Donnell told me, he's divorced. He splits his time between here and Denver, where he also has a house."

"What's he retired from?" Nate asked.

"Used to be a supervisor for the IRS."

"Please let me shoot him in the head."

JOE WASN'T SURPRISED that Blevins knew they were there before he knocked. It was quiet in Aspen Highlands, and Blevins no doubt heard the pickup turn up into his driveway.

He opened the door as Joe approached carrying the shotgun. Nate was a step behind.

Blevins was stooped and slight with a wisp of gray hair. He had close-set eyes, a thin nose, and a small mouth offset by a prominent lantern jaw. Joe thought the man gave off a palpable aura of unpleasantness.

"Can I help you find something?" the man said. "Why are you armed?"

"You're Harry S. Blevins?" Joe asked.

"Yes. And who are you?"

"I'm Joe Pickett. I used to be the game warden around here. You might have seen me wearing a red uniform shirt a week and a half ago. I was standing around on the Roberson lot with the sheriff's department. I'm guessing you could see the whole thing from here."

Blevins made a sour face and shook his head slightly, as if denying the premise of what Joe had said.

"I wanted to see what you looked like, once I figured it out. You look exactly like I thought you would."

"I don't hunt or fish," he said. "There's no need for a game warden to come to my place."

"I'm no longer a game warden," Joe said. "I'm here as a local."

"You got fired?"

"I quit. Which means I don't have to play by the rules anymore."

Blevins studied Joe's face. Joe didn't flinch. He noticed that Blevins shot several cautious glances toward Nate as well. Nate had that effect on people.

Blevins said, "It's nice to meet you, but I really don't have time for this right now."

Joe said, "When the investigation was going on, did you

see me when I turned around and looked right at your nice cabin here? Did a little bit of fear go through you that I might figure it out?"

"Really, I don't have time for this . . ." Blevins said, and stepped back to swing the door closed.

Nate lurched over Joe's shoulder and shot his arm out and stopped the closure with the heel of his hand. Nate said, "My friend is talking to you. Don't be so fucking rude."

For the first time, fear flickered across Blevins's eyes.

"You didn't want your view of the lake blocked by the Roberson home," Joe said. "You got a call from a man who said he could help you if you agreed to keep him informed on the progress of the construction."

"I don't know what you're talking about."

His voice was weak and small, Joe thought, and betrayed exactly the opposite of the words he spoke.

Joe said, "I wondered how you knew Julio Batista, but he actually contacted you, didn't he? Because you had a mutual interest? Then you and Batista set things in motion and you just sat back here in your nice cabin and let the system destroy Butch."

"That's ridiculous," Blevins said.

"Whatever. But there's no doubt you lit the Butch Roberson time bomb."

"I didn't know he'd murder anyone. I honestly had no idea that could happen."

Joe hesitated, then asked, "Did you see him pull the trigger?"

"No. I was in town the day it happened."

"Convenient," Joe said. Then: "You never spent a minute getting to know him, did you? As far as you knew, he was a redneck in a ball cap, right? You didn't know he was a local contractor who had a family, did you? To you he was a stupid gorilla who fired up his loud tractor and wanted to screw up your perfect view of the lake. And when things got out of control, you didn't do anything to stop it, did you? When Butch showed up here two weeks ago and started up his tractor after a year of leaving you alone, you got right back on the phone, didn't you?"

Before Blevins could speak, Nate growled, "What an asshole."

Joe said to Blevins, "Five men dead, one man in jail, a good family wrecked. Thousands of animals and birds burned to death. An entire forest incinerated. You're quite a guy, aren't you?"

"Look," Blevins said, panic in his voice, "I'm not responsible for all the things that happened. I was just making a call."

Joe said, "It'll be interesting when Butch Roberson's attorneys find out about you and put you on the stand. Once people find out what you did, you'll spend the rest of your life looking over your shoulder. Right, Nate?"

"And you might see *me*," Nate said in a homicidal whisper.

"You can't prove any of this," Blevins said. Beads of perspiration sequined his upper lip. He swiveled his head toward Nate and said, "So who are you?"

Joe cringed because he'd seen raw red meat tossed to problem grizzlies before—and this was the same thing.

But there was a hesitation on Nate's part. Then an explosion. Nate shot his hand out and grasped Blevins's ear and twisted. The man cried out and bent forward. Nate leaned into him with his huge gun drawn and pressed the muzzle into Blevins's temple.

"I can twist your ear off your head or blow your brains to Nebraska," Nate said evenly. "Or I can do both, one after the other, which is my preference."

Blevins mewled and choked, his head down. Joe considered stopping it, but he didn't want to.

Nate leaned in closer to Blevins, and thumbed back the hammer of the .50-caliber revolver until it locked.

Nate said to Blevins, "I've torn apart men much better than you with my hands. I've twisted their noses and ears off and I've ripped their arms and legs out of the sockets and beat them over their heads with them. I *like* doing it to those who deserve it, that's what you need to understand. You deserve it more than most. So if you don't start singing *right now* to my friend Joe, you'll be eating your own nuts in less than ten seconds. Got that?"

Joe was stunned. But he appreciated it.

Blevins mewled like a cat, then said, "I called Julio when Roberson showed up with his tractor. I never knew what would happen."

"That's why those agents showed up so fast," Joe said. "It's been driving me crazy. So when did you last talk to Batista?"

"Why is that important?"

Nate twisted the muzzle into Blevins's temple, breaking the skin. Blevins cried out.

"Answer the question," Joe said.

"A couple of days ago. He called me and asked if I knew anything about Pam Roberson giving a press conference today."

Joe knew all about it because Marybeth had written the release and emailed it to every newspaper and electronic media outlet within five hundred miles.

"What did you tell him?" Joe asked.

"That it was scheduled for this afternoon."

"Did he ask for directions to her house?"

After a beat, Blevins said, "Yes."

Nate's finger tightened on the trigger.

"Please, dear God, get him off me," Blevins pleaded.

Nate looked to Joe and grinned. Joe was unsettled. Something had happened to Nate to drive him further over the moral line he'd always insisted was there. Joe had no doubt that if he said, "Waste him," Blevins would be history. Headless history.

Instead, Joe drew his new digital recorder out of his breast pocket and checked it and showed it to Blevins.

"You'll hear this again in court."

Blevins, still in Nate's headlock, looked up with equal measures of horror and confusion.

ON THEIR WAY back to Joe's house, Nate said, "There are too many assholes like that. This is why we need a revolution."

Joe didn't respond. He'd been able to contain his red-hot anger at Blevins while he was there in order to get the

evidence, but it had been tough work. Nate's overreaction
had skewed things.

"I'm worried about you," Joe said, not looking over to
Nate in the passenger seat.

"What? You thought I'd blow his brains out?"

"Yes."

"You told me to be scary. You told me to be Nate," he
said angrily.

"Still," Joe said. "I got the impression you really wanted
to do it."

"I did," Nate said quickly. "There's nothing worse on
this earth than privileged bureaucratic assholes who work
the system. They never get caught, and if they do, there
are no real consequences. I wanted to show that asshole
some consequences."

"I understand," Joe said. "But he'll be shunned—or
worse—when his name gets out and folks find out he's the
one who started all this. He'll wish he was in jail."

"Then we're cool?" Nate asked.

Joe was unclear how to answer.

Nate said, "I saw Marybeth's post on that website, asking me for help. You don't understand or want to know my
situation these days, but when I saw that she asked for help,
I dropped everything and showed up. So cut me a fucking
break, Joe. I did it for you."

"And I appreciate it," Joe said.

"We can always go back," Nate offered. "I could blow
him away and burn his house down."

Joe shook his head and said, "I'm tired of fires. Plus,
we've got bigger fish to fry."

He drew his cell phone out and called Marybeth at home.

"Honey, are Hannah or Pam Roberson still there?"

"Hannah is here, of course," Marybeth said. "Pam's going over her statement for the press conference later. I think there will be plenty of press, based on the calls we've received."

"Good for her."

ANOTHER CALL FLASHED on the screen of Joe's phone, and when he saw who it came from, he said to Marybeth, "I have to take this—it's Sheriff Reed."

"Call later."

"I will." Then: "Sheriff."

"Joe, you were right. We pulled him over as soon as he crossed the county line and he's sitting in my interrogation room, demanding his lawyer."

"Was he packing?"

"He had a loaded twelve-gauge shotgun in the backseat."

"I'll be there in fifteen minutes," Joe said, and punched off.

Nate had an expectant look on his face.

"It worked," Joe said. "The press conference flushed him out."

Nate nodded with satisfaction. He said, "Drop me off at your place. As much as I'd love to go with you and brace that asshole, I can't be seen by all the coppers."

Joe agreed and smiled to himself.

It worked.

36

JOE PUSHED THROUGH THE DOUBLE DOORS OF
the vestibule into the reception area of the Twelve Sleep
County Sheriff's Department and nodded a greeting to
Wendy the dispatcher, who waved back. The walls inside
were decorated with elk, deer, and antelope heads as well
as mounted trophy trout that needed dusting.

"Mike in?" he asked.

"He's in his office waiting for you," she said. Then,
looking him over: "It's strange not to see you wearing your
uniform."

"Feels strange, too," Joe said. He strode around the
counter and saw Sheriff Reed wheel out of his office to
greet him.

"He's in there?" Joe asked, gesturing toward the closed
door of the interrogation room.

"We're watching him on the monitor," Reed said. "He's fidgety, to say the least."

Reed backed his wheelchair into his office and Joe followed. Deputy Justin Woods, evidence tech Gary Norwood, and Dulcie looked up from where they sat on folding chairs in front of a television monitor. The black-and-white image was of Juan Julio Batista seated at a bare table. He was aware of the camera lens above him and glanced at it furtively.

Dulcie looked concerned. She was a famously by-the-book county attorney. Joe grinned at her in an effort to reassure her she'd have a clean prosecution, that not too many rules had been broken. That this might *flirt* with entrapment but not quite cross over the line.

He held up his digital recorder. "It was Blevins working with Batista."

To Norwood, Joe said, "When you transcribe this, you'll want to leave out the threats."

Norwood smiled and Dulcie moaned.

"Don't worry, Dulcie, you can lose the tape and the transcription later. You won't even need it."

Joe turned to the image of Batista. He looked small, pale, and nervous. There was an ugly red welt over his right eye.

As if reading his mind, Reed said with transparent insincerity, "He forgot to duck when we put him in the cruiser. He doesn't like to be in handcuffs. Apparently, he still doesn't think much of us small-town Barney Fifes."

"Has he talked?"

"No," Reed said. "And I don't suspect he will for a while. That may change when he realizes he may not get out right away."

Dulcie said with caution, "He refused to answer questions and he immediately demanded his lawyer so we backed off. From what I understand, his counsel is flying up from Denver as we speak."

Joe said, "Good thing I don't have to care about that kind of thing anymore."

"Joe . . ." she said, her voice trailing off.

"I promised you ten minutes with him if he showed up and no more," Reed said to Joe. "So you better get in and get out. Be quick."

Joe nodded. "Are you going to watch on the monitor?"

"Yes, and it's being recorded," Dulcie said, obviously uncomfortable with the arrangement. "So don't . . ."

But Joe had already turned and marched out of the office for the interrogation room.

JUAN JULIO BATISTA looked up at Joe like a trapped animal. His cuffed hands were on top of the table, his fingers interlaced. His eyes narrowed as Joe sat down across from him.

Batista said, "I'm not saying a word to anyone until my lawyer gets here. You have no right to question me any further. I know my rights."

Joe shrugged. "I'm not a cop. Those rules don't apply to me. I resigned, remember?"

"Then why are you here?"

Joe said, "I've found it's more efficient to do some things when you *don't* have a badge."

Batista looked puzzled.

Joe plucked the recorder out of his pocket and placed it on the table between them. He hit the play button of his conversation with Blevins. Batista's face drained of color while he listened. Joe turned it off as Blevins said *Please, dear God, get him off me.*

"That's what was driving me crazy all along," Joe said. "How you knew to send the agents up here so quickly when Butch started working again. Now I know."

"That was obviously coerced," Batista said, his voice not as strong as he'd probably intended it, Joe thought. "It will never stand up in court."

"It doesn't have to," Joe said. "Blevins will cut a deal and throw you under the bus to save himself. And proving you called him repeatedly will be a matter of getting your agency phone records. My buddy Chuck Coon with the FBI is in the process of obtaining them now. You're going to prison, Batista. Rawlins, Wyoming, will be your new home. And no one deserves it more than you."

Something went dead in Batista's eyes.

"My wife is really smart, and she put together a timeline," Joe said. "Tell me if she got anything wrong, okay? We want to make sure we understand the whole story."

Batista didn't speak.

"You grow up in Chicago as a dweeb named John Pate. No one likes you much because you're not a likeable boy, but you have a burning desire to make something of yourself and show *them* someday. So you can't wait to leave all that behind you and you go to college out of state in Fort Collins. You kind of reinvent yourself there, right? College is a good place to do that. Am I right on so far?"

"This is ridiculous," Batista said.

"I'll take that as a yes. You major in sociology and something called environmental affairs. As a senior you act like a big shot. During orientation week for newbies, you notice a very cute and naive freshman girl fresh from Douglas, Wyoming. She looks like she's right off the ranch and she's at this big school with no friends. Her name is Pam Burridge. You become infatuated with her, and because she feels over her head at such a big school, she appreciates the attention from you for a while."

Batista broke off his gaze and swiveled his head away. Joe took it as a good sign.

"But you came on too strong with her. You were too domineering. You didn't want her to make any new friends, and you spooked her when you would go on and on about your future lives together. You told her her job would be to support you and look good on your arm. If she so much as *talked* to another male, you would go into jealous rages. You didn't know it at the time because you had such a high opinion of yourself, but she was desperately looking for a way out. She met that way out at a club in Old Town in Fort Collins. His name was Butch Roberson, a redneck construction worker who barely graduated high school, and he was passing through town on his way back to Saddlestring. He was the kind of guy you despised—blue-collar, rough around the edges, no sophistication. A rube."

Batista shook his head but wouldn't look at Joe. And here is where Marybeth's additional research into Pate had really paid off.

Joe said, "It turned out to be quite a scene that night in that club, didn't it? You grabbed Pam by the arm because you caught her talking to this redneck from back home, and the redneck wiped the floor with you. In front of your friends! The police report you filed against Butch said you had multiple contusions and some broken ribs. But the Fort Collins cops never arrested Butch because he was gone by then, and he'd taken Pam with him. She dumped you like a hot rock. Then she dropped out of school and actually married the guy."

Joe noticed the cords in Batista's neck were as tight as guitar strings.

"And it festered, didn't it?" Joe asked. "She forgot all about you, but you couldn't keep her out of your mind. Even after you changed your name and started climbing through the bureaucracy, it still burned hot, didn't it? That this silly girl had picked an uneducated loser over you?

"So a year ago you tracked her down and called her. You didn't give her your new name or tell her exactly what you did at the time, just that you were very successful. You claimed you just wanted to touch base with her and see how she was doing after all these years, but you were obviously hoping she'd hear your voice and maybe she'd come to her senses. Instead, she told you never to contact her again. She said she and Butch were happy and they had a daughter now and they were doing well. In fact, they'd just bought this piece of land . . ."

Joe sat back and waited for Batista to turn his head and look at him.

When he did, Joe said, "Pam told us all this after she saw your photo on the agency website last week. Your face brought up some bad old memories for her, but your call to her meant so little she'd forgotten about it, and she never even told Butch. That must sting a little, huh?" Joe said, twisting the knife.

"I don't have to listen to this," Batista hissed.

"Here's where my wife's timeline comes in," Joe said, pushing on. "A year ago, at the time you made that call, the Sackett case in Idaho was getting some attention. Even some of your colleagues in Region Eight were alarmed. But you didn't look at it that way. You looked at the details of what had been done to the Sacketts and saw it as a perfect way to ruin Pam and Butch. You could dish back some of the pain and humiliation they'd caused you. So from your anonymous perch behind a desk in Denver, you researched the lot they'd purchased and you found Blevins. From your position of power, you set this thing in motion and thought you'd crush them without the Robersons or anyone else ever tying it back to you."

Joe paused for a moment, and then said, "Then you sent those two agents up here to die."

Batista erupted and slammed the table with his cuffed hands. "I did not! They were supposed to serve the compliance order and come back."

Joe glanced at the camera in the top right corner of the room, as if to say "Got him." Then he shifted back to Batista.

"No, I'm sure you didn't," he said. "I actually believe

you had no idea there would be shooting. But when it happened—you panicked. You saw your world and career about to blow up if the story got out, though, so you tried to do damage control. You were determined to take Butch out because if he talked it might lead back to you. And today you were going to threaten or murder Pam before she could expose you and what you did to them. The press conference was my wife's idea to get you up here so you could be prosecuted locally. I wasn't so sure you were this desperate and stupid, but Blevins confirmed it. And he'll confirm it on the stand."

"He's a liar," Batista said.

"Maybe," Joe agreed. "But you were the one caught with the shotgun."

Batista sneered, but his face had completely drained of color.

"You know what first got me to thinking that something was hinky with you?" Joe said, sitting back. "It's when you had Underwood announce that reward. It was a desperation move, and it especially didn't make sense to me that a glory-hungry political hack like you would pass up an opportunity to get his name in the papers. But you didn't want Pam or Butch to recognize you as John Pate and put things together, right? Your only shot to save yourself was to get them both out of the picture before they figured the scheme out. And now look at you."

Joe stood and shook his head. "You destroyed a family and five people died, one by your hand. You abused your power in the worst possible way. As far as I'm concerned, nothing that happens now is bad enough for you."

"My lawyer . . ." Batista said, but didn't finish his thought.

AFTER CLOSING THE DOOR of the interrogation room, Joe leaned into Reed's office.

"That help?" he asked.

"I'm going to crucify that piece of shit," Dulcie seethed.

"That's my girl," Joe said.

To Reed: "Please tell Butch what happened. He'll want to start pumping iron for when he runs into Batista in prison."

Reed barked a laugh.

"Man," Joe said with a heavy sigh, "I think I'm talked out."

NEVERTHELESS, HE CALLED Marybeth from his pickup in the lot of the county building. "It's done," he said.

"Thank God. I'll tell Pam."

"Is Hannah still there?"

"She's hanging out with Lucy like usual and staying for dinner again."

"You're a saint."

He could envision Marybeth rolling her eyes at that. She said, "One more mouth to feed. No big deal."

"Keep her there," Joe said. "I need to talk with her."

"Joe," Marybeth said, concern in her voice, "what's this about? I don't like the sound of this."

"I can't tell you yet."

"Did Butch relay a message? They won't let Hannah in to see him, you know. They say she isn't old enough for visiting hours. So I'm guessing he wants to tell her something through you. Am I right?"

Joe closed his eyes. What he was about to do felt like the toughest thing he'd ever done. He wished Marybeth was there cheering him on instead of making it harder. But she didn't know.

He said, "Just keep her there, please."

37

WHEN JOE ENTERED HIS HOUSE, HANNAH ROB-
erson looked up from the board game she was playing with
Lucy with fear in her eyes. Lucy looked puzzled as she
turned her head from her friend to Joe.

"Hannah," Joe said, "do you want to take a walk?"

She nodded and gathered herself up.

"Dad—what's going on?" Lucy asked.

"It's okay," Hannah said to Lucy. "I'll be back in a
minute."

"Dad," Lucy said, annoyed.

Marybeth intervened from the kitchen. "Lucy, your dad
needs to talk to Hannah."

Joe gave Marybeth a look of appreciation, and Marybeth
arched her eyebrows in a gesture asking him what was going on.

Joe held up a single finger to Hannah, indicating she should wait for a moment, then took Marybeth aside in the kitchen. He leaned close to his wife and said, "That girl is going to need our help. She's going to need *your* help, Marybeth."

Then he told her.

In reaction, Marybeth's eyes got big and filled instantly with moisture as if twin tear duct valves had been opened. She covered her mouth with both of her hands.

She whispered, "My God . . ."

Joe said, "I'm hoping you can work with her. You've told me caring for horses and riding can be therapeutic. Maybe that will help her."

"It might help *some*," Marybeth said, "but this might be too big to overcome."

Joe said, "We thought April's problems were too big to overcome, but look at her now. You've worked miracles with her."

Marybeth looked back at Joe with doubt in her eyes.

NATE WAS IN THE FIELD behind their house with Sheridan, looping a pigeon wing lure through the air on a string. Sheridan's kestrel was in the smoky sky, circling, then diving at the lure. Joe heard Sheridan cry with glee, then Nate's deep laugh.

Hannah followed him through the backyard gate and Joe closed it behind them.

"This way," he said, gesturing toward the road.

She followed as if her feet were weighted down, as if she was making her trip to the gallows.

"THIS ISN'T EASY for either of us," Joe said to her.

She nodded, her eyes large and frightened.

Joe said, "You know that your father will go to prison, maybe for the rest of his life. You know that, right?"

She nodded. "I hate it."

"Hannah," Joe said, "I found the .22 rifle in the trunk of your car. You really need to get rid of it somewhere no one will ever find it."

Tears filled her eyes, but she didn't move or speak.

"The forensics team knows the agents were killed by .22 slugs. They assume they came from your dad's .223, but they may figure it out at some point."

Because she seemed frozen in place, Joe reached back and grasped her arm gently and guided her on.

He said, "You and Butch were target-shooting when those agents showed up, weren't you?"

"It was just me," she said, in a tone barely above a whisper. "Dad was doing something with the tractor."

Her voice trembled with sobs as she told Joe how happy she'd been that her dad was finally back, and how he smiled when she told him she'd like to go with him that afternoon to their property.

"Tell me exactly what happened," Joe said.

She said, "The younger man got out of the car first and started walking toward my dad. He had a gun. When I looked over at Dad's face, I saw he didn't know what was going on. Dad looked scared and angry, and I thought that man was going to hurt him. I had the .22 in my hands and . . . I just shot him. When he fell down, the older man started to reach into his jacket and I shot *him*. Dad yelled at me to stop, but it was too late. I still can't believe I did it.

"I didn't *think*," she said, crying. "I just started pulling the trigger. I didn't want to kill them. I just wanted to make them go *away*."

"They didn't identify themselves?" Joe asked.

"No. All they said was, 'Are you Butch Roberson?'"

Joe pulled her into him and let her cry.

"My dad was finally back with us and he was happy again," she sobbed. "I wanted him to stay and for everything to be normal. But when those men showed up and I saw that look on my dad's face . . ."

She was clutching him and crying and Joe didn't know what to do with his hands.

"Afterward," Joe said, "the two of you drove out to Big Stream Ranch and you dropped Butch off and took his pickup home. Then you got in your own car and drove it here. Do I have that right?"

"He didn't want me to get in trouble," she said, her voice muffled in Joe's shirt. "He made me promise I'd never tell anyone. He said he wanted me to have a second chance."

"Does your mother know?"

"Oh God, no," she cried. "Please, oh God, don't tell her."

Joe stroked her back.

"Are you going to take me to jail?" she asked.

"No. Your dad made me promise him I wouldn't when I figured it out. He's already confessed and he's not going to take it back. I just told Marybeth. She's agreed to try and help you deal with this, but you need to promise me you'll try and that you'll listen to her."

"I promise," Hannah said. "What about Lucy? She's my best friend."

"That'll be up to you," Joe said, wishing he had Marybeth's counsel on how best to answer that question.

"Does anyone else know?" she asked.

Joe sighed heavily. "The only other person who was in a position to have seen what happened wasn't home that afternoon."

"So I'm not going to jail or prison?"

"I'm not law enforcement anymore."

He looked toward the house and saw Marybeth at the window, her hand again covering her mouth. Joe feared he'd asked of Marybeth too much.

"Your dad is giving up everything for you," Joe said. "His freedom, his reputation, and his future. You need to keep your promise to him and make him proud."

"I will, I will," she wailed.

JOE STAYED WITH HANNAH until she regained control of herself, then said, "Go back to the house now."

"Thank you," she said.

"He's a good dad," Joe said.

"He's the *best*."

Joe watched her slowly walk back, her shoulders still heaving. Marybeth met her at the door.

Then he dug out his cell phone. It was time to return a call to Governor Rulon.

He needed a job.

AFTERWORD AND ACKNOWLEDGMENTS

The premise of this book is based on a true story.

The author thanks Mike and Chantell Sackett of Nordman, Idaho, not only for their courage in their battle with the EPA in a situation similar to the one portrayed in the book but also for graciously sharing their story. Readers outraged by the abuse of authority may consider a donation to the Pacific Legal Foundation (http://www.pacificlegal.org), who defended the Sacketts and won a remarkable landmark 9–0 U.S. Supreme Court Decision in 2012.

Special thanks also to Bob Krauter, Hugh Hewitt, Jake Budd, Mark and Suzi Dunning, and Mark Nelson, all of whom provided insight, contacts, settings, and assistance.

My sincere appreciation to Laurie Box, Becky Reif, Molly Donnell, Roxanne Box, Jennifer Fonnesbeck, and Don Hajicek for their support at home; Ivan Held, Michael Barson, Tom Colgan, and the legendary Neil Nyren (who wisely dialed me back) at Putnam; and the amazing Ann Rittenberg in New York.

C. J. BOX is the author of the twelve Joe Pickett novels and three stand-alones, and has won the Edgar, Anthony, Macavity, Gumshoe, and Barry awards, as well as the French Prix Calibre .38 and a French *Elle* magazine literary award. His books have been translated into twenty-five languages. He lives outside Cheyenne, Wyoming, with his family. Visit him online at cjbox.net, facebook.com/authorcjbox, and twitter.com/cjboxauthor.

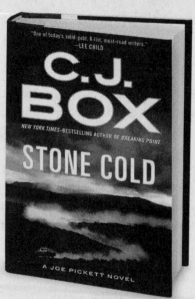